HEATHER LOWELL

NO ESCAPE

D0089910

HarperTorch
An Imprint of HarperCollinsPublishers

This is a work of fiction. Names, characters, places, and incidents are products of the author's imagination or are used fictitiously and are not to be construed as real. Any resemblance to actual events, locales, organizations, or persons, living or dead, is entirely coincidental.

❦

HARPERTORCH
An Imprint of HarperCollins*Publishers*
10 East 53rd Street
New York, New York 10022-5299

Copyright © 2004 by Two of a Kind, Inc.
ISBN: 0-06-054214-4

First HarperTorch paperback printing: August 2004

HarperCollins®, HarperTorch™, and ❦™ are trademarks of Harper-Collins Publishers Inc.

Printed in the United States of America

Visit HarperTorch on the World Wide Web at www.harpercollins.com

10 9 8 7 6 5 4 3 2 1

For Matt and Jen,
creators of the Monkey Boy,
and Miss Miraboo.
You done good!

Chapter 1

If being raped by a hulking professional football player was the price she had to pay to make it big in Hollywood, Kelly Martin figured she should pull up stakes and head back to Kansas. Even working the Blizzard machine at Dairy Queen had to be better than what she had endured over the last few hours.

With a sideways glance at the huge man driving her home in his Hummer, Kelly pressed a hand low on her abdomen to quiet the burning, grinding pain there.

She was positive Britney never had to do anything like this to get her first recording contract.

Kelly felt tears well in her eyes and pushed the thought away. When that didn't work, she bit her lip hard. *I will not let this jerk see me cry. At least not again.*

Without turning her head, Kelly checked the position of the man next to her in the front seat, then decided she couldn't move farther away from him without opening the door and bailing out. Which she would do if he made a single move toward her.

She almost laughed out loud. All of her friends at Central High School in Hays, Kansas, would probably kill to be in her position—being driven home in a luxury car after an evening spent in Hollywood with an all-American hero. Sledge Aiken was the most sought-after celebrity quarterback in the country, especially after his team's dramatic Super Bowl win last month in New Orleans.

With his slow Southern drawl, light brown hair, and wild green eyes, he would be considered a catch anywhere. When those were paired with six-feet-one inch of heavily muscled physique and a talent for football handed straight down from God, Sledge was the kind of man most girls dreamed of at night.

When Kelly had been offered a chance to go on a date with him, she'd taken it in a heartbeat. After all, every girl in the club was after him. And Jerry had told her going out with Sledge would increase her chances of being seen by celebrity photographers—which in turn would boost her prospects for getting a recording contract.

But Kelly hadn't known the price she would have to pay. She flashed back to an hour earlier, to the terror and helplessness she'd felt when she realized that Sledge wasn't going to be stopped by her tears and pleas. When she'd realized that he was going to continue to press her slender body into his velvet couch and take away from her something she would never get back. Something he had no right to take.

Kelly's lip trembled, even though she still had her teeth clamped around it hard enough to draw blood.

The car turned into a residential area and slowed to a stop in front of a modest single-level home.

"So, are you free next weekend?" Sledge's voice came out of the darkness, causing Kelly to jump visibly. She had hoped to go inside without having to say another word to him.

She shrugged her shoulders and brought her thumb up to her mouth, chewing on its lacerated cuticle.

Sledge took her silence for agreement. "Then I'll set things up with Jerry again, okay?"

Kelly shrugged once more and reached for the door handle. It was locked.

"Hey, wait a sec. I got something for you, sugar." At one time, Sledge's thick Alabama accent would have made her heart turn over. Right now, it made her skin crawl. If she'd had anything at all in her stomach, she was sure it would have come up right then. But she'd been so ill at Sledge's house after . . . she bit harder on her cuticle, then tugged again on the door handle.

Sledge released the locks and held something out to her, causing her to flinch away from him.

"It's for you. And there's a lot more where that came from. You're a gen-u-ine firecracker, darlin'."

Kelly looked at the crisp hundred-dollar bill in Sledge's beefy hand. Then she raised her wounded gaze to his for the first time since they'd gotten into the Hummer. She looked into his eyes for guilt, apology—anything. But when he smiled and winked at her she pulled the door open and bolted.

"Aren't you going inside?" Sledge called through his open window.

Kelly ignored him. She passed the house and continued running down the street in her high heels and cocktail dress, until she disappeared into the darkness of the night.

Chapter 2

"An eighteen-year-old girl was raped by a high-profile athlete three days ago, and I get the impression the officers who were first assigned to the case couldn't care less. They haven't even brought the suspect in for questioning, let alone arrested him. It's just not right."

Tessa Jacobi speared a piece of grilled shrimp with her fork to emphasize her point. She then put the bite down untouched, pushed away her half-full plate, and used both hands to tuck her dark blond hair behind her ears.

Police Officer Veronica Harris took in her friend's barely suppressed anger and chose her words with care.

"I'm sure the officers were proceeding carefully on the case, Tessa. What reason have they given you for not arresting him?"

Tessa rolled her blue-gray eyes. "They *say* there isn't enough evidence to substantiate a sexual assault. That's why I had Carmen pull some strings to get you and Ed assigned to the case."

And it must have burned like acid to do it, Veronica thought.

Tessa continued. "I hope I didn't wait too long. Apparently the football player involved is out of town and unavailable for questioning. I just hope the creep hasn't bailed out of the country to Mexico or something. Getting sufficient evidence to prosecute a date-rape case is hard enough without having the rich defendant flee the jurisdiction."

Veronica pushed aside her empty plate with regret. She was still trying to lose some of her extra pregnancy weight, and so resisted the temptation to pick at Tessa's lunch. "If the evidence is there, we can make a case. Start from the beginning. Who is this girl?"

"Her name is Kelly Martin," Tessa said. "What a sweetheart. She's eighteen, and came to LA a few months ago to pursue a recording contract."

"Like thousands of other girls, God help them. Where's she from?" Veronica asked.

"She said she was born and raised in Denver. There aren't any recording studios there, so she hopped a bus to California. I know it's tough to make it in Hollywood, but I have a feeling about this girl, Ronnie. She's got star quality. I could see that the first time I met her, even though she was a wreck," Tessa said.

"How did you meet her?"

"I was walking my brother's dog in the park early last Sunday. We went on a back trail and suddenly Roscoe took off into the bushes. When I went to get him, I found a clearing, and Kelly was sitting there in high heels and evening clothes. When Roscoe licked her face, she threw her arms around his neck and started bawling. She was in bad shape."

"And she just blurted out to you that she'd been raped?" Veronica looked skeptical.

"Of course not. I sat down with her and we talked for a

while. Roscoe is a great icebreaker, you know. One hundred pounds of pure Labrador therapy at work."

"Roscoe is an oaf," Ronnie said with a smile. On their first meeting he had taken her down and licked her face clean of makeup in five seconds flat.

"He really likes your moisturizer, what can I say? Anyway, after an hour or so of chitchat, I asked Kelly what she was doing crying in the park. She said she'd had a bad date, but I could see in her eyes it was more than that. She looked like a wounded animal. Her posture, body language—everything was screaming out that this girl had gone through something horrible."

Veronica had worked with numerous victims of sex crimes in her job with the LAPD, so she understood well the nonverbal clues Tessa had picked up. "Did she finally admit what had happened?"

"Yes. She said she went out on a date with this hotshot quarterback and after dinner he brought her to his house. He then gave her a drink, sat down on the couch next to her, and started making his moves. She was okay with it for a while, but when she asked him to stop he ignored her."

Veronica winced, knowing what was coming next.

"Kelly said she was sure he would stop if she kept asking. He didn't. She said she began crying and fighting, but it didn't even slow him down. She's a tiny little thing," Tessa said as she crumpled her napkin in her fist.

"I'm sorry. It sounds like a classic date-rape situation."

"That's what I told her. She was shocked—she didn't even know there was a name for this type of attack, let alone that it happens to young women all too often. She asked how I knew about stuff like that."

"And you told her you were a prosecutor with the D.A.'s Office?"

Tessa nodded. "When she found out, she just about bolted. She said she didn't want to cause any trouble, she just wanted to go home. I convinced her this was a serious crime and that she had to report it, or it might happen to another girl. She said no one would believe her because of the guy who was involved."

"Who is he?"

"He's the quarterback for the LA Waves," Tessa said, naming one of Los Angeles's two professional football teams.

Veronica coughed as she inhaled her iced tea. "Holy shit! Sledge Aiken? He's the man Kelly is accusing of raping her?"

Tessa nodded, cynically watching the expression on her friend's face change to one of utter disbelief. She'd seen the same thing happen with the first officers in charge of investigating Kelly's allegations of rape.

"Don't look at me like that," Veronica said, wiping tea off her blouse. "You have to admit it's a tough sell. Sledge Aiken is the single hottest commodity in sports right now—he probably has to beat women off with a stick."

"You know rape isn't a crime of sex. It's about power," Tessa insisted.

"Yes, it is. But I also know that in order to prosecute, you have to make a convincing argument of *why* the crime was committed. That's going to be very difficult with a celebrity of Aiken's stature."

Tessa looked stubbornly at her plate. "I can do it."

"I'm not doubting your abilities as a prosecutor. I'm just saying that now I understand why the other officers involved have been proceeding cautiously. And to be honest, Ed and I will have to continue in the same vein."

Tessa rubbed her forehead. "I know. But it's so frustrating to watch the police tiptoe around this case just because the accused rapist happens to make his living running around throwing a ball to grown men in tight pants."

Veronica cleared her throat and went back to the important details of the case. "What kind of physical evidence do we have so far?"

Trust Ronnie to go right to the weakest part of the case, Tessa thought.

"Not much, I'm afraid," Tessa said. "I need to get copies of the file for you, but Kelly said Aiken used a condom. I was able to talk her into having a medical exam at the hospital, but they didn't get much with the rape kit. Some bruising on her thighs, slight vaginal tearing, a few stray hairs."

"So basically there's proof of sexual contact, but not rape?" Ronnie asked.

"Yes. I didn't mention that to Kelly. I'm trying to be positive, because she needs to know we believe her and are going to help her. Especially since even the nurse was treating her like a criminal."

"Usually they have a little more tact than that."

"It wasn't the nurse's fault," Tessa admitted. "There was one strange thing that even I have been questioning."

"What?"

"During the exam, an admissions nurse pulled me aside. She wanted to show me something that had fallen out of Kelly's purse."

"Drugs?" Veronica asked.

"No. It was an envelope that wasn't sealed, so when it hit the ground the contents went flying. There were half a dozen credit cards and a wad of cash inside," Tessa said.

"Kelly's cards?"

"No, that's the weird thing. They all belonged to different men, according to the names on them."

"Geez, Tessa. Sounds like she's involved in some kind of scam."

"I know it looks bad. I made a photocopy of all the cards, then returned the envelope to Kelly's purse. I asked her about the credit cards, but she had no idea what I was talking about. She said the money was for a deposit."

Veronica was silent as she stirred another packet of sugar-free sweetener into her tea.

"I know what you're thinking, Ronnie. But I'm pretty good at reading people. Kelly was genuinely surprised about the credit cards in her bag."

Veronica frowned. "So what's her story then?"

"She said the restaurant she works at gave her the envelope to give to her cousin, the one she's staying with. She had no idea of what was inside the envelope, but thought about it and came up with an explanation. Apparently her cousin had some friends in a private room at the restaurant, and they must have left the cards that night. The cash is part of the regular deposit."

"I suppose that could be a logical explanation. But until you investigate further I'd reserve judgment."

"That's one of the reasons I'm glad you and Ed were assigned to the case," Tessa admitted. "I want Ed to look into the credit card thing, so we can decide if Kelly can be trusted. But everything else about the hospital exam and interview with a rape counselor checked out," she added.

"What happened after the medical exam?" Veronica asked.

"I took Kelly and the hospital records to the police station nearest where the attack occurred, so she could make a statement. The officers said they'd question Aiken, but every time I follow up I'm told they haven't done it yet. And really, what's this guy going to say? 'Yeah, I'm the knuckle-dragging son of a bitch who raped an eighteen-year-old girl with stars in her eyes, go ahead and lock me up?'" Tessa shook her head, causing her shoulder-length blond hair to fall forward across her face again.

"You know he won't. He's going to say that whatever happened between him and Kelly was consensual, and she's a trashy, gold-digging wannabe starlet," Ronnie said bluntly.

"Exactly. I don't want to put Kelly through that, but . . ." Tessa knew there was no choice, given the constraints of the legal system.

"What is Kelly doing now?" Veronica asked.

"She's staying in LA at her cousin's house. The rest of her family is still in Colorado, I guess. Anyway, Kelly said she needed a few days to get herself together before she decides whether to press charges."

"Wait a minute," Veronica leaned forward. "Why the hell am I coming off maternity leave a week early to take this case if Kelly hasn't agreed to testify yet?"

Tessa shifted in her chair. "She will."

"Well, shit. Tessa, you can't blame the other officers for dragging their feet if even the victim isn't sure she wants to pursue the case."

"It's a common reaction among rape victims. She will press charges, she just needs a few days to deal with what happened to her before she can cooperate fully with the investigation."

"*She* needs a few days? Or *you* need a few days to talk her into prosecuting?" Veronica asked as she arched a dark brow.

Tessa met Veronica's brown eyes. "I did have to push pretty hard to get Kelly to go to the hospital," she admitted. "I see that now. So I want to give her time to learn to trust me—and to trust the system. In the meantime, it's up to me to fill in the gaps in Kelly's story. That's where you guys come in. It means a lot to me to have two officers who deal with major crimes against persons assigned to the case."

"Has Ed been much help to you yet?" Veronica asked.

Ed Flynn had been Veronica's partner on the police force before she went on maternity leave six months ago.

Tessa nodded. "He told me he'd look into a few things yesterday. Background stuff. I guess he found something, since he wanted to meet us here for lunch today."

"He must have a light caseload while I'm out on leave," Ronnie said with a wicked grin. "Normally he gives all the chicken-shit background stuff to me."

Tessa laughed at the common complaint of a rookie partner. "I know. He grumbled about doing the grunt work." Her smile faded. "Seriously, though, it is a big imposition on him. That's why I was thinking about bringing in a local private investigation firm to work on some aspects of the case. Especially the credit card thing. I, um, kind of didn't mention that to the police when we filed the rape report."

"I'm not hearing this," Veronica said.

"I even toyed with not telling you guys," Tessa confessed. "But I can't hold back information like that. So I need to contract a little help to look into the credit cards and get that whole thing out of the way. I don't want you and Ed to have to spend any time on anything beyond what Sledge Aiken did to Kelly."

Ronnie blew out a long breath. "It's a tough call, but I guess I'd go to a private investigator if I were you. Because if we have to look at the possibility of credit card fraud, that will become the focus instead of the alleged rape. We'd have to bring in another department that deals with white-collar crime, and if they hear that Ed is poking around their territory . . . well, let's just say that police turf wars can get ugly. Going with a P.I. is probably safest."

Tessa rolled her eyes. "Please don't tell me the police would turn a rape investigation into a pissing contest because Ed stepped on their toes."

" 'Fraid so. Who were you thinking of farming the investigation out to?" Ronnie asked.

"I don't know. None of the investigators I've used previously with the D.A.'s Office have the qualifications to take on a case like this."

"Most of the banks and major creditors have private investigators on retainer for this kind of thing."

"I suppose I could ask around and see which firm my banks use."

Veronica thought for a moment. "What about Novak International? It's run by Lucas Novak, who is a former deputy with the Orange County Sheriff's Department. He's got good investigative experience in the major crimes division, plus he did a stint with the SWAT team before going private. If he's not on retainer with some of the local banks, he'd certainly be able to point you in the right direction."

"Does he have experience with cases like Kelly's?" Tessa asked. She got out her black notebook to write down the investigator's name.

"He should. Most of his business now centers on family issues, custody cases, kidnappings, ransoms in Mexico, runaways. He also has a division that provides corporate
security and bodyguard services, as well as fraud detection
and prevention. He's a bit of a renegade, but a damned good
investigator."

Tessa nodded and closed her notebook. "Thanks. I'll talk
to the owner. Hopefully he can help me take some of the
pressure off Ed. And you, when you get back on duty."

"I'm counting the days—five more. I love my baby girl,
but being stuck with her at home all day"—she shook her
head—"there are times when I spend twenty minutes on the
phone with telemarketers just to have an adult conversation."

"Wow, that's pretty bad." Tessa laughed. "Still, you're
lucky to have a healthy daughter and a husband willing to
share baby duty."

"I think Mike is freaked at the idea of a six-month leave
of absence from the force. But he loves Jordan and agrees
with me that she's too young to go to day care for sixty or
seventy hours a week. It's going to be a big hit financially,
and probably for Mike's career, but . . ." Veronica shrugged.

She hadn't planned things this way, but she hadn't
planned on dating a coworker and getting pregnant, either.
Still, they were making the best of the situation, and building a stronger relationship each day. And despite the sacri-
fices, having Jordan was a joy she'd never dreamed of
before.

Tessa saw the dreamy look come over Veronica's face and
sighed. Another good friend lost to the baby bug. She felt
like she was the only thirty-three-year-old in L.A. who
wasn't married with at least one munchkin hanging on her
business skirts.

"There she goes, off to babyland. Go ahead and call Mike
if you want to check on her," Tessa said.

"Just wait. One day you'll be responsible for a perfect,

tiny little person. Then you'll understand. I can't wait for that to happen."

"You know the Plan—career until I'm thirty-six, then focused dating, then marriage, then babies. I'm just not capable of dividing my attention like you are. I'm either focused on my career or on my private life. Not both," Tessa assured her.

"Famous last words." Veronica smiled knowingly. "Kids are remarkably resilient. The notion that you can't be a great parent and a fully productive employee is a thing of the past."

Tessa thought of her own father, how his career had taken over every aspect of his life and caused him to leave his young daughter to fend for herself after her mother had died.

"Not everyone is capable of multitasking like that," Tessa said. "Besides, I'm not even going out with anyone. Too busy trying to expand my caseload to something beyond small-time felonies and misdemeanors. I want some cases where I can make a difference."

"You'd have them, too, if you'd only accept the promotion that's been offered. Twice," Veronica said.

"I don't want anyone to think that I've cashed in on my name. I want to be promoted on my own merits, not because my father used to run the FBI."

"Tessa, you graduated *cum laude* from the University of Virginia. You set up a Legal Aid clinic here that serves thousands of people every year. You've been working piddly shit cases for the last two district attorneys for almost five years. In fact, you make it possible for the D.A. to focus on the big political cases by taking care of the meat-and-potatoes stuff. I think you've more than earned your stripes."

"I hope you're right. Because I'm going to ask to keep Kelly Martin's rape case. If this isn't big and political, I don't know what is. But I know I can do it."

"Because you're emotionally involved? I wouldn't use that tack with the D.A. if I were you," Veronica said.

"I won't. I'm going to hire an investigator, light a fire under Ed's feet, and schedule an interview with Sledge Aiken to get his side of the story. And then I'm going to close this case by using due diligence and letting the system work."

"Don't forget me. I'm with you on this one," Veronica said.

Even if something doesn't feel right about your victim's story.

Chapter 3

Los Angeles, California
Tuesday, February 23

Detective Ed Flynn pushed through the doors of Felipe's Shrimp Shack, looking for the two women he was meeting for lunch. He didn't see his girls inside, so they must be on the patio, enjoying the winter sunshine.

His girls.

That's how he thought of them, as the daughters he'd never had. And right now, he was very much afraid one of his girls was in over her head.

He sought out Tessa's familiar compact frame and blond hair at one of the tables on the edge of the patio. She always sat in that spot if possible, because his Tessa was a creature of habit. Ed smiled slightly at the thought. Those habits had turned her from a green law school graduate into an indispensable junior prosecutor for the District Attorney's Office in a record period of time.

He switched his gaze to Ronnie, his other girl, the young officer from Minnesota he'd helped mold from meter maid to an officer on the major crimes squad. Another of his works in progress, and he couldn't be prouder of either one.

But right now, something was wrong with the case they were about to embark on, and he needed answers to make sure his girls didn't get burned.

"Over here, Ed." Tessa jumped up to kiss his cheek when he reached the table, an act which never failed to make him turn red with pleasure and embarrassment. It was such fun that Ronnie stood up to do the same thing.

"You been surfing without sunscreen again?" Ronnie asked wickedly, watching the color rise higher in his face.

"Every day of my life," Ed replied.

Waking up at five in the morning for several hours of surfing before work was a ritual from his teenage years. The four decades of sun and salt water since then had turned his thinning, light brown hair almost white and given his face a weathered, ruddy appearance. His eyes were surrounded by pale wrinkles, a legacy of squinting into the sun while waiting for the perfect wave.

Right now, those serious brown eyes settled on Tessa's upturned face.

She stilled when she picked up on his tension. "Do you have something on Kelly's case? Were you able to talk to Sledge Aiken?"

"You'd better sit down for this one, Tessie," Ed said, taking a seat himself and pulling her half-empty plate to his side of the table.

"What's wrong?"

"I spent the better part of yesterday on the phone with the CBI. That's the Colorado Bureau of Investigation. They're in charge of processing civil and criminal identification files and records, among other things," Ed began.

"And?" Ronnie and Tessa asked together.

"And they have no record of young Kelly Martin existing in the state of Colorado. No birth certificate for a Kelly Martin that matches the date of birth you supplied, no driver's license that matches the Polaroid photo of her you gave me."

"What does that mean? Is it some bureaucratic mix-up?" Tessa asked.

"What it means is that there is no Kelly Martin, date of birth 12 January, blond hair, blue eyes, five-foot-two and 105 pounds," Ed read the information off a notepad he'd pulled out. "Said Kelly Martin does not exist, according to the state of Colorado."

"How can that be?" Tessa asked.

"It can't— unless your victim isn't telling the truth about something."

"Wait. At the hospital she didn't have any ID. She said her wallet had been stolen shortly after she arrived in LA," Tessa said. "Maybe there's some kind of identity theft thing going on—you know, someone creating a whole new identity using Kelly's name and social security number?"

Ed shook his head. "Could be, but there are hundreds of Kelly Martins registered with social security. It's a common name. Maybe too common."

Tessa sat back as she tried to take in the information. If it had come from anyone but Ed, she would argue that there was a mistake. But Ed was a thirty-year veteran of the force, and he simply didn't make this kind of error.

"What about the credit card data I gave you? Did anything pop with it?" she asked.

"The cardholders all have accounts in good standing. The cards weren't reported stolen," Ed replied.

"Thank God for that," Tessa said. "So maybe Kelly really was giving them to her cousin so they could be returned to their owners."

"Don't be too relieved. The owners may simply not be aware that their cards are missing yet."

Tessa bit her lip. "I'll have to contact the issuers and see if there's any recent activity on those cards."

"Good. I'd be especially interested in any activity since Kelly left the hospital. Looking to see if she's charged a bunch of high-ticket items since then would be a good start."

"Once you meet her, you'll see that she's not like that."

Ed hesitated, then spoke. "Tessie, there are several very strange aspects to Kelly's story. We need to talk to her about them. Where is she right now?" Ed asked.

"She's staying with her cousin. I don't know where—she wouldn't let me drive her home, wouldn't even tell me his name. She said she didn't want to make waves, you know, because her cousin is letting her stay in his house as long as she wants for free."

"How are you supposed to get in touch with her?" Ronnie asked.

"Kelly gave me a pager number where I can reach her. I'm going to leave a message for her right now." Tessa got her cell phone out and left the patio so she wouldn't disturb the other diners.

"You really think there's something screwy with Kelly Martin and her story?" Ronnie asked Ed.

"Yeah. She's not telling the truth—or at least not all of it. The credit card issue is a red flag for me, even though Tessie is trying to explain it away. I hope she doesn't get her teeth kicked in on this one. The case is too big and the suspect too rich for her to take him on with what she's got now."

"She can handle it. You've seen to that yourself by teaching her the ropes."

"I know. But something is going on beneath the surface here. Otherwise, Kelly's supposedly quiet, middle-class upbringing in Denver would be documented by the state of Colorado."

"So you'll talk to Kelly and straighten things out."

"I think the big problem is going to be convincing Tessa not to go balls out on this case," Ed said.

"Yeah. She told me she's going to ask the D.A. to be assigned first chair on this case. She said she wants to make a difference, to work on a case that has substance for once."

Ed shook his head.

Ronnie leaned forward, her voice low. "You think we'll be able to prosecute?"

"I don't know. Tessie understands the system inside and out by now—probably better than anyone because she started at the very bottom and learned every one of the rules the hard way. But . . ."

"But not everyone plays by the rules," Ronnie finished for Ed.

"Yeah. I wonder how she'll react when she encounters someone who doesn't give a shit about playing fair and will do anything to win."

Chapter 4

Santa Monica, California
Thursday, February 25

Tessa verified the address of Novak International, Inc. a third time. Apparently, Lucas Novak had rented space in a small medical and insurance business mall on the edge of a residential neighborhood, rather than going for the exclusive and chic real estate in Hollywood or Beverly Hills. It was a sound business decision that would keep overhead down, even if it wasn't the best marketing approach.

She rang the bell and was greeted by an efficient receptionist who showed her to Mr. Novak's office. Though he was on the phone, he waved Tessa in and offered her a seat. It was clear he was wrapping up the discussion, so she took a moment to study him while he typed an entry onto his small laptop.

He was big enough not to be dwarfed by the large executive desk he sat behind—a desk that was notable for its lack of decoration and clutter. Tessa thought of her own work surface with its overflowing piles of files, sticky notes, and memos jotted on the back of used copier paper. While the rest of her life was quite organized, her desk was a disaster. She liked it that way.

The man seated across from her caught her eye and shrugged apologetically, motioning that he would be with her soon. She smiled as he rolled his light-colored eyes. He was obviously trying to be diplomatic with the person on the other end of the line.

"That's right, Mr. Soares. I'm obligated by law to report that the theft of your coin collection was committed by your grandson. I realize you are my client and paid me to investigate the crime. But the fact is an insurance claim was filed, you collected the money, and it's now an issue for the cops. I can't stop their case now just because you don't want your grandson arrested."

Tessa watched as Novak raked a hand through thick brown hair that was turning gray at the temples. His handsome face was creased in a frown of concentration as he looked through his computer files. She saw that his eyes were hazel, a mix of light brown and green and blue that was striking even in the low office lighting. She knew he was thirty-six from her research, but he looked much younger, despite the bits of silver in his hair.

"I'm going to give you the name of a good defense attorney. It's possible with restitution of funds to the insurer and a family court sentence for your grandson, you can make this all go away. It's out of my hands, though, as I warned you it would be if you filed an insurance claim."

Tessa watched Novak shrug his shoulders. Very broad shoulders. He wore a casual oxford-type shirt tucked into khakis, which emphasized the wedge shape of his chest. She remembered Ronnie saying Novak had worked with the Orange County Sheriff's SWAT team, so clearly he was once in excellent physical shape. Life behind a desk hadn't changed that as far as she could see.

"Sorry about that, Ms. Jacobi. That particular client has a

personal problem I got involved with. I didn't want to cut him loose without giving him some ideas on how to proceed."

"I know what you mean. I often spend more time on my petty crime and misdemeanor cases because the people involved are so . . . needy. It's hard to say no sometimes," Tessa smiled.

"My assistant MacBeth tells me you're a prosecutor with the Los Angeles District Attorney's Office," Luke said. MacBeth was his primary investigator and sometime assistant, the person in the office who fielded most of the new cases to determine whether they were viable for Novak International.

"Yes. I've been there over four years. While I've never worked with Novak International, my office occasionally farms out cases to local bonded investigators."

"That's us. All of my employees are former peace officers who are able to make arrests, gather evidence for trial, perform legal surveillance, and so on. Although I have to admit, it's not the bread and butter of the company," Novak said.

"Why? There are plenty of firms that make their overhead doing that type of work."

"I don't need all the rules, paperwork, and bureaucratic ass-kissing that goes along with getting those contracts," Novak said bluntly, watching for her reaction. "If I'd wanted that, I would have stayed with the sheriff's department."

Tessa hesitated, then reminded herself that this was exactly what she was looking for. She needed someone who could discreetly investigate an aspect of the case that she wanted to soft-pedal to the police. At least for now.

"Point taken, Mr. Novak. I've kissed more than my share of ass with the D.A.'s Office, and it's something the police seem to do particularly well when it comes to certain key players. Frankly, that's why I need someone like you."

"Call me Luke. Or Novak. We're not much on ceremony around here, Tessa." He leaned back and put his feet on the desk just to see how she would react. Poking at the pretty, uptight prosecutor was proving to be the most entertaining part of his week so far. He wondered how far he could push her before she pushed back—always a good thing to know with a prospective client.

Tessa had been around enough cops to know when she was being tested. And to know that passing the test was important to earning the respect of the man casually reclining across from her with his feet on the desk.

"Luke it is," Tessa said. She pushed her chair back far enough to prop her own feet on the desk as well.

Luke's eyes goggled as he took in her pale brown suede pumps and slender calves encased in silky nylons. His gaze went up her legs, and he could have sworn he saw a hint of creamy lace underneath her business skirt.

"Is this outrageous enough, or do I have to grunt and scratch my crotch as well to play in your boys' club?" Tessa asked with an arched brow.

Luke laughed out loud as he sat up and put his feet back on the floor. "You'll do, Tessa Jacobi. You'll do just fine. I should have known better than to dare a woman with an Italian last name."

Tessa chuckled as she sat up and smoothed her skirt to cover her legs once more. "Comes from hanging out with cops. My family is actually Swiss—from the part of the country near the Italian border."

"Swiss. That explains the organized and no-nonsense approach."

"It goes far with the prosecutor's office. And it helps when I'm dealing with a complicated case and a VIP suspect that no one wants to upset with something as pesky and irritating as an investigation," Tessa said.

"I wondered what was so messy that the D.A. had to do an end run around the police. Why don't you start from the beginning."

Tessa nodded and briefly went over Kelly's story. She started with the night the attack took place, then walked him through the medical exam and gathering of evidence. Finally, she gave an overview of the stalled investigation into the rape allegations and her reluctance to have the police investigate the credit cards and cash discovered in Kelly's things.

"So you're looking for help with the investigation overall?" Luke asked.

"For now, let's focus on the investigation into these credit card accounts," Tessa said, handing him the photocopy she had made of the cards. "I don't want to break all the rules and involve a private investigator in a major celebrity case. Besides, I have absolute trust in the two officers who have now been assigned to take over the investigation. I've worked with Ed Flynn and his partner in the past," Tessa said, reluctant to divulge her personal friendship with either Ed or Veronica.

"Can I be honest here?" Luke leaned back in his chair as he studied the photocopied sheet. He noted with interest that there was a handwritten phone number at the bottom of the page, and filed it quietly away for the future. "When I was with the OC Sheriff's Department, I was involved with lots of major crimes cases—including high-profile ones. There's something highly suspect about this rape victim's story. That's probably why the guys assigned to the case at first dragged their feet."

"Look, we don't exactly have a slam dunk in terms of physical evidence, but I'd hardly call her story suspect."

"Yeah? Then why do you need me?" Luke asked.

Tessa swallowed. "Since the police have a number of other cases to pursue, I was afraid this one was going to get shelved. Or that the police would get distracted by the possibility of credit card, um, irregularities. I'm sure you can understand why I don't want the police to waste time looking into something like that when I believe that the whole mess can be easily explained."

"What else? I still don't buy the reasons for the departmental foot-dragging that's happened up until now. Something happened to get this case pulled from the preliminary investigators and handed to these new ones. Ed Flynn is the best, so I know there's something big here," Novak said. "Anything you share with me is confidential," he reminded Tessa.

"Ah, there are some slight irregularities. A few problems with the victim's identification papers."

"Such as . . . ?"

"Such as she doesn't seem to have any. Says they were stolen. But the fact is, nothing on her matches anything in the state of Colorado's databases. It's raised a red flag, and I'm afraid the police would rather focus on that than on the fact that an eighteen-year-old girl was raped by America's favorite quarterback," Tessa said, shoving her hair behind her ears.

"Sounds like you've hit more than one brick wall over this," Novak said.

She took a deep breath and blew it out slowly. "You could say that. No one seems to see what I do," she said.

"Which is?"

"A pretty eighteen-year-old girl who wants to be the next Britney Spears. Who came to Hollywood alone to pursue a recording contract, and has no friends or family in LA except for a cousin. I see a petite teenager who was raped on a date with a thirty-year-old football player weighing over two hundred pounds," Tessa said, clenching her fists in her lap at the thought of what Kelly had been through.

"Finally, I see two overworked Beverly Hills cops who would rather pick at holes in the victim's background than have the stones to confront said football player and deal with the political fallout. That's why I asked to have Ed assigned to the case, and for it to be handled as he does his other major crimes investigations."

Novak's eyebrows went up at the suppressed rage in Tessa's voice. "Why are you so concerned about a starstruck kid from Colorado? Unfortunately, her story is not uncommon in LA."

"Well maybe that's proof something really is wrong with the system."

"And you're going to be the one to fix it," Novak said neutrally.

"I'd like to try. This is the biggest case that's come across my desk in four years with the D.A. But it's not just that—there's Kelly. You need to meet her to understand. There's something about her that draws you in. Innocence, vulnerability, I don't know what it is. I just know I believe her when she says something terrible happened. I want to help her."

"Emotional involvement can be a liability in a case like this. You might discover things you don't want to believe about innocent, vulnerable Kelly during the course of the investigation. And potential credit card fraud could be the least of the situation. Are you ready for that?"

Hazel eyes looked right at Tessa, as if trying to determine whether she had the strength to do this. "I'm ready. But frankly, it's not any of your business. I'd be paying you to investigate the credit cards found in Kelly's possession. Not to monitor my commitment to finding the truth or handling whatever reality is uncovered."

"That's where you're wrong. If you hire me, my job will be to protect you and your interests while I investigate what's going on. As my last client discovered, sometimes I may have to protect you from yourself. Especially if you're wearing blinders where the victim is concerned."

"I'm not—" Tessa began.

"Sure you are—look at Kelly Martin's situation. The credit card thing could be the tip of the iceberg, yet the victim pleads ignorance. And you make excuses for her by saying she's been through an ordeal. It sounds like she and her story could lead you into a minefield. Missteps on this type of case can end your career."

"That's my risk to take," Tessa insisted.

"Not if you hire me, it's not. Then I'm in the game with you. Take it or leave it."

"I don't need a partner to share liability. I need an investigator to look into the accounts of the cards involved, gather information, and document what he finds so I can clear Kelly. And I need someone who doesn't have issues with taking a subordinate role," she said pointedly.

Novak laughed. "I've got no problem with that. But you need someone who doesn't have a brain—who will tiptoe around the tough questions. That's not what people hire me for."

"What *do* they hire you for? I find it fascinating that you're trying to talk me out of giving you this job. I was told that you wouldn't be afraid to take on a case like this one. Obviously, I was told wrong."

"Ouch—straight shot to the balls," Novak said with a grin. "But I like you, Swiss. So I'm going to skip the sales pitch. You need to hire a bonded investigator who will do exactly what you ask and never question whether there's a better way to do things. Or whether there's another explanation for how Kelly Martin ended up with a fistful of cash and credit cards on a date with a sports star."

He held his hand up to stop her when she tried to interrupt.

"People expect Novak International to get the job done, regardless of the methods—and regardless of what kind of dirt we turn up on each of the players. You need to think about whether this is the type of service you're looking for."

She stood and grabbed her bag, then took her papers off his desk. "It's not. I'm looking for someone who can work within the system and help me get justice for Kelly— someone who understands the rules."

"Then you'd better go back to hoping the police will solve all of society's problems," Luke said. "Maybe they'll buy this kid's sob story."

Tessa whipped around. "Yeah, well I won't hire an investigator who looks at Kelly and wonders what she did to bring this situation onto herself." She turned around again and crossed the room. A lifetime of good manners had her stopping in the doorway. "I appreciate your honesty, though. It saved us both a lot of trouble."

"Honesty is something you'll always get from me, Swiss. Whether you want it or not." Novak called his receptionist to see his almost client out.

He turned toward the floor-to-ceiling windows and watched Tessa cross the parking lot. He could almost hear the authoritative click of her heeled shoes on the pavement. Watching the irritated swish of her hips under the sage green business skirt, he smiled.

She was pissed.

"You're supposed to be a salesman, boss. Not drive prospective clients out the door."

Luke turned to look at the man who had silently entered the office from a connecting doorway behind him. MacBeth, as a potential future partner in Novak International, was being trained in how to handle clients and had been observing the meeting behind a two-way mirror.

"What can I say? It was too much fun watching her try to control her temper. What did you think of her?" He gestured toward the woman backing up her Honda sedan with a jerky motion.

"Not what I expected from a junior prosecutor with the D.A.'s Office. She's a pistol under the cool surface."

"Seems strange to have all that fire wrapped up in an Ann Taylor suit with matching suede shoes," Luke agreed. "I was half-tempted to take the case just to see what has her in a lather."

"Sledge Aiken had better look out," MacBeth noted.

"Yeah, but there's something wrong with the setup. How does an eighteen-year-old kid fresh in from Colorado score a date with LA's newest celebrity, especially when she supposedly doesn't have any friends here? And how the hell does she end up with almost ten thousand cash and half a dozen credit cards belonging to other people in her purse?" Luke asked.

"I thought the story sounded odd. That's why I passed Ms. Jacobi on to you."

"And why I passed, period. A celebrity case is hard enough without having to deal with the shattering of innocence, too," Luke said.

"Whose innocence? The girl who was raped or Tessa Jacobi's?" MacBeth asked.

"I think they're uncomfortably linked, my friend."

"Then it's just as well she didn't hire us. I'd hate to watch someone as nice as the deputy D.A. figure out the hard way that not everyone is as honest and straightforward as she is."

"Yeah. Watching good people get manipulated and chewed up by the system is never fun," Luke said.

And I ought to know it.

Chapter 5

"I'm sorry to drag you into this, Ed. As soon as I can find another investigator to look into the credit cards, I'll stop bugging you to come along and hold my hand every day," Tessa said.

Ed Flynn snorted and followed her through the early-morning pedestrian traffic on the sidewalk. They were headed to a popular local coffee shop where Ed would meet Kelly Martin for the first time.

"Luke Novak is one of the best investigators in Southern California. He's got a list of informants that any active cop would kill to have. I still don't understand why you wouldn't hire him."

"He didn't have the right personality," Tessa said vaguely.

"What the hell does that mean?" Ed asked.

"I need someone who can help me work within the system, in Kelly's favor. Novak doesn't want to work with the system, he wants to burn it down."

Ed coughed at the edge in Tessa's voice. She glared at him.

"Luke Novak is a cowboy. I need someone a little more . . ." She searched for the right word.

"Tame? Obedient, even?" Ed suggested.

"I don't require obedient," Tessa shot back. "But house-broken would be nice."

Ed laughed out loud. "So he pissed on your case, did he?"

"He basically said he didn't believe Kelly's story. He told me I had blinders on and might not like what I saw when reality unceremoniously ripped those blinders away." Her pride still smarted at that one.

There was a long silence. Finally, Ed said with a sigh, "Let's go meet your victim, Tessie. I want a chance to understand this girl who's got a hold on your tender heart."

She let out a relieved breath, thankful he hadn't agreed outright with Novak's analysis of the situation. "Come on, that's her in the corner booth."

They greeted Kelly—who barely looked up from the coffee she was stirring—and sat down across from her. Tessa frowned as she saw the girl was wearing a high-necked sweater despite the mild day. She had also stuffed her long, platinum blond hair under a large-brimmed hat.

When Kelly felt Tessa's eyes on her, she glanced up briefly, revealing oversized black sunglasses. The room was bright, but not enough to need them. She quickly looked back down at the table and continued stirring the cup in front of her.

"What's wrong?" Tessa asked gently.

Kelly shrugged, then lifted her thumb to her mouth and started chewing the ragged cuticle.

Tessa slowly reached across the table and pulled Kelly's sunglasses away from her face. The girl said nothing as Tessa gasped out loud.

"Your face! Who did this to you?" Tessa carefully turned Kelly's head toward the sunlight, revealing raw looking bruises around her left eye, cheekbone, and the corner of her mouth.

"I tripped getting out of the pool," Kelly said, pulling away from the gentle touch.

"What did you trip on?" Tessa asked angrily. "Someone's fist?"

Ed put his hand on Tessa's arm to silence her, then held it out to Kelly. "I'm Ed Flynn. It's very nice to meet you. I understand California hasn't been too kind to you."

Kelly looked down at the weathered hand he offered her, then up into Ed's warm brown eyes. He looked like such a dad, with an expression of concern and gentleness that made tears well up in her eyes. Instead of latching on to his offered hand like the lifeline it was, Kelly snatched the sunglasses off the table and put them back on her face.

Ed knew she was trying to put distance between them, and he let her. If she felt safer with the Jackie O glasses on, maybe she'd relax enough to tell them what had happened.

"I won't let anything happen to you now, Kelly. Neither will Tessa. But you have to trust us," Ed began. "Can you do that?"

Kelly resumed biting on the thumbnail she had been mauling. "I just want to go home," she said with a break in her voice.

"We'll take you there. Is home in Colorado?" Ed asked.

Kelly hesitated, then nodded jerkily.

"Then why don't you have a driver's license issued from that state?" Ed asked.

"My family didn't have a car for me to drive," Kelly mumbled.

Tessa's eyebrows shot up. She knew that even when an individual didn't have a driver's license, it was customary to get a photo identification card from the state. "What about your birth certificate? The state of Colorado doesn't have a record of anyone named Kelly Martin being born on January 12, 1985."

Kelly shifted in her seat. "I don't know. Maybe my mom

lost it. Maybe I wasn't born in a hospital, so they never got a birth certificate."

Ed caught Tessa's glance and shook his head slightly. "You'd need one to enroll in school, child."

Kelly thought for a moment, then said "My mom home-schooled us."

Ed had to give her credit for quick wits—or for remembering a story she'd rehearsed before. "Tessa told me that you had an envelope with a bunch of cash and credit cards in your purse, but that you hadn't known the cards were in there. She said you were going to talk to your cousin about it."

Kelly's shoulders hunched even more. "I did. He said they belonged to friends that he had dinner with. They all forgot their cards at the restaurant I work at, so I returned them to my cousin when the manager asked me to."

Same story. Ed sat back and raised an eyebrow at Tessa, silently asking what she wanted to do next.

Kelly saw the exchange, then shot to her feet. "I'm out of here. I don't need this."

"Wait—" Tessa began.

"You don't believe me," Kelly said accusingly. "After everything I told you. I trusted you."

Tessa's heart sank at the hitch in Kelly's breath, at the beginnings of a sob in her voice. "We do believe you were attacked, Kelly. We just need to understand the rest. But that can wait. Right now my priority is to get you to a safe place."

"What do you mean?"

"You can't go back to your cousin's house. Why didn't you tell me what happened when we talked yesterday?"

"I tripped and fell after I talked with you," Kelly said, refusing to meet Tessa's eyes even through her sunglasses.

"Yeah, right." Tessa shook her head. "You're still not going back there."

"I have to. I have, um, things there. I can't just leave. Jerry would worry about me," Kelly said.

"We'll call your cousin—"

"No! You can't talk to him. I have to go now, I don't want to cause any trouble." Kelly began to edge away from the table.

Tessa had had it. "Listen to me, young lady. You will not be going back to that house. Clearly there's not enough supervision for you there."

"You can't make me leave," Kelly insisted. But it was said in a tone of voice that was almost hopeful, as if she wanted the responsibility to be taken off her tiny shoulders.

Tessa jumped into the opening. "Right now, you are the only witness to a crime that's being investigated. I can have Ed take you into custody for your own protection. So you can tell your cousin you don't really have any choice."

Kelly felt her stomach muscles relaxing for the first time in days. "Whatever," she said, working hard to sound sullen.

Tessa looked at Ed, glad that he hadn't called her bluff. He stood up. "Kelly, why don't you order yourself a big breakfast. I need to talk to Tessa alone." He handed the girl a menu and steered Tessa out of earshot.

She looked back over her shoulder and saw Kelly reading through the menu with what looked to be real enthusiasm.

"That was pretty tricky, lady. She was damned relieved to have you take the decision out of her hands," Ed said.

"Comes from helping to raise Kevin," Tessa smiled, referring to her much-younger half brother. "Teenagers act like they want independence and responsibility, but when things get tough they're happy to find a way out of being in charge of their own lives while still saving face."

Ed smiled briefly, then grew serious as he thought of what he had to do next.

"Kelly's lying, you know. She's got a pretty, well-rehearsed story, but you could grind it up and use it as fertilizer," he said.

"I don't know what's going on, but I do agree there's something, er, fishy-smelling about her story," Tessa responded. "Still, someone could be intimidating her, and that's why she's afraid to tell us the truth. We need to get her into a safe environment, then she'll begin to trust us."

"You can't build a legal case on a foundation of lies."

"She's not lying about being raped," Tessa insisted.

Ed looked over her head at Kelly, who was watching people pass by the front windows—as if she were looking for someone and afraid to see him at the same time. "Something happened to her, there's no question. And I don't like the bruises on her face. Slipped on the pool deck, my ass."

"So you agree that she needs our support right now, not a bunch of questions that imply we don't believe her?" Tessa asked.

"You have to stop making excuses for the child, Tessie. Try to understand what she's lying about and *why* she's doing it, and I bet you'll uncover the truth about what happened to her."

"I know. I was thinking that we could have her take a polygraph test. That way we'll know what to focus on and be able to weed out the unimportant stuff. And you'll know for a fact that she's nothing more than a scared teenager who needs our help."

"Hell, I can see that right now. But I worry about how to figure out the rest of it," Ed said.

"I know. But can we do it my way?" Tessa reached out and laid her hand on Ed's forearm. "Please. It's important to me that we do this right—and slowly. I think it's even more important to Kelly."

Ed looked down into hopeful blue-gray eyes and felt it happening—felt himself being sucked in against his better judgment.

What the hell.

At least he'd be there to watch over Tessa if things started spinning out of control. He wouldn't let her throw away her career on this case.

"I'll call and set up a polygraph for this afternoon, off the record. Then we should talk to Sledge Aiken," he said, checking his watch.

"I'd love to," Tessa replied. "He's been traveling with his team for off-season appearances, according to his agent."

"Ah, but I checked the official web page of the Waves before leaving this morning. The team returned to LA last night."

"So while you are monitoring the polygraph with Kelly, I'll find a place for her to stay. Then we can go see Aiken," Tessa said.

"Where are you going to put her?" Ed asked.

"Well, she can't stay with me. I don't want any accusations of conflict of interest or malicious prosecution. I think I'll talk to TSS—Three Sisters Shelter. They take in battered women and children, and they have a residency program for at-risk patients who have graduated from their drug rehabilitation programs. The security there is decent, and they have good supervision. Kelly might even meet some girls her age."

"Okay. But first, we'd better get that girl some breakfast before she starts eating the place mats," Ed said as he steered Tessa back to the table. "Poor kid probably hasn't eaten in days."

Chapter 6

Several hours later, Tessa and Ed pulled into the exclusive Hollywood Hills neighborhood where Sledge Aiken had purchased a 2-million-dollar home the year before. As they studied addresses painted on the curb, they noticed a new FOR SALE sign outside the metal gate at the end of the driveway leading to Aiken's home. The property was encircled with a six-foot-high wrought-iron fence, ensuring the quarterback's privacy.

"So much for the element of surprise," Ed said, indicating the locked gate and security camera that covered the driveway.

"Looks like Aiken is moving," Tessa said, pointing at the sign. "You don't suppose he plans to leave town suddenly"

"I doubt it. More likely he's going to renegotiate his contract with the Waves now that he has a Super Bowl ring," Ed said. "Rumor has it he's been shopping for nicer digs."

"Nicer digs. Because his multimillion-dollar Hollywood Hills shack isn't good enough?" Tessa shook her head. "The more I learn about Mr. Aiken, the less I like him."

Ed got out of the car and rang the bell. When he got no response, he pushed down the buzzer and held it.

"*¿Quién es?*" The hesitant voice coming over the intercom sounded middle-aged and feminine.

"*Policía, señora. ¿Podería hablar con el señor Aiken?*" Ed asked to speak to Aiken in rapid-fire Spanish, which was a basic requirement for all Southern California law enforcement officers.

"*No se encuentra en el momento*," the voice replied. "*Debe regresar por la tarde.*"

"*¿Con quién hablo?*" Ed asked who the woman was.

"*Soy la housekeeper, señor.*"

Ed let the woman get back to work and returned to the car. "Aiken isn't home," he told Tessa through her open window. "The housekeeper says he'll be back sometime this afternoon."

"So we wait for a bit," Tessa said. "You can give me the full details of Kelly's polygraph results."

Ed sat behind the wheel again and pulled out his ubiquitous notebook. He'd taught that to Tessa, and half smiled when he saw her pull out a small leather-covered pad of paper herself. "You may not like the polygraph results. They're a bit ambiguous."

"I can take it. Give it to me straight," Tessa said.

She was starting to become annoyed with men trying to protect her from information they thought might be difficult for her to accept. She didn't think of herself as fragile, but apparently being a few inches over five feet tall, and blond, gave the impression of being delicate.

"The examiner did a baseline with the regular questions. Then he asked her whether she was raped by Sledge Aiken. She said yes, and she was being truthful about the answer."

Tessa relaxed just a bit. "I'm sorry it's true, but I'm glad she's not lying about that part."

"Yeah. She also didn't know what was in the envelope in her purse until you told her. The examiner was positive of that. Kelly also works as a hostess in a restaurant, is actively pursuing a singing career, et cetera."

"So which results were ambiguous?" Tessa asked.

"She is ambivalent about proceeding with the investigation against Aiken, for one thing. And her responses about her background before getting to LA indicated evasion. Her name is real, but not much else. Which would explain why the state of Colorado doesn't have any information on Kelly. She's probably not from there."

"Maybe she's protecting someone," Tessa said.

"Like herself?" Ed asked before he thought better of it.

"You said her answers were honest about all the other stuff. Why would she lie about her background?" Tessa asked angrily. "I'm not blindly defending her, I'm just asking you to consider that maybe these lies have nothing to do with the case."

"Tessie, anything important enough to be lied about is important enough to impact the case."

"Then I'll find out what it is from Kelly. Just give me a little more time to earn her trust."

"Time is something we have plenty of," Ed said. "Since no charges have been filed, the media hasn't caught a hint of the story yet. At this point, we have the luxury of doing things slowly and carefully."

"Maybe." Tessa checked her watch. "But how long are we going to kill waiting for football boy?"

Ed sighed at her uncharacteristic impatience. "We can see if the neighbors will talk about him while we wait."

They began with the house across the street because it didn't have a fenced driveway. A man in his fifties wearing a colorful golf shirt opened the door almost immediately.

"Good afternoon." Ed flashed his badge. "We'd like to ask you a few questions about the neighborhood if you don't mind."

The man's eyes widened, then he glanced across the street. "Is this about the noise complaint? I've been telling the police for months about the loud parties across the street. Nobody's even come out before."

"We're here now, sir." Ed took out his notebook and a pen. He didn't bother to correct the man's assumption about why they were there. "Can I get your name?"

"Ira. Ira Seymour. I live here with my wife, June, and her mother, Stella."

"Is there a lot of traffic coming in and out of the house across the street?" Ed asked.

"All the time. You know who lives there, right?"

Ed nodded. "I was wondering if you ever saw any of the people who spend time with Mr. Aiken, since everyone has to stop at the gate and be let in."

Tessa took out a Polaroid of Kelly. "We're interested in this girl in particular."

Ira Seymour studied the photo, then shook his head. "I'm usually parked in front of the TV when I'm home. And my eyesight isn't too good. But my mother-in-law is a big star watcher. She sits upstairs day and night with a pair of binoculars, even keeps a log of the famous people she's seen on this street."

"Is she home?" Tessa asked.

Ira rolled his eyes. "Always. Let me call her," he said. Then he winked at Tessa. "I love doing this."

Tessa and Ed exchanged a curious glance as Ira went to the bottom of the stairs. "Stella! Hey, Stella," he repeated, in an impressive imitation of Marlon Brando's character from *Streetcar Named Desire*.

Ira's mother-in-law came down the stairs, muttering about melodrama. An ancient Pomeranian was tucked under her arm. The dog saw the guests and immediately began growling.

Stella was introduced by her son-in-law, raising her voice to speak over the snarling dog. Tessa explained that they were looking for information on Sledge Aiken and some of the guests he might have had in his home over the last two weeks.

"That boy has a constant stream of friends coming over at all hours of the night. He's not afraid to turn up the volume on his stereo system, either," Stella said.

"Have you ever heard yelling, maybe even screaming coming from the home?" Ed asked.

"Heavens, no. Just the usual party buzz, maybe some squeals from girls in the backyard pool."

"Loud enough for you to hear from all the way across the street?" Tessa asked.

Stella looked at them sheepishly. "He has a corner lot. You can see what's happening in the backyard if you go past his house and turn onto Magnolia Court," she said, pointing toward the other street.

Tessa held the Polaroid photo out to Stella, then quickly snatched her hand back when the older woman's dog began to bark.

"Don't worry about Precious. I had to have all his front teeth removed after the third biting incident. He's harmless now," Stella said.

Ira crossed his arms with a snort of derision. He glared at the little dog, which pulled its lips back in a snarl to reveal pink, toothless gums.

Stella turned her body so she was between her pet and Tessa, then reached for the photo.

"Oh, yes, I've seen her. She's been to the house a couple of times. I recognize her hair—it's so pale and long. She came by with a man, some kind of sports person."

"You mean she came with another athlete, someone besides Sledge Aiken?" Ed caught Tessa's gaze.

"Yes. I didn't recognize the man she was with, but my friend Ruth did. She said he used to play one of those fringe sports that her late husband watched—arena football, maybe?" Stella stroked her dog's head as she thought. "I can't remember."

"When was the first time you recall seeing the girl?" Ed asked.

"Maybe a month ago," Stella said.

"What did the man she was with look like?" Ed asked, prepared to write down the description in his notebook.

"He was fairly tall. Or at least he towered over the girl. I recall he had blond hair, kind of thin in the front, but the color was much darker than hers."

"What was his build like? Husky, thin, muscular?" Tessa pressed.

"Quite stocky. You know, when an older football player goes to fat," Stella replied.

"What kind of car did they arrive in?" Ed asked.

Stella didn't hesitate. "It was a Mercedes, but one of those cheap ones. It had two doors, with a hatchback. I'm pretty sure it was black."

Ed wrote down all the information. "I don't suppose you got a license plate," he asked, half-seriously.

Stella laughed self-consciously. "No. I try to draw the line somewhere between star-watcher and stalker, you know?"

Tessa thanked Stella for her help, then strolled back down the drive with Ed. "Do you want to try another neighbor?"

"Why bother?" Ed asked. "It doesn't seem like much gets by Stella and Precious."

Tessa paused at the sound of a motorcycle without a muffler coming down the street. They jogged over to the gate at Aiken's driveway as a large man stepped off a vintage Harley Davidson and pressed the intercom button.

"I forgot my clicker, Lupita. Open the gate." Sledge Aiken turned back to the motorcycle, but stopped short as he saw Tessa and Ed. A flash of annoyance gave his boyishly handsome features a petulant look. "No autographs, please."

Ed gave Sledge a smile with lots of teeth. "We're not here for your autograph, Sledge. We want to hear about your alibi." He opened his badge and held it closer to Aiken's face than was necessary.

"Sorry, Officer." Sledge stepped back. "What's going on?"

He gave them a charming smile that had been getting him out of trouble since he was in the second grade.

"We'd like to talk to you about Kelly Martin. And what happened early in the morning on February 20," Tessa said, showing her own ID as an officer of the court.

Aiken's face immediately lost his smile. "I've got nothing to say to you. If you have any questions, talk to my lawyer."

"Not good PR, Sledge." Ed shook his head as if he were disappointed. "A beautiful eighteen-year-old girl accuses you of date rape and you lawyer up? It's not going to play well in the media."

"She says I raped her? That's a fucking lie," Sledge said hotly.

Tessa looked at his red face, tight body language, and clenched fists. She was suddenly very glad she'd brought Ed with her. Sledge caught her considering look and paused for a deep breath.

Once he had gained a little control, he smiled grimly at Tessa. "Look, anything that happens between me and a woman is consensual. Come on, do I look like a guy who needs to use force to get some action?" He spread his arms out to encompass the Harley and the upscale neighborhood.

"If nothing happened," Tessa asked evenly, "then why won't you make a statement for the record?"

"Painful experience," Sledge said. "I may look like a dumb redneck from Alabama, but even I eventually learn my lesson. Sometime after the fifth fake palimony suit, I decided it was best to let my lawyer handle complaints from lying women wanting to sponge off my hard work."

"This isn't a palimony claim, it's a charge of felony sexual assault," Ed said.

"Come on, you know how it is. There are groupies and sports fans who think if they spend the night with me, they can cash in and make the rest of their lives real cushy. They accuse me of anything from promising them a ring to fathering their bastard children, then they demand hush money to go away. I've got to protect my image, because there are always women out there fixing to take advantage of my celebrity and human needs."

"Human needs?" Tessa asked, thinking of how small and fragile Kelly was. "You son of a bitch—"

Ed clamped a hand over her shoulder and squeezed. Hard. Then he turned to Sledge. "At this point you're refusing to talk to us?"

Sledge shrugged. "I'm sorry, the instructions came straight from my lawyer. Here's his card if you want to contact him." He withdrew a business card from his wallet and handed it to Ed.

Sledge started to roll his motorcycle through the open gate. "One more thing, Officer. If you come to my house without an invitation or a warrant again, I'll have to talk to my lawyer about filing a complaint of police harassment. I'm sure you can understand what's at stake for me and the companies I endorse. For your sake, I hope you'll be doing things through appropriate channels in the future."

Tessa ground her teeth at the arrogance behind Sledge's parting comment. "I'm going to enjoy watching him lose each and every one of his endorsement contracts."

"Simmer down, Tessie. He's already picked up on the fact that this case is personal for you. It only gives him and his lawyer ammunition."

Tessa turned and got in the car. "You're right. I just couldn't listen to him talking about Kelly like that. Like she's some kind of groupie." She caught Ed's glance. "Okay, maybe she was dazzled by his celebrity. But she didn't ask to be raped. All she wanted was to go out with the man."

"She picked the wrong celebrity to cut her teeth on," Ed said. "Aiken is a snake."

Tessa smiled. "Is that what I'm going to put in my notes? 'Subject has a reptilian nature'?"

"No. You're going to put down that it was apparent the

subject recognized the victim's name, and his answers indicated evasion. You'll note that it seems the subject has something to hide."

"Yes he does. I can't wait to expose the good ol' boy, starting with any similar complaints he may have in his past," Tessa said. She was already plotting in her head the argument she would use to get her boss to support this new angle of the investigation.

"Tread easy. Sledge Aiken is a man who's got no respect for women—or anyone else who gets between him and what he wants. He has fame and a fortune in endorsements to protect, which makes him damned dangerous."

Tessa heard the tone of caution in Ed's voice.

At least he believes that Sledge Aiken is responsible for whatever happened to Kelly.

It was a start, even if Ed's warning did send a shiver through her body.

Chapter 7

Tessa got back to the District Attorney's office after seven that evening, thanks to LA's famously gridlocked freeways. Despite the hour, she was eager to begin planning her strategy for building a case against Sledge Aiken. She went into her cramped office, flipped on the light switch, and walked to the whiteboard nailed on the wall across from her desk.

Several minutes later she had a diagram of the case labeled in her notorious shorthand. She turned when she heard a voice from the doorway.

"Working after six on a Friday gets you double brownie points, you know. Especially when your boss catches you doing it."

"Hi, Carmen." Tessa turned to look at Carmen Ramirez, who at age forty was one of the youngest district attorneys in the history of Los Angeles. Carmen was dressed in a stunning red cocktail gown, apparently heading off to some political function. Tessa knew a lot of the D.A.'s work was done after hours and outside of courtrooms, so her dark-haired boss was dressed to kill.

"Working on the Aiken investigation? I already gave you the case," Carmen said. "You don't have to prove to me that you've earned it."

"I just came from talking to him, so I wanted to get some stuff down while the information is fresh."

"I've got a few minutes before the Hispanic League fund-raiser. Bottom-line it for me." Carmen perched on the edge of Tessa's desk.

"Eighteen-year-old girl goes on a date with Aiken, then goes back to his place for a nightcap. From there, the stories diverge. She says he refused to take no for an answer and raped her. He says anything they did was consensual, and he's always being pursued by groupies wanting a cash settlement for spending the night with him."

"Any witnesses or forensic evidence?"

"Witnesses can only show a prior association, starting about a month before the assault. The rape kit turned up evidence of rough sexual contact, but was inconclusive for anything else."

"You know the burden is on us—and the victim—to prove that what happened was an assault. Historically, juries don't favor the woman in this type of case."

"I know," Tessa said. "But the victim was later physically assaulted—I saw the black eye and bruises myself, even though she denies anyone hit her."

"Then what's the holdup with the police?" Carmen asked, her dark eyes impatient.

"First of all, she's not cooperating."

"Then why do we care about her?" Carmen asked.

"Because she's a scared kid. I'm working to build her trust—I'm almost there. Once she believes in us, I think the truth will come out."

"So we work on the aspects of the investigation that don't require cooperation from the victim," Carmen mused.

"Yes," Tessa said. "I'm still clearing up a couple of issues with the victim's background. She was in possession of several credit cards belonging to other men as well as a large sum of cash, and she eventually gave a plausible reason for that. The cards, along with her lack of ID, initially threw off our investigation."

"What does Flynn think about this?" Carmen asked.

"He's agreed that Kelly is telling the truth about the assault. He was, ah, concerned about the other details of the case and the effect they might have on the victim's credibility. That's why I'm trying to gather additional evidence to push forward—much more evidence than would normally be required for a rape case. But right now I can't even get another interview with the suspect. He refuses to speak to us unless we go through his lawyer."

"Who is his counsel?" Carmen asked.

"Carl Abrahms." Tessa winced, waiting for the explosion.

"*¡Santa María!* No way, do you hear me? I'm not going to tangle with that shark in my first year as district attorney. *Carajo,* the honeymoon is already over as far as the voters are concerned—this kind of bad publicity would be like declaring open season on Carmen Ramirez."

Tessa nodded glumly. Carl Abrahms was a legend for taking on seemingly impossible cases with high-profile clients—and winning them. He had a tireless staff that could turn out enough well-researched motions and other legal documents to keep the D.A.'s entire staff busy for years to come.

"Have you talked to Abrahms yet?" Carmen asked.

"No. We just wanted an informal, off-the-record statement from Aiken first. But he lawyered up right away. I'm sure we'll be hearing from Abrahms soon, though."

The D.A. snorted. "He's probably filing a police harassment case as we speak. He does that if someone even looks sideways at one of his clients."

Tessa nodded again. "I believe Aiken mentioned those words. Still, he dropped a tidbit that I just can't leave alone."

"What?"

"He mentioned some experience with palimony suits in the past. I'm just wondering what else might have been involved, and if there is enough to show a pattern of sexual abuse of women." Tessa drew a line leading away from Sledge Aiken's name on her whiteboard, then put a question mark at the end of it.

"You're going to have to be very careful—as in, don't bother Sledge Aiken or his lawyer while you do the background work," Carmen said.

"But—"

"No. Aiken and his lawyer know too many powerful people in this city. If you go after him up front, he'll take you down and me with you."

"So basically we can't disturb the famous people with pesky little things like state and federal laws, a victim's rights, or anything like that?" Tessa asked. She had known the edict was coming, but was still angry that politics would come ahead of the law and Kelly Martin's rights.

"Not until you have enough proof to make an arrest. With the Kobe Bryant and Michael Jackson cases in the past, we have to be very careful about releasing the name of accused celebrities before we have any evidence. And judges have underscored that trend in the last year by not giving much leeway to prosecutors and police who want to open up the life of the accused merely to go fishing."

"How else are we supposed to gather evidence?" Tessa asked.

"Quietly. And make sure the members of the media don't catch wind of this, or we could be looking at a lawsuit if the case falls apart. So work with Ed Flynn inconspicuously and put together enough evidence for warrants behind Aiken's back. Then we can look through his financial records and openly interview previous associates—and you can fry his ass for all I care. He went to a fund-raiser for my opponent during the election," Carmen said with a feline smile.

"You're tying my hands—how am I supposed to get proof without 'bothering' Aiken?" Tessa asked.

"It's called discretion. You guys will probably need to team up with an investigator outside the police force, one who can poke around without tripping any alarms. At this point, if we so much as do an official check of Aiken's credit, his lawyer is going to get a phone call. I'd rather lull them into a false sense of security."

Carmen stood and paced, tapping her fingers along her arms as she continued. "Talk to your father. We need an investigator who's wired into the system, but not currently a part of it. That rules out anyone we've used for recent cases. Maybe he can suggest a firm that would allow us to go private with the investigation—without having to break the rules. Just bend them a little."

Tessa bit her tongue against an instinctive protest. She hated that Carmen knew who her father was. And she really didn't want to use her personal connections to gain information, even to further a case. She'd never once done that in four years with the D.A. But that reluctance was due to Tessa's tense relationship with her father, not because she didn't understand the nature of contacts and politics. Having a father who was the former director of the FBI was a valuable thing. She just hated to cash in on it.

"I've already thought of contacting an outside P.I. firm," Tessa began. With Carmen's new edict in mind, Tessa was formulating a plan to say the private investigators would only be looking at the credit cards found in Kelly's possession. In reality, they could do the background research into Sledge Aiken's past without alerting the star or his lawyer.

"I can see by your expression that you're already plotting something new. So why don't you run it by your father when you call him? I really think he could be helpful in this situation, since he'll have contacts that will come in under Carl Abrahms's radar." Carmen raised an eyebrow while waiting for a response.

No help for it, Tessa decided as she checked her watch. "I'll do it now. I should be able to catch him before he goes to his supper club. He's big about his routines."

"Good. In the meantime, stay away from direct contact with Aiken. We can't afford to antagonize him or his lawyer any further until we have concrete evidence." Carmen picked up her jeweled cocktail purse and left for the fund-raiser.

Tessa reached for the phone before she lost her nerve. Talking to her father never went well. It was usually impossible to keep the feelings of disappointment and antagonism that colored their relationship from spilling over into anything but the most shallow of discussions.

She cleared her throat as the housekeeper answered the phone. "Hello, this is Tessa. Is Mr. Jacobi in?" She didn't refer to him as Dad—and hadn't done so since her mother's funeral, when Tessa was eight years old. That was the day Paul Jacobi had shipped her off to a boarding school in Connecticut and begun a steady relationship with a nineteen-year-old fashion model.

Tessa sat at her computer and pulled open a file, refusing to dwell on the past and her damaged family life. When Paul Jacobi's voice came over the line, there were no initial pleasantries or small talk—he knew something had to be up for Tessa to call him.

"What's wrong?"

"Nothing," Tessa said, pinching the bridge of her nose. She hesitated.

Just do it. This is no big deal, he gets asked stuff like this every day.

"I need a favor," she said baldly.

Paul Jacobi's silence was deafening. He knew something big was going on in his daughter's life to get her to ask him for anything.

"Are you all right?" he asked quietly.

"Sure. I just need to pick your brain for a good private investigation firm. We have a very high-profile case, and if things aren't handled discreetly, it could create a lot of heat for the D.A."

"The best firm in town is Novak International. They've done work for the local, state, and federal governments."

"Ah, is there another firm you can recommend?" Tessa asked.

"Lucas Novak has set up a first-class investigation firm. I'm sure he can handle whatever case you're working on," Paul said.

"No, he can't. He's already refused to take this case. Do you know of anyone else?"

"As far as I'm concerned, there *is* no one else. Look, why don't I talk to him and straighten out your little misunderstanding?"

Tessa ground her teeth. "I didn't misunderstand anything. Novak said he couldn't help me." A tension headache was building at the base of her skull.

"If he can't help you, I don't know who can." There was a tone of stubborn finality in Paul's voice. Tessa knew from experience that a full-blown argument was not far off, so she ended the call.

"Thanks for your time, anyway. I've got to get going. Oh, and tell Kevin to be ready tomorrow night at seven," she said.

"Your brother is at a football game right now, but I'll leave him a note."

Tessa hung up and thought for a moment. Then she got ready to leave, pausing to straighten the files on her desk. There was no way she'd get any quality work done after the frustrations of the day. She planned to spend a quiet evening at home trying to forget about politics, celebrities, and investigations.

And tomorrow night she would take Kelly out to one of

the city's hot spots for teens—a new pizza parlor and video arcade. Tessa wanted to take along her sixteen-year-old brother Kevin as well, to act as an icebreaker and provide some entertainment.

Hopefully the quiet weekend would be enough to help Tessa reground herself and remind everyone what the investigation into Sledge Aiken was really about. Not district attorney election politics, not star quarterbacks with multimillion-dollar endorsement deals. But a fragile, naive eighteen-year-old girl and a man who believed that his wealth and fame gave him license to do whatever he wanted to her.

Chapter 8

"Don't get too involved in the game. The pizza should be out soon," Tessa said to Kelly above the din of arcade games and teenage chatter.

"I'm just a beginner, so my games only last a few minutes," Kelly assured her. She turned and headed for the bank of full-sized games about twenty feet away from the table where Tessa and her brother sat.

"She's really nice," Kevin said.

"Yes she is. I want to thank you for giving up your Saturday night to help me out. Kelly's had a really tough time lately, and I wanted her to have some fun," Tessa said. She'd been working hard to gain Kelly's trust, and in the last day seemed to have made some progress.

"Wait until I tell the wrestling team on Monday that I spent the weekend with *two* hot older babes," Kevin said with a grin. A lock of light brown hair fell across his forehead as he turned to watch Kelly's progress.

Tessa laughed and resisted the urge to smooth the hair out of her brother's eyes. She had been the closest thing Kevin had to a mother for the first few years of his life, so it was hard for her to think that he was practically grown-up now. Still, he was a great kid—how many sixteen-year-olds would help their sisters out on the biggest date night of the week?

"Kelly's only two years older than you are," she told him.

"Maybe. But she's got a look sometimes that makes me think she's a hundred," Kevin said. "Other times she's just like any other girl in my high school."

Tessa nodded at his perception. "Like I said, it's been a tough month for her." She hesitated, not wanting to draw Kevin too far into the ugliness of the case. "Something really bad happened to Kelly, and I'm trying to help her through it," Tessa finally said.

"I'm glad she's got you on her side. You helped me through some bad times when no one else was around."

"Thanks," Tessa said past the lump in her throat. "I knew what it felt like not to have a mom, especially when Paul wasn't around either. I never wanted you to go through that."

"So you moved back in with our father and the stepmonster to take care of me." Kevin said, referring to his mother with an irreverent grin. He loved his mother, but wasn't blind to her failings. "That's sisterly dedication above and beyond the call of duty."

Kevin's mother, Lana Olsen, had been a nineteen-year-old rising fashion model before meeting Paul Jacobi less than a week after his first wife's sudden drowning death. Her subsequent marriage to him, acquiring a new stepdaughter, and Kevin's birth eight years later hadn't kept Lana from pursuing a highly competitive and international career.

Since no one else had planned to do so, Tessa returned home from boarding school at the age of sixteen to take care of her newborn brother. She'd been the focus of Kevin's world until he'd turned six, and his mother had found her first hints of wrinkles and gray hairs. Though she was still a stunningly attractive woman in high demand as a model, Lana decided to retire and take up the position of mother for

the first time in her life. She'd been at the top of her field for
too long to deal well with being passed over for the top as-
signments because she was in her thirties.

"I still remember the yelling and fighting after Mom finished her last contract," Kevin said, as if reading Tessa's
mind. "She didn't understand why she couldn't come back
home and pick up as if she'd never been gone."

Tessa thought over her words carefully. While Kevin was
very blasé about their dysfunctional family life, Tessa was
always careful never to criticize Lana in front of him. "She
wanted what was best for you. We all did."

"Yeah, right. Is that why she moved across the country
with me and Dad when I was six, and made it clear that you
weren't welcome in *her* new home?" He looked at her with
cynical blue eyes that were a mirror of his father's.

"She didn't think our relationship was healthy. She and
Paul wanted me to have a chance at a normal college life in
Virginia." Tessa almost choked on the words.

Kevin sneezed, though Tessa distinctly heard the word
"bullshit," buried in the act. At over six-four and 225 muscled pounds, Kevin had his mother's looks and stunning
physique, but he'd inherited Paul Jacobi's keen mind and biting sarcasm. No one could fool the kid about what was really
going on, even when he was six.

"That was a long time ago. You should just be happy that
you had three people who loved you enough to fight over
you," Tessa said. She laughed when he shot her an incredu-
lous look. "All right, I tried to put a positive spin on it. Anyway, let's not burden Kelly with our family baggage, okay?
She's got enough to handle as it is."

"Don't worry, I'm done rehashing ancient history. I'm
back to being Kelly's date for the evening."

"Good," Tessa said, then waved Kelly over as their pizza
arrived.

"So where's your date?" Kevin asked Tessa.

She narrowed her eyes at him. "So where are your manners? Don't you know better than to ask a woman over thirty why she's flying solo for the evening?"

"Brother's prerogative," Kevin assured her, then bit into a cheesy slice of pizza.

"Do you have a boyfriend?" Kelly asked Tessa.

"No," Kevin said. "She broke it off with Mr. Perennial Grad Student about a year ago."

Tessa ripped a piece of pizza free. The topic of her last long-term relationship was still a sore one. She couldn't believe she'd wasted four years of her life on a spineless guy who saw nothing wrong with being a professional student. At the age of forty.

"I don't have a boyfriend, Kelly. And even if I did, I'm not sure I'd call him that at my advanced age."

"Thirty-six isn't that old," Kelly assured her innocently.

"I'm hardly thirty-three. Eat your pizza, child."

Kevin and Kelly exchanged a conspiratorial smile and laughed. Tessa chuckled, too. If nothing else, her dull love life could provide some entertainment for a young girl who'd had very little to laugh about recently.

"I'll leave you here while I drop Kelly off, okay, Kev?" Tessa stood next to the video game her brother was playing and had to practically shout to be heard.

"Sure thing."

"I'll be back in half an hour to pick you up—can you be out front?"

"Sure thing," Kevin said, without looking up.

Tessa shook her head. "Come on, Kelly."

They made their way through the crowd to exit at the front of the building. Tessa steered Kelly around the side of the building and past the back parking lot. The restaurant had been so crowded earlier that she'd had to park her car in the overflow lot farther down the alley. When they reached the lot, Tessa saw that other patrons had blocked the entire row by parking behind her car and the vehicles next to it.

"Great," Tessa said. She walked around the front of her car to make sure there was no cement block or other item that would prevent her from pulling headfirst out of the parking spot. Kelly stood by the passenger door, waiting for it to be unlocked.

Standing up from her crouched position, Tessa nodded. "Looks okay. Maybe you should stay out here to spot me in case I get too close to the fence post," she said. Behind her she heard a powerful engine downshift as it slowed to a stop.

When Kelly didn't answer, Tessa looked at her across the hood of the car. The girl stood frozen with a look of horror on her face.

Tessa turned around to see that a huge black Hummer had blocked her from being able to pull forward out of the spot. Her car was effectively boxed in. The driver's side door of the Hummer opened, and Tessa squinted to see who was getting out.

"Hey, can you move your car? I'm blocked in here," Tessa said, straining for a casual tone as she saw the size of the man coming around the hood of the Hummer. He leaned casually against it. Something about the man's body language and posture made Tessa's heart skip a beat as adrenaline poured through her.

Recognition flared in an instant, and she abruptly understood why Kelly was frozen with fear.

"Get in the car and lock the doors," Tessa said sharply. "Now, Kelly!" She tossed her keys to the girl, who caught them reflexively.

Sledge Aiken folded his arms across his chest and shook his head regretfully as Kelly obeyed the instructions. "Now why would you want to do that, darlin'? I just want to talk to you."

"Stay away from her." Tessa hurried around the front of the car to plant herself next to Kelly's locked door.

"That's not real hospitable. Especially when I came all

the way across town to talk to sweet Kelly and clear up any confusion."

"She isn't confused about being raped. Back off. Or do I have to get a restraining order?" Tessa asked. Her heart was pounding so hard and fast she was surprised the words came out steady.

"Yeah? And who's going to give you one of them restraining orders?" Sledge had moved away from his car and toward Tessa. "I've done nothing wrong, I'm just here having a friendly word with the little lady. If she's real nice, maybe I'll give her another ride in my Hummer," Sledge said with a feral grin.

Tessa stomach turned at the double entendre. Kelly flinched and leaned as far away from the locked door as she could. When Sledge stepped closer to the car, right into Tessa's personal space, her chin went up.

It's like dealing with a vicious dog, she told herself. Show no fear and convince the animal that you're meaner than he is. He was big, but not as tall as her brother, so she refused to let him intimidate her with his size.

"Step away from the car, or I'll have you arrested by 9:00 A.M. tomorrow on rape charges," Tessa said. "Think how that will play on the Sunday evening news. To say nothing of the Monday morning business shows, who will be talking about the diving stock prices of the companies whose products you're endorsing."

Even in the dim light she could see Aiken's face turn hard and bright red. "You've got nothing on me, you silly bitch."

Tessa crossed her own arms and leaned against the car with a bravado she did not feel. "I've got enough information in my files to haul you in anytime I want to question you further. Once that happens, it will only be a matter of time and digging before we come up with enough dirt to bury your sorry redneck ass."

Sledge stepped closer and towered over her. "Yeah? Files have a nasty habit of getting misplaced, you know?"

Tessa caught her breath, more at the physical threat than the verbal one. Sledge turned his attention to Kelly, banging his fist on the window. "Girl, get your ass out of there right now. We're going to have a talk."

Kelly said nothing, just looked out at Tessa with huge, pleading eyes.

"Did you hear me? Get into my truck *now*," Sledge repeated.

"Don't move, Kelly," Tessa countered.

"What the hell is going on here?" The masculine voice echoed in the quiet parking lot. Tessa had never been so glad to see her brother—ever.

Kevin Jacobi approached the car and stopped, hands planted on his hips. He knew enough about body language to understand that Tessa was scared to death of the man towering over her.

Tessa watched Sledge look over at the new arrival. She knew he was seeing well over six feet of honed muscles and bristling young attitude. What he didn't realize was that Kevin was ranked at the national level in both football and wrestling, giving him the raw power and skills needed to take on a man of Sledge's size. On top of that, Kevin had done years of close-quarters self-defense training with his father, ensuring that he could hold his own in a street brawl as well as on a wrestling mat. Tessa could have kissed him at that moment.

Sledge turned toward the car again, dismissing Kevin. "Go on home, boy. This is a private matter that don't concern you."

"You're the one who needs to shove off, boy," Kevin drawled.

"Yeah, who's gonna make me?" Sledge asked, spreading his arms wide and looking around.

Kevin approached them, handing Tessa the red sweater

that he'd run out to return to Kelly. He then pushed his sister behind him and went nose to nose with Sledge, crowding him into taking a few steps away from the car.

"The ladies don't like you. I suggest you leave," Kevin said quietly.

"Fuck off." Sledge shoved at Kevin with his hands, but wasn't able to budge him. He was a couple inches shorter than the teenager, but confident and arrogant enough to think that he could take him anyway.

Kevin came back with a body slam, crashing into the older man's chest with his own. While Sledge was off-balance, Kevin reached out with a foot and whisked his feet out from under him. The professional quarterback hit the ground hard enough to drive the breath out of his lungs.

As Kevin dove onto the ground to continue the brawl, Tessa began looking around for something to use as a weapon. Kelly shouted and held something through a small opening in the window.

"Here's your cell phone, Tessa. I already dialed 911."

"Thank God one of us has a brain." Tessa grabbed the phone, which had been charging on the dashboard during dinner, and held it to her ear. "I need you to look in the backseat, Kelly. I have a big, metal flashlight lying around somewhere in there."

Kelly leaned into the backseat and began patting around for the flashlight. Grunts and swear words came to her through the open window. "I don't see it."

"Keep looking. It's long and black—like the kind police officers carry," Tessa said. She checked on Kevin, but he was still on top. She figured that meant he was okay for now.

"Got it! It's under my seat, hang on."

Kelly broke two nails tugging, but finally pulled it free. She tried to pass it through the window, but the flashlight was too wide. With shaking fingers she turned the key she'd put in the ignition enough to get power to the automatic windows again.

Tessa grabbed the flashlight and held it like a weapon as she advanced toward the writhing, cursing mass on the ground. She heard a voice in her ear at the same moment that Kevin laughed triumphantly. He had Sledge Aiken in a wrestling lock, held from behind and basically immobilized on the ground.

"Kevin? Are you okay?" Tessa asked.

"Fine. This asshole is history," he said, tightening his grip on Sledge's arms and at the same time forcing the older man's head down to his chest from behind. Sledge heaved and grunted a few times, but could not shake off his opponent.

Tessa thought fast. Yes, Sledge was immobilized. But as soon as Kevin let him go, he could take another shot and really hurt someone. She'd be forced to bash in Aiken's brains with the flashlight, and there would be a lot of explaining to do to her boss.

"Yes, is this the 911 operator?" Tessa said suddenly. She watched as Sledge froze. "There's a fight in the parking lot behind Game World. Someone just attacked a guy here, we need help. How long? Okay, I'll stay on the line."

Sledge made another effort to throw Kevin off his back. "You're breaking my neck, man."

"The police will be here in about four minutes," Tessa said.

"I can hold him that long. No problem," Kevin said. "I'm not even sweating."

"Why don't we forget about this little incident?" Tessa said, looking at Sledge. "That way, no one has to deal with the paperwork."

"What?" Kevin asked, surprised into loosening his hold.

"How about you let go of Mr. Aiken, then he gets in his car and drives away. We forget this ever happened, and he stays the hell away from Kelly. Sound like a plan?" Tessa asked Sledge.

"Fine. Whatever. Just get this dickhead off of me."

"Let him go, Kevin. We're not going to solve this tonight." Tessa checked Kelly to make sure the window was rolled back up and the door was still locked.

Kevin stood and dusted his pants off with his hands. Normally, he'd hold a hand out to help his wrestling opponent off the ground. Instead, he stood over Aiken with feet spread and arms at his side, ready to take the guy down again if he made a move toward Tessa or Kelly.

Sledge pulled himself off the ground and wiped his bleeding nose with the back of his hand. With a wary eye on Kevin, he began to edge toward the Hummer. "This isn't over. You can't get off telling lies about me to the police. No one is going to believe that little slut, so y'all had best just keep your mouths shut."

Kevin took a step forward. "I'm going to say this real slow-like, so you understand. Go on home, boy. Git!"

It might have been over a decade since Kevin had left Virginia, but the rhythms of the South could still come through in his speech. He spoke to Sledge in the same way he had addressed the sweet and stupid hound dog he had gotten as a boy.

Sledge pinned Tessa with a glare. "You know what they say about paybacks—they're a bitch. Bitch."

Tessa leaped forward to restrain Kevin. "Let him go. He's just talking trash because he can't do anything else. Let's get in the car."

Kevin waited until Aiken's taillights had disappeared. Then he opened Kelly's door and helped her into the rear passenger seat. "I think you should lie down back here."

Kelly said nothing, just slid over and slumped low in the seat so she couldn't be seen.

"Good idea, Kev. I'm going to drive around for a while so we can all calm down." Tessa met Kevin's eyes. He knew she was going to make sure they weren't being followed, but said nothing that would upset Kelly. Instead, he opened the front passenger window and adjusted the side mirror so he could watch the traffic behind them. He had no idea what was going on, but since he'd grown up as the son of the director of the FBI, he knew well the security routines that were routinely employed to ensure the Jacobi family's safety.

Half an hour later, Tessa turned down yet another residential street. She hadn't seen any cars behind them, and felt it was safe to go to the shelter.

"I think she's asleep," Kevin said.

"Good. Christ, what a night," Tessa said. "I can't believe I threatened to arrest Sledge Aiken."

"I can't believe what a candy ass he is. He wouldn't last ten seconds with my wrestling team."

"If I hadn't seen it for myself, I never would have believed it."

"Why, because he's a star quarterback? That's nothing. He knows how to throw a ball, run, and get tackled. He clearly doesn't have any experience with self-defense or wrestling. Bet he takes some lessons after tonight," Kevin said with a grin.

"God, don't remind me. Humiliated men with inflated egos make very dangerous enemies. Especially when they have media sharks as lawyers. My boss is going to kill me," Tessa groaned.

"Nothing's going to happen."

"What are you talking about?" Tessa asked.

"You just don't understand men, Tessa. He's not going to say anything to anyone. Otherwise, he'd have to admit that he got his ass kicked by me in front of witnesses. His ego can't afford that. He's probably worried you're going to say something and expose him."

Tessa hadn't thought of that. "Since I was instructed yesterday in very specific terms to leave Sledge Aiken alone and not antagonize him further, my lips are sealed. I don't want anyone hearing how we ran into each other tonight."

"Yeah, what are the chances of that happening in a city the size of Los Angeles?" Kevin asked.

Slim to none, Tessa thought grimly, though she said nothing. Apparently, Sledge Aiken had been following their movements. Since he drove a high-profile luxury SUV, she figured that meant he had someone else following them so he could arrange the meeting in a quiet location—on his terms.

"Anyway, it's just as well we left before the police arrived. No one needs this kind of publicity." Kevin checked the mirror one last time.

"The police were never an issue," Tessa admitted. "Kelly called 911, but the system was busy. I was on hold the whole time—when I said the police were coming, it was a bluff to get Aiken to leave."

"Unbelievable. Kinda makes you want to sign up for self-defense classes and a permit to carry a weapon, doesn't it?"

"Yes, it does. I'm learning the hard way that the police aren't always there to save the day." Tessa gripped the steering wheel. She needed to get this investigation moving, and quickly. She wanted to have at least enough evidence to request a restraining order against Sledge Aiken.

But what good is a restraining order? And how in hell is a legal document going to keep Kelly safe when we can't even depend on the police to enforce it in an emergency?

Chapter 9

Sledge Aiken aggressively drove through traffic on the freeway. His nose still bled sluggishly, and his neck and head were throbbing from the hold that had been used against him. He'd gotten his ass kicked, but only because the other guy hadn't fought fair. It wasn't right to use fancy tricks and holds in a parking lot brawl. Bastard.

He reached over and punched a button that activated the hands-free mode on his cell phone. "Call Jerry," he instructed the unit.

A moment later, a voice answered the phone. "You didn't tell me they were going to have a boyfriend along. That little bitch is causing problems, and you need to fix them," Sledge said.

The person on the other end sighed. "Which little bitch?"

"Both of them. That prosecutor has been snooping around for days, and she's starting to make things uncomfortable. She told me she has enough information to press charges and make them stick. If that happens, my sponsors will drop me like a sack of shit."

"I'll take care of things,"

"You do that. It's why I went to you in the first place—to avoid any difficult situations. This is one mess you're going to have to clean up, and fast," Sledge said.

"Have I ever let you down? I said I'd take care of it, and I will."

"You'd better. Otherwise, I'm going to take my business— and my friends—somewhere else. What would that do to your precious club?"

"Look, the Kelly situation will be under control very soon. Haven't I been keeping an eye on things? Didn't I tell you where she was going to be tonight?"

"That's only because you got lucky and picked up on the lawyer stopping by her office before going to the pizza place. You still don't know where Kelly is staying. What the hell are you going to do about that?"

"You don't need to know. I'm going to make the problem go away."

"Then stop talking about it and do it. I'm headed home. Don't disturb me until you have good news."

Chapter 10

Tessa pulled to a stop at the top of the long drive of Paul Jacobi's exclusive Bel Air home. She popped the locks so Kevin could get out.

"You're not getting off that easy. I called to say we were on the way. Mom has coffee and dessert ready, so you may as well come in."

"Oh, bother. Do I have to?" Tessa asked. This new trend of peace overtures from Paul Jacobi and her stepmother was disturbing, to say the least. Frankly, she preferred the cool politesse that had marked their relationship since Tessa had graduated from college.

"Quit whining. Besides, we need to plan the next time I get to see Kelly," Kevin said.

"Why?" Tessa asked baldly.

"I like her. She seems really nice."

"Ah, Kev, it might be a good idea if you forgot ever meeting her. As you can see from tonight, she comes with a lot of baggage. Paul would kill me if anything happened to you."

"So put Sledge Aiken in prison, and the problem is solved," her brother replied.

After they'd dropped Kelly off, Tessa had explained to him the situation and what Sledge had done. She felt she owed it to her brother for coming to the rescue in the parking lot.

"I'm not sure if that would do it," Tessa said. "Kelly's going to have emotional troubles to deal with for the rest of her life. Besides, putting someone with a Super Bowl ring in prison has turned out to be harder than I thought."

"So make a plan. You always have one, don't you?" Kevin opened the door and stood up. "There's Mom checking in the window—you've been spotted."

Tessa got out and locked the car, muttering. "I'll have coffee, but no dessert. Not everyone has a turbojet metabolism like you guys."

"Puh-lease. Not everyone likes skinny toothpicks, either. Besides, your butt's not that big," he said with an evil grin.

Tessa elbowed her brother in the side as they climbed the stairs. "Watch it, or you'll use up the Prince Charming points you scored tonight helping me and Kelly."

Kevin laughed and held the door open for her with a bow. She led him through to the formal salon, where the family normally had after-dinner drinks and dessert. Tessa didn't see why the three people living in the home needed a kitchen, formal dining room, breakfast room, and salon in which to eat the various meals of the day—but hey, it wasn't her house.

She mentally groaned at the sight of her place setting— rich Colombian coffee served in bone china cups, accompanied by a slice of Tessa's favorite chocolate peanut butter cheesecake. While most people might consider this a thoughtful offering, Tessa was somewhat convinced her stepmonster was trying to fatten her up. For what, she didn't know.

"Did you two have fun tonight?" Paul Jacobi asked.

Tessa tensed. She hadn't asked her brother what he was going to say about the evening. While she didn't want to put him in the position of lying, neither did she want the former head of the FBI to know that his son had gotten into a parking lot brawl with a celebrity athlete.

"The arcade was a lot of fun," Kevin said carefully. "And I really liked Tessa's friend. I hope to see her again."

Tessa opened her mouth to reply, but was interrupted by her cell phone. "Sorry, that's my business phone, so I have to answer it." She walked through the open doorway to the formal dining room before she answered.

"Tessa Jacobi?" The caller mispronounced her last name, calling her "Ja-KO-bee" instead of "JACK-o-bee."

"Speaking."

"I have some advice for you. Lay off the Kelly Martin case."

"Who is this?" Tessa asked in a low voice.

"Someone who doesn't want to see you get hurt," the male voice said. "Your boyfriend Kevin might not always be around to protect you."

She didn't correct that mistake, either. "Kevin has nothing to do with this. You have a problem, you take it up with me."

"You've done enough already. You're making things worse for Kelly by pursuing this investigation. She's going to be punished. If you want to avoid the same treatment, I suggest you drop the case."

"That's not going to happen—" Tessa began.

"Oh, and one more thing. Tell your boyfriend that people who butt in where they don't belong have a tendency to get hurt."

The caller hung up before Tessa could respond.

Chapter 11

"Who was that?"

Paul Jacobi's voice behind her caused Tessa to jump visibly. Receiving late-night phone calls with anonymous threats was unnerving to say the least.

Tessa held up a hand to silence her father as she used the last call return function on her cell phone to find out who the threatening caller was.

Caller ID blocked.

She scowled at the screen, then cleared it and dialed the women's shelter where Kelly was staying. She asked to speak to the night manager.

"This is Tessa Jacobi of the Los Angeles County District Attorney's Office. I need to talk to your security officer, then have you check on one of the new residents, Kelly Martin. Yes, I'll hold."

Paul Jacobi closed the French doors behind him, giving them privacy. He said nothing as he listened to his daughter speak to a security manager and advise that there had been a specific threat made against a recent arrival.

He saw Tessa's relief when she heard that Kelly was peacefully settled into her room for the night. His daughter's face was pale, but slightly less tense when she finally ended the call.

"What the hell is going on? Did I hear you say something about Kevin?" Paul asked.

Tessa looked at him, realizing she was as trapped as she had been earlier by Sledge Aiken's car. The thought did nothing to help calm the anger and frustration she was barely keeping contained.

"It's a case I'm prosecuting—it made for an interesting evening, to say the least. But it has nothing to do with you."

"It sounds like Kevin's involved. That makes it my business."

Tessa closed her eyes briefly. He was right—she couldn't shut him out if her brother's safety was at risk.

"Then there's the fact that you have yet to call the police about the disturbing phone call you just got," Paul continued. "And your question yesterday about finding an outside investigation firm. If this whole situation is messy enough that you don't want the police involved . . . I don't like it, Tessa."

"I know you're worried about Kevin—"

"I'm worried about both of my children, even if you choose to shut me out," Paul said.

Tessa didn't want to go there. Not on top of everything else she was dealing with tonight. She turned away to focus her thoughts. The best way to get Paul off her back would be to give him a job to do, like keeping Kevin safe.

"I can't tell you much more than I told Kevin," she began. "A high-profile celebrity athlete is being investigated for a date-rape incident involving an eighteen-year-old girl. She's the friend of mine that Kevin met tonight. Our investigation has hit a few speed bumps, mainly because of the suspect's fame and popularity. His lawyer doesn't help things, either."

"Who's the lawyer?" Paul asked.

"Carl Abrahms."

"Jesus. Ramirez must be worried about losing her newly refurnished District Attorney's office."

"Um, she's definitely not happy. I'm supposed to stay away from the suspect and not upset him—which is kind of hard to do when he pops up in front of me wanting to talk and not wanting to take no for an answer. Seems to be a theme with him."

"There was a confrontation tonight?"

"He wanted Kelly to go with him. But Kevin was able to stop the guy. He was great, as a matter of fact. You should double his allowance," Tessa said.

"But your brother's not always going to be with you. Frankly, while I know he can take care of you and himself, I don't want him involved in anything like this," Paul said.

"I don't, either. I'm going to talk to a judge about getting a restraining order on Monday morning."

Paul snorted. "You've been followed, confronted, and threatened on the phone. And this is all just tonight. I think the case is bigger than you want to admit, Tessa. So you should know a piece of paper isn't going to stop a man with a great deal to lose, not when he's already gone to such lengths to keep things quiet. Maybe you should back off for a while."

"I owe it to Kelly to keep pushing. She's been through a lot since I talked her into pursuing this case, and I promised I'd take care of her."

Paul's eyes narrowed at Tessa's tone. He knew from experience that it meant she wasn't going to budge on this argument.

"Besides," Tessa continued, "this is just some loser who intimidates teenage girls. The D.A. eats jerks like him up for breakfast."

"And craps them out before lunch, no doubt," Paul said. "But only when formal charges have been filed. And that hasn't happened yet, has it?"

"I'm working on it. Besides, I tried to get additional help with the investigation from Novak International. Mr. Novak didn't seem to believe Kelly's story, but as you can see from tonight's activities, we're certainly onto *something* concerning Sledge Aiken. I'm going to keep digging until I find what it is."

Paul knew there was no talking to Tessa when she was so determined. Frankly, he had trouble talking to her at any time. That was his fault. But she didn't need a rehashing of family communication issues right now—she needed help with her investigation. Fortunately, that was one thing he was uniquely qualified to provide.

"What is your plan?" Paul asked his daughter.

"I'm going to follow a couple of leads. Ed Flynn and his partner from LAPD have taken over the rape investigation, so I'll be able to follow it very closely. We're working together to build a case, but I've been given orders to come in under the radar on the background checks. It's going to take some time. But I'll make sure Kevin is kept out of things in the future."

"Was Kevin mentioned specifically?"

Tessa met Paul Jacobi's eyes. "They threatened him. Look, I know he's on break from school. Maybe now would be a good time to send him on a ski trip or something. Get him out of town."

Paul hadn't realized the threat was so serious, but knew it took a lot for Tessa to admit this to him. "He's been angling for it, and Lana as well. I'll take care of it."

He'd also be booking a fourth seat on the trip—for his daughter. But he wouldn't tell her that yet, because she'd only fight it. Just as she'd fight Paul when he tried to involve a senior private investigator in the case. But she'd give in, because she'd realize it was the best way to help her new friend. He knew his daughter well enough to understand that her personal integrity and desire to help were both her greatest strengths and his main point of leverage.

"Thanks. I think I'll skip the rest of dessert. I need to call some people and write up the paperwork for a restraining order," Tessa said.

"Go ahead," Paul said.

He had some calls of his own to make.

Chapter 12

Two people with the last name Jacobi contacting him in the same week could not be a coincidence.

Luke Novak turned the wheel of his vintage Mustang to enter the long driveway leading to Paul Jacobi's house. He'd received an urgent call from the man last night after eleven, requesting a meeting at his Bel Air home on Sunday morning. Anything that had the former director of the FBI worried had to be big.

Luke was willing to bet a year's worth of profits that it had to do with Tessa Jacobi.

Considering that he'd deliberately antagonized Tessa during their last meeting—and essentially talked her out of hiring him—Luke was more than curious about why he'd received a summons to meet with her father.

He parked the car and walked up the stairs, then rang the doorbell. He stepped back in surprise when Paul Jacobi himself opened the door. The man had aged extremely well. He knew Paul was approaching seventy, but his body was still lean and strong, his hair an attractive salt-and-pepper color.

The dark blue eyes that swept over Luke hadn't lost any of their sharpness over the years.

Paul stepped back and motioned for Luke to precede him into his private study. Walking behind the man gave Paul an opportunity to size him up—and it was plain that Luke Novak didn't make a habit of turning his back on anyone he didn't know. As soon as they entered the room, Luke took the seat that would give him an optimal view of the room and put his back up against a wall.

"Tell me about your company, Mr. Novak. And your qualifications." Paul took a seat behind a broad mahogany desk and offered coffee, which was politely refused.

Luke knew when he was being asked for a sales pitch, and this wasn't one of those times. The guy wanted to check him out—fair enough. "My company provides private investigation, corporate and personal security, and family reunification services."

Paul frowned. "You mean like custody disputes?"

"We handle a variety of situations which can pull a family apart. Custody disputes, kidnapping and ransom, runaways. We do whatever the client needs."

"And you were with the OCSD for how long before you left?"

"Twelve years. Then I took early retirement after being shot."

"In the line of duty?" Paul asked.

"I was off-duty depositing my paycheck when the bank was robbed. The resulting hostage standoff went bad. SWAT stormed the building, and I was caught in the cross fire trying to get civilians to safety."

"I think I remember now. If I recall, you made yourself the liaison with the bank robbers, negotiating for the release of some of the hostages and sending coded messages to your SWAT buddies. You were on the team, yourself, right?"

Luke shifted in his chair. "I had trained with most of the guys who were waiting to storm the building. We had a private communication system, so I was in a unique position of being able to help out."

"And for your trouble, you got shot. Then you were yanked off active duty and parked in front of a desk, if the sheriff's department's procedure is anything like the FBI's," Paul said.

"Yes, sir." It had been one of the reasons he'd left the force.

"Call me Paul. I can see from your face you didn't like being stuck in an administrative role. But it's standard procedure, not a case of being screwed over by the system."

Luke looked him right in the eye. "In my opinion, Paul, the question of whether I'm being screwed or not can only be answered by *me*. And I felt like I was getting fucked without getting kissed first."

Paul laughed, relaxing for the first time since the night before. "Speaking of the proverbial kiss-off, I hear you met my daughter, Tessa."

"Yes, sir. Paul," Luke corrected himself. "I don't think she liked me."

"I'm not worried about that. I'm more concerned about why you didn't take her case."

"She didn't want me to. Not really. I told her that part of my job is to look through the bullshit to see what's really going on. Tessa is in full ostrich mode with respect to some unanswered questions about the victim, so she wasn't interested in the way I work," Luke said.

"Well I am. I don't have the full details of the case, but I think Tessa is going to need an unorthodox partner for the investigation. Any time you mix celebrities, money, sex, and D.A. politics in a criminal investigation, I think there is an advantage to be had in going outside the system."

"I agree. But your daughter has made a career of defending the system. Does Tessa really want to hear that it's not going to help out this Kelly, but instead is going to stand by while her rights are trampled, all the while protecting the rich and powerful?"

"Tessa has always needed to learn things the hard way. But once she does, she never forgets. I need you to look out for her and make sure the lesson isn't any harder than it has to be."

"Sounds like the job of a parent," Luke said, with a raised eyebrow.

Paul leaned back in his chair. "Normally, it would be."

"You're not interested in that role?"

"More than anything." Paul hesitated. "I'm not in the habit of publicizing family issues, but I get the feeling that you will work better if you understand exactly what's going on. I was never much good at being a parent—I was always doing work at the FBI that I thought was more important."

Luke nodded. "I understand that—thinking that you're upholding the law and helping to save the world. Then realizing you have no personal life to fall back on when the system kicks you out of the inner circle."

"Very good, Novak. I didn't learn that until I was sixty. By then the political winds in Washington were changing. I left the Bureau to focus on family, but the damage was done with Tessa, to my everlasting regret. When I took steps to ensure that I didn't make the same mistake with my second child, I'm afraid I hurt Tessa even more. I ended up growing closer to my son, but forcing Tessa into the periphery of the family I was trying to create."

"I see why Tessa values order and loyalty so much," Luke said.

"Ouch."

"I'm sorry, I didn't mean to say—"

"The truth?" Paul asked. "That's all right. Tessa's world fell apart when she was eight. That's when my first wife—her mother—drowned while sailing. I didn't handle things well, I'm afraid. Within a few weeks of that, Tessa was shipped off to boarding school, and I was dating a young woman barely out of high school. I married her not long after that. Tessa has never forgiven either one of us."

"Sounds like she holds a mean grudge," Luke said.

"Only because the betrayal was so profound. I utterly failed my child because I couldn't handle being alone after my first wife died. I remarried, then buried myself in work while Lana traveled internationally on one assignment after another. Sending Tessa to boarding school was the only way I could think of to protect her from coming home to an empty house every night, but she saw it as a rejection of her value as a human being."

"Kids are tough, though. And Tessa strikes me as a decent and honorable person—that much was clear after meeting her. Why didn't you ever patch things up?" Luke asked.

He didn't normally get involved in the family lives of his clients unless it directly impacted the case. In this situation, he had a feeling that Tessa's decisions today were being shaped by events that had happened to her decades ago. It was important for him to know the truth.

"When Tessa was sixteen, Kevin came along. She told me she was moving back home to take care of him. Since she was mature for her age, no one saw any problems with this. On the contrary, it allowed me and my wife to continue working more than eighty hours a week with a clean conscience."

"Until your careers began to go a different direction," Luke guessed.

"Yes. I eventually left my job to spend more time being a parent, and Lana quit modeling as well. That meant Kevin no longer needed Tessa's care full-time. There was quite a power struggle between her and Lana for six-year-old Kevin's affections. I'm afraid that I sided with my wife, believing it was best for Kevin to be raised by his mother."

Luke raised his eyebrows as he thought about the damage that kind of family infighting could cause, especially to a teenage girl.

"I know." Paul sighed, catching Luke's look. "Everything I did just reinforced Tessa's feelings of inadequacy and betrayal. But of all of us, she made the adult decision and put Kevin's needs ahead of her own. She saw the potential for emotional damage to Kevin and bowed out of the fight. She even moved into the dorms on campus at the University of Virginia to ensure a smooth transition, though I know it killed her to be away from Kevin. Tessa did it all in such a way that Kevin never felt abandoned, and Lana and I picked up the job of raising him from there. But our relationship with Tessa never recovered. It's like she's always waiting to see how we'll hurt her next."

"It sounds like you've done a lot of analysis of the situation," Luke said.

"Oh yes," Paul said bitterly. "I can tell you exactly what went wrong. I'm following the Alcoholics Anonymous method of patching up family relationships, first admitting what I did wrong and then making amends. That's part of the reason you're here."

"Have you two made any progress?" Luke asked.

"None. I just don't know how to fix it. The only thing I can do is give her time. I have faith in Tessa's goodness, in her love of family, and in her decency as a human being. If I can prove to her that I'll never hurt her like that again, maybe she can forgive me."

Luke heard the naked pain in Paul's voice. Looking beneath that, he realized how much it cost the man to admit to a perfect stranger how he'd messed up his relationship with his daughter. It almost seemed like he was doing penance.

It also explained a hell of a lot about Tessa Jacobi and her approach to the current case.

"I'll tell you, Paul. I think you're on the right track here. I didn't see any pettiness or evidence of a mean spirit in your daughter. If you honestly want to heal the breach, I'm sure she'll forgive you someday."

"That's why I need you to help her with this investigation.

Recent events have led me to believe it may be dangerous," Paul said, then cleared his throat as the somber words echoed in the quiet study. "I can't have something happen to my only daughter before we get to the point that she actually calls me 'Dad' again."

"What makes you believe that Tessa is in physical danger?" Luke asked, leaning forward.

Paul was interrupted by a knock on the door. Lana Olson swept in, a stunning blond goddess in a gold silk robe. A cloud of Chanel followed her across the room as she went to Paul. At just under six feet tall, she had a powerful combination of slender curves and a youthful face that could stop traffic.

"Good morning." She kissed Paul lightly on the mouth, then perched on the arm of his chair. Luke smiled to himself at the look of both awe and adoration Paul gave his wife. It was as if he couldn't believe the exquisite creature settled next to him was really his wife.

However their relationship had started, it was clear there were deep feelings of love and affection between the two now.

"I came to see when you would be able to help me make lists," Lana said. She reached out to drink Paul's coffee, then made a face and added more cream to the cup.

"I'm just finishing up a meeting. This is Luke Novak. He owns a company that I may hire to upgrade the house security system while we're gone," Paul said. His warning look dared Luke to say otherwise.

"We've had the same system for three years with no problems." Lana shook her head. "I don't understand why we have to change now."

"Thieves update their techniques and technology every six months or so," Luke said. "It's a full-time job to stay ahead of them."

"Hmmm. Don't take too long, Paul. Once we finish sorting things to be packed and making lists, we still need to shop for outdoor gear and binoculars," Lana said. She turned to Luke. "After years of pestering, all of a sudden he wants to take us on a cruise of the Antarctic. We're going to see penguins nesting, glaciers, whales, everything. I'm so excited."

She leaned forward to give Paul Jacobi another smacking kiss. Then she swept out of the room, the scent of expensive perfume trailing behind her.

Once the door closed, the silence in the room grew thick. Finally, Luke broke it.

"Antarctica? What the hell kind of trouble is your daughter in?"

Chapter 13

Tessa knew it was cowardly, but she'd deliberately spent Monday morning working from home so she wouldn't run into her boss. It was only after Carmen Ramirez had left the D.A.'s office for a day of off-site meetings that Tessa went in to work. She hadn't wanted to show the paperwork for Aiken's restraining order to her boss before it went to the judge—because she was sure Carmen would veto the whole thing. This way, Tessa could honestly say she hadn't been able to get approval because Carmen had been gone for the day.

Never let it be said she didn't know how to massage the system.

Not that it had done her much good. Tessa had submitted the paperwork to the judge's clerk at lunchtime. By late afternoon, she had been called into the judge's chambers and chided for putting forward an "ill-conceived and inflammatory motion." The judge was concerned that the name of the accuser be protected in the same way that the alleged victim's was.

In other words, there wasn't enough evidence to proceed

with a request for a restraining order, let alone the filing of sexual assault charges against Sledge Aiken.

Tessa wasn't all that surprised, though she was disappointed. But she had closely followed legal trends over the last few years and realized that the Kobe Bryant sexual assault case had changed the way states carried out rape investigations involving high-profile suspects. In a situation where the basis of the allegation was a victim's word alone, the current tendency was to go forward cautiously and protect the accuser's name and reputation as zealously as the courts had once protected the victim's.

But even knowing that, Tessa still clenched her teeth when she thought about her discussion in chambers. Even with recent trends in protecting the privacy of celebrities, she thought that the judge had gone too far in turning down her requests and cautioning her to be careful in the investigation to ensure that the rights of all parties were protected.

She had been around long enough to wonder whether a call had been made to the judge by Sledge Aiken's attorney before Tessa's request for an order of protection was denied.

Deep breath, nice and slow. It's not like the restraining order would have done much good. The police actually have to respond to a call for help first, not put you on hold after you dial 911.

She checked the time on her desk clock, then scrubbed her hands over her face. She hadn't slept well since she'd received the threatening phone call two days ago, but at least now she wouldn't have to worry about her brother. He and his mother were headed off to Buenos Aires for a week, then were hopping a ship to Antarctica for an ecocruise. Paul Jacobi would join them in a few days.

Kevin had urged Tessa to come with them, but the thought of being trapped on a small vessel with her stepmonster for ten days was enough to bring on a cold sweat.

Frankly, she'd rather be stripped naked and thrown into a Turkish prison. But there was no need to say that to Kevin.

Feeling much better for her wicked thoughts, she decided to have dinner at a Chinese buffet restaurant down the street. It was a popular place for after-work action, so she walked down the hall to see if anyone else was interested in going. But it was after seven, and a Monday as well, so her colleagues were gone for the day. As the work week went on, people started piling up the overtime, so most employees went home at a reasonable time on Mondays and Tuesdays.

Tessa gathered some files she wanted to review at home, locked her office door, and went to the restaurant. She nursed a dry Chinese beer while making her way slowly through the steaming buffet dishes. During the meal, she flipped through her files and began consolidating information in her notebook so she would be able to give Ed and Ronnie a more coherent update the next time they met.

Two hours, three plates, and two beers later, Tessa realized she'd forgotten some important files in her office. One held Kelly's medical records and photos, including the Polaroids taken to document her facial bruises after arriving in the women's shelter. It was locked in a recessed drawer in Tessa's credenza, which was why she hadn't thought to pick it up with her other files.

She scooped up her things, paid the tab, then made her way back to the District Attorney's office. Her car was in the parking garage beneath the same building, so it wouldn't be any trouble to pick up the files on her way home. She took the elevator to the correct floor, then paused as she stepped off to search for her keys. After a moment muttering and shaking to resettle the contents of her oversized purse, she finally found the keys at the bottom.

But when she got to her office door, it wasn't locked. In fact, it wasn't even closed all the way. Curious, Tessa looked around. She spotted the night janitor cleaning an office across the hall from her own. The man was working in the dim illumination provided by the emergency lighting system.

"Excuse me, did you already clean my office across the way?" Tessa asked.

"Not yet. You want me to do it now?" The janitor barely looked up from the surface he was dusting.

"No, that's okay. Whenever you get to it."

She went back to her office and locked the door behind her. On approaching the desk, she immediately noticed that something didn't seem right.

It was too neat, for one thing. The files were stacked, but not in the haphazard way she normally kept them. And two files from the "old cases" group on the left side of her desk were now sitting on top of the "new cases" file on the right. A note that had been on the stack was now stuck to the base of her lamp, and the stapler had been moved from its position as paperweight to some loose documents in the middle of the piles.

Someone had gone through her desk in the last two hours.

Tessa froze, then told herself it was a little late for panic. Whoever had done this was gone. Besides, it could have been one of her colleagues looking for a file on a joint case. Maybe the person in her office had been spotted by the janitor.

She opened her door again and went looking for the man to put her mind at ease. He was nowhere to be found—which was strange, as it was obvious he hadn't finished cleaning the floor. She shook her head and told herself the guy was probably taking a cigarette break.

She spent the next half hour organizing her files and locking information from inactive cases in the drawer of her credenza. Unfortunately, she couldn't find the photocopied sheet with the names and numbers of the credit cards found in Kelly's possession, which she was pretty sure had been in the stack of loose papers. Clenching her jaw, Tessa decided that Kelly's files would be coming home with her from now on, at least until she had a chance to get the information duplicated.

But Aiken's earlier taunt about files going missing was

giving her a major case of the heebie-jeebies. She knew that someone had gone through her office, just as she knew she'd never be able to prove that Aiken had anything to do with it.

After stalling as long as she could, Tessa checked again for the janitor. The floor was dark and quiet, with no activity in any of the rooms. She locked her office door and took the elevator to the lobby. Once there she asked the security guard where the night cleaning staff was at that moment.

"They don't come on duty until after midnight, ma'am," the security guard told her.

"Are you sure? No one comes in earlier?" Tessa asked.

"No, ma'am. The D.A.'s office and some of the others complained about being disturbed by the cleaning crews when the employees were working late, so now none of the janitors comes in until after midnight."

Tessa clenched her hands around her black leather briefcase, which now held her only copies of the information pertaining to Kelly Martin's rape investigation.

As she walked to her car, she tried to imagine if Sledge Aiken would have the guts to pay a man to dress in a janitor's uniform and go through her desk. And what he hoped to achieve by that act.

Because all he'd really done was put Tessa on alert. And make her more determined than before to see Aiken in an orange prison jumpsuit.

Chapter 14

Tessa heard a loud, persistent noise and rolled over with a groan. She swatted at her alarm clock, then squinted at the time. Six. But she hadn't set the alarm that early—in fact, she hadn't gotten to sleep until well after two. She frowned in confusion as the noise started again.

Phone.

Who the hell was calling her number—twice—at this ungodly hour? She sat upright, thinking abruptly of Kelly.

"Hello?" Her voice was husky from sleep.

"This is Luke Novak. I was wondering if you would have breakfast with me before going in to work. I have something important to discuss with you."

"What?" Tessa asked. She wasn't anyone's idea of a morning person, and was having trouble getting her brain working after only a couple hours of fitful sleep last night.

"I have information about Kelly Martin that I think you will find interesting. I'd like to discuss the case further with you," Luke repeated patiently.

"Uhh—"

"Say 'yes,' Tessa."

"Yes, Tessa."

He chuckled. "Then I'll meet you in two hours at that little coffee shop by the courthouse. The place with the great buckwheat pancakes."

Tessa mumbled a reply, then hung up the phone and dragged herself into the shower. She turned the water on full cold and stood shivering under its stream, trying to wake up her body, if not her brain.

She'd been up late copying Kelly's medical files, rape kit report, and the details of the investigation to date. She'd also scanned Kelly's pictures into her home computer, though she knew that was of limited use. Still, it would have to do until she could get the photos professionally duplicated. That way, if any more of Kelly's information went missing, they'd have a backup copy stored in a safe place.

Which did not include her office at work. The more she thought about last night, the more she saw it as a positive thing that someone had rifled through her papers—it showed she was making someone very nervous.

Good. That meant she was digging in the right place.

Luke ordered a pot of coffee and sat back in the corner of the vinyl booth to wait for Tessa's arrival. He whistled a quiet tune and tapped his fingers in time on the table. An elderly woman seated across the aisle caught the action and smiled. He nodded and smiled back.

Not wanting to analyze too closely why he'd been looking forward to this meeting, Luke took out his notebook to review the information he had gathered since speaking to Paul Jacobi on Sunday. When a bell jingled daintily over the front door, he looked up to see Tessa removing her sunglasses. She saw him and hesitated, just briefly, before making her way to the booth.

As she got closer, Luke saw the deep circles under her blue-gray eyes. Her face was a little paler than he remembered, too. And there was a tightness to the way she carried herself that told him she was both tired and stressed.

Not that it made any difference in her efficient walk and the swing of her nicely curved hips. It just showed in the set of her shoulders and the grip she had on her black briefcase. Something was gnawing at her.

"Don't take this the wrong way, but you look like hell. Hot date last night?" Luke asked.

"Is there a right way to take that comment? Besides, you're the one who dragged me out of bed at the crack of dawn. What do you want?" Tessa was never at her best before morning coffee, which she hadn't had time to make before leaving this morning. L.A. commuters had paid the price on her way to the coffee shop and now she was happy to turn her temper on Luke Novak.

"Efficient and to the point, as always. That's what I like about you, Swiss." Luke pushed a cup across the table to her, then motioned to the carafe of coffee at the end of the table.

"I like it, too. So why don't *you* get to the point," Tessa said, snatching the carafe and pouring liquid caffeine into her cup. She could almost feel the dull headache behind her eyes easing its grip as she took a huge gulp.

"You're grumpy in the mornings—that's so cute." Luke grinned when she scowled at him. "All right, enough teasing. And I'll use short sentences with small words so you can follow. I've looked further into Kelly's story, and it seems like both of you could use some help."

Surprised, Tessa lowered her cup to the table with a thump. "Why did you look into Kelly? How was it possibly any of your business, since you turned the case down because you didn't believe me?"

"It's not that I didn't believe you—"

"But you didn't believe Kelly, I know," Tessa finished. "What's changed?"

"I'd like to help you, but I can't do that if you're grilling me. Do you want to argue about bad first impressions, or do you want to prosecute the rich jock who raped an eighteen-year-old girl in his Hollywood Hills home?"

Tessa raised her eyebrows as she took another sip of coffee. Apparently Luke Novak had done enough investigative work to realize that Sledge Aiken was a real loser, one who was more than capable of the crime of which he'd been accused.

"So now you believe us. Why?" Tessa asked.

"I don't believe the whole story."

"At which point do you get lost?"

"I believe the starstruck innocent making her way to Hollywood bit," Luke said. "I get lost at the point where she leaves the bus station."

"So you don't think this girl could be staying with her cousin while she tries to get a recording contract, then meets up with the rich jock who attacks her?"

"See, that's the first problem. Do you know the name of the person who lives with Kelly—her cousin, right?"

"His name is Jerry," Tessa replied.

"Jerry Kravitz, to be precise. And I was interested to discover he doesn't have any known cousins, nor do his parents have any siblings that I've been able to find. So much for lie number one," Luke said.

"Are there more than one?"

"I'll say. Like the credit card numbers that Kelly had. I ran them to see what popped up."

"How did you do that? I didn't give you that information," Tessa said. "You son of a bitch—were you the one who searched my office last night?"

"Back up a sec. Someone tossed your office?"

Tessa looked into Luke's eyes to measure whether he was telling the truth. All she saw was concern and anger, along with sincerity. Based on that, and his sterling reputation in the state, she figured she could relax.

"So maybe it wasn't you," she said. "But someone dressed up as the building janitor and rifled through the files on my desk last night."

"Was anything important taken?" Luke asked.

"No, just the sheet of paper with the photocopies of the credit cards we found in Kelly's bag. Everything else was in file folders locked away in my credenza. I think I scared the guy away when I came back to my office unexpectedly after a late dinner," she said quietly.

"I don't mean to doubt your story. But how do you know the janitor didn't just knock stuff off your desk and put it back in the wrong order?"

She explained about her discussion with the security guard, and the fact that no cleaning staff came on duty until much later, then told him about Sledge Aiken's veiled threat about files disappearing. "Unfortunately, I can't prove anything. I'm just looking at it as a relatively cheap lesson about keeping irreplaceable files on my person instead of leaving them at the office."

That wasn't how Luke was looking at it. To him, it meant that the players involved in this case were serious enough that they were engaging in surveillance of an officer of the court to track her movements. And they also weren't above risky behavior to get information they wanted.

"I don't like this," Luke said.

"I'm not fond of it, either. But there's next to nothing I can do except make sure it doesn't happen again. Anyway, if you didn't take the papers from my office, how were you able to look up the credit accounts in question?"

"I have a good memory. And I'm on retainer with several of the local banks and major credit card companies, so I have access to their databases. All I had to do was run the names and pull recent credit card activity."

"And?"

"Nothing too wild. Some clothes, online purchases, and a lot of charges at a place called Club Red. Most of the cards had a balance of several thousand dollars on them, not enough to set off alarm bells. But there aren't any restaurant charges on the cards, even though Kelly said they were given to her by the management at the restaurant where she works. So where did she get the cards?"

Tessa sat back as she turned the new information around in her mind. "It's still possible Kelly could be telling the truth about these men having left their cards at a restaurant—maybe the charges just haven't appeared on the cards yet."

"I suppose anything is possible," Luke conceded. "But I don't think that's all that was going on with those cards. And I think you know I'm right. So why are you making up lame excuses for this kid?"

Tessa poured a third cup of coffee—it was going to be that kind of day.

The kicker was that she believed Novak, not Kelly. At least with respect to the credit cards, and staying with her "cousin" Jerry Kravitz. She'd always felt something was off with a cousin who would let Kelly go out with Sledge Aiken, then let the girl be abused while she was living under his roof. She just hadn't pushed Kelly hard enough for answers, probably because she had known she wouldn't like them.

"How did you find all this out?" she asked Luke. "That's a lot of threads to unravel in a short period of time."

"To start, I sent MacBeth to visit Sledge Aiken at his favorite sushi bar in Hollywood. Apparently, he always heads over there when he gets back from out-of-town trips. So MacBeth hung out at the bar in his favorite undercover disguise—bleached blond, trust fund frat boy. On the second night, he was able to talk to our favorite football player. He blew MacBeth off—got really angry, actually."

Tessa winced, thinking of her boss's warning to stay away from the football player and not irritate him further until they had a stronger case against him.

"Don't worry, there's no way MacBeth can be traced back to you. He's a damned chameleon. But Aiken said something important as he was leaving," Luke continued.

"What?" Tessa asked.

"He said that whatever he got from Kelly was 'bought and paid for,' and MacBeth should ask Jerry if he didn't believe it. Even gave him a phone number and said Jerry would clear up everything. I put that information together with the name Jerry Kravitz—who, by the way, popped as the owner of the pager Kelly carries. It turns out he's also the owner of the home where we think Kelly could have been staying. The address for the phone number Sledge gave to MacBeth and the address on the pager records match. Both belong to Kravitz."

"Where did you find out about the pager? And how did you get Jerry's full name? Kelly wouldn't even tell it to me."

"When you came to my office, you had that photocopied sheet of the credit cards found in Kelly's purse. You also had a phone number written across the bottom of the sheet, with the initial "K" next to it. It didn't take much to trace that number back to a pager and the person who paid for it— Jerry Kravitz."

"You make it sound like an oversight that I didn't do the same."

"No, I figure you just hadn't gotten around to pushing Kelly for that type of information yet because you were trying to build a trusting relationship with her."

"Yes. But I also have to follow procedures. I can't just go digging into a private citizen's life without due cause—I've got to obey the rules," Tessa said.

"I know you do," said Luke. "That's why I'm a good person to have on the case. I have a freedom of movement that you don't. And I'm able to do things like talk to Jerry Kravitz without causing a stir."

"You actually talked to Kelly's cousin? Or whatever he is?" Tessa asked.

"MacBeth did, while still in his disguise. He was waiting for Jerry to get home, and had a chance to talk to some of the neighbors first. They said they started seeing a girl matching Kelly's description about a month ago, but didn't know much about her. She stayed in during the day and mostly went out at night."

"Sledge Aiken's neighbors also started seeing Kelly come to his house about a month ago. What's the connection?"

"I don't know. MacBeth tried to question Jerry when he arrived after midnight, but he was less than helpful. He got combative, talked about interference in private lives, and wanted to know where Kelly was."

"He doesn't sound like a nice person," Tessa said.

"He's not. MacBeth described him as sleazy and rude, and said that as he left Kravitz was calling Kelly all kinds of names. He was very angry at the way Kelly is disrupting his life and business, and he wants her back."

"I wonder if he's the one who hit Kelly," Tessa said. She explained to Luke about the girl's facial injuries. "Are you sure they're not cousins? I've noticed in my line of work that a lot of families treat each other worse than perfect strangers."

"There's no indication of any relatives from a basic background check of Jerry Kravitz's records. He's an only child, and both of his parents were as well," Luke said.

"Then why would a really sweet eighteen-year-old girl be staying with him? I mean, if he was her boyfriend, wouldn't Kelly have just said that?"

"Like I said, she seems to be lying about a lot of things."

"But not everything. We did a polygraph, and she passed most of the tough questions—she was raped, and Sledge Aiken was the one who did it."

"What was she lying about?" Luke asked.

"I'm not sure, but I'm going to find out."

"Let me help you."

"You can't," Tessa said. "The D.A. can't just bring in a private investigator and bypass the police completely. There are rules and procedures governing this type of case."

"Don't forget, I'm on retainer with a third party that's involved—the credit card companies. As far as I'm concerned, talking to Kelly is the first step to investigating a potential fraud case. There's no way I can look into that crime without understanding who Kelly is and what she's been up to."

"But I haven't filed any fraud charges, so there's nothing to investigate. I don't need your help."

Luke shrugged and tried to look apologetic. "Unfortunately for you, I know about the credit card irregularities. As a paid contractor for the banks, I'm obligated to pursue this aspect of the case—with or without your help. I just thought it would be best if we could work together instead of tripping all over each other. I have a feeling whatever I uncover with respect to the credit cards will be related to what happened to Kelly. I think she's a young kid in over her head."

It seemed fairly logical to Tessa. Still, she was surprised at the amount of information Luke had been able to uncover in a few short days on the case. Police channels took so long, and they had barely scratched the surface in more than a week. In a few days, Luke and his man had managed to turn up a connection between Sledge Aiken and the man with whom Kelly had been staying—information that could take the case in a whole new direction.

She was beginning to think it might be worthwhile to have Luke around to work on the case, as long as he could be controlled.

"Can any of your information be used for my investigation?" Tessa asked.

"I don't think we have anything for the courts yet, but it does let us know we're moving in the right direction. When the victim is telling lies, that's kind of tough to figure out."

"Look, I don't care whether Kelly's story has holes in it or not. I said I'd take her case. I gave her my word. I'm not going to abandon her just because things are getting tough," Tessa said.

Luke heard loud and clear the echo of pain from Tessa's childhood, which was going to make things difficult. But part of the job he'd agreed to with Paul Jacobi was to ensure that those emotional scars didn't cloud Tessa's judgment today.

"If you'd look at these pictures, you'll see that Kelly really was being abused," Tessa said, sensing his hesitation. She took out a file and let Luke read through the emergency room doctor's findings. She watched his face turn hard as he flipped through the Polaroid photos cataloging Kelly's bruises and injuries.

"Dammit. You don't have any DNA evidence, or real physical signs of rape. The only sure way to convict is to get Aiken to plead guilty or find a witness to corroborate Kelly's story." Luke shook his head. "I don't see that happening. Maybe we can try to squeeze 'Cousin' Jerry for information on what happened, but . . ."

"The police are already looking into Kelly's background and so forth. I've struck out with the judge on getting a restraining order, and am no closer to pressing charges against Aiken than I was a week ago. You're the investigator—where do you recommend we start?" Tessa asked.

"Why do I distinctly hear the word 'partner' echoing in the air?"

"Because that's what I am to you right now. If I let you on board, I'm going to be there every step of the way, pushing this investigation forward."

Luke poured another cup of coffee. It was going to be next to impossible to keep Tessa out of the active investigation, just as Paul Jacobi had warned him before he'd agreed to take the case.

"Don't look at me like that," Tessa said. "I told you I was a hands-on type of person."

"I thought you meant hands on my body, not my case," Luke said.

Tessa's mouth dropped open before she realized he was teasing. Her skin was so fair there was nothing she could do to hide the wash of color she could feel burning in her cheeks.

"You'll find I never mix business with pleasure, Mr. Novak."

Luke rubbed his chin regretfully. "Never?"

"Nope. One of my rules, developed after years of working with defense attorneys and cops."

"Well that explains it," Luke said. "You just haven't met someone who tempted you enough to break the rules."

Tessa lifted the tablecloth and peered intently underneath.

"What are you looking for?" Luke asked.

"I was wondering how there was enough room for you and your ego on that bench seat," Tessa said. Humor had always been the best way to handle the routine advances she'd encountered on the job over the years.

Luke laughed and shook his head. "You've got me."

"Good, maybe now you'll tell me why you went digging into Kelly's case even though I made it clear I wasn't going to hire you?"

"You're not going to like the answer."

"Try me."

"Your father contacted me because he thought you might be in over your head. He thought I could help, so it's now my job to be concerned about you and this case. Which I am, given that you've received threats over the telephone and someone has broken into your office," Luke said.

"My father hired you?" Tessa asked as she reached for her bag. "So much for the credit card bullshit."

"Wait. I *am* on retainer for the credit card companies, so that gives me good cover to be poking around the case. It will enable me to do a lot more work than you can. Besides, I may prove useful, especially since I have access to methods and information that are strictly off-limits to the police."

Tessa hesitated. He had been able to get very helpful information, details that she hadn't uncovered in over a week of active investigation. His facts corroborated some of the data she'd gathered, giving a view of the big picture. They complemented each other, and that could be very useful during the investigation. She shouldn't let her feelings about her father obscure that fact.

"I can almost hear the cranks turning in your brain," Luke said. "Your father trusts me to get the job done. God knows he's a cynic, so you can trust me as well."

"I don't want him paying the tab to solve my problems," Tessa said. "I've taken care of myself for a long time.

Luke knew he was on shaky ground, so he tried logic. "I doubt you can afford my daily rates. Remember, I was a public servant as well, I know what you get paid. So are you going to keep your pride intact or help Kelly? Do you want to curl up with your principles at night, or sleep soundly with the knowledge that you've helped take a rapist off the street?"

"You're basically asking if I want to follow the rules or get the job done," Tessa pointed out.

"You're right. If you can't deal with that, you're too naive to be working at the D.A.'s Office as anything but a photocopy girl."

"There's no need to get nasty," she said quietly. "I know it's not fair to ask Kelly to pay for my scruples, or to trip up an investigation of this magnitude with my pride. But I think we can help her without breaking the law."

"It's that important to you?" Luke asked.

"It's everything I believe in. I couldn't get up and come to work every morning if I didn't think I was upholding the system and the order it brings. I know that sounds stupid, but—"

"It doesn't sound stupid. I think you're a decent, honorable person. But I'm not accustomed to working with the police or any branch of law enforcement these days, despite my background with the sheriff's department. I learned there that bureaucracy gets in the way of getting things done. I'm willing to try it for a little while if that's what you want—I just hope that it doesn't handicap us too much."

"Did you just say 'us'?" Tessa asked, ignoring the bigger question under his comment.

"Yeah, I guess I did."

"Where do we start?" Tessa asked.

"I want to start with detailed questions on Jerry's background, and get some answers as to how Kelly came in under the official radar in the state of Colorado."

"I know the police are looking at that as well. Any ideas on where to start?"

Luke nodded. "But it'll cost you my per diem to find out what they are."

"I'll give you a few days—on my father's nickel—to prove that you can be useful. If we can break the case, the D.A. will pick up the tab retroactive to today," she said.

At least I hope Carmen will, Tessa thought.

"Even if the D.A. doesn't approve the charges, if I can prove credit card abuse or fraud, I can bill my time to the banks."

"We have to play this carefully—the division of labor is important because I don't want to be stepping on the toes of the police," Tessa said.

"If that's the way you want to play it," Luke said. "But I have to look at the big picture and keep the interests of all my clients in mind. That means I can't afford to ignore any aspect of what's going on in Kelly's life."

"Who takes priority if client interests are in conflict— Kelly or the credit card companies?"

"You do, Tessa." Luke ignored the way she shifted in her chair. "Your father hired me specifically for this case. If I can turn it around to do work for my ongoing bank clients, that's fine."

"So we all walk a fine line and try to keep everyone happy." Tessa stirred her coffee as she thought about how to sell this new plan to her boss.

"Not too hard with a team of two, when both members are interested in the truth," Luke pointed out.

"Don't forget Ed and Ronnie," Tessa said. "Remember I told you about pushing to have Kelly's case reassigned to officers I've worked with who have a lot of experience dealing with major crimes and high-profile cases. Ed's a veteran, and Ronnie is his protégé."

"Ed Flynn is a good cop. The best. I worked on a couple of task forces with him."

"He tried to talk to Kelly, but frankly we were so disturbed to find she'd been smacked around that we didn't press the issue beyond the lie detector test. We decided to back off while I tried to get her to trust me and understand that I'm on her side. Now that she's had a few days, why don't we start with her?" Tessa asked.

"Is tomorrow okay with you?"

Tessa nodded while Luke paid the tab for their breakfast. For some reason, she'd thought he would protest more about taking her along while he questioned Kelly. The fact that he didn't was a good sign.

She was going to have her hands full enough keeping an eye on Luke Novak, loose cannon. She didn't need the added strain of fighting with him every step of the way. Hopefully, he took orders well.

Tessa looked at him out of the corner of her eye. *Yeah, right. He jumps through hoops, too.*

She shook her head. All the more reason for her to work closely with him and keep him out of trouble.

Chapter 15

Luke pulled into the parking spot beneath Tessa's apartment and shut off the sleek Mercedes his company leased for client visits. Tessa had a second-floor unit in an older Santa Monica beach house converted to multiple dwellings in the 1980s. He trotted upstairs and rang the bell. He rang it again after there was no answer, remembering with a grin her sleepy response to his phone call the morning before.

A dog barked loudly from the other side of the door. Luke could hear the animal place its nose on the floor and snuffle noisily at the crack beneath the front door. Then he heard the distinct sound of paws hitting wood, before the dog barked again. Several times.

Luke's grin faded as he heard a deep male voice telling the dog to be quiet.

A boyfriend. He should have known that a woman like Tessa would be taken, even if she wasn't wearing a man's ring.

The door opened and Luke found himself face-to-face

with at least six-foot-four of muscled male god dressed in boxer shorts and nothing else. Light brown hair stood on end, and navy blue eyes regarded him blearily.

The man mumbled, rubbed his eye, then tried again. "Time is it?"

"Seven," Luke replied cautiously.

The man grunted, then made a belated grab for the dog's collar as it lunged toward Luke.

"Roscoe, no! He won't hurt you," he said to Luke.

Luke had shoved his knee into the dog's chest to keep it from jumping, and now bent down to stroke ears and thump the dog's sides. "Of course he won't. Labradors don't make the best watchdogs."

"Come in," he stepped back. "Tessa's in the shower."

Great. I'll be days getting that image out of my head. Luke smiled politely.

"I'm right here," Tessa said, peeking out from her bedroom. She had wet hair and was wrapped in a towel. "I wanted to make sure you checked who it was before opening the door."

"Have you had any unwanted visitors lately?" Luke asked, crossing his arms as he leaned against the door. The other man began making his way through kitchen cupboards, putting together the makings of coffee.

"I'm going to plead the Fifth on that one," Tessa said.

"Lawyers." Luke shook his head as Tessa shut her bedroom door.

"Coffee's on. Don't take any crap from Roscoe. I gotta get ready."

Luke watched the other man practically sleepwalk down the hall. It looked like Tessa wasn't the only slow starter in the mornings. Luke loved dawn, but had learned to take it easy on those whose metabolisms prevented rational thought before 10:00 A.M.

After snooping around for a few minutes, he made himself comfortable with a cup of coffee and a newspaper he'd found on the front stoop. Roscoe casually jumped onto the couch beside him and put his head in Luke's lap. Since the dog acted like it was a common occurrence, Luke let him be and scratched soft ears as he read the paper.

That was the sight that greeted Tessa when she walked down the hall—Luke Novak making himself at home in her living room while stroking the ears of her brother's adoring dog. It was such a domestic scene it gave her a start.

How long had it been since she'd allowed a man to make himself at home in her apartment?

Frankly, she couldn't remember the last time. Probably when she was in college. Sometime between law school and moving to LA, Tessa had become the queen of long-distance relationships. Which meant that more often than not, she ended up meeting her boyfriends on vacations and holidays, giving a feeling of unreality to the relationship. That was why she'd eventually broken up with her college sweetheart after moving to LA, and why her more recent long-term relationship with a graduate student cum teaching assistant from San Diego had also fizzled.

"Penny for your thoughts," Luke said.

Tessa started. "Sorry, as you know from yesterday I'm not at my best until I've had some caffeine."

"Apparently your young friend isn't, either," Luke didn't like to think how young the guy was. He wondered how Tessa could be interested in some jock at least ten years younger than she was.

It's called hormones. Men don't have the corner on the hottie-with-a-naughty-body market.

"You mean Kevin?" Tessa asked, gesturing down the hall. "Clearly that gene came down from the Jacobi side, since we both have it."

Luke goggled. "That's your brother? Your sixteen-year-old-brother?"

Tessa nodded. "I know, he's gorgeous, isn't he? I only

hope he'll ignore all the modeling agents and stay in school. I want more for him than the life Lana had."

Luke sat there in stunned silence.

"What, you don't believe we're related? Who did you think he was?" Tessa asked.

"I thought he was your boyfriend or something. He looks very mature for his age," he said.

"As if I could snare a young hunk like Kevin." Tessa shook her head. "Anyway, he's going away for a couple of weeks, so he crashed here last night. He stays with me at least once a week."

"You're very close, aren't you?"

"He's my boy," Tessa replied in a husky voice. Then she cleared her throat. "And you, Roscoe, can be replaced with a stuffed animal. What are you doing on my couch?"

Roscoe put his head back in Luke's lap and thumped his tail on the cushion. "Sorry," Luke said. "He was so confident getting up here, I figured it was allowed."

"It ends up being allowed. How can you say no to that sweet face?" Tessa walked into the kitchen and poured some coffee for herself just as Kevin came out of the bathroom.

Luke looked him over thoroughly and kicked himself for missing the resemblance. Tessa and Kevin had similar eye and hair color, with Tessa's being a few shades lighter. Several of their other features were similar as well. And Tessa interacted with her brother in a motherly way, stroking his wet hair out of his face as she set coffee and a bagel in front of him.

Jealous of a high school boy. Excellent. What a mature way for a thirty-six-year-old veteran of the dating wars to act. Luke dislodged the dog's head as he stood up to introduce himself to Kevin Jacobi properly.

"Where have you stashed Kelly?" Luke asked. He and Tessa had driven out of Santa Monica and were heading for the city center and their interview with the young rape victim. She gave him directions to get off the freeway.

"She's staying at Three Sisters Shelter," Tessa said.

Luke nodded. "I know the name, it's just off the freeway exit. They do some good work with young women."

"That's why I put her there. The security is better than most places—the only off-hours for the roving guards are midnight to 5:00 A.M."

"They probably can't afford much more than that," Luke said, looking at the shabby exteriors in the neighborhood as he pulled up at the correct address.

The shelter was set up in an old strip motel, so the residents had individual rooms. The former manager's office had been turned into a security checkpoint, which all cars had to pass by in order to park in the lot. He followed Tessa down the walkway leading to the residents' rooms, pausing while Tessa waved to the shelter manager.

Eunice Benson was a former nun from a remote East Coast order. She had given up the Church ten years ago to tend battered women in a way that ruffled the feathers of her former colleagues. Shelter residents were given freedom of movement, responsibilities and chores on the campus, and relatively few rules to live by—beyond staying clear of drugs and alcohol, obeying curfew, and not having overnight visitors.

The only other requirement was for tenants to work at least thirty hours a week once they were settled, and to pay 15 percent of their wages to cover rent and other services. The relaxed atmosphere and loose supervision had led to better results and fewer dropouts than some of the other, more strict halfway houses Tessa had visited. That was why she'd chosen to place Kelly here.

"This is her room." Tessa knocked on the door, but there was no reply. She knocked again, but there was silence. Before Luke could stop her, Tessa had pushed the unlocked door open and walked into the room. He followed her quickly, noting that the small efficiency was empty except for two unmade beds, a portable baby crib, and a load of dirty dishes in the sink.

"Kelly?" Tessa called out. She went to the bathroom, but it was quiet and dark.

"She's gone," said a voice from the doorway. Tessa turned to see Eunice Benson leaning on a broom she had been using to sweep the walkway.

"What do you mean, gone? Where did she go?" Tessa asked.

"I have no idea. Jasmine told me this morning."

"Who is Jasmine?" Luke asked.

"Kelly's roommate," Eunice replied. "When she went to bed last night around eleven, Kelly was already asleep. Jasmine said she woke up at three to feed her baby, and Kelly was gone."

"What's wrong?" Luke asked, as Tessa went to a closet and threw the door open. "Is that Kelly's stuff?"

"Yes. And her toiletries are in the bathroom. We went shopping for all these things a few days ago. Kelly was very excited about some of the clothes and makeup I bought her. I can't believe she'd leave everything behind."

"I see this all the time." Eunice shook her head. "You can't force these girls to stay off the streets or out of bad relationships. It's such a shame when they go back to the only life they know."

Tessa knew there was something terribly wrong. There was no way the girl would go without leaving so much as a note. She remembered how scared Kelly had been on seeing Sledge Aiken on the street and knew she wouldn't do anything that could lead to another encounter like that. She just wouldn't.

Tessa looked at Luke, who searched her own face with concern. "Something is wrong with this setup," she told him. *Please believe me*, her eyes begged.

He stood next to her and slid an arm around her shoulders for support. "Where is Kelly's roommate?" he asked Eunice.

"She's at rehearsals for work, I think."

"What does she do?"

Eunice pressed her lips together. "Jasmine is an exotic dancer."

Luke's eyebrows shot up at this information.

"You put Kelly in a room with a stripper?" Tessa blurted out.

"It was the only apartment available, and we had to push Kelly to the top of the waiting list to get it," Eunice said. "Besides, it's better than being a heroin junkie who works for her pimp boyfriend at a Mafia-run club—which is what Jasmine was doing before she came here. As long as she stays clean and keeps it legal, we aren't going to pass judgment on what she does to earn money."

Tessa stared at Kelly's rumpled bed while her mind tried to take in the new information. She distantly heard Luke asking the manager when Jasmine would be back, then thanking her for her assistance. She jolted as he used the arm around her shoulders to steer her out of the room and back to the car.

"I'll drop you at work while I check this out," Luke told her.

Tessa ignored his comment. "I don't like it. Kelly wouldn't ditch her new stuff. And I've never seen her bed unmade since she arrived. She wouldn't willingly leave in the middle of the night, would she?"

"You know her, I don't. Would she?"

Tessa was silent for several moments. "No. And I'm sorry I ever believed that she had. She was scared to death of meeting up with Sledge Aiken again, so I don't believe that she'd go back to Jerry's house. And she doesn't know anyone else in the city, so . . . I've got a bad feeling." She reminded Luke about their encounter with Aiken the other night, and how he'd tried to intimidate Kelly into leaving with him.

"Okay, so we know there's possibly something wrong, that Kelly was maybe pressured to leave or forced to do so against her will," Luke said.

"Thank you. For believing in Kelly."

"You're the one I believe in." He took his eyes off the road to look at her.

She didn't know how to respond to that, so instead stared out the window. At least five minutes passed in silence before she spoke again.

"Wouldn't the roommate have awakened if she heard someone moving around? Eunice said Jasmine had a baby to feed, so I would assume she's a pretty light sleeper, right?"

Luke nodded. "It's logical to think she would have heard something. And there's another thing that's bothering me. I want to check it out."

"What?"

"I can't put my finger on it yet, but hear me out. Jasmine is a former junkie who now works as an exotic dancer. Before that, she was apparently stripping and turning tricks for her pimp boyfriend."

"The one who worked with her in a club linked to the Mafia," Tessa added.

"That's the part I don't like," Luke said. "In a club like that, she would potentially come into contact with some of the figures who run other scams and prostitution operations throughout the state."

"Such as?" Tessa asked. "I don't see the connection yet."

Luke pulled over on a side street, then turned to face her. "Remember when I told you MacBeth tried to interview Sledge Aiken?"

"Yes."

"He was hanging out in a new Sushi restaurant in Hollywood—*Arigato*. The owners of that club also run a popular nightclub that Sledge likes to frequent, a place called *Ultimo*. The club also has Mafia connections if you believe the locals. In fact, many of the LA hot spots do, because they are predominantly cash operations that are attractive targets for organized crime."

Tessa sat up straight. "You think Kelly somehow got mixed up with the mob at one of these clubs? I know she worked as a restaurant hostess, but—"

"Where did she work?" Luke interrupted, though his tone said he already had the answer.

Tessa bit her lip. "At a popular restaurant. A place where she met Sledge Aiken, presumably."

"Exactly. Think back to the credit cards you found in her purse. She said she brought them from work and was returning them to her cousin, who, we now know, is actually an older man named Jerry Kravitz, and not related to her. When I pulled the charge records for those cards, the only entertainment establishment that came up for recent activity was a place called Club Red."

"I remember the name. Is that a nightclub?" Tessa asked.

Luke hesitated. "Sort of. I had to look into it, since I'd only heard the place mentioned once in the past. Club Red is billed as a 'gentleman's club' but is zoned for food, liquor, and adult entertainment. According to people I've talked to, it's part sports bar, part dinner club, part strip joint. The place is ultraexclusive. People are invited to become members, and the club itself sits on a private property spread over several acres. Imagine Hugh Heffner's Playboy Mansion with an on-site nightclub and strip joint."

"And Kelly worked in that particular club? She's only eighteen," Tessa said.

"It would easily explain how she met Aiken," Luke said.

"Because he hangs out there a lot?"

"It's his favorite place to go clubbing, according to Hollywood gossip. In fact, lots of star athletes and celebrities are members of Club Red. They can get together and not be worried about the being stalked by the press or having their stories sold to the tabloids, since each member has a stake in keeping things exclusive and private," Luke said, hating to watch the expressions of fear and disappointment cross Tessa's face.

"Listen to me, Swiss. All I'm saying is Kelly was known to associate with Aiken, starting up to a month before she was assaulted. He hangs out at various LA nightclubs every night of the week, according to a variety of sources that MacBeth talked to. Many popular nightclubs are owned by the Mafia, or at the very least pay them protection money—I know that from my days with the sheriff's department, and I doubt things have changed."

"And Jasmine, the last person to see Kelly, works in a nightclub and has dated someone with mob ties. I'm not sure about the connection, but it doesn't sound good," Tessa said, suddenly chilled.

"Hey, I'm just thinking out loud here. It could be nothing. We'll know more once we get a background check done on Jasmine and talk to her."

"Where does Jerry Kravitz fit into all this?" Tessa asked.

"I don't know. But I'm damn sure going to find out. Give me some time—I need to make a few calls and set up a meeting with an old informant of mine."

"Hurry. I'm don't even want to imagine what Kelly's doing right now."

But as Tessa wrapped her arms around herself and stared out the window, she could think of nothing else.

Chapter 16

"**D**o you want me to drop you at work? Or do you want to go home?" Luke asked Tessa a few minutes later as he drove onto the freeway.

"Neither," she said suddenly. "I want to go see Jerry Kravitz at home. Maybe Kelly is back at his place."

"I'd already thought of that possibility. We can start there."

"Even if he's not home, we can talk to his neighbors and check whether anyone has seen Kelly recently," Tessa said.

Luke drove to the only address he had been able to connect to Kravitz so far. The house was in a neighborhood of modest ranch homes from the sixties, though Luke knew they went for a premium price—at least half a million each. Real estate prices in Southern California were so inflated that as long as the home was physically sound and in a decent neighborhood, owners could demand and receive astronomical prices.

"I wonder where Jerry gets the money to afford the

monthly payment on a five-hundred-thousand-dollar mortgage," Tessa said.

"I was just thinking the same thing. Partner," Luke added
with a slight smile.

"Limited partnership. You do credit cards, I do felony
rape convictions."

Luke brought the car to an abrupt halt at the curb. "This is
more to me than a case of credit card fraud, okay? I have a
real bad feeling about what's going on—I think what we're
seeing is the tip of the proverbial iceberg. Given that, my
priority is helping an eighteen-year-old kid out of a dangerous situation."

Tessa bit her lip. "Mine, too."

"Then we're agreed. I'll help you find Kelly, Swiss." He
took her chin and forced her eyes up to his. "I give you my
word. It means as much to me as yours does to you."

Tessa looked into the hazel swirl of his eyes and found
herself believing him. As the moment stretched on, she
started to wonder what else she was feeling from him. Determination, focus, strength—those she could handle.

It was the feeling that he was looking deeply into her and
liking very much what he saw that made her want to open
the car door and escape.

She pulled her chin free of his gentle grasp. "Then let's
get started. No one takes a victim out of protective custody
on my watch."

Luke had seen the pulse accelerate in the base of Tessa's
throat, along with the slight dilation of her blue-gray eyes.
He figured his point had been made and started the car
again. Without a word, he checked house numbers. Several
minutes later he guided the car to the curb in front of Jerry
Kravitz's home.

"There's no vehicle in the carport—or either neighbor's
driveway," Tessa pointed out.

Luke nodded and cut the engine. "So we wait and get to
know each other. Got a man in your life?"

Tessa gave an uncomfortable laugh. "This is how you pass time on a stakeout?"

"It's not a stakeout, we're waiting for the suspect to get back from the grocery store or something equally mundane. Besides, it beats the heck out of singing along to golden oldies on the radio."

Her laugh was genuine this time. "I do eighties music myself." She ignored his earlier question.

"I see I've got a shy one, so I'll start. I'm not seeing anyone seriously right now. Building a business takes most of my time."

"Hmmm." Tessa looked out the window.

"I suppose you know I worked with the sheriff's department for about twelve years."

Curiosity got the better of her. "I'd heard. Why did you leave? Was it too structured for your renegade soul?" she teased.

"It was, but that's not what drove me out. I was injured on duty and wasn't allowed to resume my investigative role for an extended period of time. It wasn't clear if they would ever let me go back, to be honest, so I took a leave of absence and drew up a business plan for Novak International."

"Must have been a bad injury," Tessa mused.

"A shotgun will do that do you."

"You were shot?" Her head whipped around in surprise.

"Gutshot. But the range wasn't great, so the surgeons were able to put the pieces back together again. The rehab took over a year, though. I don't recommend it as a weight loss regimen."

"How can you joke about it?" Tessa asked.

"Beats whining. Besides, it was the best thing that ever happened to me because it gave me the kick in the ass I needed to go out on my own. I'd been unhappy with my job for a long time because I felt I wasn't helping people like I'd been trained to. I was pushing papers around to a chorus of 'Yes, sirs,' and I hated it. Just didn't have a reason to do anything about it until I got shot."

Tessa shook her head. "We're very different. I mean, in a similar situation to you, I just throw myself more deeply into my work and try to find some satisfying aspect of it. That's why I'm going after big cases like Kelly's, to tell you the truth."

"While I decided there was no point in sitting around watching the system grind up innocents like Kelly," Luke said. And you, he thought, but didn't say it out loud.

"We can help Kelly," Tessa said.

"I know. But I doubt it will be with the methods you're planning to use."

She opened her mouth to reply, but he cut her off.

"I don't want to fight about it, Swiss. I just want your word that you'll be open to alternatives if going after Kelly by the book doesn't work out. I want to hear you say that she's a bigger priority than the system and its rules."

"Done," she said without hesitation. "Just as I want your word that we'll try playing by the rules first."

"You've got yourself a deal. And we have ourselves a neighbor," he added, looking at the car stopping at the driveway of the house next to Jerry Kravitz's.

They both stepped out of Luke's vehicle and approached the woman pulling shopping bags out of her backseat. Luke showed her his identification briefly, then asked if the neighbor had seen Jerry Kravitz recently.

She shaded her eyes with her hand. "He was out this morning washing and vacuuming his car. Then he left. I haven't seen him since then. He's usually gone most days and well into the night."

"Did he have anyone with him? Maybe someone in the house?"

The woman shook her head. "He was alone. I guess the girl who was staying with him is gone," she said, referring to Kelly. "I believe I talked to someone else about him recently. Some blond guy. One of your colleagues?"

Luke smiled at the woman and gave her his card. "Lots of people are interested in your neighbor. Please call the cellular number if you see the girl or Mr. Kravitz. And don't mention this to anyone else, okay?"

"I won't," the woman promised. "This is like an episode of *Law and Order* or something."

Luke waited until the woman had gone into her house before turning to Tessa. "I'm going to take a look around Jerry's pad," he said. "Why don't you go back to the car. This will only take a minute."

"Why can't I go with you?" Tessa countered.

"Much as I would enjoy the view, were you planning on hopping his fence in your skirt and heels?" Luke pointed to her short business skirt and pumps.

Tessa thought for a moment. "Why don't we ask the *Law and Order* fan if we can look over the fence from her backyard. That way we are obeying the letter of the law."

"If not the spirit," Luke muttered, and shook his head. "Fine, let's go."

Round one. Tessa tried not to let her smugness at victory show in her smile.

A search of the Kravitz property from the neighbor's yard didn't provide any additional information. The curtains were open, and there was no activity inside. Luke and Tessa returned to his car and headed back downtown.

"So Jerry was up bright and early washing his car," Tessa said musingly as she chewed on the cap of a pen. She sat up straight as she remembered something.

"When you did a background check on him, did you pull a vehicle registration?"

Luke took one hand off the steering wheel and flipped open his notebook. "He drives a Mercedes C230 coupe, registered with the DMV last year."

"I'm not familiar with that model. But Sledge Aiken's busybody neighbor saw a girl matching Kelly's description arriving at Aiken's place multiple times in a Mercedes." She looked through her own notes. "Here it is. A two-door, one of the cheap models."

"That's the C230. It's an entry-level Mercedes."

"Then I think we can safely assume Kelly was introduced to Sledge Aiken by our buddy Jerry," Tessa said. She made additional notes in her book. "I wasn't sure about that before. Now I want to talk to him even more."

"We will. But while we're waiting to pin him down, I want to talk to Jasmine and see what information she can add to the mix."

"Why don't we talk to her at work?" Tessa asked.

"Because I need to see an old contact first. He has a lot of firsthand information on the clubs, strip joints, and bars in town. I want to speak to him so we don't walk into an interview with Jasmine unprepared."

Tessa nodded her approval of the methodical approach. "When can you set up a meeting with your contact?"

"We'll go tomorrow. I need to give him a heads-up today so he can ask around for us first."

"And then we talk to Jasmine," Tessa said.

Tomorrow was going to be a very interesting day.

Chapter 17

Luke sat in the booth where he'd met Tessa for breakfast a couple of days earlier. She was running late and had sounded distracted when he'd called her on the cell phone an hour earlier.

It was a contrast to what he'd been afraid of finding. Actually, he was pleased at how well Tessa was handling the sudden disappearance of Kelly Martin. Given her emotional involvement with the case, he wouldn't have been surprised if she'd been upset and demanding faster action from him. But instead she'd maintained control and was working the case slowly and methodically.

It beat the hell out of him why he was going along with that, but so far it seemed to be going okay.

The café's front door flew open, and the normally delicate jingle of the attached bells ended in a clatter as they came into contact with the wall. Tessa stalked over to the booth and threw her bag onto the bench seat before sliding in after it.

Luke didn't say a word, just poured a mug of coffee and pushed the cup toward her.

"Lazy bastards," Tessa said in between gulps. "They won't file a missing persons report."

"The police?"

"*Protect and Serve*, my ass. More like protect their next serving of doughnuts."

"You know there's a waiting period before Missing Persons can file the report."

"Not in a kidnapping." Tessa began, opening packet after packet of sugar to put in her coffee.

"We don't have any proof of kidnapping," Luke pointed out, then shut up when she pointed her spoon at him like a weapon.

"Don't start with me. I've heard enough crap for one morning already."

Luke smothered a grin at her tone. She was in a foul mood.

"Anyway, I talked to Ed today. He's not willing to hit the panic button yet, but will treat Kelly's disappearance as a possible case of foul play. It doesn't change a lot how he and Ronnie will proceed, except to make them more concerned about her welfare," Tessa said. "Also, he pulled the records for Jasmine Jones this morning. I can't believe Three Sisters Shelter let her stay there with such a blatant alias."

Luke shrugged. "What did he find?"

"Standard junkie arrests—possession of small amounts of heroin, prostitution, some tickets for solicitation from a couple years ago. She entered rehab several times and has been clean for eight months, according to her parole officer."

"Did Ed fax you a picture of Jasmine?"

"Right here," Tessa said. She pulled the sheet out of her bag.

"I'll keep it—we may need to show it to my contact."

"Who is this mysterious informant?" Tessa asked.

Her mood was improving as she talked with Luke, probably because she was able to tell herself that they were working toward finding Kelly. Banging her head against the wall of blue the police had around them was fruitless and frustrating—not a good way for her to start the day.

She had been spoiled by her dealings with Ed and Ronnie, leading her to believe that all precincts were staffed by competent and concerned officers. That hadn't proved to be the case today, when she'd called the police department that had jurisdiction over the area where Three Sisters Shelter was located.

"My informant's name is Alexander King," Luke said. "But he goes by Lex. He owns a small cigarette distribution business, primarily targeted to the vending machine market. He does most of the entertainment establishments in LA and Hollywood, including the clubs."

"How does he get his information?"

"He's tied into one of the small-time mob operations—the Ianelli Family, specifically."

"Is that the one Jasmine's boyfriend is involved with?"

"I don't know for sure. That's why I wanted to talk to Lex. How familiar are you with the local criminal organizations?" Luke asked.

"I don't know anything about them," Tessa said, stirring her coffee morosely. "Most of my previous cases have involved misdemeanors and lightweight felonies."

"Here's the Cliff's Notes version. One of the most popular, time-honored traditions for the transplanted European Mafia organizations—mainly the Italians—is to get involved with cigarette and gasoline distribution, because of the high government tax rate on those commodities. With the Ianelli operation, the Family distributes the product and collects the tax from the retailer, then pockets the funds and gives Uncle Sam zilch. It's an easy percentage for them, so it's very lucrative."

"That's something the ATF would be involved in," Tessa said.

"Among others. And with the focus now on terrorism and

weapons of mass destruction, small-time organizations like the Ianelli Family are operating pretty much without restrictions as long as they keep the volume low to medium. It will get to the point that their profits can't be ignored, and the Feds will move in, but until then it's a nice way to make a buck."

"It doesn't sound like a complicated operation."

"It isn't. A lot of times the cigarette and gas schemes are used to train young managers in the Family, or are turned entirely over to independents like Lex. Then the Family comes along and collects its cut of the profits, called a tribute, and everybody's happy."

"Can't these operations be shut down, especially if everyone knows what's going on?" Tessa asked.

"A lot of times there are too many jurisdictions involved because the goods are smuggled in from Mexico or elsewhere. It's not unusual to have the ATF, FBI, local police or sheriff, US Customs and Border Patrol, State Attorney's Office, US Postal Inspectors, and the Highway Patrol involved. Half the time, multiple agencies are investigating the same operation from different angles and have no idea of the work the others are doing."

"That's why there's a new focus on multibranch task forces, right?"

"Exactly," Luke said. "Unfortunately, with that many agencies, jurisdictions, individual agendas . . . you end up with a cluster fuck more often than not. So much for the system."

Tessa shook her head. "It doesn't make sense."

"That's why I started Novak International. My focus is on the victim, and I don't let the bureaucratic bullshit get in the way of that."

"And you've been able to keep some of your old informants?"

"Hell, I've doubled the number. When you're working with law enforcement, you're not able to pay the informants because that creates a conflict of interest if the information they provide ever gets to trial. As an independent, I'm able to use whatever carrot my informants respond to. The important thing is the information," Luke said.

"I hope it's good stuff."

"With Lex, it usually is."

Luke entered the slightly shabby Russian café and guided Tessa toward the table where Lex King was sitting. The two men shook hands, then Tessa was introduced, and everyone took a seat.

Lex passed them a menu. "I don't recommend the *borscht* but you can't go wrong with the *pilmeni* here."

"Why meet in a Russian restaurant? I think we're the only English speakers here . . ." Tessa's voice trailed away as realization dawned.

"Exactly," said Lex. "Sure as shit we're not going to meet any Italians in this place."

Luke hesitated. "Is that something we need to worry about?"

"If you're digging into Miss Jasmine Jones, it might be." Lex sat back as a waiter brought him a shot glass, a small bottle of vodka, and a teacup. A pot of steaming tea had already been placed on the table.

"What do you have on her?" Luke asked.

"Not much. Do you know how long it would take to check out all the potential aliases of strippers named Jasmine in Southern California?"

Tessa almost choked on a sip of water as she laughed. "I hadn't thought about it that way. I guess there are lots of them out there."

"Too many, and all with the same story. God damned depressing research."

Luke interrupted. "But what did you find?"

"A stripper named Jasmine Jones used to turn tricks to support her heroin problem. Then she got pregnant by her dog, a guy named Street." Lex caught Tessa's blank look. "Street was her pimp. He also used to collect a percentage from all the girls and dogs in the club for the Ianelli Family. In fact, the pimp boyfriend was the main point of contact for Family activity in that club."

"What's the name of this club?"

"Forget about it, the place burned down last year. Insurance scam. Now Street is working at a dance joint called Mr. Chubby's."

This time Tessa did choke. "What a name for a strip club."

"The owners aren't looking for subtle," Luke said. "About Jasmine—what have you heard on her lately?"

Lex shot back the vodka in one swallow, then followed it with sweetened tea. "Nothing new on her in particular. Seems like she dances and keeps her nose clean. She doesn't hang with Street anymore and doesn't seem to have a pimp at all. If she's turning tricks, she's doing it freelance with low volume."

"That doesn't help us," Luke said.

"This might—last few days the skin joints have been in an uproar. Management asking people to keep an eye out for some chick—I figure she must have stiffed her pimp or run off with the till, something like that. Then I talk to you, and I think maybe not, maybe this girl is into something else."

"Who were they looking for?" Tessa asked.

"Can't say. The manager caught me talking to the girls and sent them back to work. But the next club I go to, the girls are talking about the same thing. And the next one. Someone put the word out looking for this chick in bars and clubs all over town."

"No one mentioned why they wanted to find this girl?" Luke asked.

"One dancer told me she thought the girl used to work at a Family location and was running her mouth about customers. That's all I know."

Tessa reached for the hot tea, suddenly needing its

warmth. "I sincerely hope she isn't the same girl we're looking for."

"You don't know the half of it, lady. Employees don't screw over the Ianellis—or anyone who works for them. They're small-time, but ambitious. And mean."

Luke reached under the table and gripped Tessa's thigh. She wasn't sure if he was comforting her or telling her to be quiet, so she let him make the next move.

He leaned toward Lex and lowered his voice further. "What about Jerry Kravitz? Have you heard his name on your rounds."

"Oh, yeah. He's a player on the So Cal club scene, no doubt about it. He announces for the Arena Football League here, and uses that to get a foot in the door at hot spots and parties. He also plays up his relationships with other athletes and gets a lot of mileage out of them."

"He moved to L.A. recently. What did he do before?" Luke asked.

"He came out West about a year ago, following several years of playing college football and tryouts for the NFL and CFL."

"He wasn't good enough to make it as a pro?"

"No, he probably could hold his own. But he couldn't keep a position in the starting lineup because of ankle problems following a bad fracture. Finally, he went to arena ball because the level of play isn't as demanding—but even that was too much. He moved to announcing and came here shortly after."

"Does he have any links to the Mafia?" Luke asked bluntly.

"A couple of possibilities, don't know as anyone has tried to prove it," Lex said.

"Maybe we can connect the dots. What are they?"

Lex thought about it. "Back when he was in college, there were rumors that Kravitz was heavy in debt. Sports betting. And we're talking debt to the kind of people who break ankles rather than garnish your paychecks, if you know what I mean."

Luke nodded. "What about since he arrived in LA?"

"Kravitz's name is linked pretty exclusively with a joint that the Ianellis have a partnership in—it's called Club Red."

"The Ianelli Family runs it?" Tessa asked.

"No, a businessman and real estate developer runs the place—guy named Roderick Hedges. Goes by Ricky. But the rumor is the Ianellis collect a tribute, throw business in Ricky's direction, and keep him supplied with drugs and other toys to keep the customers happy. They also provide security to keep the club grounds locked down tight—it would be a disaster if the media or a photographer from the tabloids got into the place. Believe me, no one messes with the Ianelli security guys."

"Club Red is the only business venture with Ricky Hedges and the Ianellis?" Luke asked.

"No. The Family is also helping Ricky expand his operations into organized betting, prostitution, creative accounting, and the like."

"How did he hook up with the Ianellis?" Luke asked.

"Can't answer that. But from the outside looking in, I'd say Ricky and Club Red give the Family a legitimate front for some of their other business activities. And they keep Ricky's cash flow liquid. Like a regular *symbionic* relationship, you know."

Tessa cleared her throat at Lex's gaffe. Luke shot her a look with twinkling eyes, then turned back to his informant. "What are the vices of Kravitz and company? Drugs? Women? Young boys?"

"They don't seem to be his deal, no. I mean, he likes women and all. But it's more his thing to score girls for the people around him. He's like a fixer or a doer, you know? He gets stuff for others whose high profile might keep them from getting it for themselves."

"Like Sledge Aiken," Tessa said flatly.

"Exactly. He's a regular in most of the high-end clubs I service, but he spends more time at Club Red than any other place."

"And does he like young girls?" Tessa asked.

"Oh, yeah. He's hooked up with most of the girls in his favorite clubs and is always looking for fresh meat. He likes variety—and he likes to brag. Club Red caters to guys like Aiken. They get him anything he wants so he keeps coming back, bringing other high roller members with him."

Luke nodded. "That's how the place gets established as a hip location—because there are celebs in there every night, yet the clientele is very exclusive."

"Right. So the management wants to keep their VIP customers happy, and the Ianellis help them do that. Drugs, women, betting—it's like a home away from home."

Tessa bit her lip; suddenly feeling ill as she recalled Sledge's saying he'd bought Kelly.

Did they want to keep customers happy to the extent that they would offer a teenager like Kelly to Sledge Aiken on a silver platter?

She looked at Luke, saw the sympathy in his eyes, and understood for the first time that he had been right. She wasn't going to like the answers to the questions she was asking on this case.

Chapter 18

"Please don't say 'I told you so.'" Tessa fastened her seat belt and sat back for the drive to see Jasmine at Three Sisters Shelter.

"You don't know me very well, Swiss." Luke started the engine and refused to let himself get mad. Tessa was under an enormous amount of stress, and worry for Kelly had to be eating away at her right now.

"No. I can only go by what I've experienced in the past."

"That sounds pretty ominous, and one day soon we'll talk about it in depth. But until then, don't judge me based on how people in your past have acted. I haven't ever let you down, and I don't plan on doing it, either."

"Who does plan on letting others down? In my experience it just happens," she observed.

"Maybe. But I'm not going to say I was right about Kelly. In fact, I'm still hoping like hell that I was wrong."

Tessa sighed. "Me, too. I'm sorry to be such a bitch. I just can't stand the thought of a kid like Kelly working as a stripper. Or being offered as a party favor to Sledge Aiken."

Luke didn't know what to say to that, so he reached over and gave Tessa's hand a comforting squeeze. Nothing more was said as they drove to the shelter to speak with Jasmine.

When they pulled into the driveway at Three Sisters, the security guard waved them over to a spot in front of the manager's office. He told them Eunice had left a message for them to see her when they arrived.

Tessa got out of the car and gripped her bag as she went to the office. She was grateful for Luke's steadying hand at her back, because her legs had begun to quiver with nerves as soon as she heard that Eunice wanted to speak to them. Maybe she was starting to develop the instincts Ed was always talking about.

"What's going on?" Tessa asked, as soon as Eunice opened the office door.

"Jasmine isn't here anymore," the woman said.

"Where did she go?" Luke asked. "And why didn't you call us? You knew we wanted to speak with her."

"She won't do you much good in the state she's in. She fell off the wagon."

"Shot up?" Luke asked.

Eunice nodded unhappily. "Went on a thirty-six-hour heroin binge, starting yesterday morning, apparently. She never went to rehearsals, and didn't make it to work, either. She got back last night just before curfew. One of her neighbors complained today that Jasmine's baby had been crying all last night and into this morning."

"Is the baby all right?" Tessa asked.

"He is now," Eunice said. "Child Protective Services has him. He hadn't been changed or fed since sometime yesterday—that's how we know Jasmine went on a major toot."

"Where is she now?" Luke got out his notebook to write down the address.

Eunice shrugged. "Evicted. We packed her bags and dropped her off at a friend's apartment in Gardena. Nasty neighborhood. I don't imagine Jasmine will be sober for the rest of the week."

Luke took down the address anyway, then led Tessa back to his car.

"Where are we going?" Tessa asked.

"To see Jasmine."

"But you heard Eunice—she's going to be high."

"The way I see it, Jasmine has a vice to exploit right now. That will make it easier for us to get information from her. It won't be pretty. But it is necessary, so I need you to back me up and not say anything. No matter how ugly it gets."

Chapter 19

"Are you sure you want to leave your car parked here?" Tessa asked. "It will probably be stripped down to nuts and bolts by the time we get back."

The neighborhood where Jasmine was staying was the type of place where even the police would hesitate to enter. Luke glanced around, then headed for a group of teenagers hanging out on the corner. Tessa saw him wave money in front of the kids; some kind of deal was struck, and Luke returned to the car. As he walked toward her and a gust of wind caught his coat, she saw a holstered pistol underneath his right arm. Apparently, he was a lefty.

"The Mercedes will be fine. Stay close to me as we go up to Jasmine's place. Make eye contact with people you see, but don't maintain it. Don't be afraid, but try not to display attitude, either. Okay?"

"Sure." Tessa swallowed hard as they approached the group of men hanging out in the entryway of the building. They ranged in age from fourteen to twenty, and clearly spent whatever money they had on gold chains, designer denim, and the hot rods parked out front. Conversation stopped as she and Luke approached.

She met the eyes of the group's leader enough to show that she saw him, then looked away. Her skin crawled as a chorus of hoots and catcalls followed her up the shallow steps. At one point, she and Luke had to pass within inches of a man who was leaning on the door frame. He pelted Luke with a question in rapid-fire gutter Spanish. Luke responded in the same bastardized dialect, and they were allowed to pass.

Tessa could smell sweat and beer on the man as she squeezed by him in the peeling wooden doorframe. She felt his eyes on her like a violation, peeling away the layers of business clothes and leering over what lay underneath. Her skin continued to twitch as she followed Luke through the dark, damp courtyard toward the cracked cement stairs at the far side of the building.

The smell of mold, urine, sweat, and despair assaulted her nostrils. The cement walls of the building were covered with dank stains and had moss growing in the cracks. At one time the courtyard had sported planters, and a few anemic ferns struggled for life among the trash, cigarette butts, and condom wrappers that were ground into the mud.

"Breathe through your mouth," Luke advised, doing the same to cut back on the stench. He saw tattered curtains flutter in a series of barred windows and felt the eyes of a dozen people tracking their progress.

"Why, so I can taste it, too? God, how do people live like this?" Tessa muttered.

Luke just shook his head and led the way upstairs. As the cement walls of the stairway shielded her from the penetrating stairs of the first-floor tenants, Tessa breathed a sigh of relief.

"Don't relax your guard yet, Swiss. It only gets better from here."

Tessa followed his gaze as they stepped into the hallway

on the second floor. Here the groups of loitering individuals included hard-eyed women and children of various ages. Some of the women were dressed like streetwalkers, others wore faded housedresses or sweats.

If Tessa had hoped for a kinder reaction from the women, she was mistaken. As they walked down the hallway, numerous rude questions were thrown at them, most of them ending with the word "bitch." She ignored the others and focused on Luke's back.

At one point they had to pass through a clutch of women standing with cigarettes in hand and fussing babies on their hips. The same smell of beer and sweat that pervaded the downstairs was here, too, and Tessa couldn't help but ache at the thought of the children being raised in such an environment.

"This is it," Luke said, stopping in front of a scarred orange door. There was no peephole, knocker, or bell, so he rapped several times with his knuckles. A young woman with tired eyes, cornrows, and pale skin opened the door. Her eyes opened wide when Luke waved a fifty-dollar bill in her face and asked to see Jasmine.

The woman took the money fast enough to give him a paper cut, then stepped back and pointed toward a door at the far end of the apartment. Luke looked at her, then at the other three women sprawled in front of the TV. "Another fifty if everyone splits for ten minutes and forgets we were here."

Without a word, the women shuffled out, the last one taking the money and tucking it into her bra. "If Jasmine isn't in the mood, *hombre,* you just give me a call." She made a vulgar kissing noise and left, giving Tessa a dismissive once-over as she passed.

"With friends like that, no wonder Jasmine is in trouble," Tessa muttered. She looked around at the apartment with its rump-sprung and tattered couch, thrift store chairs, and a card table that served as dining surface and trash receptacle.

The sink was full of beer bottles and wine coolers, and someone had dumped used paper plates and napkins in there as well. She saw rodent droppings on the counter and turned away with a sound of disgust.

Luke had been busy checking the other rooms to make sure they were alone. He motioned Tessa behind him and slowly opened the door to the bedroom where they were told to find Jasmine. Inside there was a single lamp with a naked bulb that gave feeble light. Vintage suitcases were strewn on the floor, with clothes and personal items spilling out of them. In the center of the room was a single mattress resting directly on the floor. Fetid sheets were twisted at the bottom of the bed, and a variety of stains dotted the makeshift bed.

A woman who matched Jasmine's mug shot was sitting cross-legged in the middle of the bed, though she didn't even look up as they entered. Her long, kinky hair had been pulled back, but hanks of it escaped the messy knot to fall around her downturned face. She held a piece of rubber tubing in one hand and adroitly flipped it around her upper arm before using her teeth to tighten it. In the other hand she gingerly balanced a raggedly cut soda can and a syringe.

Tessa stood with her mouth open, watching as Jasmine carefully drew water into the syringe then squirted it into the cut-out bottom of the soda can. A small brown lump the size of a breath mint rested there.

"We have some questions for you, Jasmine. You answer, we leave," Luke said, kneeling cautiously on the mattress to get on her level. She didn't even look up as she swirled the can to mix water with the heroin rock.

Luke watched as Jasmine grabbed a lighter and held it under the can. He could see her licking her lips in anticipation of the drug, and waited until the right moment to interrupt her.

She had just drawn the dirty brown liquid into the syringe when Luke leaned forward and stopped her from plunging the needle into her skin. She cursed and struggled, but he held her arms securely and ignored her insults.

"You can shoot up in a minute, Jasmine. First we have a few questions for you."

Jasmine wet her lips and pulled her dazed eyes away from the syringe. "What the fuck you want, man? I'm busy. You wait a sec, then we can talk prices."

"I'm not here for sex. Where is Kelly Martin? What happened to her the night she disappeared from the shelter?" Luke asked.

"Fuck her. I don't know anything about her. She never trusted me, snotty bitch." Jasmine pulled against Luke's hold but wasn't strong enough to break away.

Luke wrenched the full syringe out of her hand and held it in the air above her head. "Give us information, and we'll walk out the door."

"He'll mess me up if I tell you." Tears of frustration filled Jasmine's eyes as she looked at the drugs. Sweat beaded her upper lip as some internal debate went on inside her. But the addiction was stronger than any sense of self-preservation. With a sigh, she fell back against the cushions.

Luke lowered his hand as he sensed victory. "Someone put out the word for Kelly in the clubs around town. What do you know about that?"

"I don't know who it was, but Kelly pissed someone off. Had to be high-level to get the word out like that. And they were paying good money for information. I needed the dough for smack."

"How much did it take for you to sell Kelly out?" Tessa asked from the doorway. She had been standing there as if in a bad dream, but shook herself free of the surreal fog when she realized that Jasmine had been the one to betray Kelly.

Jasmine didn't look away from her syringe. "Five hundred. I told Street about Kelly and split the money with him."

"What happened the night Kelly disappeared?" Luke held the syringe higher as Jasmine feebly reached for it.

"Nothing. She walked out."

Luke shook his head, aimed the syringe at the filthy sheets, and squirted a small stream of liquid onto them.

Jasmine shrieked in frustration. "All right, don't waste my stuff. I was smoking on the porch at about two in the morning, and these guys show up. Said they were going to take Kelly back home. They gave me an extra hundred to look the other way, so I went into the bathroom. When I came out, Kelly was gone."

"Who were these guys? Who did they work for?"

"I don't know, man. One of them looked like he could be a bouncer, you know? I saw plenty like him at the club I used to work at."

"You mean Mafia muscle?" Luke clarified.

"Probably. Street told me Kelly was working out of Club Red, so I just assumed she was mixed up with their business."

"What did Kelly do there?" Tessa asked.

"I heard she was being groomed. She had this sweet young thing going for her that's popular with a lot of guys."

"So Kelly was stripping?" Luke got to his feet still holding the drugs.

"Nah. I heard she was going to be an escort for the big spenders once she got a little more polished. Stupid little Goody Two-shoes didn't have enough experience with men to be any use, so they were, like, training her," Jasmine sneered. Then she gulped at the fire in Luke's eyes. "At least that's what I heard."

Tessa pressed a hand to her stomach to quell the sudden urge to throw up. She leaned back against the wall for a moment, but saw something move in her peripheral vision. Turning slightly, she saw a cockroach marching up the wall about six inches away from her head. It was huge.

She remembered Luke's warning not to interfere in his questioning, and barely stifled her shriek at the last second.

She pulled away from the wall and focused on Luke. He was the only sane thing in the waking nightmare she was experiencing.

Luke heard Tessa's muffled noise behind him, but didn't take his attention off Jasmine. So far, the stripper had confirmed every one of his worst fears. He shifted the syringe from one hand to the other as he thought about what to do next. Jasmine's eyes followed his motions involuntarily, pulling his focus.

Looking at her, Luke figured that anyone who would look away while a young girl was taken off in the middle of the night didn't deserve to have something she wanted so badly. He stepped off the mattress, carefully broke the syringe in two, and dropped it to the dirty floor. As Jasmine howled, he ground it viciously beneath his heel. He left her cursing and huddled over the broken pieces, trying to salvage her drugs.

He turned to Tessa, but she was already backing out the bedroom door, looking behind her to make sure there was no one blocking her way. He followed her out of the apartment and down the exterior hallway. They had to run the same gauntlet of residents as when they came in, but this time did it at double speed.

As they made their way past the group of young men out front, Luke did a quick visual inspection of his car. He felt Tessa stiffen beside him as the men began another chorus of whistles and rude suggestions. He knew she was at the point of exploding and tried to hustle her down the shallow steps in front of the building.

"They're just kids trying to act cool," he said. "Keep walking."

Instead, she shrugged off his hold. She turned and walked up to the ringleader, who couldn't have been more than eighteen. "Shut your fucking mouth, *vato*. Your mother must be really proud of you."

There was a moment of tense silence before all the men cracked up, slapping their leader on the back as they howled with laughter. Luke stood behind Tessa, made a pointed comment in gutter Spanish to the men, then pulled her toward the car. He ignored the laughing offers to take the "hot chili pepper" off his hands, and flipped a wadded-up fifty to the kids who had watched the Mercedes.

Tessa was silent as she fastened her seat belt and locked the door. Luke kept looking at her out of the corner of his eye, trying to gauge how she was doing.

"Look, I know I was a little hard on Jasmine," he began.

"The woman sold Kelly out to some mobster for $250 worth of heroin. She deserves whatever you gave her and then some."

Luke had never heard her voice so strong and steady. He realized that while she was reeling from her exposure to the ugliness of LA's dark reality, she was going to hold herself together and focus on getting the job done.

He turned her head toward him and kissed her gently on lips that parted in surprise.

"What was that for?" Tessa asked, when the soft kiss was over.

"For doing a great job. And not getting squeamish."

"I don't know about that," she said, rubbing her unsettled stomach.

"You only shrieked once. What made you do that, by the way?"

"There was a cockroach the size of a Buick on the wall next to me."

Luke looked at her. When he realized she was serious, he laughed out loud. "Tessa, you were in a heroin flophouse, surrounded by gang members, prostitutes, drug dealers—and you freaked over a bug?"

"It was a really big bug," she protested. Then she started to snicker as well. It had been pretty stupid.

And besides, it felt so good to laugh and release some of the tension and adrenaline inside. "Sorry, I didn't mean to distract you."

"You did just fine, Swiss." Luke looked at her with approval before landing another smacking kiss on her surprised lips.

He was so casual about it she didn't even know if she should say anything. Instead, she rubbed her tingling lips and looked out the window, wondering how to handle this new wrinkle in their complicated partnership.

Chapter 20

Ed Flynn leaned back in his chair at the police substation, saying nothing as he listened to the story Tessa was telling. Then he cut a hard glance at Luke Novak. He figured, since they knew each other fairly well from previous police operations, that he could speak his mind.

"You took Tessa to a flophouse in Gardena to see a junkie whore?"

"She did a great job. And I couldn't exactly leave her in the car," Luke pointed out.

"Drop it, Ed." Tessa snapped her leather notebook closed. "I'm learning more with Luke than I have since I did the two week ride-along with you."

"Just wanted to make sure he was watching my girl's ass," Ed said.

Luke fought hard against an inappropriate grin. If Ed had any idea of how he had been watching Tessa's ass—literally as well as figuratively—he figured the veteran cop would take him out in the desert somewhere and shoot him. "I watched her back. And she did a good job of guarding mine, too. Except for a minor cockroach incident, she was unshakable. You should be very proud."

"Okay, can we get back to the case?" Tessa asked, sure her pale cheeks were flushed at both the compliments and the underlying testosterone communication thing going on between Ed and Luke.

"What do you want to do next?" Luke asked. "We have a good idea that Kelly was kidnapped or at least threatened into leaving the shelter, and all roads lead to the entrance of Club Red."

"Why don't we go there and get her back?" Tessa asked. "A preemptive strike would take them by surprise."

Ed shook his head. "If we go in without backup, without a warrant, we won't be able to look for Kelly."

"She'll come with me," Tessa insisted.

"What if she doesn't? What if she's been locked away, or if she's being kept somewhere else?" Luke asked. "You could tip off the club ownership, and they could make Kelly disappear permanently. She would become a liability to them."

"So we conduct a raid," Tessa said.

"Not with the information you have so far, and you know it. We can't even say for sure if Kelly is there," Luke pointed out.

"And even if you did find Kelly and talk to her, it's possible that she's being coerced or manipulated," Ed pointed out. "If she is, and if she refuses to go with us, that would be the end of the matter. We'd have little recourse to get a warrant and go back for her at a later date unless we got some compelling evidence."

Tessa made a frustrated noise. "So how *do* we go after her?"

"We've got to focus on the other crimes involved—ones where we can gather incontrovertible proof and use that as leverage on the Club Red folks," Ed said. "Stuff like credit card fraud, Mafia connections, sports betting. That way, we can make a bust and pull Kelly out of there whether she wants to go or not."

Tessa looked briefly to Luke for confirmation, giving Ed a start. He wasn't used to her looking to someone else, but was pleased to see that Luke had gained her trust to that extent.

She thought about it. "We know there are at least several criminal activities going on at Club Red. We can try to focus on those as a way of getting to Kelly. For a day or two, anyway. I'm not comfortable leaving her there for much longer than that."

"From everything you've discovered, it seems like the club has made a big investment in Kelly. It would be foolish to hurt her and risk that," Ed said.

"He's right," Luke said. "Listen, if it looks like Kelly is in imminent danger, we'll go to Plan B," Luke said.

"Which is?" Tessa asked.

"Fighting fire with fire. We take Kelly back ourselves. No cops, no warrants, and no evidence we were responsible."

Tessa closed her eyes as she thought of how that would play with the D.A. "We wouldn't be able to build a case against the people holding Kelly if we did that," she pointed out.

Luke looked at her steadily, saying nothing.

She turned to Ed, who held up his hands in mock surrender. "Don't look at me, kid. I can't help you there. It's your case, and you have to decide how far out on a limb you're willing to go to get Kelly back. At this point, I can't even tell whether she's there against her will or not, so my hands are tied."

"Then let's work strengthening our case and untying your hands," she said. "So we don't ever need to implement Plan B. Kelly struck me as a survivor. I hope she can hold out for a little while where she is."

Unless something has already happened to her.

Tessa physically shook off that thought and began to plan the next step in her evolving strategy. "Ed, we need to talk to some of your contacts in Major Crimes and Vice to see if there are any ongoing investigations into Club Red. I find it difficult to believe that they could be up to what Luke is thinking without catching the attention of someone in local law enforcement."

"Good idea," said Luke. "I'll do the same and check with some of my sources at the ATF, FBI, and State Attorney's Office. We can compare notes."

"I also want to look further at this Jerry Kravitz," Ed mused. "How does a washed-out Arena ballplayer put together something like Kelly's disappearance? There has to be someone else involved. Someone bigger."

"That's what I'm afraid of," Tessa admitted. "I have a feeling Jerry isn't calling the shots. But I don't know who could be—I don't have experience with anything like this." She gave a short laugh. "Who am I kidding? I know just enough to know I'm out of my league. And I'm clueless about the rules of play where I am right now."

"You're doing just fine winging it," Ed said. "And Luke and I do know what we're doing."

Luke stood up. "Besides, rules are overrated."

"I'm glad," Tessa said. "Because I'm about to bend some. Do you think it's possible to send one of your employees into Club Red so we can get an idea of what's going on behind closed doors? Someone who is off duty and going in purely for his own entertainment?"

"Swiss, you corrupt so beautifully. We'll send in MacBeth."

"Didn't he already talk to both Aiken and Kravitz?" Tessa asked. "I'm afraid they'll recognize him."

"I told you, MacBeth is a chameleon. Let me call him and see if he wants to cultivate a taste for gentlemen's entertainment."

"How will he get in? The club is invitation only," Tessa pointed out.

"We did work for the custody case of a last year's Best

Actor Oscar Winner," Luke said. "He owes us a big favor. If he's not a member, he should be able to ask for an invitation and get MacBeth in as well."

"I never knew he had a custody problem."

"Like I said, he owes us a big favor. I'll cash in the chips to get MacBeth inside the club by tomorrow."

Friday morning, March 5

The next day, Tessa and Luke assembled again. This time, they were joined by MacBeth. The last addition to the team was Veronica Harris, who had stopped by to talk to Ed and stayed to participate in the strategy session.

They moved into an unused conference room at the back of the police substation. Ronnie held out several colors of Dry-Erase markers to Tessa with a long-suffering sigh. "I knew you were going to want to diagram shit, so take these. While you're drawing, why don't you bring me up to speed on the players?"

Tessa went to the whiteboard that covered most of one wall. "So far, we've got sports figures big and small. There are possible credit card fraud and sports-betting activities in a gentlemen's club, and a young girl."

"Pull back a little," Luke said. "Keep it general—we've got several named individuals, a couple types of criminal activity, a location. And rumors—lots of them."

Ronnie and Ed studied the board as Tessa wrote Luke's observations, then looked at each other. They had both worked major crimes long enough to understand what else was potentially going on.

"Over all of that, you have a cloud of rumored Mafia involvement," Ed finally said. "And I think there are probably more activities going on than you've got written down."

"I agree." MacBeth spoke up, and all eyes turned to him. "From what I saw last night, Club Red is a poorly veiled brothel. No pimps were running the show, so I imagine the management plays that role."

Tessa remembered Jasmine's comments. How she said Kelly was being groomed to provide sexual favors to high-end clients who were paying top dollar for variety and youthful innocence. She looked at Luke.

"Do you believe Kelly was turning tricks?" she asked him.

"I think we can't ignore that possibility," Luke said softly.

"That would make it almost impossible to stick rape charges on Sledge Aiken," Ronnie pointed out apologetically. "You and I understand that even the most jaded prostitute can be raped. But a jury won't make that distinction."

"I know, dammit. I've been doing a lot of thinking about that issue since we talked to Ed yesterday," Tessa said. "It kills me to say it, but we may not be able to prosecute the sex crimes against Kelly at all. So I've decided we should go after the people involved for their other crimes, and we'll have to be satisfied with whatever convictions we get. Jail time is jail time. When all is said and done, I'll do everything I can to help Kelly seek restitution in civil court."

Luke nodded approvingly. "We shift gears and focus on the drugs, financial crimes, the manipulation and potential kidnapping of a middle-class kid who could be anyone's daughter. These are things that will play to a jury, regardless of Kelly's level of complicity. And that way, no defense attorney will be able to put the victim on trial and manipulate the jury's moral indignation about rebellious youth in America. Good move, Counselor."

"Thanks. I've got several other tricks up my sleeve. I filed a missing person's report this morning and indicated that foul play may be involved. Ed and Ronnie, you're going to catch this one as well. So now I've got a couple of days to put my arguments together, and this diagram of our case is going to play an integral role."

"So let's finish it." Luke stepped up to the board next to

her and picked up a marker. "We have Kelly, Sledge, and Jerry. Off to the side, we have Street and Jasmine. What is the common thread for all of these individuals?"

"Entertainment—nightclubs, sports, stripping. Kelly working in a restaurant," Tessa replied distractedly. When she breathed in, the air was laced with the chemical scent of the markers and the musky undertones of Luke's aftershave.

"And the Mafia has been mentioned in connection with all of them at one time or another," Ronnie pointed out.

"Those are just rumors. We need to get something concrete—and fast," Tessa said, pulling her attention back to the board.

"So where do we start digging?" Ronnie asked her.

"The club," she replied immediately.

"That's the answer I was looking for," Luke said. He wrote down *Club Red* and drew a box around it. "All of the individuals have a connection to this place. It's the only physical location we can link all of them to, so it's logical to assume that we'll find what we need starting there. In effect, it's our main crime scene."

Tessa passed a pen to MacBeth. "What did you find there last night, and where does it fit on the diagram?"

MacBeth took the marker and drew two more boxes under criminal activities. *Prostitution/Illegal sex acts. Sports betting.*

"Most of the lap dances and interaction with the strippers cross the line into illegal. There's touching, full nudity, and a private booth where I'm pretty sure clients were getting sexual services. The VIP clients who came in were all escorted to an upstairs room, one I couldn't get into. I heard they were placing bets on college hoops up there."

"Okay, what else?" Luke asked.

MacBeth hesitated. "Just a feeling. When I arrived, I was taken to the lounge area by three pretty hostesses. Two of them looked very young, and they were all sweet and giggly. Not like you'd expect professionals to act. I struck up a conversation about them with the bartender, asked if the girls were available. He said no, they were being trained."

"That's what Jasmine said about Kelly," Tessa murmured.

"Yeah. And when I said to the bartender that a few of the girls looked like jailbait, he tells me that's the way some of the big customers like them. Most of the young ladies weren't for the regular customers, he said. They were being trained for the more exclusive guests."

"How the hell do they find their girls?" Tessa asked in frustration. "Is this really something these kids want to be when they grow up?"

"No," Luke said suddenly. "They're probably like Kelly—they want something very badly. They'll probably do anything for the person who says he can help."

"She wanted to work in show business," Tessa said, as understanding dawned.

"Exactly. That's probably the hook that the Club Red people use to get these girls in the door," Luke said. "The lure of all the famous club members who hang out there every evening. The exclusive, invitation-only atmosphere. Maybe the management even holds out the potential of making some celebrity connections."

"But how do they first meet the girls—how did they meet Kelly?" Tessa drew a large question mark above the word *Scam* on the board next to Club Red.

"I don't know, this all is just a theory about what's going on," Luke said. "But we need to find out one way or the other. Once we do, a lot of other pieces are probably going to fall into place. At least we now have a motive for these people to kidnap Kelly. Maybe this will light a fire with Missing Persons."

"Not if they write her off as a prostitute," Ronnie pointed out.

"I know she wasn't turning tricks. I'll just have to prove it," Tessa said.

"We will," Luke assured her, but he exchanged a serious look with MacBeth behind Tessa's back.

Chapter 21

After their meeting with Ed and the others, Tessa returned to Novak International's offices with Luke to work for the remainder of the day. She wanted to be able to follow the telephone conversations Luke was going to have with his law enforcement contacts, but also had work of her own to do. Carmen had agreed to transfer most of Tessa's active cases to other prosecutors, in order to free up more time to investigate the charges against Sledge Aiken.

Tessa still had some work to do to clear her caseload, but she also wanted to stay close to Luke in case he was able to turn up a useful contact. She decided to log into the D.A.'s secure network from Novak International and do both.

Seated at a makeshift desk in the corner of Luke's spacious office, Tessa made her way steadily through the backlog of e-mails from the last few days. Across the room, she could hear Luke start on a series of phone calls, asking old colleagues and contacts for information on who to talk to in the various agencies they had targeted. Ed and Ronnie were doing the same thing with the various departments inside the LAPD, so Tessa was able to focus on the pile of motions and documents that had been filed in the other cases on her roster.

She wrote a detailed summary of what had been done to date and what her planned strategy had been, and passed each of the cases on to a different coworker inside the D.A.'s Office. She also sent a brief, less-than-informative update to Carmen on the status of Kelly's case. She didn't want to deal with too many questions she couldn't answer yet.

All she could tell Carmen was that the judge had refused the order of protection against Sledge Aiken and that he wasn't interested in hearing any more about the case until Tessa had sufficient evidence to file charges.

She finished in under two hours, and by her eavesdropping knew that Luke had yet to come up with a solid contact at the ATF or US Attorney's Office. He was having better luck with the FBI, since he had cultivated several contacts there when he was still with the sheriff's department.

As he chatted and caught up with former colleagues, all in an effort to generate new contacts, she thought about Kelly.

Tessa wondered what the girl was doing and if she knew how hard they were looking for her. And if she had truly set out to sell her body in order to get a recording contract.

It was impossible not to consider the degree of Kelly's involvement in activities like stripping and prostitution. Tessa considered herself a good judge of people, and she felt certain that Kelly was telling the truth about being raped. But the circumstances and events leading up to the attack were still a big question mark in the logical part of Tessa's mind.

Even if the irrational, emotional part of her refused to accept the possibility that Kelly was involved in the adult entertainment or sex industry.

She considered the odds that Kelly had been tricked. The teenager had been so transparent in her desire to get a recording contract in LA. And despite all that had happened, Kelly had an innately trusting nature. Look at how she'd opened up to Tessa after meeting her and Roscoe in a city park. Tessa hated to imagine how someone more cynical and experienced could have taken advantage of Kelly's naïveté. But would that have been enough to get a girl like Kelly into prostitution?

On a whim, she opened an Internet browser on the computer and went to a favorite search engine. She typed in the words *California* and *teenage* and *prostitution*, then sat back with a gasp at the number of hits she received.

There were over thirty thousand of them. Page after page of links containing those keywords, an emotionless cataloging of the exploitation of young girls.

"What is it?" Luke asked as he approached her desk.

"Look at this," she said. "I was just doing some research on the prostitution angle and came up with tens of thousands of hits on the Internet."

Luke stood behind her and looked at the monitor. She felt his breath against her cheek as he reached for the mouse and scrolled through several screens of data. She held her breath until he stepped back and sat on the desk to her right.

"What are you thinking, that maybe Kelly got mixed up in some kind of organized prostitution ring being run out of Club Red?"

"I don't know if I'd go that far. But consider the profile of the teenage prostitute: young, blond, from the Midwest, and wanting to make it big somewhere like LA or New York."

Luke rubbed his chin thoughtfully. "She'd be ripe for exploitation."

"And that would explain a lot of things we've questioned—like why she was staying with Jerry Kravitz and why she wasn't being truthful with us about her background. My God, Luke. What if she's a minor?"

"Then she'd be a high-ticket commodity and exactly the type of girl to be recruited into this industry. And remember, Sledge Aiken told MacBeth that whatever he'd gotten from Kelly had been bought and paid for."

"Look at her face," Tessa said, pulling out the Polaroid of Kelly she kept in the file. "She hardly looks eighteen. The more I think about it, the more I feel we should contact the Center for Missing and Exploited Children, see if Kelly is perhaps a minor who has been listed as missing. Maybe she's even a runaway."

"Good idea. I'll put MacBeth on it as well, checking law enforcement databases nationally. If Kelly is a minor, it will give us some leverage to use on Jerry and his buddies."

"Were any of your contacts able to come up with information on Club Red?" Tessa asked.

"I've still got lots of work to do," Luke said. "From the little bit of information I have, I'd say Club Red is quite a profitable operation—yet at the same time the activities are very straightforward. You might even say it's brilliant in its simplicity."

"What do you mean?"

"Club Red's activities are highly diversified. We figure the club pulls in millions of dollars a year, but if you break the activities down into categories, no single one of them contributes to a majority of the profits. It's more like a little here, a little there, if that makes sense."

"Highly diversified. Sounds like an MBA business plan," Tessa joked.

"What do you mean?"

"Well, good business advice will tell you not to be overexposed in any one sector, because of market fluctuations and sector instability. In the case of Club Red, you could consider law enforcement interest and criminal prosecution kind of like a negative market variable—something that would adversely affect the bottom line of the business."

"So whoever is running the club would have to be careful not to be too successful at any particular activity; otherwise, they would draw the attention of the police or the FBI," Luke said musingly.

"I wonder if the guy who runs Club Red has a business

background," Tessa said. "What have you been able to learn about him?"

"Ricky Hedges is the owner of the club, and he's supposedly involved in every aspect of the operation. Nothing gets served that Ricky hasn't tried first, no girl performs without auditioning for him first. He even picked out paint, flooring, and fabrics when the club was being built."

"So you would think he'd know about activities of people like Jerry and Sledge going on in his own club."

"You would," Luke agreed. "I'm going to have MacBeth do a little more in-depth research on Ricky. There's not much available on him on the surface, and he's got no record of criminal activity in the state of California."

"But he might in another state," Tessa guessed.

"It's worth a shot."

Club Red
Hollywood, California

Club Red's gated and patrolled parking lot was full, and patrons could hear the music blasting long before they passed the third security checkpoint guarding the entrance of the building. Friday was one of the biggest nights of the week, especially with college basketball gearing up in preparation for March Madness and the NCAA championships.

Well-dressed members waited in line behind red velvet ropes at the final security check as they were politely searched for items like cameras, recording devices, or even cell phones with Internet and photographic capabilities. Any item that didn't pass the stringent privacy rules was traded for a claim check and stashed in a line of locked boxes just inside the entrance. Patrons who requested one were given a global satellite phone for use—free of charge—during their time inside Club Red.

Ricky Hedges made his way through the crowded foyer,

where patrons milled around with drinks in hand, watching sports action on the projection TVs. He greeted several well-known professional baseball and football players who were making their way back to the VIP lounge and the exclusive entertainment that awaited them there.

After straightening his trademark herringbone jacket and his thinning ponytail, Ricky paused at the edge of the foyer. He briefly spoke to one of the bouncers and asked that a stripper who had been learning the art of belly dancing be sent back to the VIP room to warm up the small crowd.

Ricky was always looking for interesting new ways to ensure that his guests had a good time.

Unfortunately, some of those innovations had backfired, leaving him to take care of the fallout. That was one of the many tasks on his list of things to do for the night, so he headed upstairs to the business offices to take care of it.

When Ricky entered his office, Jerry and the girl were already waiting. He looked over the cause of so much trouble, as if trying to evaluate whether she was worth it. She was stunning, without a doubt. Long platinum blond hair, with too many highlights and shades to be artificial. Her eyes were powder blue and fringed by full, dark lashes. Her frame was short—the only drawback—but she was curvy enough that most customers would happily overlook it.

Besides, she would be the perfect size for some of the Asian high rollers he was trying to attract to the club.

All in all, she looked like she would be worth the effort it would take to clean up the mess and salvage the situation with Sledge Aiken. Ricky didn't let those thoughts show as he took a seat behind the old-fashioned cherrywood desk. Without a word, he opened an expensive humidor and began to prepare an illegally imported Cuban cigar.

Kelly sat in a chair and looked down at her intertwined fingers. The knuckles were white from the pressure of holding her hands together, and she could hear the sound of her pulse over everything else in the room. She jolted slightly when Jerry spoke from beside her.

"There was no need to involve yourself here, Ricky. I've got the situation under control." Jerry crossed the ankle of one leg over the knee of the other and tried for a casual and disinterested pose. In reality, his cushy relationship with Club Red was on the line—and he knew it.

"Was it under control when this brat ran away from your house and talked to the police?" Ricky asked calmly. He raised an eyebrow and took a puff off the cigar, before blowing the cloying smoke across the desk at Jerry. "When she brought charges against one of our best customers?"

Jerry shifted defensively, pulling his thinning bangs down over his forehead in an unattractive habit that served to draw attention to his receding hairline. "No charges were ever filed, the police just investigated because it was procedure. Aiken's lawyer put their case into a tailspin, and the police aren't even supposed to speak to him directly again. Now that Kelly's back with us, it will all go away."

"That's assuming you can keep her here this time," Ricky said with a puff. "I understand she ran away even after you tried, ah, physical persuasion. So if smacking her around doesn't work, what are you going to do differently this time?"

"She's a smart girl. She can be reasoned with—watch how I handle her."

Ricky watched impassively as Jerry reached out and grabbed a fistful of Kelly's blond hair and lifted her head to meet his eyes.

"We haven't really had a chance to talk since you came back, Kelly. But I want to tell you how much you're going to regret not being nicer to me—or to Sledge. He's a stupid fuck, but he can be manipulated. He's got fabulous connections, and if you give him what he wants, he can be a very generous man."

Kelly's stomach lurched from the combination of cigar smoke and the memory of Sledge's brand of generosity.

"That's right—you really blew that one," Jerry continued, misunderstanding her expression. "One of his old college buddies is a record executive. Didn't I tell you I'd hook you up? But you had to play the frigid bitch and piss Aiken off when you cried rape. And after I'd broken you in so nicely for him," he sneered.

Kelly's face turned white at his words. When she'd been introduced to Jerry by a girl she'd met at the bus station, he'd offered to let her stay with him while she was finding her way around LA. Soon after, he'd begun to pay special attention to her. She had thought that he'd been interested in her as a girlfriend.

She'd been grateful, flattered, and completely out of her league. It had taken Jerry weeks of friendly flirtation, candlelit dinners, and overt seduction that focused on all she owed him to finally get Kelly into bed. She'd thought it was the beginning of her first serious relationship.

Until the next night, when Jerry had sent her out on a date with Sledge Aiken. *Set her up.*

The knowledge that she had been betrayed so absolutely sat in her stomach like a lead weight. In a state of shock that made the moment seem surreal, she wondered what she'd done to deserve something like this. Then Jerry began speaking again.

"When Mindy brought you to my place from the LA Greyhound station, I saw something special. I could have made you a star at Club Red, which would have opened other doors for you. Now I'm thinking you don't deserve anything that good. Unless you give me a reason not to, I'm going to have to make other plans for you."

Kelly swallowed against the dryness in her throat. "Like sending me home?"

"Hell, no. You know too much for that, and you owe me. I was thinking about Tijuana."

Kelly's eyes widened. Even she had heard of Tijuana—also known as T.J., the ragged city of sin across the border in Mexico. Historically, sailors visiting the naval port of San Diego went down there in droves, as did college students from all over California. The city was seething and swarming, the proverbial den of iniquity, where every vice had a home, and nothing was above being bought or sold. Not even people.

"I can see you like the idea," Jerry said. "Since you wouldn't be nice to Sledge, maybe I can make some money off you by sending you to T.J. Sleeping with fifteen sailors a day will teach you not to bite the hand that feeds you."

She shook her head frantically and held the back of one hand to her mouth to keep from crying.

"Oh, you'd get used to it. It wouldn't be as bad for you as it would for your little brother. What's his name—Taylor?"

"No, please," Kelly begged, as tears finally began to fall.

"Yeah, we could pick him up from his little primary school in Hays, Kansas. Maybe bring him down to T.J. to work with you." Jerry smacked his forehead. "Wait, we could make even more money selling him to a private collector on the Internet. There are all kinds of perverts online, and some have the money to pay for a private boy toy of their own."

"Please, I'll be good. I'll do anything if you leave Taylor alone," Kelly sobbed. She was his big sister, and there was nothing she wouldn't do to protect him from the hell she had already endured.

"So you'll behave and do what I say—without complaining or crying?" Jerry asked.

"I promise," Kelly said in a broken voice.

Ricky looked unconvinced, so Jerry tightened his grip on Kelly's hair. "I'll give you a week to prove that you're with the new program. You'll continue your training at the club, but will have a guard with you at all times. The girls will be told not to talk to you and will report everything you do back to me."

Kelly nodded cautiously, feeling a small spark of hope about being able to spare her brother.

"And I'll have the cell phone number of our guy in Kansas at all times. One call from me, and young Taylor will disappear from the playground and be sold to the highest bidder."

The kernel of hope inside her died with those words. Jerry saw the defeat that replaced it and smiled grimly. With a nod at Ricky, he brought Kelly to her feet and led her to the door. In the hallway, one of the bouncers stood waiting.

"Take her downstairs to the hostess station. Don't take your eyes off her until I tell you otherwise. See that she isn't alone with anyone," Jerry said to the man.

When the door closed, Ricky spoke. "I have big plans for expanding my business empire. No little runaway from the cornfields is going to ruin them. How much does she know?"

Jerry shrugged. "I never talked about anything big in front of her. And all the arrangements were made from public pay phones, so she can't know anything about the real estate and consulting stuff. Even if she did, she wouldn't talk. She spent her first few weeks here talking about how much she hated her parents but loved her brother. She'll stay quiet to protect him."

"From what? Your imaginary colleague in Kansas?" Ricky scoffed.

"Don't you love working with the teenagers? They'll believe anything you tell them. She'll be a model worker, believe me."

"Fine. But if there is any sign that she's going to be a liability, I'll take her up to the cabin and lose her in the mountains."

Jerry shrugged again. "Whatever."

Chapter 22

Tessa heard the knock on her door late Sunday evening. She set aside the papers she'd been working on and padded across the living room. After a quick glance through the peephole, she undid the various locks and opened the door.

"What's up?" she asked Luke as she pulled her comfortable old bathrobe tighter around her body.

Luke walked into the hall without permission. "Like the shoes, Swiss."

She looked down and wiggled her toes inside a pair of threadbare Tweety and Sylvester slippers. "Thanks. Kevin got them for me years ago—they're really comfy. Did you come by to discuss footwear?"

"No, I just thought it had been a while since we'd checked in with each other. In person, you know? And I've got some updates." Luke had thought of that excuse on the way over. The truth was, he hadn't seen Tessa since Friday and had found himself wondering how she was doing.

"Do you want something to drink while we go over this?" Tessa asked as she made her way to the kitchen.

"I'd love a beer if you have one."

Tessa grabbed two pale ales from a local microbrewery out of the refrigerator. She popped the lids off both and handed one frosty bottle to Luke.

"Where's Roscoe?" Luke made himself comfortable in the corner of the couch, toeing off his shoes and putting his feet on the coffee table. He stuffed a throw cushion behind his head and took a slug of beer.

"Speaking of making yourself at home?" Tessa muttered to herself. "If I know that dog, right now he's sleeping on Lana's ten-thousand-dollar damask chaise. I wasn't sure how often I'd be at home during the next weeks, so their housekeeper is watching the place and keeping an eye on Prince Roscoe while everyone else is in the Antarctic."

Luke cracked an eye open to look at her. "Why didn't you go with them? Paul said you were invited."

"Yes, but did he also tell you I'd be more inclined to sign up for a root canal without anesthesia than to get on a small boat with him and my stepmonster?" Tessa was proud of the even tone—hardly any bitterness came through in her voice.

Luke snickered. "He did mention there was some, ah, tension between you guys. But family dysfunction aside, I know you wouldn't have left Kelly behind. Even though it might have been safer, given the threat you received."

Tessa just nodded and drank her beer.

"Have you heard anything from our mystery caller since that night?" Luke asked.

"No, I would have told you. I tried to check the records with CalCell—that's my cell phone company. They said it was impossible to trace the origin if the caller ID was blocked. I just wrote the threat off to talk and shelved the call."

"But we know it probably wasn't just talk, since someone

later broke into your office. And since Kelly eventually disappeared, probably under duress," Luke pointed out.

"Yes. But with Kelly gone they now have what they want, so I'm fairly certain no one will waste any time coming after me."

"Not true. They wanted you to drop the case. Instead, you're in deeper than ever, which could get more dangerous."

"Maybe," she shrugged.

"If you want, you could come stay at my place until this is all over."

"What?" She tilted her beer bottle abruptly, then wiped foam from the corner of her mouth.

"It was just a suggestion, Swiss. I can also put a man on your place to keep an eye on things."

"I'd rather dedicate that person to keeping an eye on Kelly, if you don't mind," Tessa said. She couldn't figure out where he was going with this conversation. And the visit.

Was he actually worried about her?

"I've got my best people on it. MacBeth has been able to get some very good intelligence in the last few days."

"Like what?" Tessa asked. Then the phone rang, and she quickly checked the caller ID window. "Hold that thought, this is an investigator from the US Attorney's office returning my urgent call—from three days ago. I told him to get in touch with me, night or day."

"Put him on speaker," Luke said, handing her the receiver on the office-style conference phone.

"Hi, Bill. Is it all right if I put you on speaker?" Tessa asked. "I have one of the investigators from our team here."

"Sure," Bill Rammel replied. "But I don't have much to give you."

"Whatever you have will be helpful." Tessa picked up her leather notebook and prepared to record the conversation there. "Fire away."

Rammel cleared his throat. "I'm not assigned to the team

anymore, but there's a high-level, confidential investigation revolving around Club Red."

"What is the US Attorney looking at?" Tessa asked.

"It's not just us. There's a multidepartment task force headed by the FBI and involving a few other organizations. We're providing help with warrants and subpoenas, and will take the lead in prosecuting the federal charges when the time comes."

Tessa frowned. "Is LAPD part of the team?"

"I don't know exactly who's involved, but I got the impression the investigation is still at a high level. And there was talk about LAPD Vice being a target of the investigation—there may be a dirty cop or two keeping an eye on things at HQ for the suspects, so the FBI is playing it safe and keeping things quiet."

Luke winced. "It wouldn't be the first time a criminal organization had an informant inside the police force. The Feds would have to approach Internal Affairs and give them the heads-up, but the investigation would still be kept confidential from the rest of the department."

Rammel continued. "Once the FBI gets to the point where the rubber meets the road, officers and personnel from cooperating agencies will be assigned, and the investigation will really take off. Right now, things are still at a conceptual level. And team leads have already been changed twice, so I imagine the ultimate makeup of the group is still in flux."

"Why hasn't the D.A.'s office been notified?" Luke asked.

"Are you sure Ramirez hasn't been briefed?" Rammel countered. "The investigation is over a year old. When she came into office about six months ago, this case should have been transitioned to her."

Luke looked at Tessa. "Wouldn't Carmen have told you if she'd known there was an ongoing investigation that could impact Kelly's case?"

"Of course. But my previous caseload involved petty

crimes—nothing at the level of this current case. So I wouldn't have been in the loop on a high-level confidential investigation. And Carmen has been in Washington, D.C., at a conference for the last few days. She may not have had a chance to respond to or even read my e-mail updates yet. Maybe she doesn't know about the new lead we are pursuing, or the connection to Club Red. I'll ask her tomorrow."

Luke watched with amusement as Tessa made a note in her leather book to talk to her boss. *Bless her anal-retentive little soul*, he thought affectionately. Smiling at her still-bent head, he spoke to Rammel. "What are the activities being investigated by the task force?"

"It was initially focused on financial crimes," the other man replied.

"Like credit card fraud?" Tessa's gaze shot up from her notebook to meet Luke's.

"No, just irregularities. Some banks reported that Club Red was paying a lot of high dollar credits into the Visa and MasterCard accounts of certain patrons, and they were curious about that. That's how the club's name initially got in the system. Then when someone started digging deeper into Club Red's operation, it looked like the owners might also be looking at a lot of federal charges, including interstate prostitution, drug charges, extortion, even liquor and cigarette tax violations. That's when the task force was formed."

"What is the mandate of the task force?" Tessa asked.

"It's now empowered to look into all aspects of the Club Red, Inc. business for potential federal crimes, including tax fraud, money laundering, racketeering, and other RICO violations."

"What progress was made on the financial aspects of the investigation?" Luke asked.

"Not much by the time I left," Bill admitted. "The task force members were all involved in other cases. Hell, every agency is overextended. At the last meeting several months ago, there was talk about getting funding for a forensic accountant to go over the books to see what else they could throw at Ricky Hedges. I recommended Chantal Francoeur, based on her reputation."

"They must have something if they were able to subpoena records and such. Do you know if the task force has enough information to convene a federal grand jury?" Tessa asked.

"I have no idea. This is all I could find on the topic, so you'll need to speak to the people in charge of the case. I wish I could help you more. One person you might want to talk to is this forensic accountant, who I believe worked briefly with the team. I heard she clashed with the new lead and left to pursue other contracts. So she might be willing to fill in the gaps for you, within the bounds of the law, of course."

"I'll take her contact info, thanks. And don't worry, Bill, you've helped more than you know. Thank you for the information." Tessa hung up and leaned back on the couch. "I can't wait to find out from Carmen what she knows about the task force. I wish I'd known about this whole investigation sooner."

Luke finished his beer and set the empty bottle down hard on the table. "Me, too. MacBeth and I have probably been stepping all over their case by looking into Ricky Hedges and friends. Damn it, I hate duplication of effort. Someone out there could have saved us days of work."

"Maybe your time wasn't lost—you're probably looking at things from a different angle. What were you able to find?" Tessa asked.

"Oh, lots of good intelligence on Ricky. He might have polished his image here in LA so he's the next best thing to Hugh Heffner or Larry Flynt, but he didn't start out that way. Ricky grew up in a working-class family in Jersey, though he never talks about it to anyone. Lex didn't even know, and that man is connected."

"So Ricky wanted to leave behind his blue-collar up-bringing?"

"Fat chance. He started out a punk, and I doubt he's gotten any classier since then. This is a kid who extorted lunch money in primary school, then sold cigarettes and pot in the seventh grade. Childhood friends say he started his first protection racket with the playground bully when he was fourteen."

"Precocious little jerk," Tessa said.

"He left high school without graduating, and by the time he was eighteen Ricky was head gofer for a two-bit mobster and pimp in Jersey. He worked in a brothel in the city that catered to middle-class yuppies. He was apparently well-known for trying to learn his manners from the lunch hour customers—mostly businessmen and art students."

"Because johns make such good role models, right?"

Luke shrugged. "If you had grown up surrounded by the projects, these customers probably would have looked like the height of sophistication. And Ricky didn't lack for ambition. By the time he was in his thirties, he was a midlevel employee being groomed for bigger things. But Ricky got greedy—either that or he has a hell of an instinct for survival."

"He cashed out of the game just in time?" Tessa guessed.

"Not quite. More like he had help ending the game for his employers—help from the Feds. Ricky turned federal witness and sold out his whole operation in exchange for immunity."

"Not something that's good for your health."

"No, which is why when the federal investigation got hung up on some legal issues, Ricky went to a rival boss and sold out his family to the competitors instead. He was probably hoping there would be no one left alive to hunt him down and ice him."

"Nice guy."

"Oh, yeah, he's a peach. Part of his deal with the rival clan was seed money to start up another operation as far away as possible. That turned out to be L.A. He started with a small bar and has been steadily growing his business since he arrived a few years ago," Luke said.

"How did he go from a small bar to the Club Red empire?"

"That's the beauty of capitalism, Swiss. Ricky moved from a hole-in-the-wall operation with a liquor license to exotic dancing, and from there to a chic, members-only gentlemen's club involved with prostitution and drugs. Somehow during the transition, he was able to attract the wild child Hollywood crowd and enough celebrity athletes to turn his club into a popular place to hang out."

"I wonder if these people know what their money supports," Tessa mused.

"I don't see how they could miss it. Guys like Sledge Aiken get treated to women, food, and drugs on the house. He's helped turn Ricky's operation into a business that potentially turns over millions each year."

"The wages of sin have gone up."

"Yeah, and the operation is expanding almost quarterly. Ricky Hedges has purchased numerous other properties in California, and sources told me he's also applied for casino licenses in Reno and Las Vegas."

"He has to be getting help from Mafia friends or colleagues. You can't swing a cat in Vegas without hitting something that has an Italian last name."

Luke snickered. "I agree his Mafia ties are probably deepening. And it seems like Ricky has lots of friends in lots of places. Most of them are involved with Club Red in one way or another—like Jerry."

"Have you found a concrete link between him and Ricky yet—something beyond talk and rumor?"

"No. But Jerry moved here from New York a year ago, and that's when he started hanging out at Club Red. We just need to keep digging to see if he had any earlier ties to Ricky's East Coast operations, or anything that we can trace back to the mob. It was shortly after Jerry relocated here that the club started to become hot property—probably because of all the after-game parties and sports functions that were held there. I can't believe Jerry isn't involved in that given his background."

"And since Ricky is apparently a control-freak owner, it would be unlikely that he's not wired in to this aspect of his venue as well," Tessa said. "It all keeps coming back to Club Red."

"Yeah. That's where Sledge hangs out, it's where Kelly was working, it's where Jerry spends most of his time. It's the center of this case."

"I'm afraid it goes much deeper than shady club escapades," Tessa said in a low voice. "What kind of people would put a girl like Kelly to work as an escort or—or worse?"

"I don't know. We haven't found anything on a Kelly Martin in national missing persons databases yet. So we'll have to pull all the missing girls named "Kelly" who are in their teens and check out each one. That's going to take a while, assuming Kelly is even her name."

"It is. I told you, the polygraph for that part of the interview showed no evasion or lying," Tessa said.

"I hope so. Because every lie she's told is just another obstacle to jump over. It's a waste of our time. And that is one thing that could be running out for her," Luke said.

"We have to keep pushing. I feel like this is an onion, and every time we manage to peel back a layer we find another one." She gave a wobbly smile. "All that we have to show for it is a bad smell and tears."

"Don't lose faith, Swiss. I'm working as fast as I can."

She took the comforting hand he offered her and tried to ignore the delicate shiver of awareness she felt when he wrapped his warm fingers around her chilled ones.

"I know you're doing your best. We all are," she said.

It would have to be enough.

Chapter 23

Santa Monica, California
Monday afternoon, March 8

The following afternoon, Tessa was once again seated at
her makeshift desk in Luke's office. There were too
many distractions in her own building, with coworkers pop-
ping their heads in to socialize and ask questions about the
cases she'd transferred to them. So she had set up a tempo-
rary workstation inside Luke's company and was making
herself at home there.

That way, they would cut down on the commute and any
time needed for updates. Since they were together all day,
nothing happened to one that the other wasn't aware of
immediately.

While the arrangement did nothing for her nerves or her
unwilling awareness of the chemistry building between the
two of them, it was benefiting the case. And that was reason
enough to continue working six feet away from Luke Novak.

Besides, Tessa rationalized to herself, it was obvious that
her office at work wasn't a safe place to keep important documents anymore. Luke had been pushing her to shift to his

building since he'd heard about the break-in at her office. Frankly, he'd worn her down.

Straightening the largest of her stacks of file folders, Tessa caught herself humming. Despite the stress of the last few weeks, she was more focused than she'd been in a long time. She was working hard on an important case that was going to make a difference in someone's life. That knowledge gave her the strength to get up after only a few hours of sleep and the will to keep pushing against the wall of bureaucracy she was running into on a daily basis.

"I never would have guessed you were a slob by looking at you," Luke said from across the room.

Tessa smiled complacently. "I know where everything is."

Her cell phone rang, cutting off any reply Luke might have made. Still smiling, Tessa pulled her phone out of the charger and answered.

"This is Kelly." The voice was tense and low, so that Tessa had a hard time hearing the girl.

"Are you all right?" Tessa's voice was sharp with worry, bringing Luke out of his chair and over to her desk. "Where are you?"

"I'm at the bus station. I don't have much time to talk, just wanted to tell you that I'm okay, and not to worry."

"You disappeared from Three Sisters, and I haven't heard a thing from you since—of course I'm worried."

"I didn't disappear. I just got tired of the place, so I called my cousin to come get me," Kelly said.

"I know Jerry Kravitz isn't your cousin. What kind of hold does he have on you?"

There was a long pause. "Look, I'm sorry for causing any trouble. I got mad at Jerry, and that's why I made up the story about Sledge. Now I just want things to calm down so I can go back to my life."

"What, as a stripper? Or maybe even a prostitute?" Tessa asked, ignoring the audible and pain-filled breath Kelly took. "We know all about what's going on at Club Red. I'm not giving up until you're out of that situation and safely back home."

Kelly was silent for so long that Tessa was afraid she'd hung up. "What's your damage, lady?" There were angry tears in the girl's voice now, and a stubborn determination that anyone familiar with teenagers knew meant trouble. "You're not my mother, you're not even my friend. Why can't you leave me alone?"

"Prove to me that you're okay. Meet me for coffee and let me see for myself," Tessa said.

"No way. You're crazy, like, obsessed or something. What I do with my life is none of your business. You'll only make things harder for me if you keep trying to butt in where you're not wanted."

"Kelly, if you're being pressured into doing this, I can help—"

"God, listen to yourself. You're so prissy, you don't even have a boyfriend. How would you understand? Why don't you just get a life and leave me alone?" Kelly's voice rose on the last word, then she hung up.

Tessa closed her cell phone with shaking fingers. Up until now, she'd been sure Kelly was being manipulated in some way. But the girl's words before hanging up had been cruel and calculated. Anyone who could aim that well with verbal jabs didn't win too many points in the sweet and innocent department.

"What did she say, Swiss?" Luke squatted in front of her chair and took her cold hands in his. He could see by her expression that the conversation hadn't been pleasant.

"She said she was fine," Tessa said. "She told me to leave her alone."

"Where was she calling from?" Luke took her phone and scrolled through menus to pull up the number of the last caller.

"She said she was at the bus station. I guess she's going home."

"Let's run a check on the number," Luke said. He beeped MacBeth and gave him the information, then returned to Tessa's desk. "I'm betting it won't be from the bus station. What else did she tell you?" Luke asked.

Tessa looked up at him with shiny eyes. "She said to get a life and leave her alone. She made it sound like I was an obsessed stalker or something. Oh, and she seems to think I need a boyfriend to take my mind off her situation."

"What was going on beneath the words?"

"What do you mean?"

"What was her tone of voice? Did it sound like she was alone? Could someone have been there pushing Kelly's buttons?" Luke asked.

"Her voice sounded . . . strained. And I think she started crying after I mentioned prostitution. I could tell she was upset that I knew."

"Okay, so that doesn't make sense with what she's saying, does it? If she were happy with the situation and wanted to be left alone to turn tricks, I'm willing to bet she'd give you some story about loving sex, how the money is great, stuff like that."

Tessa swallowed around the gravel in her throat. "I read about that in some of the articles on teen prostitutes. That they tell themselves it's a glamorous life, and they are in control of their bodies."

"Did Kelly give you any of that attitude?" Luke prodded.

"No. She sounded tired. She got angry at the end, but it was more a hurt kind of angry than rebellious. At least that's my impression—maybe I'm being blinded by my emotions. She certainly knew how to stick the knife in my back."

"Don't give up on her, Swiss. She may have been coached. You have to trust your instincts and what they tell you."

"My instincts tell me to go get Kelly right now, wherever she is. But my brain says that at best I may have pushed her back into a very difficult situation."

"And at worst?"

"I may have put her in real danger," Tessa said.

"The only way to find out is to keep pushing. We'll trace the number she called from, if possible. And we'll keep looking for answers," Luke said. He would have promised to do anything to put the color back in Tessa's cheeks.

"Even if they're not what we want to hear?"

"Sometimes those are the most important answers of all."

Chapter 24

"Quit whining," Luke said. "I'm tired of talking to law enforcement agencies, too. But the information has been good enough that we can't walk away."

"Yeah, but when are we going to stop gathering information and actually do something with it?" Tessa grumbled.

"Have you been reading my cue cards? I'm supposed to be the one advocating action over analysis," Luke teased.

"I'm beginning to think that you're a sheep in wolf's clothing—you talk like a cowboy, but underneath you're as conservative as an underwriter."

Luke chuckled. "Just don't blow my cover with McKeltie and the FBI. He believes I'm one of the lucky ones who got out. In fact, I think he's angling for a job, which is why he's willing to share information with us off the record."

He held the door of the Federal Building open and escorted Tessa through security and across the lobby. They were shown up to the office of Frank McKeltie, a senior Special Agent with the FBI. Luke's networking over the previous few days had turned up the fact that McKeltie had worked part-time on the task force investigating Club Red. He had recently been reassigned to take a leading role in another case, but still had up-to-date information on the FBI's progress against Ricky Hedges.

The fact that McKeltie was reaching early retirement age and looking to get out of the Bureau gave Luke reason to hope he'd be extremely helpful. He wasn't above dangling a Novak International job in front of McKeltie to encourage that spirit of cooperation. That prospect, combined with the knowledge that Tessa was Paul Jacobi's daughter, should help smooth any issues that might arise from an FBI agent sharing information with others not officially involved with the investigation.

Luke greeted McKeltie and introduced Tessa. In turn, they were introduced to a female FBI agent who specialized in sex crime investigations, including interstate prostitution rings and teenage runaways.

"I asked Agent Beals to sit in on the discussion," McKeltie said. "Once I heard that you were looking at the potential for teenage girls being involved in Club Red operations, I figured she'd be the best resource."

Luke nodded and turned to Tessa. "It's your show. Where do you want to begin?"

Tessa still had trouble adjusting to the fact that Luke didn't mind turning the running of these interviews over to her. Most men—hell most everyone—she'd ever worked with had issues of territory, seniority, and good old-fashioned workplace competition. That meant that in nearly every case Tessa had worked with colleagues, she'd spent at least as much energy fighting her own team as working to solve the case.

The fact that Luke chose to sit back and play second fiddle from time to time was refreshing. Especially when he was actually more qualified and experienced than anyone she'd ever worked with except Ed. It spoke to his supreme self-confidence that he readily handed over the lead to her without worrying what others would think of him.

Unfortunately, she had always found confidence extremely attractive.

But there were enough potential land mines in Kelly's case to keep Tessa occupied. She shouldn't borrow trouble by continuing to think things like that about Luke Novak.

Aware that everyone was waiting for her response, Tessa cleared her throat. "I wanted to thank you for your time. While we aren't sure if our investigation into Kelly Martin's complaints is going to overlap the work of the task force, I think it would be wise to coordinate our efforts where possible. I'd hate to jeopardize an ongoing investigation of the FBI by pursuing a local case."

Luke swallowed a grin at Tessa's sincere tone. Right now, she was playing the self-deprecating novice, and Frank McKeltie was lapping it up. The FBI always liked to think that its investigations were more important than local law enforcement's because the Bureau only dealt with serious federal crimes. Tessa was delicately acknowledging the tensions that existed between federal and local authorities on joint investigations, and at the same time letting the Feds know she wouldn't dream of getting involved in their big, important case.

Luke didn't believe it for a second. But it made for a good icebreaker, and Tessa knew it.

He wondered who had given her the idea that she somehow wasn't capable of pulling her own weight, that her observations weren't as worthy of attention as those of other team members. He knew better. While she lacked experience in some aspects of criminal investigations, she learned quickly and never made the same mistake twice. And her passionate dedication to the victim kept her going long after most would have quit. He couldn't ask for more in a partner.

Plus her inexperienced prosecutor act tended to put other people off guard, as if they felt she offered no threat or competition to them. That would be very useful as he and Tessa made their way through the law enforcement agencies investigating Ricky Hedges.

She continued, "It would be helpful for us to understand what activities at Club Red are under investigation, and what you think the larger ramifications might be."

McKeltie opened a file in front of him. "I'm sure I don't have to explain to you the relationship between organized crime and the high-end food service and entertainment industry here in LA."

Tessa interrupted with a slight laugh. "I think it would be better to assume that I don't know anything. That way you can explain it to me from your point of view." She hesitated, wondering if she'd laid it on too thick. But if she had, McKeltie didn't seem to care.

"The strip clubs, nightclubs, bars, and restaurants are a prime Mafia target for a couple of reasons. First of all, they need a lot of contract services—linens, dishwashing, garbage pickup, recycling, liquor, cigarettes—and some Mafia families are heavily involved in the provision of these services. Then there are the illegal services that we believe are offered at establishments like Club Red. The Mafia wants a cut of this action as well, both in the supply and sale. This includes prostitution, drug use, extortion, credit card abuse, and so on."

Tessa knew this already, but nodded and took notes.

"Then there's the fact that these are cash businesses. That makes it possible for the Mafia families to collect tributes without leaving an accounting trail. And, of course, there's the whole money laundering angle."

"Is that what you think is going on at Club Red?" Tessa asked.

"We hadn't found any evidence of that on a large scale by the time I left, which was puzzling."

"How so?" Luke asked.

"If they were laundering money at Club Red, it would

prove to us that the Ianelli Family is involved in operations there, because that's the new focus of the LA branch of the family. But so far, nothing. At this point, we have to wonder what the Family would be getting from a possible relationship with Club Red."

"What kind of revenues are we talking about?" Tessa asked.

"That's tough to estimate," McKeltie said. "We have a hard time proving where the illegal profits are coming from, and where they're being hidden, because Club Red is a cash-based business. Ricky Hedges could be hiding all his profits in a secret stash somewhere. Or it could be in banks in Switzerland or the Caymans. We just don't know at this point."

"And you won't until he tries to spend it, either as an individual or a corporation," Luke said.

"Yes. That's why we were looking for evidence of money laundering—it's the only thing that would explain where the profits are going. So far, we've got nothing. No evidence of illegal profits, yet no evidence that he's laundering profits, either. It's a conundrum."

"Could that be because there *are* no illegal profits on a large scale?" Tessa asked.

"That's a possibility," McKeltie admitted. "If that's true, though, then the lack of capacity to absorb illegal profits is going to be a liability that holds back the growth of the Club Red empire."

"Has anyone looked at the Ianellis in depth?" Tessa asked. "For example, if they are looking around for a business partner to launder their drug profits, wouldn't that imply that Club Red isn't willing or able to provide this service?"

McKeltie flipped through the file. "I hadn't looked at it like that," he said. "We've been looking for outflow from Club Red. But as far as I know the Ianellis are always eager for someone to launder their money, and Club Red falls in their turf. They aren't major players in California organized crime, and their volume is small enough that the other clans like the Russians and Chinese just leave them alone as long as they stick to their territory."

"So if Club Red isn't laundering money, and isn't hiding illegal funds anywhere you guys have found, where do their profits come from?" Tessa asked.

"Aside from the nightclub revenues, so far it looks like smart and legal investments. We've pulled the club's financial records for the last few years, and our team hasn't found anything out of order." McKeltie pulled a thick packet of paper out of his file. "I'll admit, however, that by the time I left no one with a background in accounting had looked over the stuff. I think that's in the budget for the next quarter, though."

"Why has it taken so long to look over the books?" Luke asked. "No offense, but that seems like a first step."

"It is. But you have to understand the challenges we at the FBI have faced since September 11. We've had our resources—which were always tight—reassigned on critical national security and antiterrorism projects. How do you argue for funds to go after a nightclub and small-time organized crime family operating in the Southwestern US when you have critical budget shortfalls and terrorists living inside the US? Cases have to be prioritized. To be honest, this investigation into Club Red has ended up simmering on the back burner for the last eighteen months."

"Until it starts to boil over," Tessa murmured.

"Exactly. It's called brushfire management—nothing gets dealt with unless it's a huge wildfire. Consequently, a lot of little fires get overlooked. Some die out, while others keep growing until one day they're raging out of control," Luke said.

Agent Beals spoke up. "That's one of the reasons it's so difficult for my division to get funds and manpower. Let's face it—illegal prostitution just isn't a high-level national security issue."

"I know. It was one of the most frustrating things I dealt with at the sheriff's department." Luke glanced over at Tessa, who seemed to be lost in thought. He raised an eyebrow at her when she looked up.

"Would it be possible for me to see the financial records?" Tessa asked. "Maybe even keep a copy? I'm sure I won't find anything, but it would be such a great learning experience for me."

Butter wouldn't melt in her mouth, Luke thought.

And the FBI just handed the papers over, confident that Deputy District Attorney Jacobi wouldn't be able to find anything that would make them look bad.

"I'll have a copy made before you leave. They're public records, really, but I'm sure you'll be discreet with them," McKeltie said.

"Absolutely. Would you explain some of the terms?" Tessa asked.

As McKeltie spoke, Luke pulled his chair closer to Tessa's, and they both flipped through the financial records for Club Red, Inc. He saw Tessa focus on the company's declared assets and expenses, especially deductible ones.

"It looks like Ricky Hedges is quite the real estate entrepreneur," she said slowly. "He's made a lot of land purchases in the LA metro area. Is this a deduction on interest here?"

McKeltie nodded. "Real estate is a pretty standard way for these guys to gain respectability. They want to be able to put something like 'property developer' in the occupation section of their tax returns."

Tessa met Luke's eyes, and he could practically hear her brain processing the new information. He turned to the agents in order to buy her more time.

"What else do you have on Club Red and its operations?" Luke asked.

McKeltie watched Tessa devour the financial information. "I can't share much more than what you have. I was pulled from the case two months ago to head up another investigation, so I don't know what the team has done since then. Do you two have anything that can help us?"

Tessa looked up and shook her head. "We're not looking at any charges this serious. The FBI's case is much bigger than ours. Right now we're investigating an allegation of sexual assault, as well as forced prostitution. We're not sure if the victim is a minor or not, or whether she's actually a willing participant. It was only while we were investigating these charges that we realized some other things were going on at Club Red, where the victim in question was employed."

"Didn't you say on the phone that there was a high-profile element to your case?" McKeltie asked.

"The allegation of sexual assault has been made against Sledge Aiken, who is a professional football player. But so far, we haven't turned up any real evidence to link the guy to Club Red, the Ianellis, or any criminal activity beyond the initial allegation," Tessa said. "It's been very frustrating. We can't even prove an improper relationship with him and the victim beyond a reasonable doubt."

Agent Beals spoke up for the first time. "If there is a prostitution or pandering operation set up, this athlete probably has nothing to do with it beyond being a client."

"Can you tell me more about how these setups work?" Tessa asked. "I've been trying to understand how they are able to attract intelligent, pretty, middle-class girls into a life of prostitution. It just doesn't make sense."

"Usually the prostitution is the end stage in a fairly elaborate chain. I take it you want to focus on teenage prostitution?"

Tessa nodded. "Yes, the victim told us she was eighteen. We've recently been wondering if she might even be a minor. She came to California in search of a recording contract."

Beals shook her head tiredly. "Recording contract, acting career, modeling—it doesn't matter what these girls say they want. The fact that they want to break into an industry that requires connections and thrives on exploitation makes them vulnerable."

"But where do they come from?" Tessa wanted to know. "Were their lives so terrible that they had to run away to the West Coast?"

"Some of them, yes. But most are simply middle-class teenagers from the Midwest, usually small towns. They have stars in their eyes, they're ambitious, and they come to big cities like L.A. and New York without the social support structures that would help keep them safe. They're basically waiting to be victimized."

"I've heard about kidnappings and teenage prostitution in India, Asia, and Africa," Tessa said. "But we're talking about California, here. In the twenty-first century."

"I know it's difficult to believe," Beals said. "But there's actually an organized network to scoop these girls up at the arrival points like bus and train stations, and get them hooked up with other girls their age who are also part of the scam. Then the pimp steps in, provides a loan or a job, and the new girl is indebted. When you add the possibility of meeting important people, or the pimp's promise to help further whatever showbiz career the girl is interested in, the trap is sprung."

"Isn't there any way out? Why can't girls like Kelly just go home once they realize what's really going on?" Tessa's frustration came through in her voice, and Luke put a hand on her leg under the table, letting her know with a gentle squeeze that he was there.

"Because they usually owe their pimp too much. It's basically indentured servitude. If that isn't enough to keep the girl, the pimp will often steal her identification and money. And most of the pimps have no problem with using gang rape, violence, and threats against friends and family members to keep particularly difficult girls in line."

"My God, what kind of people are these pimps?"

"They come in all shapes and sizes," said Beals. "Some

are better than others. I'm just giving you an overview of what we've encountered while working with victims of teenage prostitution rings. Most of them are young, pretty girls from the farm belt. They're in high demand in the sex trade because of their fair complexions and good manners. On the street they're called Thoroughbreds. And since many of them come from middle-class families who have no exposure to this kind of life, it's that much easier to manipulate and humiliate the girls into staying."

"Because once they've been bought and sold, they can't go back to their old lives?" Luke asked.

"No, often they can't. The stigma is very real. Rehabilitating teenage prostitutes is one of the most difficult obstacles to breaking up these rings—really, what are the girls going to do with themselves once we close down the operations and arrest the pimps? They are usually high school dropouts and are candidates only for the most menial of jobs. Frankly, they make good money turning tricks."

"You can't tell me they stay in it for the money," Tessa said fiercely.

"No, they stay in the business for a number of reasons. A lack of other opportunities, psychological and physical abuse, low self-esteem, and the lack of legitimate work or the education record needed to get decent-paying jobs. Let's be honest, Ms. Jacobi. These girls aren't going to make rent and support themselves in Hollywood by working at McDonald's. But if they are young and pretty enough, they can make hundreds of dollars a day—tax-free—by turning tricks. It is the single most difficult problem to overcome in getting people out of the sex trade."

"How do we go from there to organized prostitution like we suspect in Club Red?" Luke asked when it was clear Tessa didn't have a response.

"The clubs need a constant supply of young, attractive girls who are willing to sell their bodies for money. This includes stripping, being escorts or eye candy, prostitution, whatever level the particular girls are comfortable with and the customers demand."

"It was my experience that girls sometimes started with stripping, but as they got more jaded they became less reluctant to do the other things. Kind of like a domino effect," Luke said.

"It can be, yes. And our psychologists believe that the erosion of the girls' self-esteem contributes to this process as well. A high-end place like Club Red has a very exclusive clientele, and it would attract the most ambitious of the girls in the trade. It's actually a street girl's dream because there might actually be a chance of meeting someone who can get her into a movie or something. If not, the clients are still big spenders, and the girls can maintain the fantasy that they are somehow better than street prostitutes."

"But would a place like Club Red actually lure girls off the streets and from bus stations in the way you've described?" Tessa asked.

"Depends on the operation, but I would think yes. They might pretty up the basic transactions, or equate the whole thing to a girl doing favors for important men in order to get favors in return. But at the core we are talking about prostitution and the commercialization of young women."

Tessa turned back to McKeltie. "Was the task force looking into anything like this before you left?"

"No," he said. "We knew we were looking at prostitution and pimping, but had no information that any of the girls were minors. Or that they might be less-than-willing participants. Of course, we knew there were strippers there, but contrary to popular opinion, not all strippers are prostitutes. Most are just making a living."

"Maybe Kelly's case is a onetime thing, then." Tessa shut her notebook. "We should know for sure soon enough."

"Can I give you a piece of advice, Ms. Jacobi?" McKeltie hesitated.

"Sure, I'm always open to tips."

"Tread very lightly. The LA nightclub world is very small and incestuous. If you're asking around, someone is going to hear about it and let Ricky Hedges know. That's one of the things that initially hamstrung the investigation when I was on the team. We had to be careful about getting information discreetly. We were restricted to dealing with outsiders and paid informants, and that made it very slow going. Similar investigations into clubs elsewhere have gone on for years."

"But we've been asking questions freely, talking to several individuals who are involved in Club Red operations at varying levels," Tessa said.

"That's my point. You might want to step back a little, or you could find yourself in the line of fire. These people that you're dealing with might seem like small-time criminals, but they have just as much interest in protecting their business as the major crime syndicates. That makes them very dangerous."

"I doubt they'd do anything drastic over a rape investigation—" Tessa began.

"Remember that the club is netting $25 million a year in profits, at least according to the balance sheet you're holding. That kind of money is worth killing for or dying over to a lot of people. Make sure that you understand that before you go poking into their business, for whatever reason."

Chapter 25

Tessa and Luke left the Federal Building with Agent McKeltie's warning echoing silently between them.

"Any more complaints about wasting our time with meetings?" Luke asked as they walked to his car.

"Nope. I'm just trying to process all the new information."

"Stop for a second," Luke said, pulling her to a halt next to his car in the quiet parking garage. "Until I saw the balance sheets, I had no idea of the size of Club Red's business."

"Neither did I," she admitted. "I'd never heard of the place until you told me about it."

"I don't like it at all. McKeltie's right—we're dealing with a major cash cow. I'm betting the people involved would do anything to protect their setup."

"I know. I can't believe the club pulls in that much money and is allowed to continue without some kind of legal intervention."

"You're missing the point, Swiss. The situation is more dangerous than I thought, and we've been thrashing around in the dark during our investigation. God knows how many trip wires we've activated."

"So we'll be more careful. You can't sit back and do the investigation at a distance when a young girl's safety is at stake. That's like trying to swim without getting wet. It's just not going to happen."

"Still, I want you to consider taking a break for a while. Let me and MacBeth be the ones to dive in the deep end."

More amused than angry, Tessa pulled her arm free. "Why? Are you going to use your penis to swim?"

"What?" Luke stared at her.

She stabbed him in the chest with her finger. "Why should you be the ones asking the questions and poking around? This is my case, my problem. If the danger is that acute—and I'm not saying it is—do you think I want it on my conscience that you're at risk while I sit home and file my nails?"

"Damn it, you're not being reasonable. MacBeth and I are both former cops. We have concealed weapons permits, and we know how to defend ourselves."

"That's typical male talk." Tessa laughed. "You think because you're strong and armed and have hang-downs, you can protect yourself if the situation calls for it. You never consider that if you used your brains instead of testosterone, things might never get to that stage."

"We're not talking about external genitalia and the battle of the sexes here, we're discussing a criminal enterprise worth tens of millions of dollars. I don't want you to get hurt. Think about *my* conscience. Not to mention the fact that your father would hunt me down and cut off my hang-downs if something happened to you."

Tessa's lips twitched at Luke's words. He looked so frustrated and worried. And annoyed. He was really angry at himself for underestimating the scope of Ricky Hedges's operation. "Your being so concerned about me is the sweetest thing anyone's said or done in a long time. But I'm not exactly your average client, so I'm going to do things differently."

Sweet. Luke winced. "Don't I know it."

"You shouldn't think of me as a regular client, either. Besides, while I may be in over my head in terms of investigative experience, I'm a really good swimmer."

"Enough with the water analogies, I'm drowning in them," Luke said. He could see there was no point in getting upset because Tessa simply didn't consider the situation to be dangerous to anyone but Kelly.

And she'd promised to help the girl, apparently no matter what the cost.

All he could do was keep Tessa close enough to watch over her. And the added benefit to that plan was the opportunity to explore the chemistry that seemed to be building between them on a daily basis.

He considered it the best possible kind of fringe benefit.

"So we're agreed that our client-investigator relationship is in no way standard, right?" Luke leaned casually against the side of his car as he spoke.

"Right," Tessa agreed cautiously. She was a good enough lawyer to understand when a verbal trap was being laid.

"And what would your evaluation of our, ah, relationship be at this point?" Luke asked.

"I think we're working really well together. I'll admit, I was spinning my wheels before I met you."

"Does that mean I'm earning my pay?" he asked, his voice deep and husky enough to send a shiver through her.

Suddenly, she wondered if they were talking about the case at all. She looked away for a moment.

"You seem to have some uses, even if you're not quite housebroken." She was trying to lighten the situation with humor, but Luke didn't smile.

She sighed, knowing she owed him complete honesty after the way he'd dropped everything and taken on a case that was so important to her. "What can I say? You've gotten great information with your contacts—stuff it would have taken me weeks to uncover alone. I can't begin to thank you enough."

That seemed to jolt him. "I don't want your thanks for doing my job."

"Well, you have them."

He ran a finger down her soft cheek. "You should be careful. A man would do a lot to have you look at him the way you're looking at me right now."

She swallowed hard. "How is that?"

"Like he's a hero," Luke said, without looking away from her blue-gray eyes. When the wind pulled several strands of dark blond hair out of the conservative bun she was wearing, he tucked them back behind her ear.

Tessa shifted the strap of her purse farther up on her shoulder, though it had been in no danger of falling. Finally, she said, "I don't really believe in heroes, but I hope you'll turn out to be one for Kelly. She needs that very badly."

"Why? She has you, Tessa."

She couldn't speak for a moment as tears burned her eyes. "Now that *is* the sweetest thing anyone's ever said to me." She placed her hand on Luke's hard forearm and gently squeezed, wanting to convey how deeply he'd touched her.

"I hope you meant it about not wanting to be treated like a regular client," Luke said as he pulled her closer. She certainly wasn't getting his attempts at subtlety.

"Huh?"

"Come here," he said quietly.

Then he kissed her. Softly, gently, at first. When she didn't pull back or resist, he slid the tip of his tongue from one corner of her tender smile to the other. Probing for entry but waiting to be asked in.

Tessa let her purse drop to the concrete floor of the parking structure as she put her hands on Luke's chest and hesitantly leaned closer. She parted her lips and gave him a hint of tongue, just enough so he would have to go looking for more. As the kiss deepened, she opened her heavy lids and met his hazel gaze. His pupils were dilated, but the blackness only emphasized the intoxicating swirls of gold, green, and blue that made up his eyes.

With a quiet sound of pleasure, she shut her lids, closing out the penetrating gaze that seemed to see right into her soul.

Luke turned slightly, pinning Tessa's hips between his body and the car. He took her soft cheek in his hand and tilted her head in order to spear his tongue more deeply into her mouth. She made another soft sound, and he was gone.

Settling more deeply into her, he nudged Tessa's legs apart and pressed his lower body to hers. She drew in a sharp breath through her nose at the sensation, then kissed him more deeply and wrapped her arms around his neck. He took that as encouragement to continue.

Tessa sighed a little as she felt the back hem of her silk blouse being pulled free of the waistband of her business skirt. Luke's hands felt incredibly warm as they stroked up and down her sensitive spine. Her own fingers clenched in the soft hair at the base of his neck in response.

He brought one of his hands slowly around to the front of Tessa's body, concealed from view by the vibrant fabric of her top. She hesitated for a moment as he cupped a small, firm breast with tiny nipple already standing at attention underneath the lace of her bra. Her breath rushed out again when Luke shifted and lightly rubbed his hips against hers in an unmistakable message. The hardness of his erection found the perfect spot between her legs, and an audible cry left her lips before she could stop it.

As the passionate sound echoed in the parking garage, Tessa grabbed Luke's hand to keep it from moving below her waist. She was breathing hard when she freed her mouth from his drugging kisses.

"Fun's fun, but I don't do PDAs." She wriggled subtly to

get free of his weight. "Besides, I don't think my father—who is currently paying your salary—would approve."

Luke gave her a hard look. After taking a moment to control himself, he realized that Tessa was afraid of him, or at least of what he made her feel. That's why she was stepping back and throwing in his face the fact that her father was technically his boss.

It was almost as if she were trying to remind herself that men couldn't be trusted by invoking the name of her father—the first man to betray her. Luke had no intention of hurting her, but Tessa didn't know him well enough to believe that or even understand what it meant. His Swiss was quite an enigma, but since he understood the deeply rooted pain and suspicion behind her behavior, it was easier to let her words go.

No matter how hard she tried to piss him off.

Luke ignored her discreet struggles and leaned in for another thorough kiss. Then he stepped back to address her comment.

"I guess it's a good thing I didn't try to kiss your father, then."

With her mind spinning, a low laugh escaped Tessa at that thought. Then she stilled as Luke took her chin in his hand again. She thought he was going to kiss her once more, but instead he stroked his thumb over the lower lip she'd just bitten to stifle her laughter.

"I know you're uncomfortable with the attraction between us, Swiss. And I know you haven't had a lot of reason to trust the men in your life."

Her chin came up at that. She wasn't sure what he and her father had discussed, but it seemed Luke was aware of the effects the emotional baggage between her and Paul Jacobi had had on the rest of her life.

She looked away from him as he waited for a response. "I can't throw away a lifetime of hard lessons because you want to get me in the sack." She forced herself to say it lightly, as if the whole subject didn't really matter to her.

"I'm not asking you to. But you should know that I'm on *your* side, no matter who's signing the checks. Think about that, Tessa."

She opened her mouth to respond, then paused as he rubbed his thumb along her lip again. "And think about what I said regarding your safety. If you want to continue being involved in every aspect of the investigation, you're going to have to compromise."

"How?"

"By letting me put a man outside your house for protection. Or coming to stay with me," he added.

"Since you just had your tongue halfway down my throat, you'll forgive me if I find that suggestion self-serving." She bit at his finger to get him to release her. "Besides, I'm the one who has to approve expense accounts. I can't authorize twenty-four-seven charges for the president of the company."

"Even if I'm worth it?"

God, he certainly is, Tessa thought. "Even then. But I appreciate the concern." She listened to his gusty sigh of frustration. "Tell you what—in the spirit of compromise, I'll ask Ed what he thinks. If he says it's a reasonable idea, I'll let you put surveillance on my apartment, and I won't fight you about it again, okay?"

Luke was smart enough to recognize an olive branch when it was offered to him. So he took it, hoping he could use circumstances and their mutual attraction to talk her into his home soon. Very soon.

He didn't like the idea of her sleeping alone at night for a lot of reasons. And not all of them were selfish.

Chapter 26

"I'm not sure if I'm comfortable with the solution you're proposing," Ricky Hedges said. He was locked in his office on a private call. Despite the air-conditioning, a line of sweat was forming on his upper lip, and his custom-tailored shirt clung to his body.

For some reason, he always started sweating when his secure cell phone rang.

"The problem is too big to deal with in the usual way, Ricky." The voice on the line was low and pleasant.

"It's being taken care of as we speak. Papa won't be bothered by these stories again," Ricky assured the caller. "Nothing has happened since the girl came back. The people investigating the charges will be forced to drop the case and move on to something else."

"Ah, but what we're asking you to do is more than a way to eliminate an annoying problem. Think of it as a test. Or maybe it's like earnest money, to ensure that you don't walk away without thinking it over real hard."

Ricky set his newly lit cigar in the ashtray without taking a single puff. He knew a setup when he saw one, and he was being set up. Papa Ianelli's right-hand man wanted Ricky to personally get involved in a serious crime so that he would be less inclined to betray his business associates in the future.

Turning on his old boss in New York had been both the best and worst thing he'd ever done in terms of his career. Yes, it had gotten him out of the city with enough money to start a new operation. But it also was something his new business associates never let him forget—the fact that he'd betrayed his old colleagues and walked away with a fat wad of cash in his pocket was something of a liability to them.

He supposed he couldn't really blame the Ianellis for wanting to ensure that it didn't happen again. But somehow that thought did nothing to provide comfort. In fact, it made his stomach clench uncomfortably as he sensed just how deeply he'd have to get in the shit in order to satisfy his business partners.

"Ricky? Do you want to continue to be a real estate developer and expand your operations?" The voice was chiding.

"Yes, of course."

"And do you want to get your casino license in Vegas someday?"

"You know I do," Ricky said. "That's been my goal all along."

"And we can help you achieve that goal. All you have to do is prove your loyalty by getting personally involved here. Then we know you'll do whatever it takes to protect our future investment in the Club Red empire."

"But I've got a lot more to lose than you do," Ricky pointed out. "So far your involvement in my club has been small, but I've spent the last ten years building this business. My stakes are much higher at this point."

"And so are the profits you get out of the arrangement. But don't worry, we're willing to expand our investment and spread the risk around. You just have to prove you're committed to the partnership first."

"So you sit back in your Las Vegas mansion and ask me to commit the kind of felony that will get me on the shit list of every cop in California."

"Think about how much the others involved have at stake, Ricky." The caller laughed lightly. "Consider how very lucrative politics can be for some of our common friends. You're not the only one with everything on the line."

"I want to continue working with you, but this is such a personal risk—"

"Oh come off it. Surely there's a way to set up someone else to take the fall for this. Show a little creativity, Ricky. But however you do it, we want the job done."

"And if I don't?" Ricky asked.

"Then the money people and influence makers will melt away at the first sign of trouble. And we'll use our political connections to crush your empire-building plans. Your Vegas and Reno casino license applications will go to the bottom of the pile."

Ricky cursed. He'd poured all of his profits into saving up for Reno and Vegas branches of Club Red. If the license applications got buried on some bureaucrat's desk, he might as well set fire to the seed money for his expansion plans, because it would never happen.

"So you'll find a way to take care of this?"

"Sure. I guess it won't be that hard. I've got a lot of loyal people working for me. But I'll need at least ten grand from you to make it happen."

"We'll send it out tonight with a courier."

The caller hung up, leaving Ricky Hedges to ponder how he was going to arrange a murder without getting his own hands bloody.

Chapter 27

"Thanks for coming over," Luke told Tessa as he closed the door behind her. "I've been putting so many hours in at work that I let the house fall apart. Since this is the first day we've had without appointments, I went in to the office early and came home after lunch. I spent all afternoon cleaning and dealing with repairmen, mail, and garden stuff."

"I need to clean my apartment this evening, too. But you said you had some new information from MacBeth, and I didn't want to wait until Monday." Tessa looked around Luke's comfortable home. It certainly didn't look like a typical bachelor pad.

He lived in a cozily chic neighborhood on the beach. Wood frame houses were mixed with modern buildings set on tiny lots, giving the area an eclectic style and feel. Tessa had stopped to admire Luke's front garden on the way in; the sprawling, free character of the plants and wildflowers suited his personality.

So did the house, with its comfortable and masculine furnishings. A leather couch sat between two recliners, and she

could see a TV and small home theatre system perched in an
entertainment center that was the focus of the living room. A
low wall separated the kitchen and dining area from the rest
of the main floor, and carpeted stairs led up to the bedrooms.

"This is a great house. How long have you had it?" Tessa
asked.

She would have killed for his home. When she first moved
to California, she'd wanted more than anything to live in a
vintage Santa Monica house like this one. But the prices
were outrageous, so she had to be content with renting her
postage-stamp-sized apartment several miles away.

"This place belonged to my grandmother. She was doing
winters here long before 'snowbirds' ever became part of the
California vocabulary."

"Where is your family from?" Tessa asked as she walked
around admiring the artwork and furnishings. Luke trailed
behind her.

"Chicago, originally."

"I never would have guessed from the accent."

Luke laughed. "I came here when I was twelve, so the accent is gone. I loved this house from the first time I visited
my grandmother, so she left it to me when she died. My siblings all had their own places already, so no one complained.
I had to mortgage a good chunk of the house to pay the
taxes, even fourteen years ago, but the value has continued
to increase every year. It's one of the best investments I ever
made."

"Oh, my God. You have a deck. This is so great—can you
see the water from here?" Tessa craned her head to look out
the sliding glass door.

"When it's not dark, yeah. There's another deck upstairs,
off the master bedroom. You can see the beach better from
there. Hey, you're getting drool marks on the carpet."

"Sorry. I've wanted a house like this for so long, but as
you once pointed out, I'm on a public servant's salary."

"I'm sure your father and stepmother would . . ." Luke's

voice trailed away at her fierce look. "Right. Feel free to visit whenever you want."

Luke left her staring enviously at the small, well-organized backyard beyond the deck. "Can I get you a glass of wine?"

"I don't think so. I haven't eaten since breakfast, and it would go straight to my head."

"Then stay for dinner. It's what I had in mind when I asked you over to talk in the first place."

"You didn't say that on the phone." Tessa's stomach had been rumbling since she'd walked in and smelled fried chicken, and it chose that moment to growl out loud.

"I know. If I had, you would have found some excuse not to come over. Here's your wine, Swiss. We've got fried chicken in the oven, along with mashed potatoes, bread, fruit, and a salad."

"A great house, and you can cook, too? Why hasn't some woman snapped you up yet?" Tessa teased, the everyday words falling out of her mouth before she'd thought them through.

"I told you, I've been working hard to build my business. And cops don't make good domestic partners."

"Sorry, that came out rude. I was just joking—"

"What about you?" Luke asked.

"You mean why hasn't some woman snapped me up yet?" Tessa asked. "I have this thing for guys."

"Oh, I think we've already established that you're deliciously heterosexual. I meant why aren't you married and happily populating the suburbs with little Tessas?"

Tessa took a big sip of wine and ignored the verbal pass. "Same reason as you, I guess. I'm busy with work, and it's hard to focus on a relationship when you have crazy hours and even crazier cases."

"Don't you want kids?"

"Sure I do. After I hit thirty-six I figure my career will be well launched, and I can focus on the home front."

"And until then you live in a cloister?" Luke asked.

She blushed. Just about, but she wasn't going to tell him that. "Of course not. I've had a couple of long-term relationships since college, but it wasn't really right to prolong things when I wasn't ready to get married."

"Especially when they were?"

"Something like that. I guess I haven't found what I want yet, and I really won't let myself look until I have more time and energy to give to a relationship. So I do the test-drive thing—that way no one gets hurt when it doesn't work out." She caught his look. "It's a good system—at least it's worked for me."

"What you mean is that it's enabled you to keep men at bay and have a safety net."

"Maybe. It just wouldn't have been fair for anyone to get too attached when the relationship wasn't going anywhere."

"Because you wouldn't let it," he pointed out.

Feeling cornered, she shrugged. "I would never want to have my marriage and family compete with a demanding law career. I've been there, and I know it's not good for the children, or the spouse. Since I have certain goals for my job, and I plan on achieving them in the next few years, it make sense to hold off on the family front. That way, no one gets hurt."

Luke was silent as he refreshed the wine she'd been steadily drinking during their talk.

She mistook his silence for criticism. "I know it sounds cold—God, don't think I haven't considered that," Tessa said.

"You're not cold—far from it. I think you were badly hurt as a child by a father who placed his job above everything and a mother who died young. Then your father and stepmother had other . . . priorities once they got married. The way you interact with people today is colored by your childhood experience."

"Thank you," Tessa said quietly. "No one has ever understood why I refuse to have a husband and family until I can give them everything. I hurt two very nice men who said they were willing to go along with my plan to put family on hold until thirty-six. After several years together, they demanded to change all the rules because they suddenly wanted to get married. Never mind what I wanted."

"Which was?" Luke asked.

"Depends. In the short term, I wanted a comfortable, monogamous affair based on respect and affection. I'm not into flings—I wanted stability and caring and companionship."

It sounded like she was looking for a dog, Luke thought, but he simply nodded. "And in the long run?"

"For once, I want to come first in someone's life. Just as they will in mine. My family will be my top priority once I have one, so I don't think it's unreasonable to ask that I be allowed to concentrate on my career for a while. Just until I get everything in order and build financial security to have a husband and kids on my terms."

Luke wanted to pull her into his arms and hug her. His organized, logical, and analytical Tessa clearly didn't understand that love seldom waited for those involved to get everything lined up in an orderly fashion. Obviously, no man had ever explained that to her.

Their loss, his gain.

But he'd have to be careful how he approached the whole topic. Before he'd met Tessa, he hadn't been looking to settle down and start reproducing, either. But that time wasn't far off, and she was certainly the most intriguing woman he'd ever met. He wanted a chance to see what would develop between them, while she was equally determined to prevent that from happening.

"So now you understand why I've been uncomfortable with . . . us," Tessa said, gesturing between them with her half-full wineglass.

"Maybe. But I don't agree. What if I'm looking for the

same thing you are—caring, companionship, monogamy, and the added bonus of fantastic chemistry?"

"Well, there's the case we're working on," Tessa pointed out.

"I'm still not buying it. I do understand your position. All I ask is the right to change your mind. Or do you think I'm so irresistible that you won't be able to stop yourself from jumping me?" Luke nudged her in the ribs and invited her to share a joke on him.

Tessa laughed, then handed him her wine for a refill. "I hope dinner's soon, or you're going to have to call a cab for me to get home."

She wouldn't be going home that night, Luke thought. But he didn't see any need to argue about it at that moment.

He showed her to the dining area and let her help set the table. He pulled warming dishes out of the oven, and soon they were seated at the table enjoying a home-cooked meal.

"So what information did you have from MacBeth," Tessa asked as she pulled the skin off her fried chicken. She allowed herself only a tiny bite of the fatty treat before setting it aside to work on the meat.

"I don't want to ruin your appetite," Luke said. "Maybe we should wait."

She gave him what he was quickly recognizing to be the Look. "It can't be any worse than what I've been imagining for the last few days. Sometimes it's better to know for sure than to wonder. We already know she didn't call from the bus station. What else is there?

"It's nothing we didn't already suspect. MacBeth found a missing persons report from Kansas that matched Kelly's description. Then he confirmed it was her by faxing the local police a picture and talking to the parents. It turns out she's a runaway from Hays, which is right on the interstate and the Greyhound bus line."

"He actually found Kelly's family?" Tessa asked as she put her food down.

"Yes. Her last name is Maarten, which is Dutch. It's spelled differently, but pronounced the same way as 'Martin.' That's why she didn't pop right away."

"Just close enough to the truth to be convincing—Kelly's a smart girl. No wonder she passed that section of the polygraph. She was telling the truth about her name."

"Yeah, but not about much else. I don't know any easy way to say this, but Kelly *is* a minor."

"We thought she might be. Just how minor is she?"

"Fifteen. She'll be sixteen next month."

"Jesus." Tessa closed her eyes and imagined being nearly sixteen and alone in Los Angeles.

"I know it's hard to accept, but does her age *really* matter in terms of what she's been through? It would be traumatic no matter how old she is."

"I know," Tessa said. She was silent for a moment, thinking about how to use the new information. "Well, her age will help us nail Sledge Aiken, for starters. He's acknowledged a sexual relationship with Kelly, which puts him up for statutory rape. I won't need to prove a thing in court."

"I hate to play the devil's advocate for that piece of dog shit, but what if she lied to him about her age?" Luke asked.

"That would muddy the waters a bit, but correct me if I'm wrong—wasn't Sledge known for liking young girls? I could argue that not only did he suspect Kelly was a minor, he was counting on it. I think if we dug into his background, we'd find a pattern of this type of behavior."

Luke stroked a finger down her soft cheek. "That's my girl. Instead of freaking out over the news, you're already planning a new strategy."

She ducked her head for a moment. "I've already done plenty of agonizing over Kelly's situation, and look where it's gotten me. I want to pour that energy into getting her away from these people and back to her family in Kansas. Hey, did MacBeth say if the parents were coming to California?"

He shook his head. "They couldn't afford to stay for more

than a few days. MacBeth told them that we knew where Kelly was and that we believe she's safe for now. He convinced them there was nothing they could do by being here. The father said it was just as well, since Kelly ran away to get out from under their strict rules. They're afraid she'll rabbit again if she sees them or hears they're in town."

"I'm sure she wouldn't run away. Even strict parents must look pretty good at this point. God, how did a fifteen-year-old kid from Kansas hook up with Jerry Kravitz and company?"

"I think the FBI agent who dealt with sex crimes had it right—Kelly was probably picked up at the bus station, befriended by someone her age who wasn't threatening, then turned over to Jerry. Her first few weeks here might have been quite pleasant until it came time for her to start earning her way."

Tessa began shredding the roll she'd been eating. "I'm going to look forward to locking Jerry up for a long time. Maybe he can make some new friends in the prison showers."

Luke winced. "Ouch. You're not supposed to know about stuff like that."

She shot him the Look again. "I've interviewed inmates from prisons as far away as San Quentin. Believe me, I understand what goes on behind bars. In some cases, I think it might even be divine justice for people who would take advantage of others."

"Don't worry too much about Kelly, Swiss. She strikes me as a tough kid—hell, she has to be a survivor to have made it this far. She'll get out, and you'll help her."

"I know she's a survivor, that's why I like her so much."

"Ditto," Luke said. He reached for Tessa's hand and brought it to his lips. "You missed a crumb."

"Did I? So what is this, you feed me, then make the moves? I thought you said I was safe."

"I said I reserved the right to change your mind. Besides, I want you to stop worrying for one night. Look at these circles under your eyes," he said as he tenderly rubbed one with his thumb. "Why don't we sit on the couch in the dark and listen to soft music for a while. You set aside the case—"

"Turning my brain off isn't that easy," she warned him.

"You should know I can't resist a challenge, Swiss. Come on." Luke pushed away from the table and went into the dimly lit living room. He seated her in the corner of the couch, pulled a light throw over her, and left to play with the stereo.

He stood looking at his extensive CD collection, then reached for one with a hand that shook ever so faintly. Dave Matthews Band? No, that was blatant make-out music. Instead he pulled out a Cowboy Junkies collection and put that on. Then Lucinda Williams. Dave Matthews would be third in the CD tray.

Tessa sat wrapped in the warm throw, waiting for Luke to come back and sit beside her. Part of her was looking forward to his inevitable pass, but, at the same time, she was dreading have to spoil the peace of the evening by turning him down and leaving.

She opened her mouth to let him know that she would not be spending the night, no matter what. Instead, he interrupted her. "I'll go take care of the kitchen. You just chill out here on the couch."

Lips pursed in a faint pout, Tessa settled back and listened to him putter around washing dishes and cleaning pots and pans. The noises were so companionable, so very ordinary, they combined with the mellow music to help her relax. Within minutes, her eyelids drooped, and she dozed with her cheek pressed against the smooth leather of the couch.

Twenty minutes later, Luke came out of the kitchen to start a fire. The March night wasn't that cold, but he figured the flames would help Tessa relax.

Of course, that was before he'd realized she was fast asleep on his couch.

Smiling at the picture she made, Luke quietly went to the deck to gather kindling and firewood. With a minimum of noise and fuss, he soon had a large blaze burning in the fireplace. He stood and washed his hands, then slipped his shoes off and crawled onto the couch next to Tessa.

If she wanted comfortable, peaceful companionship at the moment, that was what he'd give her. Maybe she'd be intrigued enough to demand more. Until then, he'd enjoy the knowledge that she was finally relaxing and letting go of the tensions brought on by the investigation.

With one arm hugging Tessa to his side, he gently settled her head on his shoulder and drifted as well.

Chapter 28

Sometime after midnight, Tessa woke to the knowledge that the CDs were on repeat play and Luke had built a fire sometime after she'd conked out. Then she realized she was curled against him, and he seemed to be asleep as well. His chest moved slowly beneath her cheek with each breath he took, and she had no idea how long she'd been using him as a human pillow.

She'd been sleeping so deeply she wondered for a horrified moment if she'd drooled all over his shirt, but a quick check showed that she hadn't completely embarrassed herself. Beyond falling asleep on the single most interesting man she'd ever met. Literally on him.

With a pained sigh at her complete lack of social graces, Tessa carefully began to untangle herself from the heap they made on the soft leather couch. The throw slid off Luke as he hooked an arm around her and pulled her back down to his chest.

"Quit wiggling. This is the best evening I've had in months," Luke grumbled.

"I have to go home," Tessa whispered back.

"Why? If you're not comfortable here, we can go upstairs."

Tessa gulped as Luke turned the full force of his sleepy gaze on her in the dimly lit room, the molten light from the flames reflected in his heavy-lidded hazel eyes. In the background, Dave Matthews crooned softly about watching his love from a distance and wanting with a physical ache. The music, combined with the remnants of the fire and the force of her attraction to Luke scrambled whatever polite words she would have said to decline his invitation to go to bed with him.

"Swiss?"

"Yes." She said it softly. Even she couldn't have said whether it was a question or a response. But Luke seemed to take it as agreement, because his eyes lit up, and his lips curved in a satisfied grin.

I can't believe I just said that. What the hell was in the wine?

But she couldn't blame it on the wine, or the firelight, or the seductive music. The person responsible for everything she was feeling was slowly pulling her to her feet, then taking her hand and leading the way silently up the carpeted stairs to the master suite.

Once they were inside, Tessa saw the huge sleigh bed and dug her toes into the plush carpeting in a sudden attack of nerves. Luke dropped her hand to pull the covers back, then returned to her and slowly pulled her blouse out of the waistband of her business skirt.

She swallowed hard as he put her on the edge of the bed and lifted her skirt hem. She grabbed his hand to stop it from traveling up her thigh.

"We haven't even kissed yet." The words didn't make sense, and she struggled to find a better way to express that things were going too fast.

"Is that a complaint? I just wanted to get you out of those uncomfortable nylons, but if you want more . . ."

"No—it's just . . . God," she said, letting her head fall back as he closed his mouth over hers, stroked his tongue around her faint frown. Then he closed a strong hand around her hip and squeezed gently. "This isn't me," she managed between kisses.

"It's new to me, too. But I'm not going to waste time analyzing things when we have this heat between us," Luke said between kisses. He caught her lips again as he put his hand between her legs and began moving his palm in slow circles against her.

Tessa cried out softly and pulled her mouth away from his to gasp for air. "I should go," she tried again. But her hands wrapped around his neck and burrowed into his dark hair.

"But coming is so much better than going," he said with a sleepy, wicked grin. Sliding his fingers under her skirt again, he stripped the nylons down her legs in one easy motion.

She giggled, the sound unconsciously seductive—not her normal laugh at all. "You're so bad."

"Bad is good, right?" Luke asked as he stretched Tessa out across the bed and laid himself down beside her. He linked their fingers together, using his hold to raise her arms above her head in a position of complete surrender.

"Bad is dangerous. I shouldn't be doing this," she said, turning her face away in a haze of indecision so he had to nuzzle her neck instead of her lips. "We work together and it's too soon, and you're too—I'm not . . ." Tessa's voice trailed away as he lowered his head to kiss and nibble at her breasts through the silken material of her blouse.

"Have you ever, just once in your life, let go of the rules? Done something purely because it felt right and good and was what you needed at that moment?" Luke asked.

She shivered at the temptation he offered. She'd never felt this way in her life and she had no idea of how to handle it— or him.

"Have you?" Luke prompted.

"No." Her serious blue-gray eyes looked so sad and wistful as she breathed the word that he wanted to scoop her against him and never let go.

"Maybe it's time to do something for yourself, then. Just relax and let me love you. It won't affect the case or whatever rules you've got in your head. No one has to know but you and me," he whispered. He released one of her hands and moved his fingers up and down her soft thigh in gentle, strumming motions. "Let go and feel, Tessa."

"I'm not, ah, very good at letting go," she said seriously. "I don't want you to build this up into something, then disappoint you."

"Darling Tessa. The only way you could disappoint me would be to get up and leave me here alone in physical pain." Luke took her captive hand and pressed it against the front of his khakis. She could feel the throbbing heat of his erection, but the fabric was too thick for her to do more.

"I'm probably going to regret this," Tessa said. She pulled his shirt out of the way and began to unfasten his pants.

"Then I'll try to make it worth your while," Luke promised solemnly. He reached under her skirt again and pulled her panties off. Then he unbuttoned her shirt and pushed the fabric aside, before she could change her mind. He laughed quietly as he studied the erotic picture she made with her open blouse, lacy bra, and the dark blond curls peeking through the folds of the business skirt bunched carelessly around her hips. She was stunning, and she was his.

"Hey," she protested as she let go of his stubborn zipper in frustration. "Laughing the first time you see someone undressed isn't exactly comforting. I told you I wasn't very good at this letting-go thing."

"I can help with that," he replied. Without warning, he laid her back on the mattress, slid her legs apart, and buried his mouth in the tender flesh between them.

The abrupt movement—the sudden change from feeling half-dressed and protected by her clothing to being completely vulnerable while Luke nuzzled her in the most intimate way possible—was too much for Tessa to bear.

Her hips surged against him, and her hands fisted almost painfully in his dark hair. He didn't complain, but instead settled in deeper and dragged his tongue across her taut clitoris. She jerked again and tugged on his hair as if to pull him away, but her throaty moan of pleasure said she was loving every second of what he was doing to her.

So was he.

"My God. Luke, no, it's too much."

Luke blew against her moist, scented skin. He gently sank his teeth into her, then used them to trap her tender flesh for his tongue, which he used like a dagger to tenderly stab at her again and again.

Her hands tightened further in his hair, and while the pain was an exciting contrast to the burning heat in his groin, he was afraid she'd start pulling out chunks of scalp soon. He reached up and linked his fingers with hers, feeling her surprising strength as she grasped his hands and held on for dear life. Her soft, choked moans continued until he withdrew the gentle vise of his teeth and used his tongue in long, firm strokes that sent her over the edge. She shuddered and twisted and cried as she came so hard she almost passed out.

When it was over, her hands slid limply from his to land bonelessly on the mattress. She slitted her eyes open, but what she saw made her close them again as a wave of heated embarrassment and expectation swept over her. Her blouse was open, her skirt pushed up, her lace bra half-on and half-off.

And Luke was lying between her spread legs, his chin resting on the pale curve of her belly. He looked at her, waiting for her to come back, and noting with amusement the flush of heat rising from her chest into her face.

"If I get up, will you promise not to move a muscle from this position?" Luke asked as he rubbed his cheek against her stomach.

"Not unless you're going to turn the lights out," Tessa replied weakly.

"The hell with that. I guess we'll go to Plan B."

"Which is?"

"To get you so worked up again you can't even think of moving when I leave to grab a box of condoms."

"I'm sorry," she said as she raised a shaky hand to push hair out of her face. "I'm not usually so, er, quick off the mark."

"I don't want to hear apologies or regrets about anything we do in this bedroom tonight, okay?" Still lying between her legs, Luke propped himself up on his elbows and met her dazed blue-gray eyes.

She just shook her head and blushed more deeply.

"Now let's see, what can we do to make the pretty Deputy D.A. let go of her remaining inhibitions?" he wondered out loud as he traced his fingers in circles around her belly button.

"Inhibitions? Look at me," Tessa burst out. "You're kidding, right?"

"Nope. Let me grab some protection, and we can find out together what it takes to make you come apart completely."

Tessa shivered as he got up and began to strip off his clothes. "If you pull a half-empty box of condoms out of the bedside table, I'm going to be seriously annoyed, Romeo."

"You'll get over it," Luke replied. He stood in his boxers and leaned over to give her a thorough kiss. Tessa got an eyeful of muscled arms, a wedge-shaped mat of hair on his tanned chest, and the taut stomach she'd only been able to imagine before. In the dim lighting, she could see a smattering of white scars from the time he'd been shot, but they did nothing to detract from his strength and raw appeal.

"I guess I could forgive you," she agreed, tentatively running her hands over the parts of his torso she could reach. He laughingly pulled away and headed to the bathroom.

"Besides, I got this box at the drugstore today. You can

check the receipt if you don't believe me." He returned and threw the brown paper bag on the bedside table.

"Today, huh? Pretty cocky of you," she said, then groaned as she heard the words out loud.

"Why, Counselor, I thought you'd never notice." Luke grinned and unself-consciously dropped his boxers, then stepped out of them and crawled into bed next to her.

Her hands and arms were trembling lightly as she wrapped them around Luke's body and pulled him on top of her. He held back long enough to strip away her remaining clothes, then settled in with a sigh of pleasure. He rubbed his face between her firm breasts and then kissed the taut pink nipples again and again.

He would have been content to linger there, but one of her soft hands trailed down his back to clench in his buttocks and trace an incendiary path between them. He jolted as she stroked his taut muscles, then groaned quietly against her breast as she rubbed and caressed and fondled inches away from where he most wanted her touch.

He pulled her hand away, bit gently at her fingers, and reached for the bag on the bedside table. She waited patiently for him to finish with the condom, and sweat popped out on his forehead as he looked at her naked and ready for him. Her blue-gray eyes were dreamy, pupils dilated, cheeks rosy. A slight smile curved her lips.

The smile faltered as he took her face between his hands and kissed her deeply, all play gone for the moment. She closed her eyes and arched against the gentle probing between her legs, opening her thighs wide to let him rub against her and spread the sweet evidence of her pleasure between them.

She gasped against his mouth as Luke pressed halfway into her, then retreated and returned several times. Her breath panted against his ear as he pressed his cheek to hers and entered her fully. He reached down to pull her legs around his hips so he could slide freely back and forth inside her.

Her sounds of pleasure were soft in the late-night stillness of the room, and he moved faster and deeper to hear those cries again and again. Her nails suddenly dug hard into his back, and her head tossed back and forth on the pillow as Luke levered up on his elbows.

"Look at me. Look at us," Luke gritted. He pushed deeply into her and ground his hips against hers, forcing her eyes to fly open as a new level of sensation was introduced.

Tessa looked down between them, and the sight of him entering her body caused the first wave of orgasm to crash through her. Luke felt her clench and contract around him and let himself go. He buried his face in the scented curve of her neck and cried out hoarsely.

She clung to him, calling his name as the world narrowed down to the tousled bed, the pistonlike motion of his hips, and the heat of his sweat-covered back under her hands.

Chapter 29

Santa Monica, California
Saturday morning, March 13

Tessa woke early Saturday morning and simply lay there enjoying the exhausted, well-loved torpor of her body as it was warmed by a patch of morning sun. Sometime during the night they had crawled under the covers, but that hadn't stopped Luke from learning every inch of her body. Her face burned at the memories of him sliding underneath the sheets before dawn to wake her with the heat of his mouth between her thighs.

And then he'd cuddled behind her spoon fashion and made love to her again, this time with his body and his hands. The memory was woven through with dreamlike recollections of the sensations he'd evoked, feelings so intense that she'd buried her face in a pillow that smelled of him and screamed.

Luke Novak was a dangerous man, no doubt about it. She hoped there was good soundproofing in his house; otherwise, the neighbors had probably gotten an earful last night.

She continued to lie there with her eyes closed, not quite sure how they would face each other in the morning light after the things they had done. Of course, since the man clearly had no shame, it wouldn't be a problem for him. But this level of intensity was completely new to her. For the first time in her life she sensed a serious threat to her peace of mind—and maybe even her plans for the future.

Disturbed, Tessa turned her back to Luke and curled up on her side.

Lying beside her, he didn't need a degree in psychology to understand that he'd rushed her the night before, and now she was pulling away. He'd been eager to take their attraction to the next level, but he should have slowed down once he understood how gun-shy Tessa was about commitment. But he'd been so sleepy and content with her on the couch, so relaxed. All of his good intentions had vanished in a heartbeat once he'd seen the awareness in her eyes,

Well, it was too late to slow down now. Lucky for him he'd always been good at damage control.

Stretching slightly to ease the kinks in muscles that had gotten a thorough workout the night before, Luke figured a strategic disengagement would be in order. He'd keep things casual but affectionate. He'd need to give Tessa the impression that he was perfectly happy with whatever she was willing to give him, while at the same time tempting her into giving more.

Kind of like fishing—the idea would be to have the net ready to scoop her up before she was even aware that she was being hooked and reeled in. Of course, she'd be furious at the analogy, or at the idea that Luke was manipulating her in any way.

If he hadn't been falling hard and willing to do anything to keep her around to explore those feelings, he might even have felt bad about his plan. For a little while, anyway.

But since he had her very best interests at heart, he figured that gave him a little leeway in terms of maneuvering around her commitment issues. She'd had little enough reason to trust men in her life—by his own admission her father had betrayed her utterly at a young age. Then the two men she'd been seriously involved with as an adult had tried to push her into marriage when she said she wasn't ready, and succeeded only in driving her away.

The key to living with someone as smart, independent, and commitment-shy as Tessa would be to make sure that wherever they went, she thought it was her idea to go there.

Luke flipped back the sheets and stood up, enjoying the sight of her curled in the middle of his bed. Keeping it casual, he covered her with the blanket and stroked tousled blond hair away from her face. Then he left the room to take a shower.

Wide-awake now that Luke had left the bed, Tessa told herself she wasn't really disappointed that he hadn't tried anything hinky in the light of day. She listened as he ran the shower, then rattled around in the bathroom for a few minutes. He came back out trailing the scent of cologne and stood bare-assed naked in front of the closet as he selected clothes to wear.

Men really had no modesty. He wasn't even sucking in his stomach or keeping his shoulders back—not that he needed to. Everything about the man was just right. Big, firm, and . . . with a shiver, Tessa rolled to her back.

"Didn't you say you had a meeting with Carmen this morning?" Luke asked with his back to the bed. He pulled on boxers, casual pants, and a sport shirt, since he would be going to the office for part of the day.

Tessa cleared her throat. "Yes. Just a quick one to find out what she knows about the task force investigating Club Red. We missed each other all week because she was out of town, then playing catch-up."

"I've got a couple hours of work to get done at the office, then some phone calls to make and a meeting with MacBeth. Why don't you swing by Novak International at four or so, and we can organize things from there?" Luke came over and sat on the bed next to Tessa to slip his shoes on.

"Okay," she said, discreetly tugging at the length of sheet that was trapped underneath Luke. When he'd sat down, the pull on the fabric had exposed her upper body. Given that he'd had his mouth all over her, it was stupid to be shy. But habits were habits.

"Towels are in the bathroom, and you should find anything else you need with a minimum of looking. I'll put on a pot of coffee before I leave. Oh, and don't worry about the door—it locks automatically. See you later." Luke leaned over and gave her a thorough kiss, but pulled back before she could respond. Then he was out the door and down the hall before she could do more than say good-bye.

She told herself that the feeling in her stomach was abject relief that he seemed to be willing to play by her rules and keep things casual.

Carmen Ramirez motioned Tessa into her office for their 11:00 A.M. meeting. "Look at you. Someone had a hot date last night."

Tessa made herself busy balancing file folders and pulling a chair up to the desk. "I actually was asleep before nine, if you can believe it." Granted, she'd been up again after that, but didn't feel the need to share her personal life with her boss.

"Darn. Well, I hate to say it, but we need to keep this short. I've got a golf game with the lieutenant governor at twelve-thirty," Carmen said.

"You're the one who called the meeting. I don't have a lot of updates. You know we talked to the FBI about the ongoing task force investigation of Club Red and Ricky Hedges," Tessa said as she took a seat. She didn't like the vibes Carmen gave off as she tapped scarlet nails on the oversized desk.

"That's one of the things I wanted to talk to you about," Carmen said. "I got a call from a Special Agent Peebles of the FBI. He's heading the task force, and his nose is out of joint that you have been 'sniffing around' the subject of his investigation without coordinating things with him first."

"I didn't even know there was an investigation until—" Tessa began.

"That's just what I said to him. Don't worry, I won't hang you out to dry. Yet. I told Peebles that while we were aware of his task force and one of our investigators had been attending the meetings, you didn't know anything about it. And since the case hadn't reached the point of being ready for prosecution, there was no way you would have known about it when you started to investigate your rape case. It was an unavoidable breach, but I also told him it was poor form on his part to be upbraiding one of my prosecutors for doing her job."

"What information do you have on the task force? I mean, what has our office done to date?" Tessa asked.

Carmen shrugged. "Nothing much. There were so many personnel changes to the task force team, and progress was slow because it was a low-priority case. Our investigators here assumed the investigation had stalled. On this type of operation, the D.A. doesn't get involved until the subpoena and search warrants phase—and sometimes not even then. Unless local and state laws are being violated, the federal investigation takes precedence. In reality, we were just getting courtesy copies of the communications until now."

"How far out of joint is Peebles's nose about our cases crossing paths?" Tessa asked.

"Pretty badly. I'm guessing from the tone of his phone voice that he's a short, balding man." Carmen waved her hand dismissively. "I told him that his task force needed to make room for my prosecutors at their future meetings. He needs to understand that we are now going to be actively involved. You've been added to the CC and e-mail lists for communications pertaining to the case and should get an invitation to their next team meeting. I have a copy of docs for you here," Carmen said, indicating three boxes next to her desk.

"When is the next meeting?"

"Next month."

"Kelly can't wait that long," Tessa said. "And I don't want to have to fight turf wars with the FBI or any other agencies. They aren't after the same thing I am."

"I know. I tried to get him to bump the next meeting up, but he said everyone had other cases to work on and would be busy. So I told them you would continue in your pursuit of the rape-and-kidnapping investigation with my blessing. I also said you would follow their lead in terms of cooperation and coordination, which I expect will mean there's going to be a lot of polite memos and not much actual collaboration."

"What about their sensitive investigation? I was told that if we keep asking questions about Club Red, it would be noticed at high levels in Ricky's organization. The implication was that I could tip him off to the FBI's task force."

Carmen looked unconcerned. "If you happen to blow the lid off their organized crime investigation by looking into these rape allegations, so be it. That's what the FBI gets for letting the case drag out so long."

"I was told the priorities of the Bureau are terrorism and national security, and this was low-priority for them."

"I don't really care why the case got hind tit, I just told him that we can't be expected to share the FBI's priorities in this investigation. We are treating it as a high-priority, high-profile case, and will be pressing forward with the LAPD."

Tessa winced. "The FBI practically accused the PD of corruption and made it clear that they are not a part of the task force."

"I know," Carmen said. "LAPD is pissed, though I'm keeping the chief as a reserve weapon. Your PD contacts will just have to muscle into the investigation if they can."

The complicated politics of the situation were enough to

give Tessa heartburn. She wished she'd had time to eat breakfast, instead of just bolting a cup of Luke's coffee before fleeing his house earlier.

"Can I be frank, Carmen?" Tessa asked.

"It's one of the things I like about you."

"This is a pretty convoluted setup," Tessa began carefully. "Lots of people, each with different goals and jurisdictions. I'm not sure if it's a workable solution."

"I don't need workable, I just need enough room for your team to move and deniability for myself if you screw up. I figure if anything goes wrong with the task force investigation, there's enough for me to lay it all at the feet of the Bureau as lead agency. Part of your job will be to make sure that they can't blame you for anything bad that happens to their case."

"What about actually solving the case?" Tessa asked. "Is that an expectation, or am I merely acting as a raised middle finger to the FBI?"

Now Carmen laughed. "You wanted to be in charge of a major case, Tessa. Welcome to the big time. I have absolute confidence you'll get a conviction and make me look good. The fact that a Deputy D.A. will get more done than the FBI could in a year will not go unnoticed, and will be a fabulous boost for your career as well."

"How long do I have to work this miracle?" Tessa asked.

"You have a week to make progress. Ideally, I'd like enough information to go for a grand jury indictment by then. If you can't come up with something in that time, then we'll use a crowbar to make a place for your case at the next multiagency task force meeting. They'll have to reprioritize and get moving. In the end, you'll have to share information and credit with the FBI, but you'll help ensure that the D.A.'s Office is there for the back patting when a local criminal organization is taken down."

"Have you ever tried to force your way onto an existing

team? It's next to impossible, unless everyone is feeling extremely helpful and cooperative."

"That's why I'm sending you. People look at the body and the blond hair and think you're harmless. I trust you'll show some teeth and use them on Peebles's fat ass when the time is right. I'm counting on you to make this happen for the D.A.'s Office, Tessa."

"I appreciate that. But what if they actively obstruct my progress?"

"Then you make sure we have enough to cover our butts. If it all falls apart, and the shit starts flying, I'll put on a Teflon raincoat and walk away."

"Gee, thanks."

"It's politics, Counselor. Nothing personal. Just make sure that the situation doesn't come up, and we won't have to worry about it, okay?"

"Sure." Tessa wondered if she had enough medicine in her desk to take on the headache she was developing to go along with her heartburn. As if her life wasn't in enough turmoil after last night, now she was being told flat out to perform a minor miracle at work, or her boss would throw her to the wolves.

But it was nothing personal.

"So what's next for our investigation?" Carmen asked.

Tessa fumbled a manila folder from the stack in her lap. "Ah, it seems that Ricky Hedges fancies himself a real estate entrepreneur. I thought I'd pull articles of incorporation and see if he has any other businesses besides Club Red where he might be hiding or laundering money. I'm guessing there are copies of personal and business records in these boxes—probably stuck in the back of the folders."

"I take it the FBI didn't look into this?"

"No. They pulled the financials for Club Red only, but the rumor I heard was that their forensic accountant clashed with the team lead and left the Bureau. They haven't replaced her yet, maybe because they didn't see the need to hurry. The agent we talked to also hinted at budgetary constraints and the fact that Club Red just wasn't a high priority."

"Contact this bean counter," Carmen said.

"I have," Tessa replied with a grin. "I didn't see any evidence of the FBI looking into the accounting side further, or into Ricky's personal accounts. To be honest, they seem kind of stumped by the financial records, because Club Red doesn't have a lot of liquid assets, and they were looking for straight drug or gambling profits."

"Sounds like the Bureau," Carmen mused. "Always going for the big stuff."

"This may be bigger than they realized," Tessa explained. "After thinking for a few days and talking with Ed about it, I realized there may be another corporation or three involved. That would explain where the funds are going. I'm hoping the forensic accountant can confirm this when we meet her in two days."

"Then take the ball and run with it. Just remember that everyone aims for the person with the ball."

"I feel sick," Tessa said, only half-joking.

"Just go like hell. You can do it, especially if you have good backup."

Tessa thought of Luke, MacBeth, Ed, and Ronnie. "I'm meeting Ed for lunch today. He's very good at making his way through the bureaucracies, so I hope he'll have a few tips for me."

"Of all the people involved, I think he's the one least likely to steer you wrong," Carmen agreed. "Just make sure you don't screw things up and cost him his pension."

"Thanks. One more thing to worry about." Tessa stood and grabbed her folders.

"Did I already welcome you to the big time?"

Chapter 30

"I love your version of a table with a view." Tessa took the hoagie sandwich Ed Flynn offered her and looked around at the LA skyline. They had parked their cars in connected lots fifty stories below, then taken an elevator to the rooftop terrace of the new California West Bank building for a picnic lunch.

"I know one of the retired cops who does security for this building. The owners said we could come up and check it out today—the view is great, isn't it?" Ed took a bite of his sandwich and stared out at the city below.

It was windy and cool up at the top of the building, and there weren't any comfortable seats except the low wall they perched on, but he'd figured Tessa would appreciate the novelty of eating on a rooftop.

"It's fantastic. Much better than the revolving restaurant at the hotel—I get nauseous up there. To be honest, I'm having enough trouble with my stomach today as it is."

"Your meeting with Carmen went that well?" Ed asked around a huge bite.

Tessa made a face. "Remember that saying about being careful what you ask for?"

"Because you just might get it, yeah. What did you ask for?"

"An important case. I'm learning that life in the fast lane isn't all I'd imagined."

"What's up?" Ed asked. "You look pretty damned good to be whining so piteously. You got a new boyfriend or something?"

Tessa inhaled her soft drink. She coughed and blotted at her streaming eyes, and Ed pounded helpfully on her back.

"Did you finally notice the sparks zinging between you and Luke?" Ed asked gleefully. "You're kinda dense where men are involved, so I wasn't sure."

She narrowed her eyes at him. "I slept with him. This morning, as a matter of fact."

"Christ, Tessie!" Ed narrowly avoided choking on his own drink. "Don't tell me stuff like that. Talk about too much information." He shook his head repeatedly, as if trying to dislodge the image that had formed in his mind.

Tessa laughed for the first time that day. Being around Ed always made her feel better. He glared at her as she kept laughing helplessly.

She finally recovered herself and smiled sweetly at him. "You're the one who brought it up. Thanks for taking my mind off Carmen, though. She kind of dropped a bomb on me a little while ago."

"What kind of bomb?" Ed asked, wanting desperately to drop the subject of sex and Luke Novak.

Tessa briefly told him about her conversation with the district attorney that morning. His playful mood evaporated as he realized how complicated the situation was. "She really expects you to just horn in on an investigation led by the FBI?"

"I think she mentioned using a crowbar to pry a space for

myself on their team," Tessa said. "I could use some advice on how to do that without totally pissing off everyone."

Ed chewed thoughtfully. "It's all a game of give-and-take. You'll need to bring something to the table, a piece of information or an angle that they haven't looked at yet."

"I'm trying. But we're looking at different crimes. The Feds won't really care about the rape-and-kidnapping charges we're pursuing. I thought about focusing on the organized prostitution, but they already know about it. Right now I'm looking at the shell corporations you and I discussed and their potential for money laundering."

"Yeah? What kind of evidence do you have?"

"Nothing yet. But I did find out today that Ricky Hedges is either an owner or board member of at least two other companies incorporated in the state of California. It makes me wonder about how many other businesses he's involved with, and whether he's using them as fronts for laundering illegal funds or something."

"What do the companies do?" Ed asked.

"The one he owns in California is a consulting firm. He also sits on the board of a property development consortium that's active in the Lake Tahoe area."

"What kind of consulting?"

"I don't know yet. I'll have to look up their articles of incorporation and dig a little further," Tessa said.

"How long do you have before Carmen starts getting impatient?"

"She wants to go to the grand jury in a week. So I have until then to get enough information on Ricky Hedges. Otherwise, I'll have to piggyback my investigation onto the task force's ongoing case."

"And you have to balance the Feds and other agencies on the task force in the meantime," Ed added.

"Nice to know Carmen has such faith in me, huh?" Tessa wadded up her sandwich wrapper and made a rim shot into the trash can. "Who am I kidding? I have no idea what I'm doing. To be honest, I'm making it all up as I go along."

"That's all anyone does. The person who tells you different is a liar."

"Come on, you know what you're doing. So does Luke."

"We're just making educated guesses based on previous experience. But you've got good instincts, girl, and you can think on your feet. That counts for as much as experience. Sometimes it's worth even more."

"I feel like everyone has a copy of the rule book, and I don't. Now I'm being told to force my priorities into an active investigation, one where I'm probably not wanted. The other team members have had a year to get to know each other and learn strengths and weaknesses. And to build a dynamic."

"You're right—you'll be starting way behind everyone else and will have only a fraction of the time to come up to speed. And no one is going to cut you any slack, either."

"Geez, Ed. Try not to sugarcoat it too much."

He chuckled. "You can handle it. You're smart, and you have an idea that could result in a strong lead for the team. You've got to use that. If you have something they want, things will go much easier for you."

"I guess Luke and I will spend the weekend online looking through the papers in my trunk. And I hope he has access to multiple state databases, because I need to look at bank and tax records."

"He will," Ed said.

"You always have a lot of confidence in him. How long have you known him?" Tessa asked.

"I was assigned to a task force he was leading eight years ago after a series of violent home invasions. That was right after I was switched to working major crimes. The team formed just before Mary passed away, but I got to know him a lot better after her death," Ed said. Mary Flynn had been

Ed's wife for fifteen years. She'd died suddenly after a short battle with ovarian cancer, and he'd taken it hard.

"I'm sure that was a tough time, with your wife so ill," Tessa murmured.

"Yeah. I was walking through life like a zombie, not handling things very well. Luke and I were having a planning session and got into the shit late one night, a few days after Mary passed. He wanted to know why I wasn't pulling my weight like I had in the first few months of the investigation."

"He actually said that to you?" Tessa asked.

"No. He asked what was wrong and what he could do to help me deal with it so I could focus on the investigation again. He said the team needed me. I told him about losing Mary, and that her funeral was the next week. I said I just needed some personal space to get through that time, then I'd try to pull it together for the team."

Tessa stroked an understanding hand down Ed's arm. She hadn't known his late wife, but she did know that he'd never gotten over her loss. "What did Luke say to that?"

"He expressed his condolences, then sent me home. The next day the team got a notice from him canceling all meetings for the next ten days. And during Mary's funeral I looked up and Luke was there with the other mourners, listening to the eulogy. He's a good man." Ed smiled faintly and cleared his throat at the memory.

Tessa blinked against the unexpected tears, then made herself busy for a moment clearing the rest of their lunch trash. She must have it really bad if she was getting all weepy over a kind gesture Luke had made to her good friend eight years ago.

"You did the right thing bringing him into your investigation, Tessie. He's got access to information and contacts that will make things a lot easier," Ed said.

"Yes. He's organized and very smart—much more so than I gave him credit for initially."

"I've never seen him so thorough and methodical, so I think that might be your influence. You two make a great team. I hope you're both smart enough to realize how rare that is." Ed leaned forward and tried to look her directly in the eyes.

But Tessa was busy turning various shades of pink, so she ducked her head. "You and I work well together, too."

"Yeah, but I'm talking about what happens after leaving work, and I think you know it. Where is this thing going with you two?"

"Geez, Ed. We got together last night, and you're already picking china patterns?"

"I'm just saying I've never seen you so flustered. Or so, I don't know, glowing. Maybe that's the word."

"Just keep your glowing observations to yourself, okay? This is all new to me. It happened too fast, and I think we both want to take it slow and easy. It may not go anywhere at all," Tessa warned.

Ed snorted. "Not likely. You're breaking all your personal rules for him. That's got to mean something."

"Why? Because I have such a great track record? I've had a couple of long-term relationships in the last ten years, and each one ended with the guy asking for too much, getting frustrated, and leaving. I don't think I have it in me to give what most men seem to need."

"Or you just haven't wanted to give it. But something tells me Luke doesn't ask for what he wants or needs. He takes it."

"So how many women has he bonked over the head with his club and dragged back to his cave?" Tessa asked sourly.

"None that I know of. He's had different lady friends during the times we worked together. But nothing serious. He was with the SWAT team part-time in those years, and that's the most demanding field in law enforcement. After a few midnight beeper calls, most women tend to vanish."

"Mary didn't."

"No. But that's love for you. And I got off my own SWAT

rotation after I fell for her. I didn't see any need to face the prospect of dying every day at work, not when I had her to come home to. Detective work was less exciting, but a hell of a lot safer. Love changes everything, Tessie."

She was uncomfortable talking about love and Luke Novak in the same conversation. She had so little experience with either one.

And yet both seemed frightening, out of control, and seductive at the same time.

Tessa checked her watch. "Darn. I need to get going. I've got a lot of research to do today before I meet Luke at four." She had about three and a half hours, and hoped to get some uninterrupted time on the library computer. It was a gorgeous spring day, so hopefully most of LA would be enjoying the outdoors, leaving the computer terminals and bandwidth to her. And if something she needed wasn't online, she could use the help of the reference librarians to point her in the right direction.

She and Ed picked up their things and took a last stroll around the rooftop terrace. He pointed some old landmarks out to her and helped her find the direction of his house off in the distance. She took a few breaths of fresh air, trying not to think about the faint brown haze on the horizon, and mentally braced herself for the next phase of the investigation.

It was a lot to ask of her—the expectation that she would bring new information or leads to a multiagency task force headed by a senior FBI agent.

"Stop worrying. You'll find something soon, or keep at it until you do."

"Really, why do I even think I can dig up something that the FBI has somehow overlooked?" Tessa shook her head.

"First of all, because the FBI is made up of people—some good, some bad. Most of them are busy, and they all bring their own preconceptions and prejudices to the table."

"So you think that might make them skip over pertinent information?"

"You bet. Plus, if I know the Feds, they're looking for something big. Something sexy. They would probably blow off anything that didn't reach out and grab their attention, or at least look like it could grab headlines. When you add to that the new culture of budget cuts, it makes for a lot of crimes slipping through the cracks."

"I guess I'll start small, then. Something tells me that Ricky Hedges isn't the type of person to plan the crime of the century anyway. You know the Ianellis, the Mafia family he's working with? Luke says they're pretty low on the food chain in LA."

"He's right. A lot of people think of organized crime and assume it has to be a big and brutal organization, like John Gotti's empire. But a lot of criminals just stumble onto something, then milk it for whatever they can get until it either runs dry, they get caught, or they find some other scheme. It's not all about 50-million-dollar drug busts."

"I'll keep that in mind. I guess the teenage prostitution angle falls under the category of minor crime. Even if it destroys the lives of the girls involved."

"Maybe you'll be able to get Kelly out before she loses her soul," Ed said as he walked with Tessa to the elevator.

They rode down to the lobby in silence, then walked out the deserted back entry to the covered parking lots. Ed paused in the long, quiet alley between the two lots. "Where are you parked?"

"Behind the wall off to the right, in the uncovered part of the lot," Tessa replied, searching her voluminous bag for car keys.

"I'm upstairs and to the left, in the parking garage."

"I'll talk to you on Monday, then. Hopefully we'll have something to report." Tessa gave Ed an absentminded kiss on the cheek and headed down the alley, still searching the recesses of her bag. She stopped to give the black leather purse a frustrated shake, and was rewarded by the sound of keys jingling somewhere in its depths. Before she could find the keys, her cell phone rang. She stopped searching long enough to answer.

"Hi, Ronnie. I'm just leaving Ed right now, so you'll have to catch him on his cell phone. Are you ready for your first day back at work?" Tessa asked.

"Can't wait. I've been looking forward to Monday for months."

"I've got lots of research for you on the investigation," Tessa said. "I got three boxes of documents this morning."

She heard a car turn into the drive well ahead of her and automatically stepped to the side of the alley. Still talking to Veronica, she walked along the six-foot-tall cement block wall that separated the alley from the lot where her car was parked.

Her friend was in the middle of a sentence when Tessa heard the distinct sound of a car gunning its engine. She looked up and saw a dark blue 1980s-model Chevrolet Caprice shoot down the alley with the sound of screeching tires.

It took two full seconds to realize that the car was headed straight toward her. With the walls of the alley taller than she was by almost a foot, and the wall of the parking building on her other side, she had no place to go.

"Are you crazy? Stop!" Tessa screamed. But the car kept coming.

She heard Veronica's frantic voice on the phone as she dropped both it and her heavy purse and turned back toward the bank building. She ran along the wall, staying out of the middle of the alley, and went right past the covered entry to the lot where Ed was pulling out in his car. She didn't even notice him.

Ed saw the stark fear on Tessa's face as she raced by and pulled his gun as he grabbed the police radio. He dropped the mouthpiece when he saw the Caprice barreling past him down the alley.

Right after Tessa.

Without hesitation, Ed floored the accelerator, smashing the arm of the parking gate with his windshield and clipping the back end of the vehicle chasing Tessa. The impact caused the Caprice to fishtail wildly, and after overcorrecting the driver was forced to pull the wheel hard to the right—away from Tessa—in order to keep from losing control completely. Ed had a brief glimpse of a large male in the driver's seat as the car sped away from them up the alley.

Then he saw Tessa sprawled near the wall and his heart skipped a beat. He threw his car into park, called in a hit-and-run to the police dispatcher, and ran the fifty feet that separated him from Tessa.

Chapter 31

Just as Ed reached Tessa, she began to move. He held her down on her stomach. "Were you hit? Don't move, wait for the paramedics." Fear made his voice sharp and commanding.

"I fell, that's all. The car didn't hit me, I just rolled my ankle and fell while I was running. Who the hell was that guy, anyway?" Tessa pushed her way up onto her skinned forearms and looked at Ed as he crouched over her.

"I don't know. It's too early for a drunk. If I didn't know better, I'd say he was aiming for you, Tessie."

She shook her head and looked at the ground. It was littered with rocks and pieces of cinder block where the car had clipped the wall, narrowly missing her. Then she saw movement in the corner of her eye, behind Ed as he crouched next to her, and knew in a heartbeat that he had been right.

The car had been aiming for her, and now it was returning to finish the job.

"He's back!" She called the warning as she tried to scramble to her feet. But the car was approaching too fast. They weren't going to be able to get out of the way.

Still hunkered down, Ed looked over his shoulder and saw the dark blue Caprice bearing down on them. There was no time to run, so from his awkward position he hefted Tessa into his arms and threw her bodily over the cement wall into the neighboring lot. He tried to jump after her, but the act of throwing her had put him off-balance, and he wasn't able to make it over the wall on his first jump. He slid down and sprawled on his back briefly before getting to his knees.

Listening to Tessa frantically call his name, Ed drew his Glock 9mm and used his half-crouching position to take careful aim at the approaching car. He got off eight even shots before the driver jerked the wheel and aimed the passenger side of the car directly at him.

Tessa tried several times to climb the wall. Finally, she jumped with all her strength and pulled herself up to lie half over the top, staring down in disbelief. As the Caprice bore down on Ed, she grabbed a loose cinder block from the top of the wall and awkwardly heaved it at the windshield, where it caused a spiderweb pattern of splintered glass. Though the car swerved erratically, the windshield held. She couldn't see inside to identify anyone.

The driver eased off on the gas when the cinder block hit. But after a moment he jerked the car back on course, hit the accelerator again, and ran down her best friend.

The Caprice hit Ed squarely in the chest, despite the fact that he continued firing shots at the oncoming vehicle— every one of them had punched holes in the windshield, but the car kept coming.

Tessa screamed again and again as she watched Ed fly down the alley into a corner of the far wall from the force of the impact.

The Caprice hesitated for a moment, then the driver gunned the engine and headed away from the scene. It clipped the front end of Ed's car and sped down the alley onto the city street beyond. Tessa strained forward from her position on the wall and saw it turn right, then listened as the sound of its engine faded in the light Saturday-afternoon traffic.

Ed didn't move.

Frantically calling his name, Tessa scrambled over the wall and staggered as she dropped down to the alley. With one shoe off, her clothes dirty and torn, she ran toward the crumpled figure of her friend. On the way, she stooped to grab her cell phone from where it had fallen.

Miraculously, she could still hear Veronica's voice demanding in worried tones to know what was going on. The whole incident had taken less than a minute, from the time she'd realized the car was headed her way to the instant it had hit Ed.

Still running, Tessa held the phone to her ear. "Officer down. Officer down. It's a bad one." She gave Ronnie the location, a description of the vehicle, and the direction it had been heading. Then she dropped the phone into her pocket as she threw herself down next to Ed.

He lay unmoving on his back, brown eyes open, his face amazingly undamaged. Except for the blood that leaked out of his nose and the corners of his mouth.

"Can you hear me? Ed? Hold on, the ambulance is coming." Tessa sat next to him and picked up the hand he held out to her. "Don't try to move," she cried as he lifted his head to check around the alley.

"Is he gone?" Ed whispered. He coughed harshly, and more blood appeared on his mouth.

"Yes. Lie still." Tessa slid his head into her lap, hoping since he was moving it around that he didn't have a spinal injury. She was more concerned about keeping him still as the blood trickled from his mouth, and she used her fingers to tenderly wipe the scarlet stream from the corner of his lips.

She only succeeded in smearing it, and more welled forth immediately.

"Tessie."

"Yes, I'm here." She stroked his hair back and looked at the gray pallor of his face. Tears leaked silently from her eyes as he coughed repeatedly, clearly struggling for breath.

"God never saw fit to bless me and Mary with children. I love you like my own daughter. Just wanted to say that."

Cough, cough.

The racking noise made her heart turn over.

"I love you, Ed. But you're going to be fine. Hold on, just hold on. Ronnie is calling an ambulance. She's here, on the phone. She loves you, too." Tessa dug in her pocket, thinking it would help Ed to hear his partner's voice.

Ed shook his head. "Don't fret, my girls. I've had a good run at it, and no regrets. Well, one. I would have liked to see you get married, Tessie girl. And give me some grandchildren to go along with the one Ronnie has."

"Please don't say that. You're going to be okay. You're too tough to give up," she pleaded.

"I'm an old cop, Tessie. And lonely. I miss Mary," he said.

Then he whispered his dead wife's name again, his tone almost surprised. His eyes closed and his struggle for breath stopped.

This time Tessa didn't bother to call his name. She heard the sound of sirens approaching as she laid Ed out in the alley and began to perform CPR.

But in her heart she knew he was already gone.

Chapter 32

Santa Monica, California
Saturday evening, March 13

"What time is it?" Luke asked MacBeth. They were spread out in the conference room, reviewing state records on income and property taxes. Tessa had called around noon wanting to look into this new angle, so they'd spent the day pulling information from online data and analyzing the results.

"Coming up on six," MacBeth replied.

Tessa had said she'd join them by four. Luke picked up the phone and dialed her cellular number. Again.

But he'd only been able to reach her voice mail for over an hour, and was starting to get worried.

The sound of the doorbell brought him to his feet in relief. MacBeth followed him through the dimly lit, glass-walled reception area, where Tessa stood with Veronica Harris. In fact, Tessa leaned heavily on her friend, which was the first clue to Luke that something was very wrong.

He jerked the door open and looked with disbelief at Tessa's battered face. She had several raw abrasions, the worst on her cheekbone and chin. A small white bandage had been taped over her forehead, just at the hairline, and even in the poor light Luke could see where fresh blood was starting to seep through it.

Then he looked down and saw the dried red streaks all over her blouse and slacks.

"My God, Tessa. What happened?" He came through the doorway and gently pried her away from Ronnie, then led her to a soft couch in the waiting room.

"I'll get the first-aid kit and change that bandage," Mac-Beth said.

"Baby, are you all right?" Luke squatted down in front of her and tried to get her to look at him. She had the shell-shocked look of someone who had been through something unspeakable.

"She's okay," Veronica said from next to Luke. "Physically, anyway."

"Someone tell me what the *hell* is going on."

"He's dead. They ran him down in the street like a dog," Tessa whispered.

Luke's head whipped around. "Who—Ed?"

Veronica nodded grimly as her own eyes filled with tears she refused to let fall. "Hit-and-run. It was deliberate."

"Are you hurt?" Luke asked Tessa.

She shook her head. "H-he's dead because of me."

"He died because of the driver in the other car. You can't blame yourself," Ronnie said. It sounded from her tone like she had repeated the phrase a number of times already.

"The car was aiming for *me*. He was trying to kill *me*, and Ed got in his way."

"What the fuck happened out there?" Luke asked. As Tessa's eyes filled with tears, he took a steadying breath. "I'm sorry, baby. Please, just tell me what happened."

She took the hand he offered her and wrapped her blood-stained fingers around it. She hardly noticed MacBeth when he sat down next to her and opened the first-aid kit he'd brought. Then she tried to relate what had happened as concisely as possible.

A few minutes later, she flinched as he peeled the soiled bandage away from her forehead. "Hold still," Luke said. "MacBeth was a paramedic before he even joined the police department. He knows what he's doing."

"She barely let the medics touch her at the scene," Ronnie complained.

Tessa exhaled a shaky breath when pressure was applied to the half-inch gash at her hairline. Then she tightened her grip on Luke's hand.

"What happened when the car came back again?" Luke prompted.

She swallowed hard. "There wasn't time to run. I was lying on the ground where I'd fallen. Ed was squatting next to me—like you are now. There just wasn't time. So he saved my life."

"He loved you," Veronica said quietly.

Tessa closed her eyes, and two tears slipped down her face. Then she looked straight down at Luke. "Ed picked me up and threw me over a wall to safety. But he couldn't make it over himself, not from the position he was in. I saw him try—his head appeared at the top of the wall, but he slipped back down before I could help. Then I heard gunshots."

Luke's hands jerked in hers, as he realized how close Tessa had come to dying.

"I tried a couple of times and finally made it to the top of the wall. I grabbed a loose cinder block, thinking I could break the windshield and make the driver stop. But he didn't. Ed fired so many shots, I couldn't even count them. And the driver still kept coming."

"We found eighteen 9mm shell casings at the scene. Ed emptied his magazine and went down fighting," Veronica said.

"I saw the car hit him. I've never seen a human being actually go flying through the air before. I—" She broke off, unable to continue.

"It's okay." Luke sat next to Tessa and wrapped his arms gingerly around her, unsure of how to offer comfort without disturbing her cuts and bruises. She leaned tensely against him, and he knew the story wasn't done. "What happened next?"

"The Caprice drove off. I had to run to get to Ed, b-because he was at least thirty feet away. He—he was still alive, but he was br-breathing blood." Tessa's teeth began to chatter as she spoke.

Luke and Veronica both flinched at that detail, and Luke said a foul word under his breath. He met MacBeth's eyes and released Tessa's hands so the other man could began cleaning the raw scrapes on her right arm.

"That's enough. You don't have to finish," Luke said.

She didn't hear him. "I told Ed he would be all right, but he knew. He said his wife's name. Then he shut his eyes and died. I tried to do chest compressions, but it just made more blood come out of his mouth. The first paramedic unit arrived, and they took over. I heard one of them say every bone in his chest was broken. There was nothing they could do, but they kept trying anyway."

In the silence that followed, MacBeth finished cleaning her right arm and gently took her left hand to inspect it for cuts. She jerked against Luke and turned even whiter than she had been before.

"Damnit, Tessa. You said you weren't hurt," Ronnie said. "You refused further treatment."

"She's in shock. Why did the medics listen to her?" MacBeth asked as he changed places with Luke to examine Tessa's left wrist better.

Ronnie sighed with self-disgust. "We all wanted to get her statement so we could go after a cop-killer. The EMTs checked her out at the scene, but she seemed okay and refused transport. Hell, an ER doc doing a ride-along with the fire department said to take her in, but she wouldn't go. She wanted to come here. Even after they took Ed away in the ambulance, trying to resuscitate him, she insisted on coming here."

"He was gone," Tessa said. "I felt him leave. And I wanted to tell Luke something."

"What, baby?"

"At lunch, Ed told me how you helped him after Mary died. He was so touched that you went to her memorial service. I wanted to tell you what that meant to him."

Now Luke was the one to close his eyes against the sting of tears.

For just a moment he could see Ed's face as it had been at Mary Flynn's funeral. The naked pain, bewilderment, and shock he'd seen eight years ago were now mirrored in Tessa's blue-gray eyes. He didn't have any experience dealing with this type of emotional pain, but was going to have to learn. Fast.

She moaned low in her throat as MacBeth gently manipulated her arm. He met Luke's gaze over her bent head. "Her wrist is broken in at least two places." He showed Luke the swelling at the point near where the wrist widened into her hand, and then another spot, a few inches above her watchband. MacBeth eased the watch off, apologizing when she sucked in a pain-filled breath.

"Shit. I'll take her to the ER. Just sit with her for a minute." Luke stood to get his keys and motioned Ronnie to follow him across the room.

"Any word on the other car?"

"No. Tessa said it was an older-model Caprice, dark blue four-door, but it didn't have any plates. Every off-duty cop from the precinct is at work right now running DMV records checks and looking at stolen blue Chevrolets. This guy had better hope the Highway Patrol finds him first."

Luke looked past Veronica to where Tessa was sitting quietly with MacBeth. "Are you going to be all right while I take her to the hospital?"

"Yes. I'll go back to the precinct. Ed had a sister in Oregon, and someone has to call her. As soon as the ME is done with the body we'll start planning a burial with full honors. He bought the empty plot next to his wife's grave years ago." Veronica clenched her hands together and dug her short nails into the palms, thinking the pain would help her focus.

"Let me know if I can do anything. I mean it. And thanks for bringing Tessa here." He leaned forward and pressed a sympathetic kiss to her cheek. "I'm sorry as hell about Ed. He was the best."

Veronica looked at him. "Take care of her. I heard the whole thing on my cell phone—her screams, the car's engine sounding like a horror movie, the gunshots. I'm never going to be the same. I can't imagine what seeing Ed die in front of her will do to Tessa. Reliving it won't be easy, but we still need to talk to her for a formal statement. The captain wants to speak with her personally."

"I'm taking her to the hospital, then we're going to ground for a few days. Until I know for sure who tried to kill her and why, I'm not letting Tessa out of my sight. If the PD needs to talk to her, tell them to come by the ER."

Ronnie nodded. "Any ideas about who might have done this?"

"It has the feel of a contract job. The guy was a pro—to come back after the first pass, then keep going despite having eighteen 9mm rounds hit his windshield. It has to be related to one of her cases."

"That's what the senior investigator on the scene thought as well."

Luke continued. "I'll bet money it goes back to Club Red, since that's the only case she's working on with players capable of arranging a hit. We found out a few days ago that the club is turning over about $25 million each year, so it's worth their while to silence Tessa."

"I'll be sure to tell the investigators to look into that angle. I guess now LAPD will get involved in that task force," Veronica said.

"Yeah. I'll call you tomorrow and let you know where we are. But just you—I don't want anyone else to know."

"Okay." She turned to leave. "Why don't you take her to the ER at La Brea Hospital? That's where Ed was taken. The people there will bump her up to the front of the line, treat her right."

"Thanks."

Hours later, Luke watched from across the room as a technician checked the new cast on Tessa's left forearm. She'd already received personal condolences, as well as a gentle interrogation about what had happened, from Ed Flynn's captain at LAPD.

Now the doctor was in the room for a final checkup and to sign her release papers. He'd pulled Luke into the far end of the room to give additional instructions.

"The fractures aren't displaced, so the bones should heal well in the cast. She'll need occupational therapy once it comes off, but I believe she'll recover fully. Her other injuries are minor—a few deep contusions, some cuts and abrasions. Keep them clean and moist to minimize discomfort. Ice should help, too."

Luke nodded. "I'd like to get her into my hot tub to help with stiffness. I'll clean the cuts after each soak."

"I've also written a prescription for painkillers. See that she takes them, at least for the first few days. It should get a lot better after that, as long as she doesn't move her fingers too much. And watch her for signs of depression or post-traumatic stress disorder," the doctor added. "She saw something terrible today. It's going to affect her deeply."

"Yeah. But if I know her, she's going to take her pain and emotions and pour them into the investigation."

"I think it would be healthy for her to work again, after she's had a few days of rest. Try to get her life back to normal as much as possible. Routine, comfort, and security will help her get through this. Understand that her emotions will be all over the place, and be patient."

"I will. Thank you, Doctor." Luke shook his hand and watched as the man went over to inspect Tessa's cast a final time. Then the doctor excused himself from the room, along with the technician.

"He's a nice man," Tessa said. "He and the captain wanted to assure me that Ed didn't suffer. Apparently there was massive chest trauma that ruptured the aorta and broke several ribs, which punctured his lungs. Even if it had happened inside the ER, there was nothing they could have done to save him. Knowing that helps a little."

Luke could see she was trying to accept the reality of Ed's death by talking about it openly. But hearing the soft, toneless summary of her friend's injuries was making the hair on the back of his neck stand up.

She might look all right, but Tessa was a breath away from emotional breakdown. She desperately needed to deal with the jumble of feelings inside her, or they would eat her alive.

"How do these people think they can get away with running down a police officer?" Tessa asked. "I don't understand."

Luke didn't argue with her assumption that Ed's death was related to Kelly and Club Red. "It's easy for them—they never signed on as law-abiding citizens."

"I want those bastards in prison."

"Or dead," Luke agreed. "As of right now, the gloves come off."

"We're going to take Kelly out of there by force?" Tessa guessed.

"Yeah. We tried making nice by working the system and building a case—and it got a good cop killed. From now on, we do things my way."

"Good."

Chapter 33

"I don't think you're supposed to mix wine with painkillers," Tessa said. "I feel like I could sleep for days."

"That was the idea," Luke replied. He was stretched out on a soft chaise lounge on the second-floor deck that connected to his bedroom. Tessa was lying between his legs, her back to his chest, his arms wrapped around her underneath a warm blanket. Less than a block away, they could hear and smell the waves that crashed on the moonlit beach.

He'd hoped that the sound of the ocean would help Tessa relax after he'd brought her home from the hospital and prepared a dinner she could barely bring herself to eat.

Her broken wrist lay gingerly braced on a pillow across her lap. He'd had broken bones before and knew there were few things that felt worse than that deep, throbbing ache in the first few days. That's why he hadn't thought twice about pouring her a small glass of white wine to go along with what the doctor had prescribed.

"The hot tub finished me off." Tessa adjusted her head

against Luke's shoulder, feeling like she was looking down at someone else instead of experiencing this moment for herself.

"I think you fell asleep while I was cleaning your cuts afterward. I wish you could have eaten more dinner. I don't want you to waste away."

She laughed without humor and gestured at her rounded hip. "Not a chance."

His hands shifted so he could squeeze her curves. "I like these just the way they are. You won't do yourself or Ed any good by not eating. I need you to stay strong so we can work the case."

"I'll be okay tomorrow. This fucking case got Ed killed, you can bet I want to close it," she said, shocking Luke with her language. He'd never heard her curse so bitterly before. "I'll start tomorrow. I owe it to him."

"That sounds suspiciously like guilt."

"How else should I be feeling? You warned me this could be dangerous, and I wouldn't listen."

"Stop it. Even I had no idea things could go south like they did."

"And I refused to consider that possibility," she insisted. "For the first time in years, I felt meaningful. I was doing something important—working on a big case, complete with tragic victim, high-profile perp, and the full support of the D.A. I'd never done anything like it, and I was loving the exposure. Even though I knew Kelly was suffering."

"I know how you were feeling before this case. Hell, it's one of the reasons I left the sheriff's department. You get caught up in the bullshit investigations and wonder if that's what the rest of your life is going to be about," Luke said. "And then you feel validated when you finally get a big case. It doesn't make you a bad person, it makes you human, Swiss."

"Do you know what my last couple of cases involved?"

"No."

"Well, there's Maria Angela Sandoval, who keeps turning tricks out of her apartment to support her five kids. The super wants her evicted, but she's got a signed lease and is very discreet with her 'dates.' Then there's Ray Barber, who may have stolen his company's software and installed it on his home PC so his kids could play interactive online games during the weekends. And let's not forget Lester Delillo—he has a frozen potato launcher that he uses after midnight to take out his neighbor's garden gnomes."

"The famous spud gun." Luke laughed unwillingly. "I did my turn as a street deputy, so I know what most of the daily calls are like. I'll admit I never thought about what happened once the police reports were filed, though."

"The cases get dumped on some junior prosecutor like me," Tessa said. "I would find myself researching the replacement value of garden gnomes so I'd know what to charge Lester with—and asking myself if this was why I'd gone to law school. But that changed the morning I met Kelly."

"Because the case was important."

"It had a direct effect on someone's life. And suddenly, my own life had purpose again. I just didn't realize the price other people would have to pay for me to feel good about my job. First Kelly, then Ed—" Her voice broke.

"Dammit, Tessa. That's not what happened. If you want to get angry, if you want to blame someone, then save it up for the guy who carried out this hit."

"Believe me, I've got plenty left over for him."

Luke gently turned her to face him on the chaise, mindful of her wrist. "After knowing Ed Flynn for eight years, I'm going to take the liberty of speaking for him."

"He respected you," Tessa said.

"By all accounts, he loved you and thought you walked on water. Both as a person and a prosecutor. He was one of the best cops I've ever known, and I'd trust his judgment about you implicitly."

"Even if you weren't sleeping with me?" Tessa asked.

"You bet. Do you believe that Ed dedicated his life to protecting others? That in the years since his wife died he was essentially married to the job?"

"Yes," Tessa said softly. "Ronnie and I kept trying to fix him up on blind dates, but after a while saw there was no use. He gave everything he had to the job. And to helping me and Ronnie learn the ropes."

"Ed died a cop, protecting a friend he cared for very much," Luke continued. "If I'd been there, I would have done the same thing."

Tessa shook her head vehemently as she blinked back tears.

"Yes," Luke said, giving her a small shake before wrapping her in his arms. "Ed left this world saying the name of the woman he loved, doing a job that made him whole. It just doesn't get any better than that, Tessa."

She continued to shake her head. "I didn't want him to die for me."

"He chose to make that sacrifice, baby. And now it's your job to make sure it wasn't in vain."

"No one is worth another's life," Tessa said.

"It's what he wanted."

"I want him alive. I want him to be here."

"I know you do. But he's gone, Swiss. We need to carry on his work for him. What drove him on this case?"

"He wanted to help Kelly. Because it was what I wanted."

Luke could barely understand her through the tears he'd deliberately provoked. He didn't think it was healthy to keep everything bottled up, but hadn't been prepared for the depth of Tessa's pain. Remembering the doctor's advice about work and getting her life back to normal, Luke said the first thing that came to his mind.

"If that's what Ed wanted, then that's what we'll do. In his name. But not tonight, okay? Tonight we cry and raise a glass to a good man."

Tessa nodded, her throat too tight to speak. She had the crying part down just fine, and couldn't seem to stop now that she'd started. She felt Luke's arms strong and warm around her, and was ashamed for the way she was leaning on him.

Normally, she didn't depend on anyone, but it had been the worst day of her entire life. Even the day she'd lost her mother hadn't hurt this badly, because she'd been too young to understand what it all meant. But now she did, and she didn't have the strength to pull away from Luke.

"Just cry it out, baby." He seemed to be reading her mind. "Ed wouldn't mind at all. It shows that you loved him, that he had an impact on your life. He had an impact on everyone who met him," Luke's voice was gravelly because of the lump in his own throat. "If I could be half as good a man as Ed was, I'd be happy."

She looked at Luke and saw his hazel eyes shimmer with moisture. Reaching to wipe away the wetness on his cheek, she felt the dam inside her bursting.

Without another word, Tessa buried her head in Luke's neck and wept.

Chapter 34

Tessa woke up at nine on Sunday morning, disturbed when Luke left the bed. She rolled to her back and winced at the pain in her wrist. Before she could do more than open her eyes, Luke was bending over her, shifting a pillow so that she could rest the cast on it.

"Don't get up. I'll get you a snack and some painkillers. Let me get the door first, though. Some jerk has been banging on it for the last two minutes."

She watched in a daze as he paused to pull sweatpants over his boxers, then finger-combed his hair. When the pounding on the door started again, Luke cursed and left the room.

Tessa gingerly piled another pillow behind her back and looked around. She vaguely remembered coming in from the porch late last night after crying all over Luke. He'd helped her wash her face and brush her teeth—he'd even opened the toothpaste and applied it for her, something that would have been difficult to do with her wrist so sore that moving her fingers caused sharp pain.

Then he'd tucked her into bed, sliding in beside her to warm the sheets and hold her close. And when she'd drifted off, only to jerk awake with a cry of protest on her lips, he'd understood the demons haunting her. So he'd turned a light on and talked to her into the night, telling funny stories about his experiences on various task forces and stakeouts. She'd fallen asleep curled against Luke's side in the middle of one of those tales.

In all, Luke Novak had taken better care of her than anyone had. Ever. And for some reason, it felt like pity was the last thing motivating his actions. But she really wasn't ready to deal with how she felt about that. It was too much, too soon.

For now, she had to think about finding Kelly and building a case against the man who had killed Ed. She hoped Luke would understand that she simply didn't have anything else to give until those tasks were done.

"Someone's here to see you," Luke said from the doorway, surprising her out of her thoughts. She saw his eyes linger on her tousled hair and bare shoulder where his oversized sheriff's department T-shirt gaped off her.

Then she sat straight up in bed as she saw her father move into the doorway behind Luke. Her eyes were still gritty from last night's tears, but they weren't deceiving her.

"What the hell? You're supposed to be in Argentina," Tessa told him.

"I made arrangements to come back as soon as Luke called me yesterday. Are you all right?" Paul looked at the raw scrapes on her face, the visible bruising on her cheek and jaw, and the pristine cast on her left forearm.

Tessa shifted under her father's silent regard and resisted the urge to adjust the neckline of the T-shirt she was wearing. She probably looked like crap.

"He wouldn't wait for you to come downstairs," Luke said, stepping into the room and sitting on the bed next to Tessa.

He handed her a breakfast bar and put a glass of water on the nightstand, then leaned against the headboard to get comfortable. It was clear Paul was pissed beyond words at finding Tessa in bed with a half-dressed man, but Luke figured it was no less than the guy deserved for barging in unannounced on a Sunday morning.

Paul let the silence stretch, wondering who would cave in and break it first. But except for the sound of a wrapper crinkling as Tessa consumed the granola bar, no one seemed willing to break the uncomfortable quiet. In fact, his daughter tried very hard to act like sitting on a bed with a bare-chested man sprawled next to her was nothing new. But as Paul looked at the casual strength of Luke Novak—whose scarred abdomen and careless pose gave him the appearance of a warrior after battle—he realized that nothing about the scene was normal for his daughter.

He'd never liked the men she'd dated previously, because they were, quite frankly, pussies. Nothing about Luke gave that impression, so he had to hope his daughter's taste in men was improving.

With a sigh, he entered the room and threw his coat down on an end table. Then he took a seat in an overstuffed chair meant for reading or getting cozy in front of the fireplace on a winter night.

Sliding his daughter and her lover a glance, he wasn't sure if he was ready to go there just yet.

"You flew all the way up here to see me?" Tessa finally asked. Her curiosity got the better of her determination not to be the first to give in.

Paul Jacobi gave a sigh. "Things between us must really be in the toilet if you have to ask me that. Of course I came to make sure you were okay. I have to admit, I hadn't considered that you might have someone to, ah, take care of you."

Luke smiled complacently and handed Tessa a painkiller and the glass of water off the bedside table. She counted to ten in irritation while she took the pill and swallowed. She didn't want to start fighting with her father—frankly, it took too much energy. But he did know how to push her buttons.

Besides, nothing had happened with Luke last night—at least nothing along the lines of what her father was thinking. But she'd bite through her tongue before giving him the satisfaction of watching her defend herself.

Seeing his daughter's shoulders tense and face go expressionless, Paul could have kicked himself. Here she was, bruised and battered, and he fell right back into their old pattern of bickering. He knew how close she had been to Ed Flynn—had, in fact, been jealous of their easy relationship. He shouldn't let those feelings color his behavior now that the man was gone.

"I'm sorry about Detective Flynn. I know how much he meant to you."

"Thank you," Tessa mumbled in surprise, and took another bite of the granola bar.

"I didn't realize how dangerous this case might become. I don't think anyone did," Paul said, holding a hand up to stop her when she would have defended herself against some imagined criticism.

"We won't underestimate the players again," Luke said.

"I want you to come back to Buenos Aires with me," Paul said abruptly to Tessa. "Come on the cruise to Antarctica. Let Luke and his company follow up on the investigation and leave tracking Ed Flynn's killer to his fellow cops."

"I appreciate the offer," Tessa said. "But I can't run away from this, no matter how tempting it might be to consider. I owe it to a lot of people to see this case through to trial."

"Your friend and mentor was killed trying to do just that. Doesn't this tell you how serious the people you're investigating are about not being caught?" Paul asked.

"Yes. And it only emphasizes the need to stop them. I couldn't live with myself if I let someone else do my job in this situation."

"You're too personally involved to be objective—" Paul began angrily.

"You're right, it is personal. And because of that, I'm going to be like a dog with a freaking bone. I'm not going to let go until these guys are in prison, preferably on death row."

"You're going to work in your condition?" her father asked, pointing to the cast on her arm.

Luke jumped in to defuse the simmering tension. "You never know when a cast will come in handy—that thing's heavy, believe me. She could use it as a weapon if she had to. Besides, her wrist is the only thing that's broken. Her brain works just fine."

Paul checked his watch and got to his feet. "Dammit, I don't have time to argue. If I don't catch the noon flight, I'll miss the boat in Argentina. I haven't made other arrangements to look out for Kevin and Lana."

"So go. I want you to. These people made a threat against Kevin. However improbable it is, you should be there with him to make sure nothing happens," Tessa said with a sigh.

A throbbing pain in her head began to rival the one in her broken wrist, and she could have sworn that each of the shallow abrasions on her face and arms was suddenly a gaping wound. Something about arguing with her father took the energy and will right out of her.

Paul watched her shut down. Jet lag and worry got the better of him, finally causing him to lose his temper with his daughter's stubbornness. "Why can't you be reasonable? Are you trying to punish me?"

"I'll be perfectly safe," she insisted, ignoring the bait. "That's what you're paying Luke for, remember?"

"Yeah, well from where I'm standing it looks like he's doing a piss-poor job," Paul said coldly.

Tessa jumped out of bed with a gasp of outrage. "How *dare* you? Luke's taken better care of me than anyone I've known. *Anyone*. So go back to your family, Paul. You've got no right to play the heavy-handed parent at this point in my life."

"You don't have to defend me, Swiss." Luke got up and put a hand on her shoulder to restrain her, but she shook him off.

She was too angry to care about the pain that movement cause, and instead focused on her father. "Why do you look so shocked? You weren't there when I needed you as a child, so don't act surprised if I don't need you at all anymore."

"Are you saying that Luke is going to be there for you in the future?" Paul asked calmly, not revealing the pain he felt at her statements. "After all, you haven't known him long. You're willing to let him come between you and your family?"

Tessa lost whatever fragile hold she'd had on her tongue. "How well did you know Lana before you married her and banished your only child to a boarding school in another state?"

Luke winced at Tessa's direct hit. He knew she had no idea how deeply that accusation would wound Paul, or she wouldn't have said it.

She wasn't a cruel person, but her heart was breaking over Ed. She was ready to lash out at the first person who asked for it, and Paul had provoked her to the point that he became a target.

"How long have you been waiting to throw that in my face, Tessa? Did it feel good to get it off your chest?" Paul asked wearily.

"Don't turn this around on me—" Tessa began.

"Fine. I did a terrible thing when I married a woman I had fallen in love with at a time when I was afraid I'd be spending the rest of my life alone." Paul held up his hands in mock surrender.

"That wasn't what I was talking about. I'm not such a bitch that I would begrudge you happiness. I just don't think it should have come at the expense of mine." Her stormy blue-gray gaze met Paul's directly.

"So I was a bad father. Sue me, Counselor. But Lana is a good woman. However badly things began between you two, as my wife she deserves your respect. You have no right to hate her for something I did twenty-five years ago."

"How about I hate you instead?" Tessa spoke in a half whisper, faintly shocked at the depths of her own emotions. But she was helpless to stop the words from coming out—it was as if a dam had broken, and she couldn't hold back the flow.

Luke held his breath, wondering if he should step between them and stop the conflict. But he knew that the only way to get over the pain of the past was to deal with it and move on. Paul and Tessa had probably never openly discussed their estrangement before, and hopefully this could be a way to begin healing the breach.

If they didn't rip each other to shreds with their words first.

Paul had his eyes closed as he tried to focus on why he was there in the first place. However, the prospect of finally having things out with his distant, elusive daughter was too tempting to give up. He knew she was hurting—both emotionally and physically—and it was wrong of him to add to her burden.

But this was the first honest emotion she'd shown toward him in decades, and he wasn't going to back off now.

"Listen to me, Tessa. What I did to you was wrong. I didn't realize it then, though, because I'd just lost your mother and was hurting so badly. I was just a shell of a man, and I let you down so completely that sometimes I still have trouble looking at myself in the mirror."

Tessa took a half step backward, running into Luke's solid warmth. She'd never actually heard her father admit that he'd done anything wrong. Instead, he'd always gotten defensive and protective of Lana, which had served to drive Tessa even further away.

Paul sat down again, the energy his anger had given him

completely gone. In its place was a weary resolve, and the knowledge that if he didn't make some effort to fix things he was going to go to his grave without his daughter ever forgiving him.

"Why the surprise?" Paul asked, correctly interpreting Tessa's silence. "I know what I did was unforgivable. It was wrong to send you away, and even more wrong to let you step in and do my job with Kevin once he was born. I only hurt you worse when I realized what I had given up and tried to be a father to both of you again. I wasn't prepared for the possibility that you two might not need me, so I panicked and forced the issue."

"You were trying to do what was right for Kevin," Tessa said hesitantly. She'd never seen her father look so old and tired. Every one of his six-plus decades was etched on his face.

"Believe it or not, I was thinking of you. I wanted you to get out and meet people, to have a normal college life, maybe find a husband. Not be tied to your five-year-old brother because Lana and I were too wrapped up in our jobs to be real parents."

"I don't know what to say to that," Tessa admitted. She felt Luke's hand settle on her shoulder again, this time offering comfort.

"Why don't you say you'll give me another chance?" Paul asked wistfully. "I've wanted to make it up to you for a long time. But you've been so angry. I'd hoped you would get past it, once you moved out to LA, and we could start interacting as adults. But it hasn't happened, and neither one of us is getting any younger."

"I had no idea."

"Because you haven't wanted to see it. The ability to be willfully blind to the truth is something you no doubt get from me," Paul said.

Tessa's chin shot up in an automatic rejection of being

like her father in any way. He recognized the gesture and shook his head.

"Isn't it time to stop looking behind us? I want to look forward to something for once, instead of focusing on the past. I know I set you aside as a child, and if I could take it back, I would. But you have my love and attention now. It's all I can do. Is it enough?" Paul asked.

"I don't know." She looked away from his intense blue gaze. It was so tempting to get sucked in by his sincerity. She'd never seen him so earnest or open before. But the wounded child inside her remembered too well the pain of being pushed from the center of her father's life.

Paul cursed.

"I'm sorry," Tessa cried out. "I had no idea you felt this way. I need some time to think about it—I can't just let go of everything that I've known for the last twenty-five years." She felt bad about the obvious pain her words caused, but her sense of self-preservation was strong after repeated disappointments from her father.

"Don't be sorry," Paul said as he got to his feet. "I should have known it wouldn't be that simple to bury the past. You're too damned stubborn to let me off easy."

"That's not it. Don't make it sound like some kind of petty game I'm playing."

"You're right. It's not a game," Paul reached a side pocket of the jacket he'd thrown down earlier. "Forget about us for a minute. I know we can't solve a lifetime of problems in the time I have before my flight. The best I can do is help keep you around long enough so that we can have it out later."

"I'll take care of her," Luke said.

"You can try," Paul agreed. "But I figured my daughter would be too pigheaded to listen to reason. So I've called in a few favors. You're going to be the guests of honor at the next meeting of the multiagency task force investigating Club Red Inc."

"But that meeting isn't scheduled for another month," Tessa said.

"Wrong. I talked to the head of the FBI's West Coast operations, and in light of recent events he's agreed to convene a meeting on Wednesday. It will take that long to give the out-of-town people sufficient notice and travel time. And it will also give you and Luke a chance to come up with some concrete evidence."

"What do you think we've been trying to do?" Tessa asked from between clenched teeth.

"Try harder. I can get you into the meeting, but from there you're on your own. Either you bring something good to the table on Wednesday, or the investigation will move on around you. You won't get another chance."

"No pressure there," Luke muttered under his breath.

"She can do it, Novak. If you didn't believe that, I don't think you'd be standing behind her."

"Hell, I know she can. I'm just concerned about putting more pressure on her when she's in pain and grieving for a lost friend."

"Are you saying you believe in me?" Tessa asked her father. "You trust me to get the job done?"

"Of course I do. I always have, I just don't know how to express it when you get all prickly and distant with me," Paul said. He continued speaking over her protest at his choice of words. "If there's someone out there who needs help, I can't think of a better person to come to the rescue than you, Tessa. But you've got a tender heart and trusting nature, which is why I'll feel better if you have a renegade like Luke Novak along."

"I don't know what to say," Tessa murmured.

"Well, that's three times I've had you speechless today—and all before noon. Things might just be looking up for us, my girl. Unfortunately, I have to leave now."

"Go take care of them. Send Kevin my love. And—and

give Lana my best," Tessa said, glad she barely stumbled over the words.

"We're all very proud of you." Paul said. He cleared his throat and picked up his coat. "I'll see myself out. You can reach us on my satellite phone."

In the silence that followed, Tessa stared at the floor and wondered how she had come to this point in such a short space of time. A month ago her life had been quiet, orderly, and slightly boring. Now she wasn't sure how much more excitement she could survive.

"Well, that's it," she said. "My life is officially out of control."

"Look at the bright side." Luke lightly massaged her tense shoulders as he spoke. "I'm guessing that your wrist doesn't hurt right now."

"What wrist?"

"I thought so. Let's get dressed and take a walk on the beach before it gets too crowded, okay?"

"Fine."

Chapter 35

"Who were you talking to?" Tessa asked as she looked out over the line of waves coming toward her. Luke had just caught up with her on the beach, having paused to answer his cell phone a moment earlier.

"Chantal Francoeur, forensic accountant and money laundering expert extraordinaire. She said the documents from the task force had arrived, and she was going to review them tonight. Hopefully she'll be ready when we meet her tomorrow morning, but only if you're feeling up to it."

"I'll have to be. We don't have much time." Tessa sighed.

"We have as much time as you need. If you're hurting, you won't be in any shape to provide the information that Chantal is going to need."

"My wrist is fine, I barely think about it." Her heart was hurting much more. Watching the surfers catch waves into shore had made her think painfully of Ed and his morning surfing ritual.

Luke slipped a casual arm around her shoulder and used it to nudge her into walking along the beach again. "I'm sure it wasn't easy to have the discussion this morning with your father, but I'm glad you did. He loves you, and I know you feel the same way. You two have just forgotten how to express that to each other."

"I know he told you what happened in our family—his side of it, anyway."

"Actually, he was pretty harsh on himself when he told me. It's been eating him up inside for years. You, too."

"I guess I didn't realize how much until recently," Tessa admitted. "It's been such a part of my life, I didn't see how it was affecting my relationships with others. Like Lana. And probably other men in my life, to be honest."

"You're always honest, Swiss."

"So is it wrong of me to say that I thought less of my father for falling in love with Lana less than a month after my mother drowned? I mean, he was supposed to love Mom forever, right? I felt betrayed, and I'm sure she would have, too. That's not something you forget, no matter how much time has passed or how sincere the apology."

Luke had known that Tessa had issues revolving around trust and commitment. He just hadn't realized how deeply rooted the pain was in her whole family dynamic. To be honest, with his happy childhood and loving parents, he was out of his league.

So he tried with Tessa what had always been an important aspect of his family relations—unconditional support and acceptance.

"If that's the way you feel, it's not wrong, baby. You just need to figure out a way to get past that and salvage the relationship with your father and the rest of your family— because they're the only one you've got. Try putting yourself in his position. I can't imagine what it would be like to lose my wife and be left alone to deal with my young child. Some men would react better than others. Some people out there always need to have a partner in their lives—it's just the way they are. Maybe your father is one of them."

"It wasn't just the way he got over my mom. It's like he walked away from his entire life, me included. I needed him so badly, and he wasn't there—he never was." Tessa broke off and looked at the water again. "I was about thirteen years old when I realized I was on my own. I swore to myself I would never need anyone again, and I haven't. How sad is that?"

"What about Kevin?" Luke asked. She smiled, a faint and sweet curve of her lips that made his insides flutter.

"He was so young and needy himself. He kind of snuck into my heart," Tessa said.

Good going, Kev. I think there's a lesson there.

Luke was silent for a moment. He thought about bringing up Ed and how Tessa had relied on him as a friend, but knew she wasn't talking about that kind of need. She was talking about not letting herself need a man to be happy or make her life complete.

The more time Luke spent with her, the more he wanted to be that man. The only problem was letting her know in a way that didn't scare her off forever.

"Besides," Tessa continued, "Kevin would never abandon me, no matter what. Other people in my life have not proven to be so steadfast."

"I realize you don't know me well enough to believe this, but I will never disappear from your life. I want you to trust me; I just wish I knew how to prove it."

"I wasn't talking about you," she said in a low voice, but she continued to walk down the beach and wouldn't meet his gaze.

"Stop for a second." Luke turned her to face him. He was about to tell her that he wanted to be a part of her life, long-term, when he saw the absolute panic in her eyes. He realized that a confession like that could end up pushing her away from him with very little effort. He would have to take it slowly.

"It's okay, Luke—" Tessa interrupted.

"No, listen." He spoke firmly, choosing his words carefully. "You have to know that I care about you very much, and respect you as both a prosecutor and a woman. I would do anything to keep you from getting hurt. And like Kevin, I would never abandon you. For once in your life, you don't have to go it alone. I'm in this with you until it's done, all right? We're partners."

She breathed a sigh of relief. For a second, she'd thought he was going to talk about what was going on between them outside of the case.

Since going to bed with him, Tessa had been unable to categorize or even define their relationship in her own mind, because too many things were going on. She'd been afraid that he was going to be like the other men she'd known and start pushing her in an effort to formalize things so he could feel better or more secure—or whatever motivated her previous boyfriends to try to tie her down. But Luke seemed to be content to leave things as they were, which was fine with her.

Really.

The fact that she felt like a complete coward for avoiding a discussion of the issue was just something else she'd have to deal with.

When she focused on him again, he was waiting calmly for a response from her. "I believe you, Luke. But I've never had a partner on a case before, so you'll have to forgive me if I don't know quite how to act." Tessa hesitated, wondering if Luke would realize that the statement applied as much to her personal life as to the case.

He smiled, almost sadly, and kept his arm around her as they began walking back toward his house. "Neither have I. But don't worry, baby—I'm a patient man. We can learn together."

For some reason, it sounded almost like a warning to Tessa.

After a long walk on the beach, Tessa and Luke returned to his house for a late breakfast. Wanting to do something for

Luke after the way he'd taken care of her since the day before, Tessa was frustrated by the constant restrictions of the cast on her left wrist. She'd had to settle for talking Luke through the preparation of her famous blueberry pancakes, Kevin's favorite special breakfast.

Once they'd eaten, Luke had done the dishes without complaint, then gone outside to get the oversized Sunday edition of the paper from the driveway. He turned on some music, then pulled Tessa down onto the cushions on the living room floor, where they'd amicably argued over who got to read which sections of the paper first. Tessa scored the comic section and graciously turned the main news pages over to Luke.

Which was fine with him, because he wanted to make sure there were no upsetting articles about Ed's death for Tessa to stumble over and read.

He flipped through his section and kept one eye on her as she lay on her back, holding the folded comics high above her with her good arm as she read. Flipping quickly through his own section, Luke came across a piece buried in the middle of the paper. The article announced that a local city councilman from Los Angeles had formed an exploratory committee to research the possibility of a run for governor of California.

What caught Luke's eye was the picture of Sledge Aiken and several of his teammates at the councilman's kickoff cocktail party and fund-raiser. They were presenting the councilman with a team jersey and signed football.

"What?" Tessa asked, looking over at Luke as he flipped onto on his stomach to read the article in depth.

"It looks like Sledge has friends in high places with respect to state politics," Luke remarked, sliding the article closer so Tessa could read once she rolled over and came to rest against his side.

"We guessed he did, just from the way his lawyer was able to stifle almost every aspect of the initial rape investigation."

"It seems to me that two things are remarkable about Sledge's presence at this fund-raiser," Luke mused.

"And they are . . . ?"

"First of all, it's obvious no news of the investigation into rape charges against him has made it to the media. Otherwise, the councilman would have dropped Sledge like a sack of shit."

"Probably," Tessa agreed. "The judge said he expected us to guard the name of the accused as zealously as we guarded the name of the alleged victim. And we haven't been doing any investigating of Sledge at all. Our files have effectively been sealed, no warrants were issued, and no official charges were ever pressed, so I'm not surprised that word hasn't gotten out yet."

"Give it some time, the media will figure out that something is going on. But the second thing that interests me is this—what is the councilman doing shilling for money with a pro athlete we know has Mafia connections?" Luke asked.

Tessa was silent as she considered the possibilities.

"Exactly," Luke said. "It's enough to make me wonder what the *hell* is going on in local politics."

"Maybe the councilman doesn't know what we know," Tessa pointed out.

Luke slanted her a cynical look.

"Okay," she laughed. "Maybe that's exactly why he's hanging out with Sledge in the first place."

"That's more like it. Definitely something we'll need to follow up on with the FBI."

"What is this politician's claim to fame?" Tessa asked. "You know, his pet projects and stuff."

Luke scanned the article, stopping when he got to the second to last paragraph. "It seems our councilman favors growth initiatives that increase municipal tax revenues. It says here that he's focused on changing real estate zoning laws and selling off tracts of city land in order to make the existing municipal resources work harder for the taxpayers."

"City land?" Tessa asked. "You don't suppose that's tied into Ricky Hedges's real estate development business, do you?"

"I have no idea. But that's something else we'll have to talk about with Chantal Francoeur. Tomorrow," he added, folding up the news section and setting it aside. "For the rest of today, I think you should rest."

Tessa started to get up, but Luke held her back with a gentle hand on her back. "Where are you going?"

"To get my notebook. I want to write this down so I won't forget. Then I can relax for a while."

Luke laughed. "You don't need to write it down. I'm not taking painkillers, so I can promise you I won't forget."

She relaxed under his hand, which began a gentle stroking and kneading motion on her lower back. "I haven't taken one since this morning. That's actually the worst time, along with late at night. Other than that, I feel pretty good."

"I'm glad. I still want you to rest, though. How about a nap upstairs—I can open the sliding glass door and let the sea breeze in," he said, soothing her with visions of dozing in the gentle winter sunlight, lulled by the sound of waves and seagulls.

Tessa closed her eyes for a moment. "I'm not all that eager to go to sleep, to be honest. My dreams have been scaring the crap out of me."

"What if I slept with you?"

"That might help," she said softly.

Without another word, she let him help her to her feet and they went upstairs. She changed into his soft, faded sheriff's department T-shirt and joined him under the covers. After some initial squirming and adjusting of her position, she laid her head on his shoulder and drifted off to sleep.

Two hours later, Tessa jerked awake in an instant. At least it had felt jerky to her, probably because her dreams had been going somewhere she hadn't wanted to explore. Luke hadn't noticed, apparently, as he stayed sprawled comfortably on his back, an arm flung over his pillow and the other curved around her.

As she watched, Luke's eyelids opened, and he immediately focused on her. "Bad dream?"

She nodded solemnly. "But it's okay. I kind of made myself wake up before it got too hairy."

He used the arm locked around her to pull her closer to his warmth. "I wish I could make it all better. You're taking this really well now, but I'm worried how things are going to hit you once the case is over."

Her insides fluttered, responding to both his soothing touch and the concern in his hazel eyes.

"Just knowing you understand helps," Tessa said. "And I'm not going to lie—I can't deal with it all right now. I'm pushing everything to do with Ed to the back of my mind. But knowing that Ed lived a full life, and that somehow he's together with Mary again . . . that more than anything is what's helping me get through the day."

That, and Luke. He'd done everything he could for her, including helping her shower and even eat for the last thirty-six hours. While at first she'd been too deeply in shock to do anything but accept what he offered, now she was beginning to feel very selfish. As if he were the only one giving in the relationship. The idea didn't sit well with her at all.

"I'm glad you've found some comfort in that. I worry about you, Swiss. You're very good at keeping the pain bottled up inside."

Too good, sometimes, which made Luke wonder what would happen when that little compartmentalized cerebral storage area filled up.

Tessa smoothed her cheek against his shoulder, realizing the quiet affection he offered was completely new to her. Luke was certainly being honest, letting her know his feelings silently as he showered attention on her, as well telling her what was going on inside his head.

He cared about her.

Her half smile faltered for a moment. At least he was brave enough to admit it. If she were honest, she'd say that she cared for him as well. But as had happened her entire adult life, she choked when it came to expressing her emotions. She was sure this was partially because of her lousy experiences with trusting men. But in this case it was also because she was flat-out terrified to examine her feelings for Luke and see if they went deeper than what she'd already admitted to herself.

And frankly, she hated herself for being afraid. Luke had done nothing to deserve the kind of neurotic insecurities that came to the surface whenever she looked at her own feelings. The problem was her and her issues with trust, but he was the one being punished.

The hell of it was she didn't know how to change. She just knew that she wanted to try.

With that thought, she rolled over. Under his steady gaze, she hesitantly reached up with her good hand and drew Luke's head down to hers.

"What?" Luke asked softly, knowing that she was thinking something deep by the look in her eyes.

"Just this," Tessa said, and kissed him.

Luke closed his eyes and let the sweetness of her wash over him. When she began to pull back, he tightened his grip and deepened the kiss. She hummed a quiet sound of pleasure, deep in her throat, and moved against his body.

The kisses went on and on, until her mouth was wet and throbbing, and Luke's muscles had taken on the tautness of arousal. He finally pulled his mouth away from hers and dragged it down her throat, using his lips and tongue and teeth against the tendons there. He barely refrained from marking her skin, and instead ground his teeth as he rubbed his face this way and that against her scented neck.

She'd kill him if he gave her a hickey before their upcoming series of business meetings.

Instead of carrying out his possessive fantasies, he brought Tessa's good hand to his mouth and pressed a hot kiss into the palm, then nibbled the sensitive pad of her thumb. When she moaned softly and moved against his body, he realized that her shirt had ridden up during their nap. And his shorts were no longer containing his cock.

From there, it was a simple matter to pull her hand down and press it against the tented front of his boxers. He watched her cheeks flush a glorious shade of pink. She was breathtakingly beautiful in the full light of the California afternoon sun as she hesitantly reached inside the fly front of his shorts and encountered the potent heat of his erection.

To distract her from her shyness, Luke ran both hands up under her T-shirt and squeezed both cheeks of her bottom hard, then released. Then squeezed. She let out a gasping little cry and tightened her grip, making him grunt in pained pleasure. To retaliate, he traced the crease between the globes of her bottom and found an erotic line of soft, smooth, incredibly sensitive skin. Her eyes slid closed as his fingers moved farther forward, down between her legs, and found her wet and ready for him.

She moaned out loud that she needed him, and that was all it took for Luke's control to snap.

He pulled off her shirt, ditched his boxers, and grabbed for the box of condoms on the nightstand in a jerky series of moves. As he slowly slid the latex sheath onto his cock, she watched in wonder, too aroused to do anything but stare at the throbbing hardness he handled so matter-of-factly.

She wanted to eat him alive. She reached a bold hand out to cup his testicles and finish adjusting the condom. It took long enough to get the perfect fit that she made Luke throw back his head and pant out loud.

"Watch your cast. Here, lie down." His urgently whispered instructions had Tessa on her left side, facing him, her broken wrist slid safely under the pillows for the moment.

They were face-to-face, breathing heavily, when Luke bent her top leg and raised it to the level of his waist.

Tessa felt his warm hand close over her bottom as he urged her closer, until she could feel him probing her body. She reached down to grab his erection, then hiked her leg higher and thrust forward at the same time, driving him into her. The feel of him sinking to the hilt inside her caused her heartbeat to hesitate, just for a moment, at the glorious shock of being filled.

"It will take a while this way," Luke whispered as he began a gentle rocking that brought him into contact with her lower body.

Good, Tessa thought as she savored the luxurious slide and friction of his body against hers. *Good.*

She turned her lips to his and followed his lead, rocking against him slowly, so slowly. Every once in a while, her breathing would accelerate and she'd move more urgently against him, but he kept the steady and purposeful rhythm until the lesser peak had passed. And still he moved, his lips to hers, his body against hers—building the feeling again, starting her out higher each time.

Until silent tears ran down her face, and she cried out loud as she moved against him harder, faster, and he rocked them both into ecstasy.

They stayed wrapped around each other, lying in bed until evening.

Until MacBeth called to report that Kelly hadn't shown up for work at Club Red for the second night in a row. And no one seemed to know where she was.

Chapter 36

Chantal Francoeur's first thought on meeting Tessa Jacobi was that she looked like hell. It was more than the bruises and abrasions on her face, more than the left wrist encased in a new cast. The woman had deep shadows in her eyes and a tightness about her that said she was under extreme stress. It made her appear very pale and fragile. The fact that she was just under average height with a figure more suited to an artist's model than a deputy district attorney probably didn't help dispel the initial impression of frailty.

That stress was also evident on Luke Novak's face, but he was harder to read. She could see he was concerned about Tessa, and as she watched him pour her a glass of water from a nearby pitcher, Chantal began to pick up on the undercurrents passing between the two of them. It set off warning bells in the accountant's head, because it was never a good idea for team members to be involved with each other.

Sex was so distracting, especially when the people involved had other concerns as well.

And apparently this case was worth concern. Chantal had been told by Luke Novak that a veteran police officer was killed in the incident where Tessa was injured. The investigation was dangerous enough that she didn't like the combination of personal and professional entanglements she was seeing in front of her.

But as Tessa began to describe the case from the beginning, Chantal was finally able to see the steely resolve, the determination in Tessa's face as she explained what they knew already and why they needed a forensic accountant. The strength in her voice, and her commitment to solving the case came through loud and clear. Having clawed her way out of the slums of Kingston, Jamaica to earn a double master's degree from Harvard, Chantal could appreciate determination and commitment. She decided to give the deputy D.A. a chance.

Tessa finished her briefing and waited for a response from Chantal. She was beginning to feel like she was the one on trial—the accountant was visibly analyzing Tessa and her summary of the case to date. Looking at Chantal's power suit, stiletto heels, and the breathtakingly expensive layered haircut, which drew attention to wide-set amber eyes, Tessa was having no trouble at all imagining that the other woman was a top-notch forensic accountant in high demand for her analytical skills.

At the moment, Chantal was undoubtedly weighing everything she'd read in the task force files over the last twenty-four hours versus the case as Tessa had described it. She could almost hear the woman's brain sorting through the information and finding the parts that interested her.

Finally, Tessa cleared her throat and continued. "So now you can see why we need the help of someone like you. It doesn't look like we'll be able to get enough evidence to go to trial on the rape charges anytime soon, and frankly, the other sex crimes are also going to be difficult to prove without a confession. But we can't let these people get away with what they've done to Kelly and Detective Flynn. So we're going to need some leverage in order to force the defendants into a plea bargain situation."

Chantal tilted her head. "This whole scenario is incredible. You started with a high-profile case of date rape, then uncovered a forced prostitution scam, and now we're looking at racketeering, organized crime, illegal gambling, and money laundering going on in a duly licensed establishment?"

"Exactly," said Tessa. "And I want to use the leverage of federal charges to get certain people in the criminal organization to testify against the others who were responsible for Kelly's rape and subsequent kidnapping. Plus anything that's happened to her since. I don't want a single person to get off the hook or leave his subordinates to take the fall—I want everybody to pay for their role in the operations of Club Red, Inc. as they pertain to Kelly Maarten."

"What do you think?" Chantal asked Luke. "It sounds quite ambitious to me."

Luke stroked his chin and wondered about Chantal. Her melodious voice was low and cultured, holding a hint of the Caribbean. He was intrigued about her background, which obviously included the islands, along with a strong dash of New England. Boston, if he wasn't mistaken.

When she raised a challenging brow at him, he grinned and returned to the discussion. "It is ambitious," Luke agreed. "But I think if we apply the right kind of leverage to the weak links in the operation, the whole chain is going to fall apart. The plan is to set these guys up on federal felony charges like racketeering and money laundering, and make it clear that we have an airtight case. Then we give them the choice between two hundred years in federal prison or confessing to their crimes against Kelly in exchange for reduced sentences. They'll be lining up to plead guilty to the rape charges."

"We hope to offer these reductions in the federal charges with the agreement that the defendants will do the full time for state charges regarding the rape and kidnapping of Kelly Maarten," Tessa continued. "The defendants will still do plenty of time behind bars, but it will be a moral victory for Kelly and other victims like her. We could even establish precedent with respect to these pimps who essentially treat young girls as sex slaves."

"What about Detective Flynn?" Chantal asked.

Tessa's mouth flattened. "Whoever set up that hit and carried it out gets a needle in his arm."

"There's not much sugar in that offer," Chantal pointed out.

"It doesn't matter. We'll get others to implicate the person who arranged the hit by offering *them* the sweet deal, as you say. We just need corroborated testimony to do that."

Luke nodded encouragingly, then looked at Chantal again. "We have the knowledge of what's going on in that club, we just need to prove it so we have some bargaining power. That's why we asked for your help."

"Has the FBI agreed to this division of the defendants?" Chantal asked. "Usually they want criminals to face any federal charges first. By the time all is said and done, it's not worth the time of the state to go after what's left. Frankly, it's often not even an option for the state to hold an expensive trial to prove that someone who is serving one hundred years in a federal prison is guilty of a sex crime that carries a sentence of five to eight years."

"I know," Tessa said. "That's why I want to give the Feds several big fish in what we suspect is a racketeering operation and use them to negotiate for the state maintaining control of defendants like Sledge Aiken and Jerry Kravitz."

"What about Roderick Hedges?" Chantal asked. "Is he not the biggest fish of all, aside from the organized crime family?"

Tessa sighed. "I'd like to have first crack at Ricky, but understand that just might not be realistic. We've got to compromise somewhere and offer the Feds a bone. Ricky may be the sacrificial offering, because the evidence to date hasn't shown that he was personally involved in what happened to Kelly—but if I find anything to the contrary, then I want him to face state charges first."

"Well the legal decisions are your call," Chantal said as she took out a pad of paper for notes. "My job would be to give you the ammunition you need—the leverage, so to speak, to force a deal. Is that correct?"

"Yes," Tessa nodded. "We understand that you were involved with the early stages of the multiagency task force. That could give us a huge advantage and will cut your learning curve."

"And you did hear about how I left the previous task force? I guess it's no secret that Special Agent Peebles and I despise one another. Such a small man, in more ways than one." Chantal spoke slowly, her faint accent becoming more pronounced.

Tessa gave a feline smile. "The thought that you might have a bone to pick with the new head of the task force never entered my mind."

Luke laughed quietly and shifted in his seat. He loved it when she got that smug look—it made him want to jump her bones right there on the conference table. Come to think of it, the last time he'd seen that particular expression on her face, she'd been sprawled across his bed.

When individual beads of sweat began to pop out along his forehead, Luke made a visible effort to restrain himself and focus on the conversation.

"So you know that Peebles and I disagreed on what the focus of the investigation should be, yes?" Chantal laughed, unaware of Luke's internal struggle. "I don't wish to sound arrogant, but if I'd remained on that team, they wouldn't need any help from you and Mr. Novak. They would already have enough to charge all of the players involved."

"What did Special Agent Peebles want to focus on?" Luke asked.

Chantal shrugged her shoulders beneath her elegant Armani suit. "He had no respect for number crunchers, as he called the consultants with accounting backgrounds. He was enamored of subpoenas for wiretaps, undercover work, and other active surveillance tools. I'm sure he believed that these methods were much sexier than poring over balance sheets and income tax returns. But in doing so, Peebles lost sight of one very important thing."

"Which is?" Tessa asked.

"The fact that the federal government will overlook many criminal acts, but it simply cannot abide those who cheat it out of tax revenues. Look at all of the organized crime figures who went to prison in the last seventy years—the vast majority were locked up on tax evasion or other financial charges. Accounting might not be sexy, but the tax laws are much more strongly enforced than any other legal codes on the books. That applies to criminals as much as upstanding citizens."

"So all income is taxable, even illegal income?" Tessa asked.

"Absolutely. It's not uncommon for drug dealers and others engaged in criminal acts to declare their profits honestly on tax returns out of fear of the IRS. So if the FBI gives you any trouble, you can threaten to talk to the Criminal Investigation Division of the Internal Revenue Service. I'm sure they'd be happy to get involved."

Tessa nodded. "We'll keep that in mind as a backup plan. For now, I want to give the FBI a chance to play nice. Where do you recommend that we start in terms of the financial information on Club Red, Inc?"

"First of all, we need to prove that money laundering is actually taking place as you suspect. There are certain legal requirements to establishing this, namely that the defendants are attempting to take profits gained from specified unlawful activities and 'launder' them so that the funds appear to be legitimate revenue."

Luke spoke up. "We have a bunch of specific examples.

Take Jerry Kravitz, who last year spent five hundred thousand dollars cash on a house. But when we looked into it, we found he only declares an income of fifty thousand dollars a year on his tax returns, money he earns as a sports announcer."

"Perfect." Chantal nodded. "This is a tip-off that the money he spent isn't from legitimate sources. Maybe he underdeclared his legitimate income, in which case he is guilty of tax evasion. Or he has another source of income that he's hiding, which would be my guess in this case. But this is an example of an individual engaged in lucrative illegal activities. I think you are more interested in a whole company based on this concept, because the penalties are much harsher. It becomes a conspiracy, punishable by strict sentencing requirements and seizure of assets, with fairly limited burdens of proof on the part of the government."

Tessa nodded. "So we look at Club Red, Inc. and charge that the entire business is based on illegal gambling, prostitution, drug sales, excise tax evasion for the liquor and cigarette violations, and so on."

"Yes," said Chantal. "Club Red, Inc. and all those responsible for managing the corporation engage in illegal acts, which generate high profits. But these profits have the stigma of their illegal origin attached to them, and law enforcement knows exactly how to prove this. So the profits must be laundered. This has to be done so the money can be spent without the government being able to trace where it came from. Without this laundering of funds, the individuals and the criminal organizations can't use their money, and it doesn't do them any good."

"We've already identified a list of illegal activities going on at Club Red, now what?" Tessa asked.

"Let me explain the most common steps of money laundering, and that will help us focus here on the best way to proceed," Chantal said. "Do you have a pen for the whiteboard over there?"

Luke laughed when Tessa immediately opened her bag

and pulled out six different colors of markers to use on the board. "I think you two are going to get along just fine. Tessa's got a thing for whiteboards and diagrams."

Chantal smiled and started drawing on the board. "It is very helpful to see things in schematic form, where they are more logical."

Tessa gave him the Look, modified in this case to signify "So there."

"There are three steps to money laundering in most traditional criminal organizations—placement, layering, and integration," Chantal explained. "More specifically, we have *placement* of the illegal funds into the financial system, *layering* of these funds in a series of steps which distance the dirty money from its illegal source, and finally *integration* of the layered funds back into the national or international economy so that it is difficult to distinguish them from legitimately earned money."

Tessa spoke up. "I've been reading up on money laundering, but most of the examples pertain to narcotics and smuggling. I don't think that's what we have here, at least not on a large scale. The mechanics of this case are very confusing."

"Don't worry, you are meant to be confused. The more complex the process, the easier it is for the criminals to continue undetected. Let me give you what I feel is a realistic example based on my review of Club Red's books." Chantal flipped the whiteboard over and began again.

"Thanks. I just want to be sure I know what I'm talking about when I meet with the FBI later."

"You will. I will keep it simple, as long as you understand that there are as many ways to launder money as there are to earn the illegal funds in the first place. But we will focus on likely activities in this case, so let's talk about the revenues we believe Ricky Hedges earns from illegal gambling and so forth. Let's say that in a particular two-week period, Ricky earns five hundred thousand dollars by running card tables and sports-betting operations, as well as prostituting his women."

Tessa winced at the phrase, thinking of Kelly.

"I'm sorry if I offend you," Chantal said softly. "But it's best not to sugarcoat the process."

When Tessa nodded, Chantal continued. "Ricky has no way to declare these ill-gotten funds as legal profits because an audit of the club's books would show that his legitimate sales cannot possibly account for a million dollars of profit in a month."

"So he has an extra million bucks and no place to spend it. Poor guy," Luke drawled.

"Indeed," agreed Chantal. "It is a very frustrating situation. If he tries to spend the money, he risks an audit that could result in his losing his whole business. Government seizure laws are positively Draconian when it comes to racketeering and organized crime. So Ricky must launder these funds. But a million dollars is a lot of money, and doubtless it is mainly in small-denomination bills. He must have a way to get this money into the banking or financial systems without drawing attention to himself."

"That much cash would be suspicious," Luke pointed out. "And heavy. A million bucks in tens and twenties would weigh around three hundred pounds. Despite the movies, cash isn't exactly a portable instrument in those sums."

"He can't just deposit the money?" Tessa asked. "Maybe in his personal accounts?"

Chantal shook her head. "The Federal Bank Secrecy Act, or BSA, requires that paperwork be filed for any deposits of $10,000 or more that banks receive. And the details from any such paperwork are then entered into a nationwide database—which has computer programs running algorithms designed to flag suspicious deposits and law enforcement officials trained to see patterns that could indicate illegal activity. So BSA regulations create complications for those who have dirty money to place in the financial system, who want to deposit the funds without drawing attention to themselves."

"How do they get around the regulations?" Tessa asked.

Chantal sighed. "Unfortunately, there are literally dozens of ways, with varying levels of sophistication. The degree of complexity employed in placing funds is often directly related to the level of sophistication of the criminal organization."

"How sophisticated is Club Red?" Luke asked.

"About middle of the road, based on my review of the financial records, though that seems to be changing over the last year. It's my belief that Ricky has been using a couple of the more popular methods to place his money, which you will recall is the first step in laundering it. One of his methods is an old favorite for cash-rich businesses—inflating legitimate revenues. He simply says that some of the illegal funds come from cover charges, stripper revenue, drinks, food, parking, etc."

"But you don't think that could be the case?" Tessa asked.

"I don't believe so. From my initial calculations based on his deductible expenses—which include overhead like liquor and food—Club Red would have to be charging outrageous sums per drink, or serving about two to three thousand people every night of the week to account for the amount of profit he's indicated in the club's financial statements. I'd have to do an inspection of his inventory and observe the activity at the club, but it seems clear to me that he's padding the books."

"Not very well, if all it took was a twenty-four-hour audit," Luke pointed out.

"Well, I can suspect it, but proving the crime would take subpoenas and warrants. To get those, I need proof. The legal system here is quite complicated sometimes," Chantal said. "It didn't take me long to spot the potential for this activity, though, because I've got a lot of experience looking for it. This is not a sophisticated system that Ricky uses, but it's also not his only method for placing illegal funds. He's also engaging in some labor-intensive methods—structuring, it's called. He uses runners or smurfs to structure his deposits in such a way that they come in under bank radar."

"Smurfs? What do cartoon characters have to do with this?" Tessa asked.

"Picture a beehive of activity, or a herd of smurfs running here and there doing work. This is where the name comes from—many, many low-paid runners who take small cash deposits to banks all over the city and state, then put them into a series of accounts held by Club Red or other companies owned by Ricky Hedges. This is all these smurfs do, day in and day out. I call them the worker bees."

"I get it," Tessa said. "These smurfs deposit money in amounts under $10,000 to avoid the reporting requirements of the banks. They do a high volume of low-value transactions so they don't trigger the suspicions of the banks."

"Very good. This is the preferred method of many drug smugglers, who try to 'structure' their deposits to avoid suspicion. It's also a crime in and of itself, but it is almost impossible to prove without a tip-off from the banks and intensive surveillance to catch them in the act," Chantal said.

"Pretty clever," Tessa said, taking notes as she spoke.

"Yes and no. It is a very popular method, so I've learned to look for it. And it seems that Ricky Hedges realized this potential, because in the last year or so he's been trying to incorporate more complex methods for placement of his money. Do you remember the credit cards you told me about?"

"The ones we found on Kelly?" Tessa clarified.

"Yes. When you said that the cards hadn't been reported stolen—that in fact Club Red had been crediting those accounts for several months—I started thinking. I believe Ricky is taking illegally earned profits and depositing the cash in the credit accounts of people who frequent the club, possibly as payment for services rendered," Chantal said.

"Or it could be another way for Ricky to sweeten the pot and get people into the club. What if they were paying off gambling balances with those accounts?" Luke asked.

"You are a very cynical man," Chantal purred. "I like that. I will have to dig further to verify, but what you suggest is very plausible. It seems that Club Red has been increasing its sophistication in the placing of funds in numerous ways."

"Now that the mystery of the credit cards Kelly was holding has been solved, we can investigate those individuals and build a case against them if it's warranted," Tessa said. "How else does Ricky play the shell game with his money?"

"Another way he's placed funds has been by starting a real estate development company, which enables him to play with property in a system we call reverse flips."

"I take it we're not talking about gymnastics here," Luke said.

"No, this involves buying property, then flipping it, or selling it again immediately."

"Lots of investors do that," Tessa pointed out.

"Yes, but the trick with reverse flipping is for Ricky to buy property at a price that is well below its actual market value. Say he buys a retail property for $500,000. But if we did research on other plots of land in the same area, we would see that the true market value of Ricky's purchase is closer to $1 million."

"Maybe Ricky's just a very good negotiator," Luke said dryly.

"Not when he pays the difference between the documented sales price and the market value to the seller under the table. The documented price he pays in clean funds, and the under-the-table amount is paid in dirty money."

"That's pretty slick, as long as the seller is in on the deal," Tessa said.

"Oh, it gets better," Chantal replied. "In other permutations of reverse flips, Ricky could take a mortgage out for part of the documented sales price. Then he can turn around and sell the newly acquired property to a legitimate buyer for its true market value, realizing a profit of $500,000. He pays off any mortgage with this profit, which is clean money. He even gets a tax deduction on interest and any closing costs for the deal. And he looks like a legitimate real estate entrepreneur."

"How does law enforcement keep track of this kind of activity?" Tessa asked.

"It's very difficult, which is why it's so popular. And there's more going on with Club Red, I'm afraid. I believe that Ricky has begun to incorporate international aspects, particularly shell corporations and offshore banking, into his strategy to place, layer, and integrate his dirty money back into the economy."

"How do things like shell corporations help out with money laundering?" Tessa asked. "I mean, I know they do, I just don't understand the mechanics."

"Well, so far we've only discussed placement of the funds in depth. There are two more stages in the equation," Chantal said, over the sound of Tessa's groan. "You can place all the money you want in the financial system, but if you don't fully launder it, you still can't spend it."

"So how does Ricky layer, then integrate the funds?" Luke asked, giving Tessa a sympathetic pat on the back. The complexity of the financial schemes Ricky was involved in was requiring all his attention to follow. He could only imagine how tough it was for Tessa, with everything else going on in her mind, to say nothing of her injuries.

"That's where these shell corporations come in. Let's go back to the funds deposited by smurfs into local and state banks. These accounts undoubtedly belong to companies other than Club Red, Inc. They are probably held by numerous phony corporations that are in reality owned and operated by either Ricky Hedges or individuals acting on his behalf," Chantal said.

"Are these legitimate business partners or underlings?" Tessa asked.

"Probably a combination of both," Chantal replied. "So when Ricky's illegal profits are shipped out in small amounts all over the state of California, they are deposited by smurfs into the accounts of Company A. This Company A may very well be a wholly owned subsidiary of Company B, which in turn is part of a consortium headed by Company C, which is part of a limited liability joint venture as a junior partner with Company D, and so on to Company M. Company M is owned and operated by Ricky Hedges or someone he trusts with the task."

"Sounds like a lot of people would have to be involved," Tessa said.

"Not at all," Chantal corrected her. "Each company would be set up in various offshore havens by a single individual in the name of owners who may or may not actually exist. It costs less than five hundred dollars to file articles of incorporation in most states and countries. Many criminals have a dozen or more related shell corporations to layer the funds, that is, to distance them so far from their illegal origins that it would be almost impossible to follow the trail unless you knew it was there."

"What is it exactly that they do to muddy the waters?" Luke asked.

"A popular method of layering would be to have Company A take out a loan from an offshore bank, let's say the Bank of Curaçao. Company A will secure the bank loan with the illegal profits that smurfs have deposited into its accounts in California. With the loan from the Bank of Curaçao, Company A can then buy certificates of deposit—or some other highly portable monetary instrument—and sell them to Company B for cash. Company B can do whatever it wants with these monetary instruments—for example, it can liquidate them and buy property, which is then flipped, or it can take out another loan with the CDs as collateral."

"Doesn't anyone follow up on what's done with loan funds to make sure there's nothing illegal going on?" Tessa asked.

"No. Certainly not at international banks, where investor privacy is guaranteed. And so the layering of funds continues," Chantal said. "Once the monetary instruments are liquidated, Company B can also buy luxury consumable items from Company C, which are sold back to Club Red at a cut rate, or it can invest the money on the stock market and generate legitimate profits, which are invested in Company D or parked in its accounts, and so on. The possibilities are virtually limitless. Every transaction further layers the money and makes it almost impossible to trace."

"So the money is pumped back into the economy in the form of 'clean' funds that are impossible to connect back to the original deposits made by Ricky's smurfs," Tessa said. "The lightbulb just went on."

"This concludes my lecture on the basics of money laundering," Chantal agreed with a smile.

"These last steps you're talking about, the layering and integration—they seem much more complicated than placement itself," Luke mused.

"They are," Chantal said. "However, the placement of funds is often the most vulnerable and dangerous step. It's a simple idea, but there are many ways for it to go wrong. This is why you hear tales of illegal enterprises that literally have suitcases or boxes full of cash lying around—they don't have the know-how or sophistication to place and launder their dirty money."

"But you also said the level of sophistication of Club Red's operations seems to be increasing, right?" Tessa asked.

"It does. The credit card activity, real estate ventures, and reverse flips—these are new. The linking of Club Red with companies incorporated in the Caribbean and Mexico is also new. If I had to guess, I'd say that Ricky has been getting investment and financial advice, starting sometime in the last nine or ten months."

"Who would do something like that?" Tessa asked. "Does Ricky just start advertising for a crooked financial advisor?"

"Certainly not. He would need to find a legitimate financial advisor, because that individual would be able to shield his illegal operations on behalf of Club Red with his genuine and legal investment activities. Unfortunately, many accountants and money advisors out there are willing to turn a blind eye to the provenance of funds given to them to invest, as long as they get a good cut of the profits."

"I don't know," Tessa said. "I would think in this case that the financial advisor would have to be deeply involved in where the funds come from, because as you said, it seems that Ricky is being guided in some way. At least in the last year or so, you said he seems to have an investment partner. Someone who's helping him deepen the level of his money laundering."

Chantal considered that for a moment. "I believe you could be right. One thing we've found about these shady financial advisors is that the primary service they provide is the use of shell corporations. Many of these accountants will incorporate various shell companies around the world, then just park them—meaning they stand inactive until a client needs to use them. Then the system of shell companies is already set up, and the advisor can quickly get things started with particular transactions when there is a need." She tapped a marker on the whiteboard as she considered that. "I think you are definitely right, and I know what might have happened to Ricky and Club Red."

"What?" Luke and Tessa asked together.

"You said the Ianelli Family is a potential business partner. This is where I believe Ricky is getting his financial assistance," Chantal said simply. "They are not one of the big-time ethnic flavors of Mafia here in Southern California. They're the offshoot of a small Midwest family, and they make their living by taking a skim of ongoing criminal operations in their territory. They do have a small drug-running and smuggling ring based out of the Inland Empire in the desert, but that's because the other profitable routes between Mexico and San Diego to L.A. were already taken."

"From my time with the sheriff's department, I remember that the Ianellis were involved in extortion and excise tax violations more than anything else. They would go around to the small-time local operations in prostitution, drug running, strip clubs, and cigarette sales, then extort the people running those schemes for a cut of the profits. Basically, a high-volume protection racket with many individuals paying small amounts of money."

Chantal nodded. "Yes. The Ianellis have been able to squeeze their way into small-time operations that other, bigger criminal organizations have written off as too tiny or not profitable enough. These small-time operations have become the niche of the Ianellis, but what if they also wanted to start growing and getting a bigger slice of the action?"

"They would form alliances like any other company," Tessa said. "In this case, with Club Red, Inc. And Ricky Hedges."

"Yes, indeed. I think we may be onto something here," Chantal said. "What if Ricky needed help expanding his business, and the Ianellis needed an organization that can absorb some of their illegal profits as well? Wouldn't it behoove them to combine forces and create some sort of joint venture?"

"Maybe in the short run," Luke said. "But it's been my experience that criminal alliances never last. And that's good news for us—it shows us exactly where the weak link is with Club Red. After a while, especially under close scrutiny by law enforcement, the criminal partnerships start to fracture under the pressure. If we exert specific force in carefully chosen places . . ."

"The whole conspiracy falls apart," Tessa finished with a grim smile.

"I don't wish to be a wet blanket," Chantal began. "But I must advise you that it is extremely difficult to prove the type of money laundering and racketeering activities that we are talking about here. It's one of the reasons that law enforcement officials build the case in other ways, first."

"What do you mean?" Luke asked. "We see evidence of the FBI and the Treasury Department targeting these criminal conspiracies all the time. People go to prison for this stuff."

"True," Chantal agreed. "But these task forces have years to investigate. You have, I think, only a very short period of time. That is if Kelly Maarten is your true focus."

"She is," Tessa said.

"So you need information on the money laundering and other federal activities to force people to return Kelly and to testify about what was done against her. I just don't see how we can do this quickly. With enough time and money, we could uncover what is going on in California and in the US banking system, because we have regulations that assist law enforcement. But to understand the full picture, I would also need full access to international bank records and transactions, including offshore banks."

"And they don't share this information with law enforcement?" Luke asked.

"No. Look at the Swiss, sitting on bank records predating World War II. It's worse in the new world, in the Caribbean and South American offshore banks. Inevitably we would come up against the roadblock of bank secrecy, and so far no agency has found a good way around that."

"There has to be something," Tessa said.

"Maybe I could look unofficially into records through old colleagues, or we could pay someone to hack into various systems. But we would not be able to take that information to trial. I'm sorry," Chantal added, when she saw Tessa's expression.

"We haven't come this far to turn back," Tessa promised. "How are these cases normally resolved expeditiously, if tracking the financial records through shell corporations and offshore banks doesn't work?"

"We must have inside information," Chantal said simply. "It is the only fast way to do things."

"We can do that," Luke said. "We need to get enough leverage to force someone to roll over on Ricky, the Ianellis, and the shady financial advisor. And to get that leverage, we have to figure out which of our players to squeeze hard enough that he starts singing."

"Jerry Kravitz and Sledge Aiken," Tessa said instantly. "We have the Kelly connection, and proof that she was a minor runaway living under Jerry's roof when Sledge paid to have sex with her. We'll have to use that to get them talking and make up the rest of the strategy as we go along."

Luke stepped aside to take a call on his cell phone, and Chantal began to gather her things. She handed a card to Tessa. "This has my home and cellular numbers, as well as my e-mail address and a secure FTP site for large document transfers. In the meantime, I will go back over the financial records you sent me and begin to draft text for subpoenas on other documents. I must see more detailed information on the workings of Club Red, Inc., in order to finish the accounting investigation."

"Get me the subpoena text as soon as you can. Carmen gave me the name of a federal judge whose campaign was based on stamping out corruption and corporate crime. He should be sympathetic to our case and will issue subpoenas and warrants if we get the paperwork in order."

"Let's go see Jerry at home right now," Luke said to Tessa as he hung up. "He just put in an urgent call asking Sledge to meet him there in an hour."

"I'm probably going to regret asking, but how do you know where Jerry is and what he said on the phone to Sledge?" Tessa asked.

"I've had a team doing surveillance on his house with a parabolic microphone for a couple of days," Luke replied.

"Shush. I didn't hear you," Tessa protested. "We don't have a warrant for that."

"I don't want to take him to court with the information, baby. I just want to know where he is so that we can, um, talk."

Chapter 37

Luke and Tessa cruised to a stop in her car several houses down the street from Jerry Kravitz's property. Luke looked around and caught sight of his surveillance team in a white utility van. He hesitated as he removed his seat belt, then spoke. "I suppose it's useless to ask you to stay behind."

"Pretty much."

"You may not like some of the methods I have to use. At least if you stay in the car, you have some deniability if it gets to a trial," Luke pointed out.

"As you said, I'm not looking for information I can take to court. Lots of legal arm-twisting goes on during the plea-bargaining process. Most of it is off the record," Tessa said.

"I want to warn you right now that Jerry might take some serious convincing. I'll do my best to keep it clean, but at this point it's really up to Kravitz how we come to a deal. It could get ugly," Luke warned.

"Uglier than someone trying to run me down with a car?" Tessa asked. There was no heat in her voice; she just sounded determined.

"I give up. But bring your poker face." Luke got out of the car and adjusted his light jacket. Tessa knew it covered a holstered handgun, though she hadn't seen it closely enough to identify it.

She figured that gave her plausible deniability if it came down to it in court.

"What's the strategy going to be to get Jerry to talk?" Luke asked. He took Tessa's hand and gave some prearranged signal to his surveillance team in the van. There was no sign of a response, but he knew they'd gotten the message to start the tape recorder attached to their surveillance equipment.

"I'm going to use a popular old auction trick—going once, going twice, sold to the person who cooperates first." Tessa gave his arm a squeeze and cuddled up to his side, figuring they were meant to look like a harmless couple as they approached Jerry's front door.

"Good plan. I think the whole Club Red empire is tottering on the edge of collapse right now. Kind of like a display of oranges at the supermarket—pull out the right one, and the whole thing comes tumbling down."

"And at this point, I don't even think it's important who we squeeze—as long as someone starts talking. The rest will come from the momentum created by that one person caving," Tessa agreed.

She followed Luke as he walked up the drive, ignoring the path to the front door. Instead, he walked under the carport, passed Jerry's black Mercedes coupe, and stopped at a side door that opened into the kitchen. He knocked twice sharply, then dropped Tessa's hand to brace for Jerry's reaction.

"It's open!" Tessa heard Jerry's voice, looked at Luke, then followed him as he went into the house.

"Hiya, Jerry. Expecting someone?" Luke asked.

Standing at the sink washing dishes, Jerry whipped around with a curse. He looked at Luke, then stared at Tessa for a moment. "You're that prosecutor who was spreading Kelly's lies. What the hell are you doing here?"

"You said to come in," Tessa pointed out.

"I thought you were someone else. Get the hell out of my house," Jerry said, dropping the glass he was holding back into a sink filled with soapy water.

"We're here completely off the record right now. Just a couple of people having a chat. I think you're going to want to hear what she has to say," Luke said. He looked around the kitchen, which was littered with dishes, cartons of Chinese food, and old pizza boxes.

Tessa also checked out Jerry's kitchen—it was bachelor chic, all the way. Formica table, mismatched chairs, and a grimy film on vinyl flooring that hadn't seen mop or bucket for months—if ever. The appliances sported a pumpkin-and-avocado color scheme that was so old it had come into fashion again, giving everything a weathered retro look that a better decorator might have been able to pull off. But not Jerry.

"I said to get out of here. You've got nothing on me, and I'm not talking to you without a lawyer present," Jerry said. He casually turned his back to them and continued with the dishes, but Luke didn't like the tension that was tightening the line of Jerry's shoulders.

Without a word, Luke motioned Tessa to step to the rear of the kitchen. "That's handy. We've got a lawyer right here. We'd like some information from you, and we're willing to cut you a sweet deal for being the first in line to tell it to us."

"Fuck off. If you had anything, you'd have arrested someone already. But I hear the judge shot your case full of holes and told you to back off. I guess pretty little blond girls who want to be singers don't make reliable witnesses, eh, *Counselor*?" Jerry snorted at his own wit.

"Oh, I don't know. I thought Kelly was remarkably composed—for a fifteen-year-old rape victim," Tessa said.

Jerry froze with a dripping sponge in one hand, but didn't look at anyone. "So you know." His tone said he knew it was over.

"That Kelly is a minor? Yeah." Luke kept sharp hazel eyes pinned on Jerry's back. His own back was feeling twitchy, and the hairs at the nape of his neck were beginning to stand on end. Without a sound, he reached under his jacket and pulled his gun, coughing once to cover the sound of the weapon leaving its holster.

Tessa's eyes widened and she took another few steps backward until she was standing in the doorway that led to the rest of the house. With the look on Luke's face, the last thing she wanted to do was stand between him and the other man.

"Last chance—get the fuck out of my house, or a lying little bitch like Kelly is going to be the least of your problems." Jerry fished around in the water-filled sink for a moment, then he whipped around with an eight-inch-long chef's knife in his dripping right hand. He went still as he realized that Luke had a gun pointed directly at his head. His eyes then skittered over to Tessa, as if waiting to see what she would do.

"How do you want to play it, Jer?" Luke's voice was even. He didn't want to shoot the man, because they needed him to testify against the others. But at the moment, Tessa was Luke's main concern. Nothing was more important than her safety. While Luke stood between her and Jerry, he'd learned a long time ago never to underestimate an opponent. He'd seen men charge into a loaded gun and do plenty of damage before they finally went down.

"You won't shoot—you need me," Jerry breathed as he tightened his grip on the knife.

"I need to breathe more," Luke shot back. "And I'm not going to go for some flesh wound on your arm, asshole. Once a cop, always a cop. When I draw this gun, it means

I'm prepared to kill someone. You want to be that person to-day?" Luke asked.

Tessa held her breath as Jerry studied the room. He finally seemed to realize that Luke would pull the trigger and drop him without a second thought, so he threw down the knife. He put his hands up in the air and mentally began to curse Ricky Hedges.

"Kick it over here, Jerry. Gently." Luke didn't move a muscle, nor did he relax the hold on his gun.

There was absolute silence as Jerry balanced on one foot and gingerly kicked the knife forward about six feet. When he looked back at Luke, there was no change in his stance, no softening of his guard.

"Can you pick up the knife without getting between the gun and the asshole, Swiss?" Luke asked the question but didn't look in her direction.

"Yes." Her voice was a lot steadier than her hands as she crouched down and came forward to grab the knife. The ticking of the clock and Jerry's labored breaths were the only sounds she could hear above the pounding of her own heart.

Carefully staying out of Luke's line of sight, she crept backward with the sudsy knife in her left hand, using her right hand on the floor to keep from wobbling in her awkward pose. As Tessa reached the back of the kitchen and stood up again, she considered putting the weapon down on a bookcase. With a brief glance at Luke, she decided against it until Jerry was completely under control.

Though as she watched beads of sweat roll down his face, she figured Jerry was pretty much hers. *Lucky freaking me*, she thought as she blew hair away from her face.

"Lace your hands behind your head, fucko. Then get down on your knees," Luke instructed Jerry.

Luke watched Jerry the way he would a rattlesnake as the other man complied.

"My lawyer is going to hear about this," Jerry muttered.

"Facedown on the floor," Luke said. "And he's not going to hear about it from us. I tried to do this the nice way, even offered you a carrot. But some people only understand the stick." He sighed with mock regret.

Tessa spoke from her position in the doorway. "I was even willing to offer you an exclusive deal. Now you'll have to wait until Sledge gets here, and we'll see who gives me the best information. That person will get the sweet offer."

"While we're waiting, why don't you look in the carport and utility room to see if Jerry has any duct tape. That should hold him while we talk," Luke said.

Without a word, Tessa walked through the living room and headed to the laundry area, where she began opening cabinets. When that didn't yield any tape or rope, she decided to go out the door leading to a side yard to see if Jerry had some kind of utility shed, since she already knew there wasn't a garage on the property.

"Why did you call Sledge and ask him to come over?" Luke asked Jerry, as they listened to Tessa rummage through cabinets. "What was it that you couldn't say on the phone?"

Jerry was silent as he lay facedown on the floor.

"We really need to work on your concept of rewards for good behavior, Jer. You help us out now, things go easier on you in the future when we bust the whole damn operation."

"She's gone," Jerry muttered. "I called Sledge to let him know that Kelly is gone."

"What do you mean by 'gone'?" Luke asked softly.

"I don't know where she is. Last time I saw her she was leaving Club Red with Ricky's assistant, and she was in big trouble. That was two days ago. I heard she got caught trying to pass a letter to one of the strippers in the club. Apparently it was a message for your girlfriend there. Ricky blew a fucking gasket," Jerry said.

Luke heard a door slam and the sound of Tessa's footsteps rushing back.

"Here's the duct tape, and some rope I found," she said breathlessly.

Luke didn't want her anywhere near Jerry, so he carefully handed his gun over to Tessa and took the rope himself. "Keep the gun pointed at Jerry's head. There's no hammer to cock, so it's—"

"A double action, I know," Tessa said, sounding confident. She handled the gun with ease, though it had been years since she'd fired one. At Luke's surprised look, she gave him a wry look. "Paul used to run the FBI—do you think he'd let me grow up without a ton of firearms training?"

Shaking his head and smiling, Luke bent over Jerry. Prudently keeping away from the other man's head—where Tessa held the gun with unwavering attention—he quickly taped his hands behind his back and hog-tied him with the rope.

"Is he secure?" Tessa asked.

"I'm getting there," Luke grumbled, giving the knots a sharp tug to make sure they would hold.

"Hurry, I have to show you something."

Luke glanced up at her serious tone and saw that Tessa was upset. Her eyes were dark and stormy, and he could see that she was clenching her jaw, but her hands were steady as she held the gun.

"What is it, baby?" Luke walked up to her and took the gun away, shoving it in his holster as he studied her face.

"Follow me." She led the way through the small and shabbily furnished living room. She preceded him through the laundry room and out into a paved side yard that would normally be used to park a camper or motor home.

Instead of a recreational vehicle, there was a large car covered with a tarp. Tessa led Luke around to the far side, where she'd pulled the tarp back to expose a crushed right front end with grille damage and a shattered headlight. Scrapes and deep gouges scored the sides of the dark blue vehicle.

Without a word, Luke flipped the tarp back more to reveal

a gaping space where the windshield should have been on the Chevy Caprice.

"This is the car that killed Ed," he said. "Do you think Jerry was driving?"

Tessa shook her head. "I don't think he has the guts. But he knows who did it. This changes everything."

Chapter 38

After placing an urgent phone call to Veronica asking her to join them within the quarter hour, Luke and Tessa went together to question Jerry Kravitz in earnest.

"Jerry, Jerry. What have you been up to in the last few days?" Luke began, as they returned to the kitchen.

"Can you sit him up straight?" Tessa asked. "I'd like to see his face while we talk."

With a lot of grunting and assistance from Luke, Jerry was able to get back onto his knees, then sit on his heels and face Tessa with his arms tied behind his back. Luke pulled a chair over for Tessa, then turned one backward and took a seat himself.

"That's a big blue Chevy you've got in the side yard," Luke said, once everyone was seated.

Jerry shrugged and refused to meet their eyes.

"Who does it belong to?" Luke pressed. "I didn't see a license plate."

Jerry lifted angry brown eyes to them. "Who cares about

that heap? It belongs to someone at the club who's going out of town. I'm watching it for him on account of Ricky asked me to."

Luke laughed with real humor and leaned forward so his face was only a few feet away from the other man's. "You're not too fucking bright, are you, Jer?"

Brown eyes flicked nervously between Luke and Tessa as Jerry at last began to pick up on the vibes in the room. "Why do you say that?"

"Because Ricky is setting you up for the hit-and-run murder of a veteran police officer. And the attempted murder of an officer of the court," Tessa said quietly.

Jerry laughed nervously while his eyes continued darting back and forth. "What the fuck? You're crazy."

"No, and since I was the one who survived the encounter with that Chevy, I can identify it with absolute certainty as the vehicle responsible for Detective Ed Flynn's death and my injuries." Tessa waved her cast at him to underscore the point. "That lines you up for accessory after the fact, at the very least. At worst, you go down for murder one."

Jerry met her eyes with an expression of dawning horror. "Someone killed a cop and tried to kill you?"

"Give the man a cigar," Luke drawled.

"Holy shit. I don't know nothing about any cop being run down. I swear, I just agreed to watch a car belonging to a buddy who's going out of town. You can't pin the rest of that on me." Jerry's pale face took on a green tinge as he finally began to understand what was going on.

And how easily he had been set up.

"I don't know about that," Luke said. "Every law enforcement agency in California is looking for that car right now, knowing it will lead to a cop-killer. If they can't find the guy who did the driving, or the guy who set the hit up, they'll be happy to take a sacrificial lamb instead."

"And from where I'm sitting, you're looking downright

wooly," Tessa finished. "Ricky screwed you over good, didn't he?"

"Can we still talk about deals?" Jerry asked. "I've got a lot of information that would help you, but you got to give me immunity. And I want protection from the rest of the players at Club Red."

"Tell me why I should deal with you when we're holding all the cards," Tessa said.

Jerry moistened his lips. "Because I can give you the name of the guy who gave me that car, and testify as to how he was doing this big hush-hush job for Ricky a couple days ago. Saturday afternoon. Would that be when this cop was killed?"

Gotcha.

Tessa kept her face calm, even though her heart was pounding. "It might be."

"So you give me immunity, I serve up this guy and Ricky on a platter."

"You have to understand a couple of things first, Jerry. I'm not the only one looking at Club Red right now."

His eyes darted between Luke and Tessa in a way she was beginning to find slightly creepy. "You talking about the cops?" Jerry asked.

"No. As we speak there's a multiagency task force headed by the FBI that's getting ready to take Club Red apart brick by brick to see what kind of cockroaches come scuttling out," Luke said.

"So I can't make you any promises on immunity from federal charges," Tessa explained. "And I've got my own bone to pick with you about Kelly. There won't be any dealing on charges related to her."

"Maybe I ain't too bright, but even I can figure out that you wouldn't be here if you had everything you needed. I can help you, but you don't get nothing for free," Jerry insisted.

"If you turn on Ricky and the driver of the Chevy, I can guarantee you immunity from charges related to the death of Detective Flynn," Tessa said. "But you've got to give me something really beefy if you want me to go to bat for you with the Feds. If the information is good enough, then we can try to get the federal charges reduced. But you'll have to serve up a lot of other people, enough so it's worthwhile for the FBI to go easy on you on the racketeering and gambling activities."

Jerry started visibly. "How'd you know about that?"

"Like I said, Jer. Law enforcement has been watching your organization for a long time," Luke said. "Enough to know that you and Ricky are in bed with the Ianellis."

"Don't ask me to rat them out," Jerry pleaded. "They'll kill me. Papa Ianelli wants to be taken seriously in the Southwestern US and there's no fucking way I'll be his example."

"You'll do it. And be happy about it," Tessa said over the sound of knocking at the front door. "Or you'll be looking at so much time in a federal lockup that death by Ianellis will begin to look pretty attractive."

Luke got up to open the door, surprised to see Ronnie standing there smiling brightly at Sledge Aiken. They'd obviously arrived at the same time, and she wanted to make sure that Sledge had no idea she was a cop and that his life was just about to get very interesting.

"I can't believe I ran into you like this," Ronnie cooed to Sledge as she followed him into the house.

Sledge came to a halt as he saw Luke standing in the entryway to the living room. He'd clearly been expecting to see Jerry and had no idea who the big man standing in front of him was.

Ronnie ignored Sledge's surprise and shoved the door shut, locking it with a flourish. "My husband is a big fan of yours, Mr. Aiken. Even though I tell him that your arm sucks on the long passes, and you run like a girl instead of holding your ground and picking out a receiver half the time."

"Huh? What?" Sledge's head whipped around to Ronnie. "Who the hell are you two? And where's Jerry?"

"He's kind of tied up at the moment," Luke said with a smile. "Why don't you join us in the kitchen and we can see who gets to make the deal of a lifetime with the District Attorney's Office."

"I'm outta here, man." Sledge turned to leave, then came to another abrupt halt as Ronnie smiled and flashed her badge at him.

"Believe me, you're going to want to hear what we have to say, Aiken. And don't worry about your lawyer. This conversation will be off the record, so you've got nothing to lose. Except a reduced sentence on state and local charges," Luke said.

He stepped aside and let Sledge and Ronnie pass him and head toward the kitchen. He used the pretext of greeting Ronnie with a hug and a kiss to whisper a warning in her ear. "Just go along with whatever Tessa says and don't show any emotion, okay?"

She nodded and went into the kitchen, stopping short when she saw Jerry trussed on the floor and Tessa sitting casually in a chair writing something on a yellow legal tablet. She looked better than the last time Ronnie had seen her— the scrapes on her face were healing, the bruises fading, and she no longer looked like she was on the verge of falling apart.

In fact, she looked pretty damned pleased with herself, something that Sledge picked up on right away.

"What have you done now, you prick?" he asked Jerry. "Did you set me up?"

"No!" Jerry protested. "But somehow they know everything. About Kelly, and what's happening at Club Red, and—"

"Shut up, you stupid shit. My lawyer told me they don't have anything unless someone talks. We'll all be fine if we just keep our mouths shut."

"I'm not keeping quiet while Ricky sets me up for killing a cop," Jerry insisted. He nodded frantically as Sledge looked at him in shock. "That's right. He went too far, and now he's trying to stick it on me. I got news for you, pal of mine, I'm not going down alone."

Tessa looked up from her pad of paper. "What he's saying, Sledge, is that you can kiss your endorsement contracts and your future political career good-bye. That's a given. The question you have to face now is how much time you're going to do, and how much of your personal fortune will be waiting for you when you get out of prison."

"But I didn't do anything," Sledge said. "Just went on a date that Jerry set up for me and Kelly. He said she was hot for me but kinda shy, he's the one who—"

Jerry interrupted with a howl of protest, insisting that Sledge had been fully involved with setting Kelly up and many other criminal activities besides.

Both Sledge and Jerry turned to Tessa and began shouting to be heard, each eager to cut the best deal in exchange for talking about the entire Club Red operation.

Ronnie leaned against the doorway next to Luke. "Don't you just love it when the bad guys realize that they've been screwed by their confreres and can't wait to return the favor?"

Luke watched Tessa trying to referee and take notes at the same time. "Yeah. It's great when the dam bursts."

"One confession at a time, please," Tessa said with a wry look at Ronnie and Luke. "But I'll be happy to reward the person with the best information. Right now, that means telling me where Kelly is."

Sledge shrugged. "I haven't seen her since that night I talked to you . . ." He trailed off at Tessa's fierce look. "Since a couple of weeks ago. I had nothing to do with her disappearance."

"Then how did you know she was missing?" Tessa asked.

Jerry leaned forward eagerly. "I told you, I saw her yesterday getting into a car with Otis. That's Ricky's bodyguard, and the guy who towed the Chevy over here a couple nights ago."

Tessa looked at each man as if trying to judge his sincerity. "You're not helping me here—or yourselves. If you want a deal, I need information that can actually lead me to Kelly."

"There's a girl at the club who might know where Kelly is," Jerry said slowly. "Crystal is always plugged into what's going on. She kind of took Kelly under her wing, was showing her the ropes, you know? And she was there yesterday, so she might know where Otis was taking Kelly."

"Crystal who? How do I get in touch with her?" Tessa asked.

"She's a dancer at Club Red," Sledge offered. "You can't miss her."

"Yeah, she has blue hair. Goes by the name Crystal Bleu," Jerry added. "Ricky trusts her—she's been with him forever. Well, a couple of years, anyway. She's the one who trains the girls and helps them pick out costumes, nicknames, and their particular trademarks, like her own blue hair."

"You told me she was helping to train Kelly," Tessa said. "What for? If you want to cut any deals, you're going to have to break down the operation for us and help us prove what was going on."

"What do you mean?" Jerry asked.

"You'll have to reveal how you entrap young girls and force them to become strippers and prostitutes for your little club," Luke said from the doorway. He and Ronnie finally came into the kitchen, figuring that since the information was flowing there was no need to hang back anymore.

"It was Ricky's idea," Jerry said reluctantly. "I just helped him get what he wanted."

"Which was?" Tessa asked.

"Thoroughbreds," Jerry replied. "Prime, young girls—preferably blondes—who didn't have the hard edge that a lot of the strippers and prostitutes get after a few years in the business. To keep the high-rolling customers happy, Ricky needed a constant supply of fresh meat—girls," he corrected himself with a wince.

"Girls you were happy to provide to men like Sledge. How did you do it?" Tessa asked. "How did you get a fifteen-year-old girl like Kelly to turn tricks for you?"

"By lying to her," Jerry admitted. "She thought she was going on a date with a star who had Hollywood connections. She thought Sledge was going to help her get a recording contract."

"And what did Sledge think he was getting?" Tessa asked as she looked at him.

"A date," he said. "Jerry assured me that Kelly had been broken in and knew what was expected of her. In return for sleeping with me, she gets to hang in my circle, maybe goes to a few parties where she could make some contacts."

"You both are disgusting," Tessa said tiredly. "But that's beside the point right now. How did you meet Kelly in the first place, and how many others like her are there?"

Jerry sighed. "We can only train one or two girls at a time. Keeping the supply low ensures a high demand, you know? It's a business decision."

"And when you're done with the girl?" Luke asked.

"Once a girl has been around for a while, or is no longer in high demand with the customers, we usually sign her up for dancing shifts if she's over eighteen. Or maybe ship her to another club where she'd be a new commodity. If the girl is young, we'll use her to recruit others like Kelly from bus or train stations, maybe even the beach and the malls."

"That's how you found Kelly," Tessa said. "At the bus station."

"Sure. One of the girls who knows the score was waiting for new arrivals at the downtown bus terminal. You can pick the runaways out from the crowd real easy. So she befriended Kelly, bought her coffee and a sandwich, talked with her about how rotten parents can be, you know. Then she invited Kelly to crash with her at my place until she found her own pad. When I opened the door and saw Kelly's face, I knew she was going to be a great addition to the club."

"So you groomed a fifteen-year-old runaway to service men like Sledge Aiken," Tessa said.

"Hey, I'm not the bad guy, here." Sledge ran an agitated hand through his trademark red-brown hair. "Why don't you ask Jerry about how he broke her in for me? I don't do virgins, so Jerry gave her a little on-the-job training. Don't make it sound like I'm the only one using these girls."

Tessa looked at Jerry. "You slept with that child, too? What on earth did you have to promise to get her into bed?"

Jerry was beginning to get angry. "Nothing. She was in love with me, thought we were going steady or something."

Luke got up and leaned over Jerry. "Bullshit. She owed you for putting a roof over her head and promising to introduce her to people, and you played on those feelings of obligation and hope. Then you showered her with attention and new clothes, getting her deeper and deeper in debt. She probably was confused and felt like she had to sleep with you because of all you had done. It certainly wasn't an act of love on her part. We know she didn't have a choice."

"Look, I'm not one of these stinking rich athletes who comes into the Club angling for underage girls."

"Look, I think it's a dead heat for which one of you is the most pathetic, revolting excuse for a human being on the planet," Tessa said. "I'm just looking for facts, documentation, and testimony to back up what we already know. It'll save you a couple of decades on federal charges, but you have to do all the time for charges relating to Kelly and any other young girls you prostituted and used. Understand?"

"My man Jerry is jerking you around with the chickenshit stuff—the girls and sex for money at the club? That's nothing compared to what's really going on there," Sledge said. "Ricky and all of the club's managers, including Jerry, are in it deep with the mob. He's holding back on the one aspect that you guys should be investigating."

"Now who's being a stupid shit?" Jerry asked. "That is my ace. If I don't get a walk, they don't get that information. So keep your mouth shut, or I'll tell Ricky who's doing the talking about Club Red, Inc."

"Are you talking about the money laundering operation, Jerry?" Tessa asked. "We know everything but the name of the guy setting up the shell corporations and overall financial strategy. And we've got a forensic accountant working on that information right now."

Once again, the only sound in the kitchen was the clock on the wall and the labored breathing of the man who was watching his plea deal go down the toilet.

"I can help you," Sledge said slowly. "But I had nothing to do with the killing of a cop, kidnapping, rape, or organized prostitution. I want your word that I won't face any charges for those things. And I get full credit in the press for aiding the investigation—maybe you could even make it sound like I was an informant and cooperating with you. Finally, I get to keep all of my money."

"You think you have something good enough that I'm going to let you off the hook for date-raping a teenager?" Tessa asked musingly.

"I did not rape her!" Sledge said, his face turning a dusky shade of red. "And yes, I can give you something that will make the rest of it look like high school games."

"Would you be talking about purchasing the loyalty of local and state politicians, by any chance?" Luke asked, thinking about the article they'd read the day before.

Tessa had to give Sledge credit for not flinching, though she could see he was shocked that they knew about the public corruption. "Is that a yes, Aiken?" she asked.

A tight nod was all Sledge could bring himself to do in response. His teeth were clenched, and his throat was closed at the thought of his career and ambitions going up in flames.

He knew without a doubt that he'd never work in Los Angeles again. Or any other town. All the teams and corporate sponsors who made professional football such a lucrative field had morals clauses in their contracts. The conservative middle-class base that supported the NFL would never accept his participation on a team once the details of Club Red, Inc. came to light.

"Forget about Sledge. I can give you the name of the financial guy," Jerry said in the tense silence. "I even have a bunch of communications that can prove he knew we were giving him dirty money. That's got to be worth something."

"Only if you can tell us with certainty in which banks the illegal funds were parked," Tessa said.

Jerry swallowed hard, knowing that meant the assets would be forfeited. "I can tell you where he stashed my personal funds. I'm pretty sure that Ricky's profits are in different accounts at the same banks."

"The money will all be confiscated," Tessa warned. "But your information will smooth the way for a plea bargain on the federal charges. I can't promise anything to either one of you, but I'm fairly certain the Feds will cooperate in exchange for your testimony."

"And if they don't?" Sledge asked.

"Then you can recant your statements. But that's not going to happen," Luke said. "The FBI won't turn away from the big-time busts that your information will make possible."

"What about the charges related to Kelly?" Jerry asked Tessa. "You have control over those."

"Yes. But frankly, they're the least of your worries. I won't negotiate on those. However, I guarantee that the formal deal I will propose to your lawyers will be one they advise you to take."

"What kind of time are we looking at?" Jerry asked.

"Five to eight years on each of the state charges—and no early parole. You *might* be able to do the sentences concurrently. Trust me," she said over the sound of Sledge's cursing, "that's the best deal you're going to be offered. You can't expect to walk away after what you've done. Once you accept the fact that you'll have to do some time behind bars, you'll see that my deal is very generous."

"No rape charges," Sledge insisted. "You can't prove them, anyway."

But I can prove statutory rape, you sick piece of crap. It's an entirely different crime. Tessa merely shrugged her shoulders. "The first person to give me the name of the accountant who plays hide the money for Ricky will get a walk on sexual assault charges. That's the best I can do."

"Tristan Rothschild," Jerry blurted out.

Sledge sighed. "His firm manages my money, too. And he arranged the structuring of donations to the campaigns of several local and state politicians. I'll give you their names and a record of transactions for the same deal Jerry gets—no sexual assault charges."

"Done. I'll give you each five minutes to contact your lawyers before we arrange for you to be taken into protective custody as witnesses. I won't finalize the pleas until you've talked with them. And with the agreement of your lawyers, I'd like employees of Novak International to provide for security and housing for the next thirty-six hours, until we can make our presentation to the FBI-led task force."

"I'll monitor them while they're on the phone," Luke offered. "Have Ronnie go bring my guys in from the van. I want Sledge and Jerry in a secure location within the hour."

Chapter 39

*"*All right, girlfriend. Spill it." Veronica sprawled on Luke's leather couch and ran an envious hand over the soft grain of the coffee brown leather. Toddlers and fine furniture weren't a good combination, so she and her husband made do with a thrift store couch upholstered in a psychedelic floral pattern similar to something found on hotel room bedspreads.

In the kind of rooms that were rented out by the quarter hour.

She'd encountered such classy and refined things since joining the police department a few years ago, Veronica mused sarcastically, hot sheet operations among them. Somehow, working with Ed Flynn had helped make it all bearable. But now he was gone, and she didn't think she'd be able to go back to the squalor without him to back her up.

Fortunately, that was a decision for another day. Right now, she worried about how Tessa was handling Ed's loss and what kind of role Luke was playing in taking her mind off it.

"What am I spilling?" Tessa asked as she settled into her own corner of the decadent leather couch with a cup of tea.

"Details about the oh-so-concerned and handsome Mr. Novak. And what's going on between the two of you."

"Geez, I don't know if I should say anything. It seems kind of juvenile to kiss and tell."

"Juvenile, hell! The only action I get is if Mike and I manage to be home at the same time for more than fifteen minutes, the kid's asleep, and we're not seeing double from sheer exhaustion. Believe me, it doesn't happen very often."

"No wonder you're so interested in my sex life," Tessa said.

"So you've got to give me a little nugget here, something to get me through the current drought."

"All I can say is that he's just . . . well, he's *wonderful*. And it all just kind of happened."

"What do you mean, it just happened? You usually analyze everything to death," Ronnie said.

"Yeah, well, there wasn't time. And there were no stray thoughts about depositions, no pondering the décor of the room, no wondering if my butt looked big enough to need its own zip code from his angle. It was—" Tessa broke off with a little shiver. "It was awesome."

"Sounds like your ex was a real prize, if that's what you used to think about. But we'll get back to that. Where is this thing with you and Luke going?"

Tessa's smile faltered as she remembered the last person who had said those words to her. "Ed asked me that. On—on the day he died. I didn't have an answer then, and I'm even more at a loss now."

"What's to be confused about? You obviously feel something, or you wouldn't be sitting here waiting for Luke to come home. You're not a casual person, and it seems like he really cares about you."

"Why do you say that?"

"Please." Ronnie shook her head in frustration, then held

up a finger to begin listing things. "No matter what subject you're talking about, he treats you like a cross between his partner and a goddess, which means his brain is engaged along with his body. He goes out of his way to show his interest—taking care of you, little strokes and touches, the concern in his absolutely gorgeous eyes."

"He's just being a gentleman," Tessa insisted.

"It's more than good manners," Ronnie insisted. "He does all those things in a way that doesn't make you all prickly and distant. It's like he can see how important it is to you to stand on your own, and all he wants is for you to know that he's there with you. To me, it means he cares."

"Maybe. He says he does, and I want to believe him." Tessa bit her lip. "God, I've got baggage, Ronnie. I've never made a commitment to anyone in my life."

"Maybe that's because no one was right for you until now."

"But how do I tell?" Tessa asked. "I mean, did you just *know* things were going to work out with Mike?"

Ronnie laughed with real humor. "We've been together a little over a year—how would I know? I'm just a dumb hick from Minnesota who got married because I ended up pregnant by a guy I'd been dating for less than a month."

"You must have known there was a risk," Tessa said, thinking about her own lack of long-term birth control with Luke for the first time.

"Think again. The Pill is over 99 percent effective, but I somehow turned out to be the one in one hundred to get knocked up while taking it. Mike and I buy lottery tickets every week now," Ronnie joked.

Tessa winced. "But you've made it. You guys are a family now."

"We didn't really have a choice, though. We got married because we wanted to do right by the kid, you know? Don't get me wrong—I love Mike. But if you're asking me if he's the Love of My Life, I have no idea. I know we wouldn't have chosen to do things this way if given the opportunity."

"Don't tell me that," Tessa groaned. "You guys were the one example I had of a successful relationship."

"It is successful," Ronnie said. "But only because we're both pouring everything we have into it. Marriage is hard work, and it takes a lot of time."

"What Luke and I have is so new, and it came out of nowhere, with no warning. We haven't had time to build anything like the trust you have with each other . . ." Tessa trailed off, not sure how to explain it.

"How did you deal with trust before? Forget the college sweetheart, because you guys were just kids then. What about the grad student?"

Biting her lip, Tessa shook her head. "It was never an issue. I didn't let myself go enough—or feel things deeply enough—that I had to worry about trusting him and being let down. We were more friends than anything else, because I didn't let him get close enough to do real damage."

"And you get mad at me for impugning his masculinity?" Ronnie muttered.

"Don't make it sound like he was completely spineless, because that's not fair. I can't put him down now for being laid-back, when that's what I was looking for in a boyfriend in the first place."

"Sweetie, laid-back is one thing. Being a doormat is another." Ronnie held up a hand to stop Tessa's protest. "All right, I'll stop. I know how hard it is to be vulnerable. You seem all independent, but I think you feel things more deeply than you let on.

Tessa smiled mistily. "Luke said something like that to me."

"I told you he was smart. I think your new man is perfect for you, because he's not the type to let you wallow in the past," Ronnie said.

"You're blowing things way out of proportion."

Ronnie shook her head. "Don't try to minimize this by saying you just spent the night together. He's been at your side nonstop since Ed—since Saturday. If Luke hasn't pressed you since then, it's because he's more worried about you than his own needs. I told you, there's something different about this guy."

Tessa set her cup aside at the unpleasant flip her stomach took.

Yes, Luke is different. That's probably why he scares me— bad. And why I can't even get myself to say out loud what I'm feeling when I'm around him. I could say the words before, when I didn't really feel them, but now that I am experiencing those emotions my throat closes up.

How messed up is that?

"What are you looking so queasy about?" Ronnie asked, interrupting Tessa's thoughts. "Is your wrist hurting?"

"Huh? No. It's something Paul said the other day. He had me pegged when he said I've gone through life looking backward, living in the past. God, don't you hate it when your parents are right?" Tessa groaned.

"So what are you going to do about it?" Ronnie asked.

"That's the kicker. I have no idea. What with Ed and Kelly, this case, what's been going on with Paul . . . I don't have any spare energy to deal with that question right now. Besides, what if the baggage has become so much a part of me that letting go isn't possible? What if I'm defined by it?"

"Then we're doomed as a race. And as the mother of a young child I can't afford to think that way. So you need to work things out in a grown-up way with those you care about."

"What, now I'm immature?" Tessa asked with a scowl.

"Growing up isn't something that happens magically when you turn eighteen. Don't kick yourself for being human and stumbling along that path."

"I'm supposedly an intelligent person, you'd think I would have managed to work through these things before now. God, why is he even interested in me in the first place?"

"There's no accounting for taste," Ronnie said.

Tessa groaned.

"Come on, you know I was kidding. Look at it this way— Luke is a smart guy, right?"

"Very smart," Tessa agreed.

"Well, he obviously sees something in you that rocks his world. You have to have enough faith in him to believe that he knows what he's doing."

"You're right. I know you're right," Tessa said. "But how do I keep from messing this up?"

"First of all, stop struggling against it so much," Ronnie advised.

Tessa absently massaged the base of her fingers where the cast dug in. "I admit, I've fought this thing with Luke every step of the way. Not fighting Luke, you know, but my feelings for him. He's had to make every overture so far. Much as I've enjoyed that, I tried to not even let things get this far. If I'd had my way, they wouldn't have."

Ronnie shook her head sympathetically. "That's what chemistry is there for, sweetie. It overcomes our logic and intellect and makes us obey the biological imperative to reproduce."

"We are more than our animal impulses," Tessa argued.

"Not when we're talking about a man as gorgeous as Luke," Ronnie said with a wink. "There he is now."

They both heard an automatic garage door opener activate, then the sound of the engine being turned off.

"Finally. It's after eight," Tessa said as she looked at her watch in concern. "He must be exhausted. I'm going to turn on the hot tub, order some takeout, and make sure we have an early night."

You have it so bad, girlfriend. Ronnie smiled inwardly as

she gathered her things. "I want you to promise me that after dinner you two will go at it like bunny rabbits."

"Get out of here, you freak." Tessa grabbed the phone to order dinner, hoping her red cheeks would fade by the time Luke made it inside.

Chapter 40

Downtown Los Angeles
Wednesday morning, March 17

As Tessa and Luke left the parking garage and crossed the street to the Federal Building, she gave herself a mental pep talk to prepare for the upcoming meeting. Finally, the day had arrived when she would make her pitch to the multi-agency task force that was responsible for investigating Club Red, Inc.

Too bad she was shaking in her shoes.

They joined Ronnie, who had arrived earlier with Mac-Beth and the rest of the players in the morning's meeting. As Luke and his employee went over the logistical plans and timeline for the meeting, Ronnie pulled Tessa aside.

"Any word on the whereabouts of Ricky Hedges?" Ronnie asked. She'd been so focused on planning Ed's memorial and investigating his death in the last two days that she'd had little time to keep tabs on the movements of the people who were involved.

"Just what I last told you. He was last seen leaving Club Red Monday night, and MacBeth hasn't seen him since."

"So how did things go with you and Luke the other night?"

Tessa pursed her lips. "Not the way I'd planned."

"What do you mean?"

"He was so tired he fell asleep," Tessa said. "I went out to pay for the dinner I'd ordered, but when I got back with the food I found him out cold in the recliner."

"What about the next day?"

"What about it? He was gone when I woke up, and Mac-Beth was in the kitchen waiting for me," Tessa said. "I met Luke later at the office, but we both had a ton of work to do. We took it back to his place, after a brief stopover at my apartment so I could get some things. We were still at work around 2:00 A.M. when I fell asleep on his couch. I woke up in his bedroom, but we had just enough time to make it here for this meeting—nothing else."

"You at least moved forward on the case, though, right?" Ronnie asked, frustrated that her advice for opening channels of trust and communication hadn't been put to use.

"Sure. We found and talked to the financial advisor for both Ricky Hedges and Club Red. It took some arm-twisting, but with Chantal's help we finally convinced him that we have enough evidence to shut down the whole operation and send him to a federal prison for the next eighty years. He was able to see that it's in his interest to cooperate with the investigation," Tessa said. "In fact, he and his lawyer should be here with Chantal any minute."

"Well at least the case is coming together. You've done a great job with everything for today," Ronnie said. "Ed would have been strutting like a peacock."

"Thanks," Tessa said huskily. Yes, the work aspect of her life was right on track, while her personal life was, in a word, hosed.

Typical.

"You ready, baby?"

Luke's voice pulled Tessa from her huddle with Ronnie.

"Yes. But I don't think you should call me that during the meeting," she said, trying to lighten the mood. She felt sure Luke would be able to tell they had been talking about him by the serious vibes they were giving off.

"No problem," Luke replied. "I won't do this, either." With that, he tipped her face up for a lingering kiss.

"Wretched man," Tessa muttered a moment later as a laughing Ronnie dragged her away in the direction of the building.

But she did look over her shoulder to exchange a final glance with Luke before they reached the security checkpoint.

I guess we'll just have to wait until this whole case is over to work things out. It wasn't what Tessa had had in mind, but since when did her life go as she'd planned?

Fifteen minutes later Luke stood with Tessa in what he was calling the staging room—a smaller meeting room just off the main conference suite where the task force was gathering at that very moment. He could see that Tessa's nerves were winding up, which was why he'd kissed her earlier and tried to take her mind off of what was about to happen.

She'd been working so hard in the last few days. They both had. The only time they'd been alone and not putting together the plan for this morning's meeting, they'd been sleeping. Often in different places. One night he'd passed out in the recliner before even getting to eat dinner.

Then last night she'd drifted off on the couch. He'd taken her upstairs to his room, and she'd readily turned into his arms . . . but she'd still been asleep. In a way, it was a good thing—they hadn't had time to discuss anything but the case. Hadn't had time to feel their way blindly around a situation where they were both without precedent.

And frankly, he hadn't had a chance to say something stupid and send Tessa running for her life.

Which was a good thing, right?

So why did it feel so wrong to leave everything hanging,

to have their entire situation unresolved and up in the air? He'd never been one to push for structure and formality in a relationship.

Frankly, his current compulsion to do so was giving him heartburn.

"Carmen! I thought you weren't going to be able to make it."

At the sound of Tessa's surprised voice, Luke stood up and turned to see a stunning Hispanic woman in a sexy, lipstick red suit approaching them.

"You didn't think I'd leave you to face the wolves alone, did you?" Carmen Ramirez asked with a slight smile.

Tessa stood there organizing her notes, not sure of whether she was pleased or not with her boss's presence.

"Don't sulk," Carmen said. "I'm not here to steal your thunder. Quite the opposite—I'm going to back you up. There's no way the head of the task force or the US Attorney's representative would recognize any deals you make with them. They expect me to give my explicit approval to any arrangements. It's simply a matter of protocol."

"I didn't mean to imply that you're not welcome to attend—" Tessa began.

"No, you just want to protect your case, which I can understand," Carmen said. "Trust me, I won't say a word. I'll just nod at the appropriate moments and expect you to do all the work."

"Typical boss behavior," Luke joked. "Are you sure you didn't work for the sheriff's department at one time?"

Carmen gave Luke a thorough, head-to-toe assessment in a single glance. "No wonder she's feeling so possessive. Tell me," Carmen spoke to Tessa, "who is this?"

"This is Lucas Novak, Carmen. He's been instrumental in getting us to this point in the case," Tessa said, clearing her throat a little at the glowing words that came out of her mouth. She meant them, she just hadn't meant to say them in that tone.

Luke shook hands with Carmen and made all the appropriate noises and gestures, but his gaze was strictly for Tessa. She felt it on her like a caress.

Enough.

Tessa shook herself free of the spell. She was going to have a hard enough time being taken seriously in the next room once the time came for the spotlight to fall on her. She had no doubt she'd be one of only a few females at the conference table, and most probably the youngest by a good decade or more. It was one of the reasons she'd chosen her most conservative blue pin-striped suit and navy pumps, and worn her hair in a businesslike bun, with the old standby pearl earrings and brooch.

Women at her relatively low level in government work weren't able to get away with being sexual creatures, whether that meant dressing like Carmen in a suit designed to bring a man to his knees, or having a man look at her the way Luke just had.

Someday, Tessa would get to that point—the way her boss and even Chantal had. But in the meantime, she had to pay her dues and ensure that everyone knew she'd gotten to where she was through brains, hard work, and ambition.

Ronnie kept insisting this was a conservative—even reactionary—approach. But Ronnie had never had to make a presentation to a roomful of patronizing and territorial men who had reached their positions the old-fashioned way—through backstabbing, office politics, and the old boys' network.

"Are you worrying about how they'll react to you because of who your father is?" Ronnie whispered to Tessa, breaking into her thoughts.

She hadn't been—until that moment. "Now I am. Thanks."

Ronnie looked chagrined. "Sorry. I just wanted to tell you that Chantal and Ricky's accountant, Tristan Rothschild, are here. So are the various witnesses and their attorneys. I'll keep an eye on everyone over here while you're at the meeting. It looks like the entire room next door is full, so you and Luke should get over there."

Tessa took a moment to acknowledge Chantal with a nod, then smoothed her hair while Luke gathered his briefcase and hers. He winked at her and refrained, just barely, from blowing her a kiss.

"One last bit of advice," Carmen said. "There are at least twenty people in that room. Don't worry about getting everyone's name and organization right, okay? There are really only two people you need to worry about."

"And they are?" Tessa asked.

"First off is Assistant United States Attorney Gilbert Rabani. He'll be in a power suit—dark hair and complexion, just under six feet, midforties or so. He'll have the final say with respect to the federal charges."

"AUSA Rabani," said Tessa. "Check. And the other, I'm assuming, is Special Agent Peebles?"

"Yes. My assistant did some research because I've never met the man. His first name is Dieter, and I understand he's got the Nordic look going for him. He's in his forties, and very ambitious. This is his first time heading up a task force, and word is he's being so cautious in dotting his i's that the investigation is moving at a snail's pace. Expect him to be pissy. He didn't want you here," Carmen said bluntly.

"I know. I'll just have to make it worthwhile for Special Agent Peebles."

"Don't forget, he's a very small man." This last bit of advice was given by Chantal as Tessa made her way out the door and into the hallway that separated the staging room from the conference suite. Tessa gave her a smile that held all the confidence she didn't feel at the moment.

"I'll worry about bringing in our guests when the time comes," Luke said as he handed Tessa her briefcase. "If you want to switch the order we agreed to, just let me know."

Carmen led the way into the tightly packed conference

room. A slim, pale-haired man seated at the head of the table was speaking to the group, reading off a list of action items from the last time the task force met.

Special Agent Peebles waited with obvious annoyance as Luke, Tessa, and Carmen entered the room. Tessa saw with some dismay that every seat at the table was occupied, and there were no extra chairs in the room.

She hesitated, assuming that someone familiar with the facility would offer to find some additional seats. Peebles looked at her, then at his watch.

"You must be Ms. Jacobi. I'm sorry, but you're seventy-five seconds late. I like to begin my meetings promptly. You'll find a copy of the minutes and action items from the last meeting on the table in the corner behind you. Okay," he addressed the room, "on to the next subject on the agenda."

Clearly, no one was going to get any other chairs, meaning they would have to move to the corner and stand there for the length of the meeting. Tessa watched Carmen's mouth pull into a flat line and wondered how to avoid the inevitable fireworks.

Luke made his way toward the head of the table. He touched the shoulders of the two men sitting next to Peebles, bent down between them, and spoke loudly enough to be heard by everyone in the room.

"I'm sure you gentlemen won't mind giving your chairs up to my colleagues here, right?"

"Excuse me, sir." Peebles stood up and glared at Luke.

"Don't mind me. I'm Luke Novak, nice to meet you, Dieter. Just making a place for the ladies at the table before we continue."

Forced into the spotlight, neither man could gracefully refuse to give up his seats. Luke smiled warmly and held the chairs out for Tessa and Carmen, then stepped back to lean against the wall behind them. The other men made sure there were several feet between Luke and them as they stood in front of the wall and waited to see what he'd do next.

Round one of the pissing contest goes to Luke Novak.
Tessa did her best to look professional as she silently
gloated.

"Please continue, Agent Peebles," Luke said graciously.
"I'll let you make the introductions."

Carmen coughed out loud. She and Tessa settled into their
leather executive chairs and waited to be presented to the
group.

But Special Agent Peebles clearly had other plans. He
went right back to where he'd left off, checking action items
and dealing with administrative details.

A dark-haired man Tessa guessed to be Assistant US Attorney Gilbert Rabani cleared his throat. "If I could interrupt
here, Dieter."

"I'm going to ask you to submit any questions to my assistant, and we'll get to them at the end of the meeting," Peebles replied. "However, I'll make note that you're first in
line, Gil."

After that, Peebles spent the next five minutes going over
a laundry list of relatively insignificant items from the previous meeting. As Luke started to twitch, Peebles switched
over to a lengthy discussion of the issues involved with getting wiretaps for the phones at Club Red and several other
locations where Ricky was known to reside.

"So because of the overlapping jurisdictions, including
Nevada and Mexico, I wanted our lawyers to spend an additional month tightening the text of the wiretap requests." He
paused to take a sip of water, then continued on about the
wording of the requests for subpoenas related to the case.

Tessa couldn't believe the rudeness. First of all, the man
had neglected to introduce them to anyone. Second, he was
spending valuable time going over the nitty-gritty details of
the investigation, which was clearly inappropriate given
Carmen's presence. The district attorney of Los Angeles did
not involve herself in the minutiae of ongoing investigations.

"Excuse me, Agent Peebles." Carmen held a hand up to

stop the man in midsentence. "I'm sure the items you're discussing are quite important to the operational aspects of this task force. But I didn't come to hear about alterations in the draft text of your subpoenas and search warrant requests."

"And you would be . . . ?" Peebles inquired.

The dark-haired man who had tried to speak earlier stood up. "Allow me to introduce Carmen Ramirez, District Attorney for Los Angeles County."

Peebles turned an unattractive shade of brick red. The color in his face was so deep it made his eyebrows look pure white against his forehead. "Pleasure."

Carmen smiled her cat smile. "Likewise. I've got a tight schedule today, so I was wondering if I could impose and have our little discussion bumped to the top of your lovely, organized agenda." She waved the document in question. "Then we can get out of your hair and leave you to work at the ant's ass level of detail. I'm really only interested in the satellite view, if you get my drift."

"Certainly." Peebles cleared his throat, several times. Then he turned the meeting over to Carmen. She indicated that Tessa should take the lead. Luke shoved his hands deep in his pocket and grinned.

Tessa stood and took refuge at the whiteboard. "You may not be aware, but the district attorney has been pursuing rape allegations made against a high-profile athlete by a girl who subsequently disappeared. The athlete in question is a regular at Club Red, and we've been given reason to believe that those who run the establishment are involved with the sexual assault and a number of other crimes. I was unaware, until recently, that this investigation had crossed paths with the case your task force has been preparing against Club Red."

"For over a year," Peebles pointed out. "And there's no compelling reason so far for why we should jeopardize our investment of time and man-hours to help you make a state case against some of the same players."

"Bear with me for a moment, Agent Peebles. I think you'll

find our information very helpful. It seems we've been going at the same case from different angles. While our goals are, of course, different, I think we would be wise to assist each other."

"I don't mean to be rude, Ms. Jacobi. But why should we give a piece of our investigation to you and your colleagues," Peebles said, with a glance at Luke.

"You'd be pretty foolish not to," Tessa said. "We have information that is critical to your organized crime and racketeering investigation, but I'm not interested in RICO violations. My main concern is getting Kelly Maarten away from Club Red and shutting its operations down. My goal is to press state charges against the individuals who kidnapped, manipulated, raped, and prostituted a fifteen-year-old runaway."

"It's my understanding you don't have enough evidence to press the sexual assault charges, let alone any others," Rabani said, though his manner was almost apologetic.

"Only because the suspects threatened and bullied the primary witness before finally making her disappear. But we know all of the individuals involved are connected to Club Red. In the course of our own investigation, we have come across incriminating evidence that relates directly to your task force," Tessa said.

"And you want to bargain with this?" Rabani asked.

"Yes," Tessa said simply. "I'll need the US Attorney's Office to allow for plea bargains and sentence reductions on the federal charges for defendants Aiken and Kravitz. In exchange for these reduced federal prison times, we expect these defendants to plead guilty on all state charges related to Kelly Maarten."

"That's impossible," Peebles said with a dismissive wave of his hand. "The federal charges are more serious, and traditionally these take precedence over parochial interests like those you are discussing. We hold all the cards, so why should we give out any sentence reductions or plea bargains?"

"Because you'd be able to build a case against everyone

else you're interested in—and you can have them all, except for the individuals I've named," Tessa said. "This includes several members of the Ianelli crime family. In exchange, I want leverage to force guilty pleas out of the individuals responsible for kidnapping and prostituting a minor."

Rabani cleared his throat again. Tessa was starting to figure out that's what he did when he was sure people weren't going to like what he had to say. "I understand you had some recent difficulties, Ms. Jacobi." He gestured vaguely at her broken wrist. "Surely you wish to press additional charges related to these happenings?"

"Yes, but I can't. I'm a witness as well as a victim, and as you know that unfortunately means I can't be involved in prosecuting the death of my good friend," Tessa said.

"No, there would certainly be a conflict of interest if you didn't recuse yourself and your office from the prosecution," Rabani said. "You couldn't be a witness, plaintiff, and prosecutor all at once."

"True, but the US Attorney's Office would have had jurisdiction anyway, as we believe the incident in question was a contract killing, and I was the intended target."

Rabani's dark eyebrows shot up, and a speculative gleam entered his eyes.

Tessa knew she had him. "Think about it—you'd be getting a murder-for-hire case involving the death of a cop. The prosecution would require very little legwork on your part."

"So the US Attorney is free to pursue the murder of Detective Flynn, outside of any deals we are making here today," Rabani mused.

"Yes. I'll give you all the evidence we have to date relating to this incident. It should be an open-and-shut prosecution," Tessa said. "I'd expect your boss to allow for no plea bargains, though. I want the death penalty for the killer. And for Ricky Hedges, as we have proof beyond a reasonable doubt that he planned and paid for the hit against me that went wrong."

She waited for a response, but there was silence in the room. Rabani was no doubt contemplating being handed a high-profile case without having to give up much in return.

"Both the Flynn murder and the Club Red investigation and prosecution would be a huge PR opportunity for this task force and all of your organizations," Carmen finally said.

"Maybe, but we could achieve that ourselves, without Ms. Jacobi and her information. It might take a little longer, probably a year or so. But we wouldn't have to negotiate on charges or share credit with latecomers," Peebles said bluntly.

"Are you high?" Luke asked in disbelief. "Maybe you're just stupid."

Ignoring the titters in the room, Tessa hurriedly spoke. "I'm not talking about accelerating your investigation by a few months, I'm talking about handing you the entire thing on a silver platter. Do you get it? I'm going to give you a case, complete with witnesses, that could go to the grand jury tomorrow."

"That would be for me to decide. So far your father has thrown his weight around to get you in here, and your boss came along to back you up. But while we've heard a lot of talk, we have yet to see a single compelling piece of evidence," Peebles said as he sat back in his chair. "You want a deal, you're going to have to prove you've got the goods."

Chapter 41

Tessa reined in the urge to throttle Special Agent Peebles of the FBI. Instead, she nodded to Luke to indicate that she was ready for the witnesses to be brought to the room.

"I think you'll find the guest speakers who are about to come in will more than satisfy the burden of proof," Tessa said.

There was silence in the room as the back door opened and eight different people shuffled in to stand along one of the walls, including all of Tessa's witnesses and their legal counsel. Ronnie and Chantal brought up the rear of the group, and Tessa wished she'd had a camera to capture the expression on Dieter Peebles's face when he saw the forensic accountant he'd essentially fired from his team months earlier.

Chantal, who was dressed in a show-stopping burnt orange suit with matching Jimmy Choo mules, waved cheerfully at Peebles when she saw him.

Smothering a grin, Tessa turned around to write the names of her witnesses on the whiteboard. Then she addressed the curious members of the task force. "If you wouldn't mind holding any questions until the end, I'd appreciate it. I don't want to have to repeat any information and waste your valuable time."

Rabani exchanged a look with Carmen, then sat back to watch the show. He knew it was going to be good by the expression on the D.A.'s face—anticipation and pride mixed together.

"Our first witness is Sledge Beauregard Aiken, quarterback for the LA Waves professional football team," Tessa began. "He faces state charges of statutory rape and unlawful sexual contact with a minor, as per section 261.5 of the California Penal Codes. In addition, he's looking at charges of providing an intoxicating agent to a minor, solicitation, intimidating a witness, and making false statements to the police."

She paused and looked over at Peebles, who shrugged.

"On the federal level, you're going to want to talk to him about racketeering and illegal campaign contributions to local politicians. Also he's confessed to being involved with influence peddling, lobbying to alter zoning laws to unfairly benefit Club Red, and real estate fraud."

Rabani cleared his throat. "I had hoped for something more substantial."

"You've got it," Tessa said. "For his finale, Mr. Aiken is ready to talk about acting as a secret intermediary in activities involving Ricky Hedges, the Ianelli crime Family, and several local politicians. He's also involved in a whole host of other RICO violations," Tessa said, citing the Racketeer Influenced and Corrupt Organization laws used to prosecute organized crime. "Finally, he will testify to what he knows about the money laundering operations at Club Red, which will corroborate the statements of our other witnesses."

Rabani's eyes glazed over as he began to realize the magnitude of the case he could build. Even Peebles had come to attention in his chair, and his assistant was taking notes furiously.

"You get all this," Tessa continued, "in exchange for letting the state of California have first crack at Mr. Aiken. Once he's been sentenced on the state charges, you're free to use him as a witness in exchange for a plea bargain on federal charges. But he does the full eight to ten years for what he did to Kelly Maarten—nonnegotiable. He understands that this is a fantastic deal, considering that he was looking at decades in federal prison on the RICO violations alone."

Sledge said nothing, just looked at the ground with his jaw clenched. The new lawyer he'd been forced to acquire after Carl Abrahms had dropped him had spent the last two days telling him what a generous deal he'd been offered by the D.A.—all he had to do was plead guilty to charges that would see him living as a registered sex offender for the rest of his life.

His lawyer had pointed out that he could always move overseas once his prison term was over. Sledge had refrained, just barely, from knocking the guy's teeth down his throat.

Tessa put a check mark next to Sledge's name on the whiteboard and moved on. "Next we have Jerrold Mihaly Kravitz, who has served as a manager of Club Red for just over a year. Mr. Kravitz is facing state charges including statutory rape and sexual contact with a minor, pimping and prostitution, unlawful imprisonment, battery, kidnapping, witness tampering, and conspiracy to kidnap a minor child in Kansas."

Tessa indicated to Luke that he should explain the other charges Jerry was facing. Luke didn't move from his position against the wall. "Mr. Kravitz is a known associate of the Ianellis, and this long-standing relationship predates his involvement with Club Red. We believe he served as an intermediary to deepen the relationship between Ricky Hedges and the Ianelli crime Family."

"What evidence do you have against him?" Peebles asked.

"We have enough to make federal charges, including gambling, narcotics distribution, running a multistate prostitution ring, racketeering, and a number of tax-reporting discrepancies. He's confessed to structuring deposits in violation of the Bank Secrecy Act, as well as smuggling currency and helping run an elaborate money laundering operation," Tessa said.

Chantal spoke up. "Mr. Kravitz is also willing to help the task force track the illegally deposited profits from Club Red, as well as identify the various shell corporations Ricky Hedges used to hide the money. He's been assisting me to that end for the last day, and his information has been useful. More importantly, it corroborates the details given to me by Tristan Rothschild."

"Rothschild?" Peebles asked. "I don't know anyone in the organization with that name or alias."

"That's because you haven't penetrated the organization very deeply," Luke said. "Mr. Rothschild was presented to Ricky Hedges almost a year ago by the Ianellis. His objective was to diversify the financial operations of Club Red and set up a variety of schemes that would be capable of placing and laundering millions of dollars in illegal funds."

"That's millions with a capital 'M,'" Chantal pointed out. "So far, I've turned up over thirteen million in illegal but laundered funds. And Mr. Rothschild tells me Ricky Hedges is planning a big placement of funds in the next few weeks."

"How much money are we talking about overall," Rabani asked.

They all looked at Rothschild, a slender man of medium build with thinning gray hair and pale blue eyes. The accountant removed his horn-rimmed glasses and began to polish them with a cloth he pulled out of his blazer pocket.

Luke nudged the guy, who spoke as if the words were painful. "Ricky Hedges is a hoarder. He has been sitting on the profits from his business and real estate operations for over three years. I estimate, from statements he's made and my review of the books, that he's got around eighteen million dollars in cash to be placed."

"My God! That would be one of the largest seizures in Bureau history," Peebles said.

"Amen," Rabani echoed. "Why on earth is he sitting on that much money?"

"Because he's a fool," Rothschild said. "He's afraid of losing control, and, frankly, he doesn't have the technical abilities to launder that amount of money. That's where I come in."

"In exchange for his testimony," Tessa said, "Mr. Rothschild expects to avoid any type of stay in the federal prison system. He'd also like to enter the witness protection program, because of his association with the Ianellis."

"I'd like to move to the Caribbean," Rothschild added. "Someplace where my financial acumen can be appreciated."

"That's it," Tessa said. "These are the witnesses that I can turn over to you."

Carmen leaned forward and met Peebles's gaze. "I'm giving my full endorsement to the plea bargains and back-scratch deals that my prosecutor is proposing. Ms. Francoeur, whose help has been instrumental in the financial aspects of the investigation, will stay behind with Mr. Rothschild and your team to lead you through the maze of shell corporations and money laundering schemes that Ricky Hedges set up. She'll do this on our nickel."

"Who is she?" Peebles asked, indicating Ronnie. "One of the girls involved with Club Red?"

Tessa coughed while Ronnie laughed out loud. "I'd like to present Officer Veronica Harris from LAPD. She's on point for the investigation into the murder of her partner, Detective Flynn, so we'll expect her to be involved with the prosecution of Ricky Hedges and his personal bodyguard Otis for that crime. Both of these men have been implicated by Jerry Kravitz, and we're confident we'll find corroborating evidence when we get inside Club Red."

"But it was so sweet of you for thinking I was a stripper,"

Ronnie said, with a wink to Peebles. "And me still trying to get my figure back after having a baby."

As the FBI agent squirmed in his chair, Tessa fought for his attention again. "Can I assume that we have a deal?"

Rabani spoke up instead. "Am I to understand that you are willing to turn over the lead on all aspects of the investigation into Club Red? And in return you simply want to ensure that we go easy on some of the federal charges these defendants are facing in exchange for guilty pleas on the state charges?"

"That's it," Carmen agreed.

"I don't get it." Rabani frowned and looked over his notes. "You'd be turning over a huge case. Why? What's in it for you?"

Carmen shrugged. "Many of my constituents don't really understand money laundering and other financial crimes. To them, organized crime is something they encounter when they watch *The Sopranos* on HBO each week. But most of the voters I represent are parents, and they do understand the impact of sex crimes on our community. The state charges revolving around what happened to Kelly Maarten are something that will resonate with them. They will also form the cornerstone of my upcoming efforts to raise the awareness of crimes against women and children."

"So it's a political coup for you," Peebles sneered.

"And a moral one," Carmen snapped back. "In addition to being a hard-fought victory for my prosecutor. You can't take away from her the fact that she put this whole thing together from a chance conversation with a distraught young girl."

Tessa cleared her throat. "I would consider this a victory for Kelly and other girls like her who have been victimized. And if I can't push straight-up sexual assault charges, maybe we can stir up enough outrage so that the laws are changed to better reflect the reality of exploitation today."

"I see. We have a political and legal mission here. That's

good enough for me," Rabani said, then looked at Peebles
for agreement.

"But I would like one more concession from your team. It
shouldn't be too difficult," Tessa said.

"What do you want?" Rabani asked.

"We're willing to give you this case, and let you run with
it. But in return, we want to be able to get Kelly out safely."

"How does this impact us?" Peebles asked.

"We don't want the FBI tagging along, for one," Luke
said.

Tessa spoke quickly. "I know that your next step will be to
serve the owners of Club Red with search warrants and subpoenas," she began. "I'd like to request that you wait a couple of days. We can't afford to have Ricky Hedges tipped off
about how far this investigation has come. If there were to be
a raid and search of the property, I'm worried about our ability to ever discover what's happened to Kelly Maarten."

"What did you plan to do in these next few days?" Rabani
asked.

Luke spoke up again. "I've had someone inside Club Red
for some time, to verify each day that Kelly was safe. But
she hasn't been seen as of a few days ago. We know Ricky
has moved her, and she could be in grave danger, so we have
to move quickly. Jerry Kravitz gave us the name of a woman
who works at Club Red, and said she probably knows where
Kelly has been taken."

"So you want to interview the woman, then go to where
this minor has been taken and free her before Ricky Hedges
is tipped off about the investigation," Rabani said.

"Yes," Tessa said. "It's the only way to guarantee her
safety. She also may know a great deal about what is going
on inside Club Red, which only makes her more vulnerable."

"That's probably true," Peebles said. "But I'm afraid we
can't help you."

"Why?" Tessa asked baldly.

"Because as we speak the task force operational unit is

preparing to raid Club Red. The whole thing will go down in a few hours."

"No."

"I'm very sorry." Rabani seemed sincere, so Luke figured he wouldn't mess up the guy's nice suit by giving him a bloody nose.

Tessa shut her eyes in real despair as she realized that Kelly's time had finally run out.

Chapter 42

Carmen Ramirez looked around at the roomful of silent people. "It looks like we might have a deal breaker, Gil. Isn't there some way to compromise?"

Rabani shook his head regretfully. "We found out two days ago that Ricky Hedges's private pilot filed flight plans for an upcoming trip to Rio de Janeiro. Our concern is that he may attempt to flee the country and live overseas. The revelation that he has millions in cash only underscores that fear."

"He's going to kill her," Tessa said.

"How can you be sure of that?" Peebles asked.

"Tell them," Tessa demanded of Jerry Kravitz. "Tell them what you told us about Kelly's attempts to get a message to me."

Jerry looked uncomfortable. "I don't know what Ricky is going to do. As far as I know, he's never killed anyone before. But he's been crazy in the last few days, thinking his whole empire is being threatened. I heard that Kelly was caught trying to get a letter to Ms. Jacobi through one of the girls. Ricky blew a gasket, and next thing I know he tells me he's leaving Club Red and taking Kelly with him. I didn't get a good feeling about what was going to happen."

"And we know Ricky has already been involved with the recent death of one other person—Ed Flynn," Luke said. "It sounds like he's starting to crack under the pressure."

"All the more reason to raid his operation now, before anyone else gets hurt," Peebles insisted.

"Wait," Tessa said. "It doesn't have to be all or nothing. What if you give us a chance to talk to the woman who may know where Kelly is? We could go in just ahead of the raid and see what she has to say. We can even be inside when the raid goes down."

"No. It's too dangerous," Luke said.

"No more so than the situation Kelly is facing. I haven't come this far just to give Kelly a Christian burial. I want to send her home to her parents alive and well." Tessa looked at Luke and silently pleaded with him to understand.

"You've got until four this afternoon," Peebles finally said. "After that, we will be giving the signal to serve the papers and search the facility."

Rabani cleared his throat. "I'll give you my cell number and advise the team that you will be inside—as of yesterday, we've had a few of our own people in and around the facility, so I'll give them your information as well. I wish I could do more. But we don't want to deal with a bunch of patrons, so we have to do the raid before this evening's rush."

"It's already going to be packed because of March Madness. The college basketball championships," Luke explained at Peebles's blank look. "The games are on East Coast time, so there are bound to be fans inside the club already."

"Is there any way to keep the bust low-key after it happens?" Tessa asked. "I remember last fall that the Coral Room in Miami was raided a couple of days before news ever got out about it. The Feds were able to set up several wiretaps and taped conversations using individuals who were swept up in the bust. These inside people set up colleagues who hadn't been arrested yet and were able to provide valuable information to investigators."

"You've done your homework," Rabani said. "We were modeling our raid on that operation, and planning on getting additional information in the hours or days before the news leaked out. With current antiterror legislation, we can hold suspects incommunicado for twenty-four hours or even longer, which should help keep things quiet."

"Give us twenty-four hours, then," Luke said. "If you keep the bust quiet for that long, I'm sure we can get Kelly back."

"Do you know where Ricky Hedges is?" Peebles asked. "If you do, I think it's only fair to share that information."

"We haven't got a clue," Luke said honestly. "But we may have a better idea once we talk to our source inside Club Red."

"Just as long as we get first crack at Hedges," Peebles said. "He is one defendant that we won't turn over to face state charges first."

"What are you talking about?" Tessa asked. "I thought we'd agreed to share the defendants and our information."

"We'll share the people you've brought here today. But you haven't given us any reason to turn Ricky Hedges over to you first. In fact, you said that the D.A. won't be able to prosecute him for the murder-for-hire incident, and that he fell under the jurisdiction of the AUSA," Peebles said. "To me, that means we get first crack."

"Listen, Tessa. We don't really care who gets Ricky, as long as the man faces the death penalty, right?" Carmen asked.

Tessa did care. Deeply. But she wasn't willing to throw away the entire case just for the chance to stick it to Roderick Hedges of Club Red, Inc.

"How about another deal?" Luke asked. "Possession being nine-tenths of the law, what's say we agree that whoever captures Ricky gets first crack at him?"

"That seems fair," Rabani agreed, confident that Ricky would be turned up in their sweep at the club. "Done."

Peebles wanted to argue, but Luke cut him off. "Come on, where's your faith in the team you've put together, Dieter? If you catch him, you fry him. Pretty simple."

Tessa began to gather her things, hiding her expression. Somehow she knew, with absolute faith, that whatever plan she hatched with Luke would end up with the capture and conviction of Ricky Hedges.

But she would feel a lot better if she had some indication that Kelly would still be alive at that point.

Chapter 43

"I don't know how I'm going to sit on the way over to Club Red," Tessa said as they left Ronnie's house. "This borrowed dress is so tight across my behind that I'm afraid the seams will split wide open if I put any additional pressure on them."

She was wearing one of Ronnie's old party dresses, left over from the prepregnancy days. Luke was in torment, walking behind Tessa down the driveway and trying—sort of—to pull his eyes away from her shapely ass. "Quit tugging. You're torturing me, baby."

Tessa gave him a surprised look, then a slight smile curved her lips. "Any last-minute advice besides not adjusting my clothing? This is my first undercover operation. I don't want to mess up."

They were dressed like wealthy members of the party set, with plans to get inside Club Red and find out where Kelly had been taken. Luke and Tessa were going to play the role of a swinging couple eager for action, and Jerry Kravitz was going to get them in the door so they could talk to Crystal

Bleu without tipping off any employees about what was going to happen to the club later that afternoon.

"It won't exactly be a deep-cover operation, so don't get too excited," Luke said. "The place is going to be raided within half an hour of our arrival, so all we have to do is hold it together long enough to speak with Crystal."

"But what if someone gets suspicious and calls Ricky or something?" Tessa asked. "What if he's even there? I'm afraid he'll recognize me somehow."

"If he is there, the guy is staying out of all the public areas. Relax—MacBeth said the gossip around the club is that Ricky has gone out of town for a few days. I'm not worried about anyone recognizing us, or I wouldn't let you go in there."

She narrowed her eyes at him. "It's not like I need your permission to do my job."

"No, but you do need my help. Don't piss off the consultants, baby, or you could end up doing their job as well as yours. Didn't anyone ever teach you that?"

Tessa picked up her pace on the way to the car, muttering under her breath about high-handed, arrogant, domineering *men*.

Luke watched the irritated jiggle of her butt underneath the skintight silk of her borrowed turquoise dress and grinned.

He just loved it when she got all prickly with him.

Ronnie caught up with them as they stood at the door of the rental limo they were using for transportation. Inside waiting for further instructions, Jerry Kravitz sat sweating heavily in his black sports jacket with white T-shirt underneath. Ronnie would be his escort, to ensure his good behavior and discourage any attempts to escape or spread word about the upcoming bust.

Jerry sat up front, with one of Novak International's employees serving as driver and bodyguard. Luke pointedly closed the privacy shield so he could speak freely and coordinate their plan on the way to Club Red.

"Darn it," Tessa said. "My left boob just slipped down my side."

Luke's head whipped around, and he closely examined Tessa's strapless bodice. All but licking his lips in anticipation, he reached for her. "Allow me . . ."

She smacked his hands away while Ronnie snickered. "It's not my fault you're built along more delicate lines up top than I am, Tessa. You're just lucky that my neighbor had those silicone inserts from Victoria's Secret to fill out the built-in bra on the dress. Although I have to admit you don't need anything to fill out the seat area. I certainly never looked that good in it."

"Amen," Luke murmured, watching Tessa as she reached down into the top of her dress and went fishing around for the warm gel insert that she needed to fill out the bodice. With some judicious stuffing and a discreet shimmy, everything settled back into place. She just hoped it would stay there.

Luke hoped it might slip again, just so he could watch the fishing expedition.

"Okay, one last time. Jerry gets us in the door, then Ronnie goes with him to the bar to watch the game and keep an eye on our backs," Tessa said. "Luke and I will request that Crystal join us somewhere private for a threesome, and then once we get her alone we drop the act and ask her about Kelly."

"When you have the information, give Rabani the signal via cell phone to start the raid," Ronnie continued. "Just remember—signal or not, they are going to come through the doors at twelve minutes past four."

Luke checked his watch. "It's going to be tight, but I think we can swing it. The timing really depends on Crystal and how quickly she goes with us."

"From what Jerry says, she's a pro," Tessa pointed out. "Your job is to look so rich that she won't even hesitate to get you alone."

"Just keep that fur wrap over your cast," Luke advised Tessa. "Or Crystal is going to think I'm a wife beater."

Twenty minutes later, Luke and Tessa were waiting at the bar inside the club. Jerry was next to them, speaking in low tones to the bartender. His job was to set up an opportunity for them to be introduced to Crystal, which would apparently be preceded by a "girl parade."

Tessa wasn't sure what that involved, but took the opportunity to study the infamous club while they waited. Somehow, she'd been expecting something more . . . forbidden, maybe.

But Club Red was decorated in a fairly generic fashion. In fact, it could have passed for a hunting club somewhere, with an interior design dominated by wood and dark carpets and muted earth tones on the walls. She could tell the hardwood flooring and carpet were expensive and made to withstand wear and tear, but she frankly couldn't imagine paying that kind of money for something that would be exposed to stiletto heels, cigarettes, and the inevitable spillage associated with bars and restaurants.

Woven through the wooden interior were many different sizes and shapes of mirrors, as well as comfortable-looking chaises and chairs.

"This place is really nice, honey." Tessa spoke loudly, adopting a Jersey girl accent for her role as Luke's bimbo.

"My man Jerry says we're on the VIP side of the house," Luke said heartily. "I'm sure the part for regular customers doesn't look nearly as nice. Look at all these girls, baby. See anything you like?"

Mindful of the bartender watching her, Tessa adopted a pouty expression and scanned the room. Though it wasn't yet four in the afternoon, there were close to a hundred people lounging in the VIP area—more than half of them women. The Club Red girls were dressed provocatively, though their clothing was of relatively high quality. Considering that they were strippers and prostitutes, anyway.

Tessa let her eyes rest on one beauty, who was seated next to a man old enough to be her grandfather. The girl wore a silk spaghetti strap top and tight black skirt, a fairly simple outfit that she'd spiced up with knee-high black boots and a leather riding crop.

Turning to Luke, Tessa shook her head. "Dominatrix chic doesn't do it for me, Booboo. If you want me to make out with a girl, she's got to be interesting. Exotic."

"You heard the lady, Jer. Who do you recommend?" Luke asked.

Jerry looked at the bartender, who nodded agreement. "I think your lady is going to love Crystal. She's very experienced and loves women as much as she does men. She'll be the perfect teacher, and her look is exotic."

"I'll call the girls and let them know it's time for the parade," the bartender said. "You just pick anyone who catches your eye and go upstairs with her. You won't regret taking a walk on the wild side at Club Red."

Tessa gave Luke a scrunched-nose smile while a shiver of disgust went through her.

Within a few minutes, a group of twelve women made their way slowly down the stairs. Just looking at them, it was easy to see that these were the pride of Ricky's club— Thoroughbreds, as Jerry had called them. They each wore fashionable cocktail dresses that showed a maximum of cleavage and thigh, and their dancers' legs were showcased by perilously high heels.

Tessa was beginning to feel like a frump, at least until Luke slid an arm around her waist and discreetly stroked her hip.

"What do you think, baby? Pick whichever one you want."

She swallowed hard, mindful of the description Jerry had given them of Crystal. The former stripper was easy to spot, with her trademark mane of powdery blue hair and silver accessories.

Though Crystal was only Tessa's age, there was a hardness about her eyes that told Luke she'd been a pro for a long time. Still, he could see that she took a lot of pride in her appearance, and took her role of mentor to the younger girls seriously.

The other women stood to one side of the bar, fussing with their clothes, some of them lighting cigarettes in European-style holders. Obviously, the American Lung Association's message that smoking isn't sexy hadn't made its way inside the club. Crystal walked along the line of girls, smoothing one's hair, encouraging another to stand up straight. Then she turned to the bar with a sultry smile.

Tessa, in the meantime, was feeling vaguely ill at the presentation of the women like prized livestock at the 4-H tent of the county fair.

She knew that Ricky Hedges made money on the retailing of women, as if they were devoid of souls or feelings. But the reality of seeing the girl parade brought that fact home with a resounding thud. The thought of Kelly being groomed to serve men like this was devastating.

As the silence stretched, and people looked expectantly at her, Tessa heard Ronnie knock her drink over with a loud giggle, then an apology. The uncharacteristic act served to bring Tessa back to the present and reminded her that she had a job to do, however distasteful.

"I think I need someone experienced, honey. And I need a lot more champagne before I can go through with it," Tessa said in her breathless Jersey girl voice. "You pick for me, okay?"

In short order, Crystal had been selected, and the other girls moved away to mingle with the remaining VIP customers. Tessa listened as Luke explained to Crystal what he and his "wife" were looking for, but was distracted by a touch on her bare left shoulder. She turned around quickly, barely remembering to keep the fur wrap over the cast on her wrist.

Standing in front of her was a black man who was only a few inches taller than she was, dressed in a football jersey, baseball cap, and gold jewelry. A lot of it.

"Yes?" Tessa asked, looking at the man's thousand-dollar sunglasses, worn despite the dim lighting of the VIP lounge.

"I'm Maurice. My man Julio want to party with you." The man smiled at her, and Tessa's eyes were drawn to his front teeth. He had what looked to be a diamond glued to one of them, and it winked merrily at her as he waited for her answer.

She looked over at Julio and found an Afro-Hispanic man who couldn't be more than eighteen. He wore more gold, a sleeveless basketball jersey, and a cap turned backward on his braided hair.

"Sure thing," Tessa said with a forced smile. She didn't want to cause trouble, and the place was going to be busted soon. Might as well keep the natives happy in the meantime. "First I have to go do something with my man, here, but I'll be back later."

"How long you gonna be gone?"

Long enough to get a restraining order. Tessa smiled vaguely and shrugged. "As long as it takes for my man to get busy."

"Ready to go upstairs?" Luke asked, unaware of the discussion Tessa had been having with Maurice.

"And leave my new friend?" Tessa asked under her breath as she followed him out of the bar.

"Lucky girl," Crystal said. "Julio is one of the biggest names in hip-hop right now. He treats the girls a little rough, but always tips nice. You might not want to start out with someone like him, though. He's into bondage and domination."

"Maybe I should stick to one new experience at a time," Tessa bubbled. She swallowed hard when Crystal took her hand and began a slow, stroking motion as they climbed the carpeted stairs to her private apartments. Giving Luke a panicked look over her shoulder, she caught him gaping.

"Don't worry, I'll take good care of you," Crystal purred. Keeping hold of Tessa's hand, she led the way down the hall. Her hips were tiny—she couldn't have been more than a size 2—but they nevertheless swayed seductively as she approached a private sitting room and opened its door.

Luke rubbed a hand over his mouth to hide his grin when Crystal pressed Tessa's hand against her improbably large breasts and offered to get her a drink.

"Vodka. Double," Tessa squeaked.

When Crystal went to get the drink, Tessa glared at Luke and made an encouraging motion, signaling him to end the ruse before it went any further.

Damn, Luke thought. *Duty calls.*

"Actually, Crystal, we aren't here for a threesome," Luke began.

The other woman looked back over her shoulder. "Cops. I knew it." She sighed.

"Not really," Tessa said. "If you'd just hear me out. I swear we're not here to arrest you."

Crystal took a seat, but warily kept to the edge of her chair.

"Is this a private room?" Luke asked. "Can anyone hear us?"

Crystal nodded, then stood up and beckoned them to follow her through another door. "This is Ricky's private office. He's not here right now, and he lets me in to use the secured phone line when I need to."

"We're here about Kelly," Tessa began, watching as Crystal leaned against a huge mahogany desk. "I work for the District Attorney's Office, but right now I'm here as Kelly's friend. We need your help to find her and get her away from Ricky."

"I should have figured a girl as pretty and sweet as Kelly would cause trouble. I told Ricky to let her go, that the kid would never adjust to this life. Stubborn bastard was sure he could threaten and bully her into staying."

"We've been led to believe that you consider Kelly a friend," Luke said. "Do you want to help her?"

Crystal nodded. "I even told her which girl would take a letter out of the club and mail it for her, but Ricky found out somehow. Luckily, he didn't know I was involved, but he came down on Kelly hard. Too hard. She's just a scared kid, way too soft for this life."

"What about you, Crystal?" Tessa leaned forward earnestly. "Do you want out, too? We can help get you away from prostitution and living your life as some man's *thing*."

Crystal laughed bitterly. "What do you think I used to do in Reno? That's where I met Ricky, you know. A couple of lifetimes ago. I'd just graduated from high school in Carson City, and thought Reno was the center of the universe. I started out dealing cards, but there's more money in stripping. And even more money in being a high-end escort. I'm into shortcuts," she added, with a shrug.

"If you want a fresh start, all you have to do is ask," Tessa said.

"It's not such a bad life," Crystal replied. "The money is great. Ricky treats me okay, and I've got seniority here. I get to meet a lot of famous people, drink nice booze, smoke the finest grass money can buy. Life here is a twenty-four-hour-a-day party, and I'm a party girl. It's a good deal for someone like me."

"But not everyone is cut out for the life," Luke said.

"No," Crystal agreed. "I could see Kelly was destined for better things right away. You ever hear her sing? She's got a real pretty voice."

"So she told you her dreams," Tessa said. "She must trust you. I hope you'll help us find her."

Crystal lit a cigarette she found inside the drawer of Ricky's desk. "Ricky was furious when he found out Kelly had given Tina a letter bound for outside. He didn't even stop to read it or anything, just ripped it to shreds. Then he said he'd had it with her—said she needed to learn to appreciate the things she had instead of whining for what she couldn't have. When he put her in a car with Otis, I figured he'd be taking her to the mountains for a little lesson in obedience."

"And you just let him take her?" Tessa asked.

Crystal shrugged. "What could I do? I've got no power to override him. But I did let Ricky know how much money I thought Kelly could bring in. It was the only way I could think of to make him reconsider hurting her. Look, Ricky has a temper. But he's kind of spineless, you know. He'd never really do damage to Kelly."

"What if she threatened his club?" Luke asked. "What if Kelly stood between him and something he wanted?"

"If Ricky wanted something bad enough, he might get violent. But I don't think so. He's real big on having other people do his dirty work. I think Kelly is still okay."

"Why do you say that?" Tessa asked.

"Because if someone is going to do an unpleasant job for Ricky, that someone would be Otis. And I heard Ricky promising Otis he could stay at the Reno Casino for a couple of days, on Ricky's nickel. Kelly is in the area with them—I saw her get in the car. There's no way Ricky would do anything to Kelly in his favorite casino, that place is like his church. And there would be too many witnesses."

"So the plan was to go up and play some cards at the hotel?" Luke asked.

"Sort of," Crystal replied. "Ricky also has a cabin up in the area, between Lake Tahoe and Reno, actually. It's very isolated, in the mountains. If Ricky were to take Kelly there, then I'd be worried."

"What's to stop him from going there after he sees the sights in Reno?" Tessa asked.

"Nothing. I mean, that was their plan, I think. Ricky's got a real connection to the cabin near Tahoe. He goes there to think, to solve problems, to woo a new girlfriend. Also—" Crystal paused to wet her lips.

"What? Has anyone ever gone there and disappeared?" Tessa asked.

"No, it's not that. I think that's where Ricky keeps his stash. It's supposed to be a big secret, you know, but I heard Ricky is sitting on a lot of money. Millions, even."

"Why would he advertise something like that?" Luke asked skeptically.

"He doesn't, that's why I think it's true," Crystal said. "No one knows where that cabin is except Ricky. There's no address."

"What's the closest town to the cabin?" Tessa asked.

"Reno and Lake Tahoe. I told you, it's out there."

"And you think he's taking Kelly to that place?" Luke asked.

"I don't know. All's I know is that *he* is going there at the end of this trip to Reno. He's probably got some cash to drop off or something."

"Crystal, do you understand that Ricky in all likelihood is planning on getting rid of Kelly—permanently?" Luke asked bluntly.

Crystal looked confused. "He really isn't like that. He's is like the school bully, you know. But he's never killed anyone. He talks big and all, but he's closer to Hugh Heffner than Jack the Ripper. He likes refined things, and this club is his baby. Why would he do anything to risk that?"

"Exactly our point," Tessa said. "He'd do just about anything to protect it. Right now, Kelly is a threat to him."

Crystal chewed on an acrylic nail extension as she thought. "I suppose he could be dangerous if enough money was involved. Or if someone else was pushing him."

"I heard Papa Ianelli has been trying to deepen their business relationship," Luke said.

"Sure," Crystal nodded. "Ricky wants to expand his operations to Reno and Las Vegas, which would require help from the Ianellis. I heard of them even before I moved to California."

"You said Ricky was going to the Reno Casino, then his cabin in the mountains. How do we find this place?" Tessa asked. "We can't sit around and assume Ricky is harmless, not when he's holding Kelly against her will."

"I've never been to the cabin. But when Otis had to go there on his own last year to drop off something, Ricky gave him a set of numbers. I have no idea how these helped, but—"

"They're probably GPS coordinates," Luke said. "Do you know where they are?"

"Right here, on the inside of his desk drawer," Crystal said. "He keeps his computer password and bank PIN code there as well." She rolled her eyes.

Luke ripped out the piece of paper taped into the drawer, then turned to the blue-haired woman standing uncertainly at the edge of the desk. A quick check of the clock confirmed that the task force would be coming through the door momentarily.

"Listen, Crystal. The FBI is going to raid Club Red tonight—in a few minutes, actually."

"Oh, man."

"They're not here to charge the girls, but I'm afraid everyone is going to be arrested and held for a few days. Just do whatever the agents tell you, and you'll be out soon," Luke said. "Don't say anything about what you've told us tonight. Just say that you don't know where Ricky is for sure, and we left after talking to you and finding that out. Can you do that?"

Crystal nodded with a little grin. "It won't be the first time I've lied to the police."

"We'll make sure they know how helpful you've been. Believe it or not, we're on the same side," Tessa said, giving Luke a frown.

He shrugged. "We just need a head start to find Kelly. I'm sorry about needing to arrest you, but we have to make sure no one can alert Ricky about the raid."

Crystal smiled ruefully. "Okay, I guess. But you may be interested to know that we all have instructions to call the same lawyer in the event of a bust. The guy's crooked, and in on everything that's going on at Club Red. If you want Ricky to be kept in the dark until you get to Reno, you'd better make sure no one calls the Krugman law firm."

"Thanks," Luke said. "That information will help a lot. I'm going to give you my business card. Show it to Gil Rabani, tell them you have information about the Club Red lawyer, and he'll see to it that you're treated like royalty. Just don't say anything else about Ricky, okay?"

"We'll call him to make sure you're treated well," Tessa assured her. She took Luke's business card before he could hand it to Crystal and wrote something across the back.

Crystal took the card and read the writing, then tipped her head back and laughed with real humor.

Get out of jail free.

"Thanks, miss. I hope Kelly's all right when you find her."

"Me, too." Tessa's head jerked up at the sound of orders being shouted over women's screams downstairs. "It's showtime. Let's go get Kelly."

"Follow my lead, okay?" Luke said as he pulled her down the hallway. "We can't let on that we know where Ricky is."

"I got that, but is it—" Tessa began.

"Our best chance to get Kelly back safely is to go in alone. No cops, no police, no SWAT team. We have to be able to move quickly, change plans, and make decisions in the field. If we're dealing with four different agencies, multiple jurisdictions, and competing egos we can't do that."

"What about Ronnie?" Tessa asked faintly. How could she lie to her friend?

"We hope she doesn't see us as we leave."

Tessa was silent as they made they're way down the stairs, stopping several times to confirm their identity with the federal agents swarming the premises. Once they got outside, she pulled Luke to a stop. "I'm not sure if I can do this."

"Which part?"

"Lying to Ronnie. And the police. And my boss—"

Luke turned her toward him and gently grasped her shoulders. When he spoke, his voice was low and serious. "Do you believe I'd ever do anything that would put you or Kelly at risk?"

"No. Never," she said with absolute conviction.

"Then I need you to work with me on this, baby. I've done a lot of extractions in the past, in a lot of different ways. You have to believe me when I say it will go down better without involving any major branches of law enforcement."

"I know I said that getting Kelly back was the most important thing, but . . . what you're planning might be illegal. Certainly it's unethical. How on earth are we going to pull it off?"

"Quickly," Luke said. "The clock is ticking now that the bust has occurred. We run the risk of the media hearing about this and reporting it on the news in the next few days. Even though the officers here are all in plain clothes, and there are no marked cars outside, someone is going to spill the beans soon. It will only be a matter of time before word makes its way to Ricky."

"And you truly believe that bringing in the police or FBI would limit our ability to move quickly?" Tessa asked.

"I know it. And then there's the fact that their priority will be Ricky. Ours is Kelly. I don't want to get into a situation where that girl is sacrificed to their desire to make a big bust. We already warned Rabani and Peebles that we were going to do things our way. This won't be a surprise to them, trust me. I need you to trust me, baby."

She looked into his eyes and thought about all they'd been through together. When all was said and done, making the decision was easy. "Okay, let's go to Reno."

Chapter 44

Reno, Nevada
Wednesday night, March 17

Tessa stood on the balcony of a hotel suite in the Reno Casino and looked out at the rolling hills surrounding the small city with big ambitions. The "strip" section of town could have been Las Vegas, for all the flashing lights, glowing marquees, and pedestrian traffic.

But the Reno skyline was abbreviated, and the town had only a fraction of its more famous sister city's population. Instead of being surrounded by searing desert, Reno was located at five thousand feet, not far from the crystal blue depths of Lake Tahoe. The wilds of California's Sierra Nevada Mountains were a stone's throw from the luxurious casino where she would stay the night with Luke and his team until they could get Kelly back.

According to Luke's research, the GPS coordinates for Ricky Hedges's cabin placed it squarely in the middle of the rugged Sierra Nevadas. They knew that getting Kelly back was not going to be an easy proposition.

Luke had called a local hunting and backpacking guide earlier in the evening, and the man had told them there were no accessible roads around the cabin. Rugged backcountry roads could be traveled using a four-wheel-drive vehicle, but the final two miles of approach to the cabin required trekking in on foot, using all-terrain vehicles, or driving in on snowmobiles, depending on the season.

Since large, heavy snowflakes had been falling steadily since their arrival at Reno's tiny airport a few hours ago, it seemed like snowmobiles would be the only way to get to Ricky's mountain hideaway. There was a base of six feet on the ground at the higher elevations, thanks to a late-winter storm that had come through ten days ago. The temperatures hadn't been above freezing since.

"It's hard to believe that just a few hours ago we were in sunny Los Angeles." Luke came up behind her and looked out the window. He raised his hands to massage the knots of tension from her shoulders. With a sigh, she let her head fall back against his chest, knowing that it was pointless to be so taut and ready for action right now.

Part of the stress was due to guilt about dodging Ronnie and the FBI when they left Club Red. Luke had let her make a call to her friend from a pay phone, saying that they were all right and following a new lead that might be a dead end. Tessa had promised to update her the next day, and hoped that they would already have Kelly out by then.

But after surveying the area surrounding Ricky's cabin, it had been agreed by the entire team that trying to get the girl out without detailed planning would be foolish.

So despite the urgency screaming through her system, and the knowledge that as the hours went by Ricky might discover that his club had been raided, they would have to wait until the following evening to attempt a rescue.

He stopped the massage on her shoulders and dropped his chin down to rest on her soft hair. "I know you wanted to go in tonight and get Kelly. But we're not even sure she's at the cabin. And if we don't plan the extraction operation carefully, we could end up doing more harm than good. Mac-

Beth and Stone are getting gear together to scout the property and set up our escape plan."

"I know," Tessa said. "And we meet the hunting guide tomorrow morning at eight to pick his brains on the best roads to take in and out. That will leave all day tomorrow to set things up, rent equipment, and so forth. But I'm still concerned about news leaking before we're ready to move. The clock is ticking."

"I talked to Rabani an hour ago, and he assured me that everyone swept up in the raid is being held incommunicado. The task force operations units cut the phone lines to Club Red before they went in, and they were able to disrupt cell service to that area for a couple of hours. It's an isolated property, and no one was rubbernecking as the vans pulled into the parking garage beneath, so it looks like we're okay."

"Do you think he knows what we're doing, or where we are?"

Luke shook his head, the point of his stubbly chin ruffling her loose blond hair. "After the deal we made regarding Ricky, the AUSA and FBI both realize we aren't going to share any information with them. I'm sure they have no idea where we are, and by the time they figure it out, we'll have Kelly back here."

"It feels wrong, even though I understand your reasons for wanting to do this with a small team of people you know you can trust."

"Listen, baby. When the army or Marines have a delicate, time-sensitive operation, do they send in a battalion to do it?"

"No," she whispered. "Special Operations forces get the call. They're the new military paradigm since Afghanistan and Iraq."

"There's a reason. It works. I'm not worried about jeopardizing the legal case, because we have guilty pleas from most of the players involved. With that in mind, Kelly is my one and only concern. Of all the players out there working on this case, I'm comfortable that my team is the one best suited to getting this done quickly and cleanly."

"I trust you. I do," she repeated when he was silent. "I wouldn't be here without that trust, and you know it. I'm just . . . turning my back on a lifetime of working to support the system, and letting the system work the way it's supposed to. It's a foreign concept to me to circumvent it."

"Don't worry, I'm getting pretty damned good at that part," Luke said with a light squeeze. "There are a lot fewer variables to control this way."

"The only important one is Ricky," Tessa agreed.

"He's in town gambling, thinking that everything is going as he planned. No one has seen Otis, which means he's probably at the cabin with Kelly, keeping her out of the way."

"I don't like the idea of Kelly being alone with someone who works as Ricky Hedges's loyal bodyguard," Tessa said. "Let alone the man who probably ran down Ed."

"I felt the same way, so I talked to Jerry about it. He told me something that I think will ease your mind just a little."

"What?"

"Otis is gay. Ricky found him at a bodybuilding competition a couple of years ago, so he's a big strapping guy. But not interested in women—which is probably why Ricky sent him ahead with Kelly. Apparently, Ricky was worried about sweet Kelly manipulating men into letting down their guard, as she did when she tried to sneak the note out with one of the girls."

"She's a smart kid," Tessa said, with a half smile.

Luke removed his hands from around Tessa and stretched. "It's just before midnight. We've got about eight hours before our next meeting, so I'm going to take a shower and crash. You should try to get some sleep."

"I think I'll watch TV in bed for a while. I'm too keyed up to sleep. I wish we'd had time to grab some things before running to the airport—like a good book."

"There will be time tomorrow to get some ski gear, warm clothes, and any other supplies we'll need. The hotel brought a bunch of toiletries up, so grab whatever you need." Luke gestured to several bags of items on the console by the suite's front door.

"At over five thousand dollars a night for this suite, we've paid for whatever's in there," Tessa grumbled.

"I know it was expensive, but we need the extra bedroom and living space. And this is Ricky's favorite club, so being here will help keep an eye on him. We just have to stay out of sight unless we know exactly where Ricky is." Luke absently kissed her forehead, then went into the bathroom. The thundering sound of water soon came through the closed door, accompanied by a cheerful tune.

Apparently Luke was a whistler in the shower. Who knew? Tessa shook her head as she considered that there were a lot of things about him that she didn't know.

But so far, discovering them had been kind of fun.

Refusing to examine the matter any more deeply than that, Tessa turned on the TV and selected a news channel. With the sound turned low, she went over to the bags of toiletries and rifled through them. In the last bag, she found a small cardboard box with the picture of a couple embracing on a sunlit beach.

Ribbed for her pleasure. With raised eyebrows, Tessa tapped the box against her palm and wondered how to slip the bellboy a twenty without either one of them dying of embarrassment.

She heard the water shut off in the bathroom and hurriedly set the box of condoms on the table in plain view. With a barely suppressed grin, she waited for Luke to come out of the steamy room.

He strode out with wet hair and moisture condensed on his broad torso. Tessa visually followed the arrow of hair from the pads of his muscled chest down to the knotted white towel around his waist. The widely scattered, puckered scars left from his encounter with a shotgun blast never failed to jolt her—not because they were ugly, but because he'd somehow survived such a grisly injury.

Luke caught her staring. "What?"

"Nothing," she mumbled, with a sudden burst of shyness.

It was one thing to contemplate jumping the man by surprise. It was another thing entirely to actually do it.

Tessa escaped to the bathroom for a little pep talk while she brushed her teeth.

You are a mature and attractive woman. What's more, he's not going to say no. So get to it!

She fluffed her pale hair around her face and held a cool cloth to her burning cheeks, telling herself it was time for her to make some moves. She couldn't sit back and let him do everything in this relationship.

Or whatever this *thing* between the two of them could be called. Luke was so generous with himself—he deserved to know that he wasn't alone in terms of feeling the pull between them.

With a deep breath, she yanked the bathroom door open and went into the suite's bedroom. Luke was wearing one of the other robes from the closet and was pulling on a pair of dark socks in the chilly air of the hotel room.

No! Not the socks!

Tessa grinned as she contemplated how to incorporate everyday issues like cold toes into the seduction she had in mind. Somehow, it was just easier in the movies, where no doubt the air on the sets was heated to an agreeable seventy-four degrees.

Done with the socks, Luke leaned against the high-backed upholstered chair and rested his head with his eyes closed for a moment. He had no idea that he was being stalked.

"Tired?" Tessa asked softly.

Luke's eyes popped open and widened when he saw her standing right in front of him, close enough to touch. But it wasn't her proximity that made his nostrils flare, it was the heated look in her eyes, which were positively navy in the subdued light of the room.

And even more than her eyes, it was the warm blush on her cheeks and the way her lips parted to compensate for her altered breathing that brought him to attention.

"Yes and no. What did you have in mind?" Luke asked. He took both of her hands in his, stroking gently around the edges of her cast. Surprised to feel a slight tremor, he realized she was nervous.

With his heartbeat kicking up in anticipation, Luke leaned back in the chair and continued to stroke his thumbs over her captive fingers.

Tessa looked into his eyes and saw nothing but acceptance of her, along with frankly lustful eagerness. That supplied the extra confidence for her to shift down until she was sitting in Luke's lap and facing him, practically nose to nose. A mere second later, they were lip to lip as she slowly pressed her mouth to his in a series of soft kisses. The tip of her tongue slid along Luke's mouth, she realized he was smiling, and she was lost. The tone of the kiss changed to hunger and passion and shared greed.

He dropped her hands and wrapped his arms around her, bringing her into gasping contact with his body from groin to mouth. The only thing keeping them apart was the plush cotton of their robes.

Tessa opened her mouth more fully on Luke's and reached behind her with her right arm to grab one of his hands as her tongue dueled with his. Breathing rapidly against his mouth, she guided his captive hand inside her robe and pressed it against a silken breast.

Luke took it from there.

His hand was warm against her, and the heat spread from where he touched to the rest of her body. Rubbing his thumb gently around her taut pink nipple, Luke gently kneaded and massaged the delicate weight of her breast with his fingers. He brought his other hand into play and used it to untie her robe, pushing the lapels back so that her upper body was exposed. Another tug and some shifting of her weight, and the robe was on the floor. Then Luke used both palms on her, shaping and fondling and caressing her goose-bumped flesh.

She was so delicate, Luke thought. So pretty. Confident in her work, yet sometimes shy as a woman. Tough, persistent, stubborn, softhearted. She intrigued him.

Tessa rocked unconsciously against him in a move that incited both of them. She freed his mouth and tugged on his head, while at the same time arching backward. She felt Luke lean down and take as much of her breast into his mouth as he could, using teeth and tongue and breath in an erotic combination that had her thighs clenching tight around his hips in response.

As he moved to her other breast and treated it to the same tender-rough caresses, Luke enjoyed the flush of red that was climbing from Tessa's chest toward her neck. She squirmed against his straining erection again, and he couldn't control the almost pained sound of anticipation that came from his throat.

"What do you want me to do, baby?" Luke pressed her breasts tightly together and breathed the question against the resulting cleavage, then rubbed his face back and forth on her soft skin. "Say it."

Tessa could only moan and press more tightly against him as she rocked into his hardness. She just wanted to hold him, wrap her arms around him and squeeze against him with all her strength. Sure that she was going to combust, she grabbed at one of his hands. With more desperation than seductive precision, she plunged it into the moist, heated space between their lower bodies.

In hushed silence, his fingers gently sifted through dark blond curls to trace soft, slick folds. The edges of Tessa's vision dimmed to gray for a moment until she remembered to breathe. Despite his need, he was tender and loving with her body—just as he was with her outside of the bedroom. The

thought made her throat tighten for a moment before she
swallowed the lump and ran her lips over his face in a series
of fluttering caresses.

The chair creaked ominously beneath them as Luke re-
adjusted her feet high around him, spreading them so they
ran along the arms of the chair and opened her to him fully.
Then he hooked the sturdy ottoman closer with his feet and
used it to brace his own legs, groaning when the motion
shifted her against his aching cock. Finally, he gently
pushed her away from him so he could see her without restrictions. Before she knew it, Tessa was spread wide and reclining back against Luke's hair-roughened thighs.

Really, the man seemed to delight in putting her in the
most exposed of positions when they made love. He gave
her a charming smile before she could think to protest.

But that thought flew from her head when Luke used one
hand to slowly, possessively stroke her from neck to stomach, then back up again. Muscles trembling faintly with anticipation, he shifted and pulled the bottom half of his robe
apart, so it no longer acted as a barrier between them. Tessa
lay back against his legs and watched from under heavy lids
as Luke's erection thrust up between them, its pulsing heat
mere inches from her body.

Saying her name softly, he brought a hand to her mouth
and ran the sensitive pads of his first two fingers around her
lips. Obeying the heated request in his hazel eyes, she
opened her mouth to kiss and lick his fingers.

He groaned when she took his fingers into her mouth to
lave and suck them. Hard. His cock twitched visibly in response, and Tessa's eyes widened in anticipation. Then they
closed in delight when Luke pulled his wet fingers from her
mouth and slid them straight down to the entrance of her
body.

Though her lids were closed, she knew he watched himself stroking her, dipping into her wet heat, then sliding up
to circle her clitoris before dropping back down again. The

sensation of being consumed and explored at the same time was unbearably intimate. Tessa's breath hitched in, then came out in a long, low cry when Luke finally slid his fingers deep inside her.

"So tell me about this famous G-spot," Luke teasingly whispered as he stroked. "Where is that puppy?"

"God!" Tessa cried out in response to his touch. "No idea. Look for it. There," she moaned brokenly, and arched against him.

"You sure?" He returned to circle the area again.

"Mmmmm," she said, rocking against his hand and fingers, no longer capable of speaking.

The sweet, slippery teasing continued until she lay arched and panting in his lap, feeling her muscles pull taut in anticipation of the climax he'd carefully built up.

"Come, baby. I want to feel you come right now." Luke's teeth were clenched and his forehead was covered with sweat as he concentrated on the woman spread before him in complete abandon.

With a throaty sound of ecstasy, she let go and felt the waves of orgasm crash over her like a hot downpour of tropical rain, washing her away. Her body shuddered again and again, and the hidden warmth between her legs contracted around Luke's fingers in a way that nearly undid him.

For a moment, there was nothing but the sound of rapid breathing and the hotel room's heater kicking in. Then Tessa heard a door close and the murmured voices of MacBeth and Stone through the connecting door.

The door that was about five feet away from where she was performing sexual acrobatics in a chair with Luke.

In a heartbeat, he felt all of her muscles tense, and she looked at him with such an expression of horror that he chuckled out loud. She was so tightly wrapped sometimes—a trait which he delighted in loving her out of—that Luke knew she'd be hesitant about continuing in their current location.

"Don't worry, they'll probably just think we're watching hotel room porn," Luke whispered.

Tessa's gave him the Look even as she bit her lips to keep from grinning. She knew when she was being teased, and he was letting her have it for being uptight. Okay, so maybe it did take her a while to unwind about having sex with him. But she did eventually get there, or else she wouldn't be in her current position.

Actually, it was kind of fun letting loose with Luke now that she finally trusted him enough to do so. Too bad he didn't realize what he'd unleashed when he'd coaxed her sexpot genie out of the bottle. He would, though.

She smiled and laughed in a way that told Luke he was in serious trouble. Suddenly, her fingers began to move down from his shoulders to stroke his stomach. Then she latched gently on to the jutting flesh that still pulsed between their bodies. Before he could say anything, she had wrapped both hands tenderly around him, careful to keep the edge of the cast away from his skin. She made several quick, pumping movements that wrung a loud groan of pleasure out of his throat before he remembered his employees next door.

There was a stunned silence through the connecting door, which was broken when Tessa bent down to wrap her lips around the head of his cock. He gasped out loud and locked his hands in her hair to pull her away. But she wouldn't move, except for her tongue and lips and . . . He groaned again, quietly this time. She laughed low in her throat, and the feel of that vibration against his painfully sensitive flesh undid him.

With a hissing sound, he shifted and scooped up a now-giggling Tessa. He flung her over his shoulder and secured her with a proprietary hand on her bare bottom, then headed to the far end of the suite—away from the connecting door. He paused to turn up the sound of the TV to cover her breathless laughs, then made his way to the oversized shower for the second time that evening. He barely remembered to grab the box of condoms and a plastic bag to cover her wrist before he shut the bathroom door and locked it behind them.

He turned on the water, peeled off his socks, and muscled her inside the stall. Soon, Tessa was no longer laughing. In fact, she was the one clenching her teeth and biting Luke's shoulder to stop the sounds of ecstasy from traveling any farther than the warm, foggy confines of the luxury bathroom.

Chapter 45

Reno, Nevada
Thursday evening, March 18

The planning phase of Novak International's extraction operation continued into the next day. They would be moving to rescue Kelly within a few hours, and yet Tessa wasn't sure if she could stand another minute of the anticipation.

She sat alone in the suite, laying out the clothes she would wear that night. Four times. With a sigh, she went into the living room and turned on the TV. But she didn't find anything to hold her attention and resumed pacing.

Since she couldn't take her angst out on Luke at the moment—in ways that were both new and addictive as far as she was concerned—she decided to take a turn around the casino floor. She picked up her cell phone to call Luke and let him know what she was planning.

"We're sorry, but your phone does not have roaming privileges in this service provider's area. If you would like to place a call, please enter a credit card number now, then press pound."

Tessa looked at her ultrathin, very expensive cell phone in disgust. Apparently, CalCell didn't have an agreement with the local wireless company to allow her automatic out-of-area rights in Reno. So what good did it do her to have this wafer-thin piece of electronics, if she couldn't use it when she needed to?

Looking around, she decided there was no way she was going to pay bloated roaming rates when a local phone call was only a quarter from the room phone. Better yet, she could call Luke's cell number for free if she used her long-distance calling card.

Muttering under her breath, Tessa picked up the hotel phone and dug around in her purse for her seldom-used telephone card.

"Hey, it's me. I was thinking of going downstairs and buying some long underwear before we leave. If I have to sit in the car like the damn family dog, I want to be warm while I'm doing it," Tessa said.

"I thought we were done arguing about this." Luke sighed.

"Huh," she said. She was still smarting about Luke's decision to allow her only as far as a few miles from Ricky Hedges's cabin. Tessa would be waiting in the weather-proofed Suburban they'd rented, like some kind of flunky getaway driver who couldn't be trusted to carry off the heist. The rest of the team would go forward on foot to the cabin to effect Kelly's rescue.

While it was only logical that she should be the one to stay behind, since she had no SWAT or hostage-rescue training, it still irked her. And she wasn't above letting Luke know it, even if logic had led her to agree to the indignity of waiting in the car while everyone else did the real work.

After all, it was either that or wait in the hotel—as Luke had pointed out. As he pointed out one more time right then.

"Do you get carpet burns from dragging your knuckles on the ground all day long like the early hominid that you are? Mr. Cro-Magnon Man."

Luke snickered, not offended in the slightest. Of course, he'd won the argument, so he could afford to laugh off her insults. Just wait until she had him spread before her on a bed again. She'd show him a thing or two.

"Anyway, I just wanted to run the idea of shopping by you," Tessa said after a long silence. "You said Ricky was checking out, so I figured I'd be safe."

"Probably," Luke agreed. "But do me a favor and keep on your ski cap and sunglasses. And wear a bulky sweater so no one recognizes that amazing ass of yours."

"You're just saying that because MacBeth is standing right there, aren't you?" Tessa asked. Luke was still trying to get back at her for teasing him within earshot of his employees. No doubt they'd given him hell for whatever they'd overheard through the connecting door last night.

"Can I help it if you find me irresistible?" Luke asked. "But yes, MacBeth is here. He and I are picking up some, ah, gear. And we're running through the plans one final time, so everything goes smoothly. In about ten hours, Kelly will be safe and warm in our suite at the hotel."

"Good," Tessa said huskily. "I'm so glad you sent Stone out to reconnoiter this morning. It was a real relief to hear that he'd spotted Kelly in the cabin and that she seemed to be unhurt."

"Which one of these do you want to bring, Luke?" Mac-Beth's voice traveled clearly over the phone line, telling Tessa that she was needlessly monopolizing his time. He should be working out last-minute hitches in their plan, not holding her hand.

"Call me when you get back to the room, okay?" Luke asked.

"I'll try. But my cell phone doesn't have roaming privileges here, so it's a real pain to make calls at all."

"Then send me a text message," Luke said. "Those often get through because they only require a fraction of a second of airtime."

"Cool," Tessa said. "I'll remember that. I'll see you guys later."

She hung up and grabbed the winter clothing, dutifully wrapping herself in the warm layers in an effort to pad her figure and hide her blond hair. She went downstairs to the arcade shops that took up the entire subterranean lower levels of the hotel. In addition to several expensive clothing boutiques, salons, and jewelry stores, there was an outdoor outfitter that should carry the thermal underwear she wanted to buy.

After several minutes of browsing, she made a selection and went to the register. She added earmuffs and gloves to her purchases as she waited in the checkout line. It was sweltering inside the heated store with all her winter clothing on, so Tessa looked casually around before pulling off her brand-new parka and warm hat, items MacBeth had purchased for her earlier that day.

At least it seemed like the stuff would keep her warm while she was waiting in the car later that night.

She'd take her silver linings where she found them.

"You had enough gambling, boss?"

Ricky Hedges turned away from the craps table where he'd indulged in a little last-minute play after checking out of the Reno Casino's hotel. He checked his watch and agreed that it was time to leave.

"Yeah, Bobby. Let's get the truck and head out to the cabin. I don't want to have to ride the snowmobiles in a blizzard if we can avoid it—the trip is already long and cold as it is."

"You complain," the other man replied as he grabbed Ricky's rolling suitcase, "but you love that place."

Ricky companionably cuffed his long-term assistant as they walked out of the casino. "I do. It's where I do all my thinking. I've got a lot of business decisions to make, and some peace and quiet will be very welcome."

"To say nothing of that hot little piece waiting for you," Bobby said.

"She's very pretty, yes. Even though she's not my type. I've never gone for jailbait, but as a businessman I've learned to give the customer what he wants. Hopefully, she will be feeling more, ah, grateful now that she's had an opportunity to think things over. I think she can make us a lot of money in the future if she gets with the program."

"Hopefully," Bobby chorused. "I've got everything packed in the truck, just waiting for your bag and stuff."

Ricky nodded, then paused in the hallway that led to the underground parking garages as his cell phone rang. He answered, turning toward the glass fronts of the boutique shops to better hear what was being said to him.

"What do you mean you found tracks? Like a bear or something?" Ricky asked.

Bobby looked at a display holding a hundred-thousand-dollar diamond-and-sapphire necklace while his boss talked.

"Just keep an eye on things until I get there," Ricky ordered. "Make sure the cellar is locked and the alarm is activated. And keep that girl out of sight."

Bobby looked up as Ricky called his name. "Come on, we have to get to the cabin. It looks like there have been people trespassing on the property. It's probably nothing, but I'll feel better once I check it out." Ricky headed down the hall toward the truck waiting in the parking garage, cursing at having to personally handle yet another potential crisis.

Tessa came out of the outdoor outfitter's shop, trying to juggle packages, her bulky parka, and the hat she'd taken off in order to keep from overheating in the warm store. She stopped in the hallway outside the shop's entrance to adjust her things and put the hat and jacket back on, mindful of Luke's warning to keep her hair covered.

She'd just slipped the dark fleecy fabric over her head and grabbed her sunglasses out of the neckline of her sweater when the ringing of a telephone caused her to look up.

She was sure that everyone around could hear the sound

of her heart rate doubling when she recognized Ricky Hedges standing not fifty feet away, talking on his cell phone. At least she thought the man looked just like the pictures of Ricky that Luke had put in the case file. After two horrified glances she was sure of it.

He was supposed to have checked out. What was he doing in the hallway chatting on the phone?

Ricky turned with the phone to his ear and seemed to look right at her.

With a gasp, Tessa turned to her right and started walking. Had Ricky seen her before she'd managed to get her hat and sunglasses on? More importantly, had he recognized her? Presumably if he'd had people tailing her—and if he'd tried to have her killed he must know what she looked like.

All she could do was hope that he wasn't a suspicious kind of guy.

She continued walking down the extended hallway, trying unsuccessfully to catch a glimpse of what was happening behind her. Finally, she paused as if to look at a sweater displayed in one of the storefronts—an act that gave her the chance to peek down the hallway in the other direction.

All she saw was Ricky, looking angry and purposeful, striding quickly right toward her.

Tessa abandoned the shop front and all attempts at casualness, picking up her pace with the hope of escaping into the parking garage. She pushed open the heavy metal door and paused to pull it shut behind her, wincing at the scream of the hydraulic hinges.

Looking frantically around, she saw no one to help, no other exits, and very few places to hide. Since she was right by the entry to the building, all the parking spaces around her were reserved for handicapped use—and almost every one was empty. There was only an oversized gold Cadillac and a dark blue pickup truck to hide behind.

Tessa ran toward the pickup, figuring she could hide in the bed in back until Ricky and friend gave up and left. As she rounded the vehicle, she found that the tailgate was open, and the whole back was covered by an all-weather tarp that was folded back at one corner to allow access to the storage area.

With seconds to spare, Tessa threw her stuff into the darkness underneath the tarp and dove in after it.

She heard the heavy metal door open, and footsteps echoed loudly in the parking garage. She listened, but didn't think they sounded like running footsteps. There was no shouting or sounds of a search.

With a deep breath of relief, Tessa told herself that Ricky and his friend would soon give up looking for her—if indeed they'd seen her at all. Maybe she had overreacted completely.

That relief lasted about ten seconds, which was the amount of time it took for two sets of footsteps to approach the truck.

She held herself frozen as a pair of blue-jeans-clad legs appeared in the narrow gap of the open tailgate. An overnight-style bag was hefted into view, then shoved into a space not two feet from where she was huddled. Another followed seconds later. A thick jacket was then thrown over the baggage, and the tailgate was closed with a metallic *thunk* that echoed in the quiet garage.

She watched in real despair as the heavy-duty tarp was flipped closed and, from the sound of it, fastened securely so it wouldn't flap in the wind.

"Don't worry, Ricky. We'll be there in an hour or so. Otis can hold things down at the cabin until then."

Tessa held her breath, but there was no reply. Just the sensation of doors being opened and closed on the truck where she had sought refuge.

The truck was in a handicapped spot! They're not disabled, the bastards.

Tessa could not believe what she'd done. Not only had she overreacted and run at the thought that Ricky might have seen her, but she'd panicked and hidden in the one vehicle in the entire parking garage that belonged to him.

Jammed into the space between several boxes and the small suitcases, Tessa gingerly maneuvered around until she could reach the seams of the tarp. She pressed up against the canvas material, but it was securely fastened. There wasn't even enough space for her to wedge her hand out and try to open the tailgate.

Hell.

She was trapped.

Chapter 46

Reno, Nevada
Thursday evening, March 18

"Hey, Stoner," Luke greeted his employee with his customary nickname. "Any problems with the rental?"

"Nope. We're gassed up and good to go. I even managed to stock it with a first-aid kit, some snacks, and a couple of warm blankets. Figured the kid might need 'em when we get her to the car."

Luke nodded his approval. He and MacBeth were just coming out of a lodge belonging to the hunting guide who had been helping them become familiar with the land surrounding Ricky's cabin. They had bought topographical maps of the area from the guide, as well as snowshoes and pack gear suitable for the frigid, snowy night.

They had also arranged to borrow several rifles, automatic pistols, and a flare gun from the guide, who had been told only that they were going in to end a case of custodial interference of a minor girl by a man who wished to abuse her sexually.

The great thing about Nevada, Luke thought, is that people weren't inclined to wring their hands and wait for the police to help out in such a situation. Once the guide had heard that a teenage girl and sexual abuse were involved, he had been only too eager to lend Luke and his team the firepower they would need to carry out the mission tonight. He hadn't even waited to receive the fax from Novak International with details regarding the licenses and permits necessary for Luke and his team to carry concealed weapons.

He'd just handed over his "varmint guns" and asked Luke what else he could do to help.

They'd agreed that the guide would spend some time in the forest near the far edge of Ricky's property line that night, playing cards with his brother and waiting on-call to see if additional assistance would be required by Luke and his team. The guide's commercial Hummer would be hauling a trailer with several snowmobiles, which could be brought in like the cavalry if it all went from sugar to shit.

Luke sincerely hoped it wouldn't, because he hated to rely on unknown elements and outsiders for help if his team got in trouble. But it never hurt to have a backup plan.

"Good deal on the rig, Stoner. Let's pack it tight and go back to the hotel. I want to pick up Tessa and get some chicken-fried steak in our systems before we head out."

"Pop the locks, would you?" MacBeth asked. "I'll throw our gear in the back."

The three men arranged the gear in the cargo area of the Chevy Suburban to their satisfaction. Luke paused as his cell phone gave a long beep followed by two short chimes, a code that indicated he'd received a text message.

"It's probably Tessa," Luke said. "No one else ever uses the paging feature to get in touch with me."

"She's probably sending you a dirty message—ooh, baby, do it again," Stone said, mimicking the voice of a woman in passion with surprising skill.

"Can I help it if my woman can't get enough of me?" Luke asked with a smug grin. "Just cut the jokes around her, will ya? She's kind of sensitive about—"

"What is it?" MacBeth asked, all joking gone as he watched the humor drain out of Luke's face.

"Something's wrong. You can only send about thirty characters per message. I've got ten of them, starting with *TROUBLE*." Luke scrolled down to piece together the abbreviated characters in the rest of the messages.

"Call the hotel," MacBeth ordered Stone. "Page Tessa in her room."

"Shit, shit, *shit*." Luke slammed the back doors to the Suburban. "Forget it, she's not there. Change of plans, guys. We go in now."

Tessa sat in the back of the truck as it bounced over the rough and icy road. She was shivering convulsively, though the ride was a bit more bearable now that they'd left the freeway and the truck wasn't able to travel at high speed. Still, she was being jostled and banged about every time they hit a pothole, and the cold metal of the truck bed was leaching the heat right out of her body.

She'd already snagged the jacket one of the men had stored in the back with her. But she wanted to be able to return it quickly to its previous location once they stopped, so she was afraid to sit on it. Instead, she spread it over herself, but that still left her with the cold metal beneath her bruised butt.

At first, she'd tried to distract herself by punching out messages to Luke on her cell phone, one character at a time. Concentrating in the dark made her nauseous, but she didn't know what else to do to let him know what had happened to her. Unfortunately, coverage was spotty where they were, and she wasn't even sure if her messages were going through.

But she'd continued to send them, willing him to receive her pages and understand that she'd really screwed up. She only hoped that she hadn't done permanent damage to the operation, but that was milk spilled all over the place at this point.

Right now she had to focus on getting out of the mess she'd made. She scrolled through the log of sent messages to make sure she'd given Luke the best and most complete information possible. Hopefully he'd understand the code she'd used.

Stck in trck. Rcky sw me @ Rno Csno @ 7pm. Hid in trck, but it was his. In bck now. Cld. Hwy thn drt rd. 2 Rckys cbn. Whn thy lv wl hik to mt u. B thr @ 3am.

She wasn't sure if the messages would make sense, but hadn't wanted to waste time hunting for vowels using the number pad on her cell phone. She also didn't want to run down the battery scrolling through everything again and again. So she decided to send one more message to Luke, then quit.

Sorry.

She'd splurged on a vowel for that one.

Tessa waited for several minutes, but no replies came. She then set the phone aside and felt around in the dark, figuring it was time to come up with a plan for when the truck stopped. If nothing else, maybe she'd find a weapon to defend herself. But after a brief search, it seemed like the cell phone was her only piece of luck for the evening.

She turned around and felt along the boundaries of the pickup bed. It felt like there was a plastic bin or something attached to the front of the bed, which ran the length of the space behind the cab. The plastic didn't come all the way down to metal, leaving a fair-sized gap. As she reached into the void, she realized she would probably be able to squeeze her body in there.

That way, she could hide when Ricky and his companion

finally came to a stop. If she stayed where she was, they would discover her when they unloaded the truck.

She knew that when Ricky traveled to his Tahoe-area cabin, he left his street vehicles parked at the edge of the property line, where he had built an oversized garage. Inside it were several snowmobiles and ATVs, which he used to complete the one-and-a-half-mile trip to the cabin. Apparently the roads were too rough and narrow for even a four-wheel-drive vehicle to get through.

So she decided to wait, wedged into the little crevice she'd found, until Ricky and his friend left for the cabin. Then, she'd do something that seemed pretty foolish, but in actuality was her only option.

She'd follow them. Or at least she'd follow their tracks in the snow.

She'd been over the plans for tonight's extraction enough times that she'd memorized a lot of the details of the land surrounding Ricky's cabin. And while she knew the location of the clearing where she had been told to wait in the Suburban for the team to return, she only knew how to get to that location from Ricky's cabin. She had no idea of how to reach the area from the garage where the snowmobiles were parked.

So she'd have to follow the fresh tracks left by Ricky and his friend, and use them to get close to the cabin. From there, she would skirt around the building until she found the path Luke and the others were planning to take back to the Suburban once they retrieved Kelly. She'd use the trail to find their escape vehicle and wait for them there.

It made perfect sense. And if she *happened* to see Kelly, she'd grab the girl on her way by.

After a final reconnoitering of the area around her, Tessa decided that the hastily conceived plan was her best way out of the situation—unless, of course, Ricky left the keys to the truck inside the vehicle, and she managed to drive back to Reno. But they'd have to leave the keys behind for that to work, because her hot-wiring skills were, quite frankly, nonexistent.

Tessa felt a change in speed once again, then the vehicle hit a particularly deep pothole. Gritting her teeth against the pain of being briefly airborne, then hitting metal as she landed, she managed to wedge herself into the space underneath the plastic storage bin. She held her breath when the cast on her left forearm clanged into metal, but hoped the men in the cab wouldn't hear the noise over the road sounds.

Once she was in place, she grabbed her cell phone to adjust the ringer. After squinting at the lighted display, she realized that they must have crossed over the border into California, because she apparently was in CalCell territory once again. Cheered by the news that she would be able to call Luke once she was left alone in the truck, she went through menus to turn the ringer off on her phone.

A brief review told her the relevant ringer options were *silent* and *meeting*, so she chose the meeting mode. That ought to disengage the ringer, which would hopefully keeping her from being revealed by an untimely phone call. But her cell would buzz soundlessly if Luke managed to receive her frantic series of pages and sent her a message with instructions in return.

Once the ringer had been set to meeting mode, Tessa took the time to type out one last text message to Luke. She wouldn't send it yet, but instead would keep her finger on the button, ready to do so at a second's notice. That way, if the men did happen to find her, she could immediately hit SEND and let Luke know what had happened.

For whatever that was worth.

Hell, she'd probably better start coming up with a backup plan to cover that contingency, too.

The vehicle began to slow down, then threw her to one side as it made a wide turn and came to a stop. She waited with breath held as both doors opened and closed. She heard muted conversation and clenched her teeth against both the numbing cold and the tension building inside her.

A minute, maybe two, and they'll be gone. Hang in there. She concentrated on keeping her breathing shallow but even, telling herself that even though every noise felt magnified a thousand times to her, the men could not really hear her breathing. They had no reason to suspect that there was a stowaway aboard.

No reason, that is, until one of them slammed shut the plastic bin she'd hidden beneath. She hadn't even realized they had opened it until the whole thing reverberated half an inch from her nose.

The bin's momentary sound and motion were enough to cause her to jump visibly. That in turn jostled her cell phone off her belly, causing it to fall onto the metal truck bed with a clatter.

"What was that?" A male voice demanded.

Of course, Tessa thought bitterly. *Of course I couldn't drop the freaking thing onto my padded body. No, I had to drop it on god damned metal.*

"Shhhhhh," the other voice hissed.

Oh, God. I'm toast.

At that moment, her cell phone received a text message. It lay against the metal of the truck bed and vibrated like a crazed hornet. Two short buzzes, then a long one. Under her horrified gaze, it actually moved several inches in the dim light, propelled by its vibrating battery away from her body. She snatched it up, hoping that no one had heard it.

But of course they had.

Ricky Hedges threw back the black tarp covering the pickup's bed and shined a flashlight inside. Tessa flinched away from the brightness and knew she'd been caught.

"Well look right here, Bobby. She don't look much like her picture, but I think we've got ourselves a deputy district 'orney hiding out in the truck."

Chapter 47

Near Lake Tahoe, California
Thursday night, March 18

Tessa eased her finger over her traitorous cell phone and hit the SEND button. Since she was apparently in CalCell territory, she prayed that Luke would quickly receive her emergency message and understand things had just gone from bad to worse. She sat blinded by Ricky's flashlight and decided that it would probably be a good time to come up with a new backup plan.

Unfortunately, it didn't seem like the earth was going to open up and swallow her anytime soon—so much for that idea. She'd have to come up with something else, and soon.

Using the pretext of turning away from the light, Tessa managed to curl away from the men. She took a second to slide her brand-new, wafer-thin cell phone between the plaster of her cast and her wrist. Hopefully, they wouldn't think to look for it there.

"Come out of there, Miss Jacobi."

Gritting her teeth, she managed to slide out from under the storage bin and make her way across the truck bed. She made a big deal out of favoring her broken wrist, hoping that the sign of weakness would put Ricky and his colleague off guard.

"What am I going to do with you?" Ricky asked. "You wearing a wire or something?"

"No," she shook her head. "My boss doesn't know I'm here. I came for Kelly."

"What if I told you that Kelly was dead?" Ricky asked.

"Then I'd say you're a liar," Tessa shot back.

Ricky cocked his head. "The tracks around the cabin—you make those?"

She didn't say anything, just tried to look chagrined and defiant at the same time. Maybe if he believed that she was an overzealous prosecutor out here on her own, he would be taken by surprise when Luke and his men raided the cabin after midnight.

That is, if Luke stuck to the plan. She had no idea what he would do now that she had been taken as well. She'd have to think about that—surely there was something in the careful plans they'd been working on that she could use to help in the current situation.

"Put her in front of you on the ride to the cabin, Bobby." Ricky turned away and headed toward the garage. "If she gives you any trouble, kill her."

Luke sat in the front passenger seat of their vehicle as Mac-Beth drove over the icy, rutted road. Stone had just taken a GPS reading, and they were less than ten minutes away from the clearing where they would park the truck and head toward Ricky's cabin on foot.

They were going to have to mix things up a bit, leaving Stone behind in the truck to wait for Tessa, even help her if needed. Luke and MacBeth would continue toward the cabin as planned, and if there was no sign of Tessa, they would hike down to the garage where Ricky usually parked his vehicles and pick her up there.

If she was all right. If something hadn't happened to her first, like hypothermia.

Luke kept going over one of the jerky messages in his mind, the one where Tessa had indicated that she was hiding in the back of a truck. And she was cold.

His cell phone, which was being charged on the console, gave a series of beeps to indicate another message. Luke snatched it up and pressed the button to read Tessa's latest page. This one was in regular English, as if she'd taken time to write it.

But the contents were urgent, and his gut clenched in fear as he read.

They found me. Escape. Love you.

"Kick it into high gear, MacBeth. Ricky's got Tessa," Luke said. "We'll have to move to our contingency plan."

Chapter 48

Near Lake Tahoe, California
Thursday night, March 18

Tessa got off Bobby's snowmobile and made her way through calf-deep snow and slush to the front door of Ricky Hedges's cabin. Although why anyone would call it a cabin was a mystery—the thing was probably bigger than Luke's whole house. It was two stories and had to be pushing two thousand square feet.

Maybe it was the log-style exterior that earned the cabin title? She tiredly pushed aside the meaningless thoughts and slogged up to the icy front steps. The clothes she was wearing were completely inappropriate for the heavy snow conditions outside, and the cold was beginning to sap her strength. She had a parka and hat, but beyond that was wearing jeans and running shoes.

Thankfully, she'd managed to grab the shopping bag containing her new long underwear and gloves, and had put the gloves on before the snowmobile trip. But she was still shivering convulsively after being chilled in the back of the ᵤuck. At that point, she was almost eager to get inside ᵥ's cabin.

"Get her pager," Ricky ordered his assistant, as they climbed up the stairs to the porch.

"I l-left it in the t-truck," Tessa said through chattering teeth.

"Frisk her," was Ricky's reply.

She stood there shivering as she was stripped down to her jeans and T-shirt and patted down by Ricky's assistant. He didn't have her remove her gloves, so she was able to conceal the cell phone jammed inside her cast—for a bit longer, at least.

"Nothing here, boss."

Ricky motioned them into the cabin without a word. She put her sweater and parka back on and made her way painstakingly up the stairs.

When she opened the front door, the two people inside looked up. Kelly had been sitting curled in the corner of the sofa, watching a movie on television. Ricky's bodyguard, Otis, was sitting at a table cleaning the disassembled parts of a large handgun. Tessa tried not to stare at it.

"Tessa!" Kelly said as she launched herself off the couch. For a moment, everything was forgotten as the teenager flew into her arms and hugged her tightly. Then Tessa pulled back to look at the girl.

"Are you all right? Has anyone hurt you?"

Kelly shook her head. "I've just been bored."

The prosaic teenage complaint made Tessa shake her head, then she hugged Kelly again before turning to look at Ricky.

"You may as well let us go now," Tessa said.

"You're outta your fucking mind," Ricky replied. "No way this little bitch goes anywhere."

"Her family is looking for her. The police are looking for her. You won't get away with this."

"She wants to stay with me." Ricky shrugged. "It might not be her mama's idea of a good life, but the kid wants to be an entertainer. Right, Kelly?"

The girl said nothing as she huddled at Tessa's side.

"That's a very cute defense, Ricky. But for one fact—Kelly is a minor. According to the law, she can't make that decision for herself."

Ricky began to look less relaxed. "How the hell am I supposed to know she's a minor? Kid's a liar. She told me she was eighteen and wanted to sing like Britney Spears."

Tessa shrugged. "It doesn't matter. We'll find witnesses to counter whatever lies you tell. Let us leave, and things will go easier for you in the courts."

"You're full of it, lady. If you had any evidence, you'd be here with the police to arrest me. No, I think we've got some kind of vigilante thing going. Or maybe you want Kelly for yourself? Yeah, I can see the headlines now—prosecutor and her young lesbian lover discovered dead in Tahoe cabin."

Tessa laughed confidently, even though her grip tightened on Kelly in a spurt of panic. "I'm not gay, and neither is Kelly. No one will believe it."

"They will if you two die in some kind of tragic murder-suicide. Hey, Bobby, I'm starting to like this idea. Think how the media would eat it up. District attorney's star prosecutor visits Club Red and falls in love with one of the acts. Society can't accept their doomed affair, and they commit suicide," Ricky said.

"There's a Movie of the Week in that," Bobby agreed.

"I'll tell you why this discussion is pointless, and everyone will know that you are responsible for anything happens to us. First of all, your club has been busted. So everyone will hear the kind of disgusting crap that's been going on there for the last few years."

That got his attention. Ricky turned pale and gaped at her. "The hell you say?"

"The FBI has been following your operation for over a year," she said, hoping to impress upon Ricky the fact that the game truly was over. And that there would be no point in killing either her or Kelly at this time.

"No way, I would have heard from—"

"Jerry? Crystal? Or maybe your lawyer, Krugman?" Tessa finished. "They've all been arrested."

Ricky turned to Otis. "Get on my cell phone. Tell the pilot to have the plane ready in two hours, then start calling people from the club to check this bitch's story."

"Getting the Learjet ready to fly to South America?" Tessa asked. "Rio, isn't it? Don't bother, the FBI knows about that plan as well."

Ricky jerked his head to indicate that he wanted to speak to Bobby in the kitchen, only a few steps away. Even though Otis ran upstairs, and they were left alone, Kelly stayed glued to Tessa's side.

"Don't worry, sweetie. I don't want you to say anything, but there are a bunch of my friends who know exactly where I am right now. In fact, they were coming here to rescue you," Tessa said. She ignored the little voice inside her head pointing out that she had no confirmation Luke had even received her text messages.

"So I don't have to be scared of him anymore?" Kelly asked.

Tessa shook her head. "Have some healthy respect for the fact that he has a gun, but don't be afraid. We're going to get you out of here tonight. We've been planning for a couple of days now, and my friend Luke is a very thorough guy. We'll be out in a couple of hours, and we'll call your parents once we get back to L.A."

"And my brother? I really missed him," Kelly said. "Ricky and Jerry threatened him. That's why I said those mean things to you on the phone. I'm sorry, they made me do it."

"I know, sweetie. I need you to be brave for just a little while longer. If we can convince Ricky that the police know everything, then he has no reason to hold us. Hopefully, he'll leave us here and run for the border."

Which meant that she would have Kelly, but wouldn't be able to prosecute Ricky Hedges for his numerous crimes.

Tessa looked down at the platinum blond head nestled against her shoulder and decided she could live with that.

"Be careful, Tessa. He's acting all cool now, but he can be really scary. He turns bright red, and screams and yells at me sometimes. I just opened the door to the basement here and he flipped. I think he's got a bad motherboard," Kelly whispered.

Tessa choked on a laugh, but took the advice with a grain of salt. After all, Kelly was a kid and easily intimidated. Crystal had painted a picture of Ricky Hedges as a basically spineless rich guy who preferred to let others do his work. And Tessa was gambling that Ricky would be more interested in protecting his money and his freedom than settling any scores with her or Kelly.

In fact, she was betting their lives on it.

She knew she had to find the right balance between confidence and the willingness to bargain. That she had to hammer into Ricky's thick skull the idea that the best thing for him to do would be to give up. Her job was to convince him that there was no way for him to escape, but an infinite number of ways for him to make his inevitable capture and punishment much harder than it had to be.

What she couldn't do was let the man know that they were aware of his involvement in a murder for hire. If Ricky realized that he was facing a death penalty case, he might become desperate.

Desperate men had been known to do horrific things, but she tried not to think about that.

"What do the police know?" Ricky stalked back into the living room and stood in front of them.

"Everything," she said. "They know about the drugs and prostitution. The catering to celebrity athletes so that your club became a city hot spot. The, um, contributions that you gave to city council members through third parties to ensure favorable zoning changes around your clubs."

Tessa thought fast while Ricky absorbed the information.

She had to get across the point that there was a major case being made against him—one that didn't necessarily include her or Kelly. That way, she hoped to avoid giving him any further incentive to make them disappear.

"It's over, Ricky. The FBI was looking at you going back to last year. They have information on money laundering, illegal shell corporations, and your accountant cooking the books," Tessa continued.

Ricky shook his head sadly. "I have no idea what you're talking about. Maybe I didn't manage my employees closely enough, and they engaged in these activities outside of my knowledge."

"Put your hip boots on, folks," Tessa drawled. "The B.S. is getting deep in here."

"Shut up, you vindictive bitch. I run a legitimate business in Club Red. And while the morality police might want to shut me down as a smut peddler, I'm only serving a need. If people didn't buy it, I wouldn't sell it."

"Come off it. You make money selling teenage girls," Tessa said as she stroked Kelly's soft hair. "We have corroboration from multiple individuals inside your operation who will testify that you make millions and millions every year off of the wholesale commercialization of women, among other things."

"I'd be happy to open my accounting books and let the FBI review them. They'll see that I run a business with decent profit margins, but certainly nothing like you're insinuating. If young girls seek out employment in my club," Ricky sneered, "it's because they're greedy and into shortcuts."

"Shut up!" Kelly screamed the words as tears started to fall. "Jerry tricked me. I was willing to work hard for what I wanted, but you guys lied to me."

"Kids are so emotional," Jerry said ruefully. "I hear they make terrible witnesses in court."

"Yeah?" Kelly yelled. "Wait until I tell them about the boxes of money in the basement." She turned to Tessa, wanting to be believed. "I saw them—all these banker's boxes filled with twenties and hundreds."

"I told you not to go down there!" Ricky bellowed.

Tessa grabbed Kelly in an attempt to defuse the situation. But the teenager had apparently had enough of being victimized. She'd believed Tessa about help being on the way, and that gave her the confidence to finally defend herself after all these weeks of abuse.

"And he killed a man," Kelly said defiantly. "He was trying to get you, and this other person got in the way. Ricky wasn't even sorry—"

Tessa pinched Kelly, hard. But the damage had been done.

Ricky yelled for Otis to come down and begin packing, then he ordered Bobby to take the women upstairs to Kelly's bedroom and get them ready for a nighttime hike in the California wilderness.

Kelly began to sob, finally overcome by the emotional outburst.

"Cry all you want, little girl," Ricky said. "You and your nosy friend are going to become tragic examples of what can happen when inexperienced hikers tackle Lake Tahoe. You'll get lost and freeze to death—so sad. Probably won't be discovered until spring."

Bobby shoved them up the stairs in front of him. "And don't even think about escaping. We're miles from any home in this area, and the temperature is below freezing out there. We're supposed to get a foot of snow up here tonight. I hear it's real tough to make a shelter out of Sierra snow because of the high water content."

"It will be all right," Tessa promised Kelly under her breath as they headed up the stairs. "I've got something up my sleeve. Literally."

Chapter 49

Near Lake Tahoe, California
Thursday night, March 18

"I don't feel good," Tessa announced a few minutes later. She and Kelly were sitting on the bed in a small upstairs room, with Bobby guarding the door nearby. As far as Tessa could see, the man wasn't armed.

But the two men downstairs were.

And Bobby outweighed her by a good fifty pounds. Catching him off guard was her only chance. She just hoped that Kelly got with the program quickly enough that they were able to prevent their guard from sounding the alarm.

"I think I'm going to be sick," Tessa said, and bolted for the double sink at one end of the room. Next to it was a small door that led to the toilet and tiny shower area—no help there.

Thinking quickly, Tessa leaned over the sink. She could see Kelly out of the corner of her eye, the teenager's face a mask of concern and faint disgust. Taking a deep breath, Tessa hesitated as if in surprise.

"What the hell is that?" She pointed to an imaginary item in the sink.

"What?" Bobby asked as he cautiously approached.

"That," Tessa repeated, watching the man approach in the tiny vanity mirror.

With his brow furrowed, Bobby approached the sink and peeked over Tessa's shoulder. "What?"

"This!" Tessa hauled back her casted left forearm and struck Bobby with it—right on the bridge of his nose. Blood sprayed out immediately, coating Tessa's face in red droplets.

With a juicy, whistling sound of surprise, Bobby fell to the ground and lay there, unmoving.

"Oh my God!" Kelly breathed. "You killed him!"

"Shhh. Oh, God," Tessa moaned in pain. The force of the impact with Bobby's nose had sent shock waves of unbelievable agony through her broken wrist. She staggered to the bed and sat down, putting her head between her knees and taking several deep breaths.

"You okay?" Kelly asked. "You didn't hit him that hard, why did he go down like that?"

"Not hard, but I got the sweet spot," Tessa ground out between deep breaths, then motioned for the teenager to lock the door.

"We've got to keep him quiet," Tessa said through her teeth as the pain in her wrist began to subside to a rotting-tooth level of throbbing. "Give me a pillowcase. And something to tie him up with."

After a few more deep breaths, Tessa pushed to her feet and approached the man whose nose she'd broken. Using the recent example of Luke immobilizing Jerry Kravitz in his kitchen, she and Kelly rolled Bobby onto his stomach and made a gag out of the pillowcase. Once that was tied, she had Kelly take a leather belt and bathrobe sash that she'd pulled from the closet and immobilize his hands and feet.

"He'll be all right," she assured a dubious Kelly. "But we have to get out of here, now."

She reached inside her cast gingerly to pull out the cell phone she'd hidden there, congratulating herself on her cleverness at keeping it concealed. Unfortunately, she'd cracked the thing clean through when she'd slammed her cast into Bobby's face. The screen was dented in and the unit refused to turn on.

Tessa stared at her mangled phone and thought about crying. "If I could catch a break here, I'd really appreciate it," she muttered.

"What?" Kelly asked.

"Never mind. On to my next backup plan." Tessa made her way to the window and used the little knob to crank it open. The rush of frigid air was welcome on her heated face, and she drew in several deep breaths to steady herself.

It was still touch-and-go as to whether she was going to hurl from the pain in her wrist. The cold air helped tip the balance toward not throwing up—for the moment. She looked outside and saw that the roof of the cabin's wraparound porch provided a perfect escape route from their second-story room.

"Do you have your coat and gloves?" Tessa asked. Kelly nodded. "Good girl. I want you to crawl out the window and slide on your butt along the roof of the porch, going all the way to the corner of the building. I'll hold on so you don't slip."

"What about you?" Kelly asked.

Good question. "Um, when you get down there, brace your feet in the gutter. I'll hold your arm, and you can help me down to the edge of the roof. Then we can scoot along until we find a place to jump off."

"Let's go to the side yard," Kelly suggested. "The snow is really deep there, and underneath are some bushes."

They both managed to get to the edge of the roof without incident. From there, they were able to use the gutter to help slide along. Once they made it to the corner, both surveyed the ground below.

"It's a long way," Kelly said.

"Not that far," Tessa lied. "I'll go first, then help catch you, okay?"

Kelly nodded and began to shiver. The snow was coming down in fat, heavy flakes, and she hadn't had any suitable clothes to bring along. She was lucky that Ricky had let her pack a suitcase at all the day she left Club Red, and she hadn't known they were heading up to the snow. So she was wearing a pair of jeans, with sweatpants and a wool sweater over them. She had a ski jacket, but the rest of her clothing, like Tessa's, was not going to stand up well to the bitter chill of the Sierra Nevadas during a winter storm.

They had to get out of the cold—and soon.

Tessa swung her legs over the edge of the roof and twisted slightly to the right. She knew her injured left arm wouldn't be any help at all, so she planned to swing down and grab the gutter with her right hand as she went by it. Hopefully, that would be enough to break her fall while she maneuvered over what looked to be a nice, deep hump of snow.

With a last, squinting look into the dark below, Tessa eased her hips over the edge. When she started to fall, she twisted around and reached for the gutter with her gloved right hand.

It caught for a second, then slipped off as if the metal had been greased.

With a muffled cry, Tessa felt herself flatten out with the momentum of her move. Before she could do anything about it, she was heading straight down into the snow—butt first.

At the edge of the tree line that surrounded Ricky Hedges's cabin, Luke and MacBeth paused to scan the house and make sure there was no one outside to be alerted to their presence.

Luke pulled out the pair of night-vision glasses he'd borrowed from the guide and scanned the property. He felt MacBeth tap his shoulder and saw him point to the northeast corner of the cabin.

In silence, he watched two slight figures huddle on the edge of the roof covering the wraparound porch. Then one of them slid feetfirst off the roof, trying and failing to catch hold of the gutter with one hand on the way down. The person's left arm hung like deadweight, and Luke knew in an instant that it was Tessa.

He threw the glasses at MacBeth and was running across the yard in a heartbeat, heading to where he'd seen Tessa's body fall into the darkness at the side of the house.

"Tessa," he whispered roughly as he reached a chest-high drift. "Baby, can you hear me?"

A gloved hand appeared out of the deep depression in the snow. "Right here, and am I ever glad to see you. I'm going to throw up now."

Luke reached over and hauled Tessa out of the deep drift, then stood and supported her as she retched convulsively. He knew that only the most severe pain could make a person do that. Unfortunately, there was nothing to be done but hold her head and stroke her back until the spasms passed.

"Hey, Kelly!" MacBeth called softly to the teenager who still clung to the roof. "Jump down—I've got you."

The girl looked down from her porch, then squinted over to where she could hear Tessa throwing up.

"I don't think so," Kelly replied dubiously.

"I'm a friend of Tessa's. We're here to take you home," MacBeth promised.

Her little face appeared over the edge. "Yeah?"

"Hays, Kansas. Right?"

Tears welled in Kelly's eyes as she nodded. "Here I come."

MacBeth grunted as he broke Kelly's fall, then he pulled her under the protection of the roof. They waited against the side of the house while Tessa composed herself.

"Sorry. It's been a hell of an evening," she said weakly.

Luke pulled out a flashlight and began to look her over for injuries. He stopped short when he saw the spatters of blood on her face. "Are you hurt?"

"No, but you should see the other guy." She held up her cast, which was also smeared with Bobby's blood, and gave a halfhearted grin. "Broke his nose. He's tied up, but I'm afraid I stunned him more than anything else. We should get Kelly out of here fast."

Luke nodded. "I want you two to cross the yard over there. Go beyond the woodpile, and follow the path to the creek. Once you cross it, you'll head out at about two o'clock until you pass—"

"A twisted pine tree with a double trunk," Tessa finished. "I remember the way to the Suburban. Did you park it where we originally planned?"

"Yes," Luke said. "Stone is there waiting. He's got blankets and food for you. Once you're settled, if it's safe, I want you to send Stone back this way. MacBeth and I may need his help."

"What do you mean? Aren't you coming with us?" Tessa asked.

"Not yet. We're going to take Otis and Ricky into custody first."

"No," Tessa said. "I heard him say he's going to the airport. They're packing up as much money as they can carry right now. Let the FBI stop him when he goes to his plane."

"No way. He killed Ed, he kidnapped you. He's hurt too many people for me to take the chance that he might get away."

"They're armed," Tessa protested.

"So are we, baby."

"I don't want you to get hurt," Tessa said. "You're more important to me than any arrest."

"I love you, too. But this guy is not going to get away. Not this time."

Tessa made a frustrated noise. Luke took her arm and began to walk with her in the direction of the woodpile. "MacBeth and I are two guys with SWAT training against Ricky and his bodyguard. You've got to trust me."

They reached the cords of stacked wood with the others right behind them. "Maybe I should stay here and—"

"You and Kelly aren't dressed for the cold. Hypothermia clouds your judgment, baby, so you don't have long to get to the car. Stop arguing and take that girl to safety. I need you to do that so I can do my job—the one you hired me to do."

Tessa looked over at Kelly, who was standing next to MacBeth and shivering miserably. The knowledge that she was suffering made the decision a little easier. When it came down to it, she'd just have to trust that Luke knew what he was doing and would get his job done. Her job was to keep her promise to Kelly and get the girl home safely.

She threw her good arm around Luke and hugged him tightly. "Please come back safely. You said you wouldn't abandon me. I'm holding you to it."

Luke leaned down and kissed Tessa's blue, trembling lips. "I've got your back. We're going to bring Ricky and Otis to L.A. to face charges, then you and I are going to have a long talk."

She nodded and shivered at the same time, then kissed him again before pulling away. "Come on, Kel. Once we get moving you'll warm up."

Chapter 50

Luke watched as Tessa and Kelly disappeared in the trees. MacBeth cleared his throat. "While Tessa was puking her guts up, I checked out the windows. Wired, all of them."

Luke frowned and turned to study the house. "Did you see the box for the alarm or wires anywhere?"

"No. My guess is they're buried."

"So we'll have to go in on the second floor," Luke said. "So nice of Tessa to discover that the gutters are slicker than snot and save us some trouble."

MacBeth chuckled. "She's a pistol, that one. Smart, too. So if you're not serious—"

"Get lost, buddy. She's mine."

Luke led the way back to the edge of the cabin and stopped out of view of the windows. "Tessa said she left her guard incapacitated upstairs. I say we go in the window they left open—I mean, we know it's not wired for the alarm."

MacBeth agreed. "A lot of homeowners don't wire the second floor. You're taller than I am, so why don't you give me a boost. Once I'm up there, I'll reach down and help you onto the roof next to me."

"Let's go." Luke bent down and boosted MacBeth until he could grab the edge of the gutter. With a grunt of effort, he lifted and guided MacBeth's slushy feet to his shoulders.

"I'm going up," MacBeth advised in a whisper. Using Luke's shoulders for thrust, he heaved himself up until the lip of the roof was at his waist. Then he lifted his right leg sideways and levered it over the edge.

"Ricky! We've got company. The girls are gone, too!"

MacBeth looked up at the shout and saw a man he recognized as Otis the bodyguard standing in the open window.

"Let go," Luke hissed from below, knowing his friend was completely vulnerable in his current position.

"Ah, fuck."- Even as MacBeth began to throw himself backward, the other man drew a silver-plated Glock—goddam sissy gun—and fired. He groaned at the sudden burning pain in his thigh. The other man continued to fire at him as he disappeared over the edge of the roof.

Luke tried to catch MacBeth and break as much of the fall as he could, but gravity brought them both down into an awkward pile in the deep snow. He'd heard the gunshot, and realized his friend was hit when he didn't immediately move off the ground.

"You all right, man? MacBeth?" Luke rolled his friend over and clenched his jaw in protest as he saw the glossy black gleam of blood on the snow.

"Almost there, Kelly," Tessa panted as they jogged awkwardly along the poorly defined trail that the men had made earlier with their snowshoes. "At least we're warmer now, right?"

"Whatever," Kelly huffed. "Please tell me there's a tall mocha latte waiting for me at the truck. Or chocolate."

Tessa laughed in response, then pointed ahead. "Look, there's a little clearing, just past the path between those big rocks. And see the slight rise that goes up through the trees—Stone and the truck are just down the hill from there. We'll be inside in another minute."

"Thank God," Kelly said.

Tessa muttered agreement under her breath, but came to an abrupt halt at the distant booming sound she heard.

"What was that?" Kelly asked, only to have her question answered by a series of muffled sounds.

"Gunshots. Oh, God." Tessa immediately turned to the way they'd come, then stopped. She was torn between wanting to rush back to Luke and needing to escort Kelly the last quarter mile to safety.

Luke won.

"Okay, listen to me. I need you to follow the trail like we've been doing. Keep going until you see the truck, then shout to Stone who you are. Tell him we need an ambulance, or a medevac helicopter if weather permits. He'll make sure that you'll be safe. I'll get back to you as soon as I can."

"You're not leaving me?" Kelly asked.

"I have to go help Luke and MacBeth," Tessa said.

"You said you'd help *me*. I don't want to walk in the forest alone, I'm scared. You said you'd stay with me."

"Luke needs me right now, and you'll be fine. You should be at the truck in less than ten minutes. Think how good it will feel to get out of the cold."

Kelly sniffled.

"I need you to do this for me," Tessa said. "We have to get word out that someone might be hurt, and that's going to be your job. Can you handle it?"

The teenager looked hesitantly over her shoulder, to where

the trail disappeared into darkness. "I think so."

"Good. I promise we won't be long. Go now, run!"

Tessa watched as Kelly took off at an awkward, loping pace. Then she turned around and headed back toward the cabin.

Luke had managed to lift MacBeth in a fireman's carry and got him as far as the woodpile before he heard more gunshots. Puffs of snow flew up where the bullets had struck close to his feet.

Too damn close.

He dove behind the stacks of wood. From the tension in MacBeth's body, he realized that his injured friend was conscious.

"You all right?" Luke asked as he drew a borrowed handgun from his jacket.

"Fuckin' A," MacBeth replied grimly. "I'm going to save the California taxpayers the cost of Otis's death row appeals process though."

"Why don't you stop bleeding all over the place first," Luke advised. "Take my belt and make a tourniquet while I watch the front door."

MacBeth reached up and unfastened Luke's belt, fumbling for a second with the metal buckle. "Watch the hands, big guy. Tessa will get jealous."

"It would be the best piece you ever had." MacBeth gave a raw laugh and wrapped the makeshift tourniquet around his middle thigh, just above the wound.

Luke shot him a worried look, knowing that for all the tough talk and macho jokes, his man was hurting. "Did it hit an artery or vein?"

"I don't think so." MacBeth hissed in pain as he tightened the leather. "Right, I'm good to go."

Luke dove down as a series of gunshots peppered the area around them. "Too bad we're trapped here. I don't think we'd be able to make it across that clearing and onto the trail before they shot us both in our tracks."

The cold sweat on MacBeth's face gleamed as he lifted his head to study the woods behind them. A movement caught his eye.

"Ah, shit. Here comes the cavalry," MacBeth said.

Luke whipped around and saw Tessa's familiar ski jacket at the edge of a the tree line—just for a moment. Then she melted back into the darkness when shots rang out from the house once again.

"Did she see us?" Luke asked.

"Yeah."

"Jesus, I hope she doesn't do anything crazy."

The clearing was quiet for a long stretch. MacBeth worked his way to a standing position, breathing through his teeth against the pain. "If you cover me, I can make it to the edge of the forest. Then I'll drop to the ground and lay down a suppressing fire so you can pull back."

Luke glanced at the tourniquet. "Can you make it that far?"

"Adrenaline is a beautiful thing, my friend."

At that moment they heard the anemic sound of a horn from one of the two snowmobiles Ricky had left parked in the yard. They looked at each other, trying to figure out what was up.

Or better yet, what the hell Tessa was up to.

Luke grinned when he heard a booming voice—or her best efforts at one—echo across the compound.

"Roderick Hedges, this is the FBI. We have your cabin surrounded. Throw down your weapons, and you will not be hurt."

Luke heard scuffling noises, then realized Otis was retreating from the second floor.

"I repeat, this is the FBI. Throw down your weapons, lie on the floor, and wait for us to come to you. We have orders to use lethal force to subdue you."

After scanning the house to be sure there were no guns pointed at them, Luke scooped MacBeth up over his shoulder and headed down the trail as fast as he could under their combined weights.

Chapter 51

Near Lake Tahoe, California
Thursday night, March 18

Tessa waited until at least a minute had passed from the time she'd seen Luke and MacBeth disappear into the dark cover of the trees. They should be a good distance up the trail by now.

Or at least they would be, if one of them wasn't shot.

She bit her lip, wondering if it had been Luke. Then she decided that it didn't matter, because either way they weren't leaving any member of the team behind. She'd bought them some time with her bluff, but Ricky Hedges was a gambler.

And gamblers always knew when it was time to call an opponent's bluff.

Tessa pushed away from the snowmobiles she'd hidden behind. She'd managed to disable one of them by ripping at every exposed wire she could find, but had been unsuccessful in her attempt to start the other one. So much for riding to the rescue.

She looked up and saw the shadow of a man's form silhouetted in the window and decided that she'd done all she could. She reached for the wires on the remaining snowmobile, but saw that it was a different model and had a plastic box covering the electronics panel. She didn't have time to figure it out, so she took off running on a course that she hoped would intersect with the trail she'd used earlier.

After realizing how dark and unfamiliar this part of the property was, Tessa abandoned the idea and backtracked until she joined the path Luke and MacBeth had taken.

She knew she was on the right trail because she was able to follow spatters of blood that looked black in the night.

At least it stopped snowing, right? There's a silver lining for you.

She looked up and saw the shapes of Luke and MacBeth ahead of her in the dim light. She realized that Luke was the one carrying his employee at the same moment that she heard the distant sound of a snowmobile starting.

"Coming up behind you," she panted.

Luke kept moving, aware that they were about to be hunted down from the back of a snowmobile. "Only a few more minutes," he panted.

"There's one snowmobile—I disabled the other." She ran behind him, astonished that she could barely keep up with him despite the burden he was carrying. "Is MacBeth all right?"

"Fuckin' A," both men responded at once.

Tessa shook her head, wondering if it was some kind of SWAT thing.

Suddenly Luke stumbled, and Tessa held her breath for a moment before he managed to right himself.

"Hold up," MacBeth panted. "My tourniquet is too loose."

"Keep going," Tessa said. "I recognize the clearing just past those rocks. We're almost there."

"Unfortunately, so is Ricky. The snowmobile is right behind," MacBeth said. "I can see the light. We have to make a stand."

Luke knew his man was right. He made it up the path just past where it narrowed between a series of boulders, then studied the clearing dotted with trees beyond. "We've got about a minute to come up with an ambush plan."

Tessa watched as Luke carefully set MacBeth down behind one of the boulders. "Is that rope clipped onto his backpack?"

"Yeah."

"What if we strung it across the path right here at the rocks? We could pull Ricky and Otis—"

"Right on their asses," Luke finished. "Except that they'd see the rope and try to avoid it. Then we're toast, unless we just shoot them."

"What if I stood up at the edge of the clearing?" Tessa asked. "They'd see me when they crested the hill and would be distracted. They'd never notice the rope you two have strung across their path."

"No way," growled Luke. "If we need a decoy, I'll do it."

She held up her cast. "There's no way I can hold the rope taut enough, even if I wrapped it around the tree. Besides, they won't get close enough to hit me, and we don't have time to argue."

Before Luke could respond, Tessa took off running up the path. She made it to the halfway point, then slowed down, taking the time to carefully scan the path ahead of her. She didn't want to run into any obstacles if someone was shooting at her.

A quick glance over her shoulder told her that Luke had helped MacBeth to his feet and taken up a position next to him, sheltered in the darkness of the boulders that loomed at the edge of the trail. She could barely see the faint outlines of the rope they'd tied around a tree on one side of the path. On the other, they both braced themselves for impact.

At that moment, she heard a shout, then the sound of the snowmobile gunning its engine. She'd been spotted.

As she started to run across the rest of the clearing, there

was no need for her to feign being afraid. Ricky was driving
the vehicle, and Otis was half-standing behind him, taking
aim at Tessa with a shiny handgun.

Luke heard the sound of the snowmobile racing toward them
and met MacBeth's gaze. The other man nodded grimly, to
say that he was ready, and tightened the grip of his gloved
hands on the rope strung across the path.

When the sound of several shots rang out, Luke jerked as
if he'd been hit himself. His head whipped to the left to try
to follow Tessa's progress. She was making no attempt to
find cover for herself, and he gritted his teeth against the effort it took not to shout after her.

Another volley of gunshots, then a whoop of triumph
from Otis as Tessa went down hard. Luke pulled his eyes
away from her. He could hear the snowmobile enter the tiny
canyon of rocks. It was time.

He and MacBeth threw their considerable combined
weight backward until they were held up only by the pull the
tree exerted on the rope. The snowmobile's front end went
flying by them, and then Ricky and his henchman were the
ones doing the flying.

Luke gave a roar of effort, conscious of the fact that Mac-
Beth would be the weak link because of his injury. The rope
was nearly torn from his gloved hands as the men on the
snowmobile ran into it and were jerked to a stop.

Otis fired several wild shots with the gun he was holding
before he became completely airborne. Luke and MacBeth
were both jerked forward but managed to hold on.

The snowmobile plunged forward, then crashed into a tree.
Ricky and Otis ended up in a moaning heap on the ground
about ten feet away. Luke grabbed the rope from MacBeth's
slack grip and drew his weapon as he got to his feet.

"Don't fucking move, boys," Luke said.

MacBeth pushed himself upright and drew his own
weapon. "I've got them, Luke. Go check on Tessa."

"If they give you any shit, I want you to plug them. It'll save us the cost of a trial," Luke said coldly.

Ricky moaned on the ground but stopped thrashing around. He knew he was done.

Luke holstered his weapon and ran across the clearing even though his legs were burning with fatigue. His entire being was focused on the motionless figure of Tessa in the snow ahead of him.

"Tessa? Please, baby." He threw himself down next to her.

"Did it work?" she asked, rolling over to her side.

Luke stared at her, mouth gaping open. She grinned and threw her arms around him. Hard.

"Jesus. I thought you'd been shot."

"No, I slipped in the mud. Tennis shoes aren't made for snowy, icy conditions."

"Oh, thank God." Luke's arms closed around her, and he pulled her against him as he sprawled in the snow on his back.

They lay there for a moment, slowing their breathing and basking in the fact that everyone was alive. A flash of red streaked into the sky above the treetops and pulled their attention away from each other. "What is that?" Tessa asked.

"Stoner. He's signaling to the backup team with a flare that we're ready to go home."

"Home," Tessa mused, as they both got to their feet. She was soaking wet, had snow crusted on her feet and lower legs, and her broken wrist was throbbing like nobody's business. "It doesn't snow there, right?"

"No, baby, it doesn't."

"Let's go home, love."

Epilogue

"I like this cast much better," Tessa said to Luke, as they made their way up the broad steps of her father's home.

Luke eyed the glaring purple of Tessa's new forearm cast with some suspicion. He'd secretly labeled it Moby Grape. "I guess the important thing is that no permanent damage was done when you bashed Bobby in the face."

"Nope," she said gleefully. "The other cast did its job, and gave its life for my wrist. I'll think of it often and fondly."

"You seem pretty cheerful," Luke said.

"Why wouldn't I be? The case is closed, and the bad guys are all in jail waiting for charges to be filed and plea bargains to be made. MacBeth will be out of the hospital tomorrow and can recover at home."

"In short, you did it."

"We did it. All of us. But yes, I'm very happy." In a rare display of spontaneous affection, Tessa stood on tiptoe and landed a smacking kiss on Luke's smiling mouth.

Of course that was the exact moment that Paul Jacobi

chose to open the door. She pulled away from Luke, aware that she was blushing, and greeted him.

"I'm sorry you guys had to jump ship and come back home," Tessa said. She stood there awkwardly as she was carefully examined by her father. The knowledge that she looked a lot better than the last time he'd seen her didn't help much.

Finally, Tessa moved forward and gave him a quick hug. "I'm glad you came back to see us."

Paul Jacobi's blue eyes closed with something that looked very much like relief, then he returned his daughter's light embrace. "Come inside. Everyone is already on the back patio."

Tessa moved ahead, and Paul took the opportunity to corner Luke. "Thank you for taking care of her."

"She took care of herself, so I guess you should take some of the credit. I just followed in her wake trying to keep up."

"Hmmph. I have a feeling you're going to be running after my girl for some time to come."

There was a question there, probably regarding his intentions. But Luke ignored it. "As long as I catch her once in a while, I'll be fine with that."

They made their way onto the backyard patio just as Tessa was being greeted by her brother, stepmother, and Kelly.

"Excellent cast," Kevin said as he hugged his older sister.

"Thanks, it's the latest color. I was just glad that there was no further damage to my wrist, so I was feeling like celebrating when I picked the new cast."

"Kelly was just telling us that she's going to be staying in Los Angeles to make statements to the police and stuff, then wait for the trials to start," Kevin said. He spoke casually, with the complete disregard a teenager would have for a difficult subject.

Kelly smiled at him, obviously smitten and grateful that he was treating her so normally.

"My mom is going to work part-time helping Luke's assistant keep the books," Kelly said shyly. "And my dad is going to look for work selling agricultural equipment up in the north county. If we can manage, we'll try to move here so I have a better chance of getting a recording contract."

"That's great news, kiddo." Luke tugged on Kelly's ponytail like an older brother and smiled when she jerked away to smooth her platinum hair.

"How are things with the FBI and the US Attorney's Office?" Paul asked as they all took a seat.

"They're, um, cordial." Tessa tried to keep the smugness from her voice. "We're working together to file the appropriate charges. No one is going to walk on this case. Best of all, the AUSA is going to seek the death penalty against Ricky and Otis. It means Kelly will have to testify, but it also means that Ed's killers won't go free."

Luke took her hand, knowing how much it cost Tessa to speak in an even tone about her best friend's death a week ago.

But it didn't feel like a week ago to her. So much had happened in such a short space of time, it seemed like she'd skipped over the initial phases of grieving and settled straight into acceptance. With the odd, lingering moments of anger when she thought of the men who had killed him.

She squeezed Luke's hand in return as tears welled in her eyes. "It's okay. I'm going to miss Ed, very much. But I really believe that he's happy now. He's spent the last eight years grieving for his dead wife, and he never got over losing her."

Tessa stopped speaking as she realized her words could seem like a criticism of her father. At one time, she might have kept quiet, but now she tried to set aside the last of her resentment toward her father. "Not everyone is as strong as you are," she said, looking at Paul. "Or as lucky, to find happiness twice in a lifetime."

Paul looked at Lana and smiled. "I've been very lucky to have all of you."

Lana stood up and hesitated for a moment. "I'm sure

you're very busy today, Tessa. But I've prepared lunch if you'd like to stay . . . ?"

"We'd love to," Tessa assured her stepmother. "Thank you."

As Lana left the patio, Kevin turned to Tessa. "I heard there were mobsters involved. What's going to happen to them?"

"I don't really know," she said with a sigh. "Most of the higher-level Ianellis are making themselves scarce in Mexico right now. It's up to the FBI and their organized crime task force to follow up."

"You're taking their escape pretty well," Paul said. "I'm sure it helps to know that their financial advisor is singing falsetto, and most of their bank accounts have been frozen."

"Yes. And I got what I wanted out of the deal," Tessa replied, watching Kevin and Kelly as they headed across the lawn to play badminton. "I made a promise to Kelly, and I feel like I've kept it. And we got all of the men who were directly and indirectly responsible for hurting her. The bastards are going to fry, and even if they get out of prison, their lives will never be cushy and privileged again."

"Almost every state in the union takes a very dim view of rapists. Once they get out of prison in a decade or so, Jerry and Sledge will have to register with local authorities as medium-risk sex offenders," Luke said.

"I thought you wouldn't be able to prosecute for sexual assault," Lana said as she came back out from the kitchen.

"We don't have to. Both men have agreed to plead guilty to statutory rape and sexual contact with a minor. That means they'll have to live as registered sex offenders for the rest of their lives," Luke explained.

Tessa smiled grimly. "It's some comfort. I hope it helps Kelly to know that those two will never hurt another teenage girl again. I'm also going to help her file civil suits against Sledge and Jerry. That should give her a nest egg while she kicks off her career. If that's what she still wants."

"I hear you were very determined in the case," Lana said.

"Wouldn't take no for an answer and didn't let anything get between you and these men. It reminds me of Paul."

Just a few weeks ago, Tessa would have bristled at being compared to her father. Now she just smiled. "I guess I am a lot like my dad."

Luke smiled into the iced tea Lana handed him. Yes, there was still a great deal to be worked out between Tessa and her father. But he knew that Tessa hadn't called Paul "Dad" in a long time. That had to count for something.

Lana jumped up as a timer went off inside. "Lunch will be ready in about half an hour. I'll just pop the quiche in the oven right now."

Luke swiveled his head to look at Tessa. "Quiche?" he mouthed in feigned horror.

"Why don't I show Luke around the property while we're waiting for lunch," Tessa said. "There's a beautiful gazebo on the little hill over there."

They held hands as they walked up the grassy slope to the redwood gazebo. The climbing roses that covered the structure gave off a sweet smell in the late-morning air. Tessa took a deep breath of scented air and looked around at the manicured gardens showcased by the perfect Southern California spring day.

"That was a nice thing to say to your father," Luke said as they stepped into the gazebo. "What brought that on?"

"I don't know. I guess I've realized that we both have made mistakes. And maybe it's time to stop letting my life be ruled by the painful things that were done over twenty years ago. Maybe I'm finally just ready to move on, to be a real adult who takes responsibility for her own feelings and actions instead of blaming the past."

"And maybe you're just happy," Luke said, and nudged her with his arm.

She laid her head on his shoulder. Expressing affection was getting easier each time she did it. "Maybe I am. I think I've got a good thing here."

"In that case, would you mind very much allowing me to formalize this *thing* between us?" Luke asked. He took a small black velvet box out of his pocket and held it out to her.

Tessa couldn't have been more horrified if he'd offered her a snake. The expression on her face said so, and it made Luke laugh out loud.

"The look on your face, Swiss. It can't be a surprise that I love you."

"You've been saying it for the last two days," Tessa breathed, unable to lift her eyes away from the box he held.

"You said it first," Luke pointed out. "I'm not letting you take it back now that the heat of the moment has faded."

"I do love you," she said mournfully. "But this is just so . . ."

"Cool? Wonderful? Unexpected? Scary?" Luke supplied. She gulped.

"Look, I didn't want to rush you, but I do want a couple of things here. One, I want you to wear my ring as a commitment to me—a commitment you've never made to anyone else."

"That sounds kind of primitive."

"You have no idea. Two, I want to have children while I'm still young enough to keep up with them. So sometime before I'm forty. That's a couple of years from now, which should give you time to get used to the idea of marriage."

"Marriage," she repeated, before raising her blue-gray eyes to him. "I think we should slow the heck down and talk about this."

"So talk. I'm listening. But you can't tell me this is a surprise."

"The idea of marrying you? I guess not. Not really," she said, pleasing him with the knowledge that she'd considered their relationship in a serious light. "But not now, not yet. Remember the Plan?"

"Why wait another year or so? You know it's right, and so do I. Will waiting a predetermined period of time make it more right?"

Tessa was beginning to feel slightly trapped. "I thought you understood how I felt and why. You're the first person to really comprehend what makes me tick. You should realize that I might be feeling hesitant about . . . this."

"I do understand, and I sympathize. But I won't be an enabler."

"What?"

"That's what love is all about, baby. Understanding the pain and helping the person you love move beyond it—not be trapped by it. If I continued to dance around your fear of commitment, I'd be helping you stay trapped in the past."

"Instead, you're going to drag me somewhere I'm scared to go?" Tessa asked.

"You're not scared. Not really. You're just looking back and thinking that you've been hurt in the past. But I've never hurt you, and I never will."

"I know you haven't, but how can you be sure about the future?"

"You can't. There's no safety net in this situation, not with the way I feel about you. And the way I hope you feel about me."

Tessa looked at him while her heart pounded with both fear and something else. Something good.

She should have known Luke would pull a stunt like this. Ever since they'd met he'd been carefully, persistently trying to pull her out of her self-constructed shell.

To be honest, it was one of the things she loved about him. The fact that he looked inside her, understood her, expected more from her—and got it. He'd been doing that in so many ways, both physically and emotionally, for the few weeks that she'd known him.

Why on earth had she thought he would stop?

"Do you understand, baby?" Luke asked. "Ours is not going to be some comfy weekend relationship. So just decide if you want to be with me, and we'll hop in the car and go to Vegas."

"Vegas?" She squeaked in surprise. "What happened to being engaged?"

"We will be engaged. All the way to Nevada," Luke pointed out with a smile.

"You're crazy," she said.

"Crazy in love, maybe. Crazy about the woman I want to have kids with, and build a home with, and get senile with."

Tessa laughed and grabbed for Luke's hand—the one holding the box.

"No one gets married after two weeks," she said. "We'd be insane to try."

"Here you go, quoting that invisible book of rules again. Who wrote that sucker, anyway? I want to beat the jerk up."

"Shut up. You're ruining my proposal," she said. "Are you going to get down on your knee and finish this?"

In a heartbeat, Luke was on bent knee in front of her, holding her hand to his heart. "Will you be Mrs. Crazy in Love with Me?"

Looking at his gorgeous hazel eyes, Tessa caved in completely.

Sometimes, she figured, you just have to throw out the rule book.

"I will." She leaned down and kissed him thoroughly. "But we'll get to Vegas that much faster if we take a plane."

The hauntingly beautiful
Draycott Abbey novels from

CHRISTINA SKYE

HOUR OF THE ROSE
0-380-77385-6/$6.99 US/$9.99 Can
Secrets and intrigue gather in the shadows of
Draycott Abbey—and astonishing mysteries of
a star-crossed love from centuries past.

BRIDE OF THE MIST
0-380-78278-2/$6.99 US/$9.99 Can
In a savage age of chivalry, a knight defended
a mysterious lady from danger and swore to
be her champion for all time.

KEY TO FOREVER
0-380-78280-4/$6.99 US/$9.99 Can
A British earl with Gypsy blood, Alexei
Cameron once shared one extraordinary night
with a beautiful stranger who vanished with the
dawn. And now, inexplicably, she has returned.

THE PERFECT GIFT
0-380-80023-3/$6.50 US/$8.50 Can
The tranquil English manor soothes Maggie's troubled
soul—until her peace is shattered by the tall sexy Scotsman
who claims he's been sent to protect her.

Fall in love with *New York Times* bestselling author
SUSAN ELIZABETH PHILLIPS
THE CHICAGO STARS/BONNER BROTHERS BOOKS

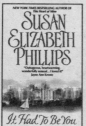

IT HAD TO BE YOU
0-380-77683-9/$7.50 US/$9.99 Can

When she inherits the Chicago Stars football team, Phoebe Somerville knocks heads with handsome Coach Dan Calebow.

HEAVEN, TEXAS
0-380-77683-9/$7.50 US/$9.99 Can

Gracie Snow is determined to drag the legendary ex-jock Bobby Tom Denton back home to Heaven, Texas, to begin shooting his first motion picture.

NOBODY'S BABY BUT MINE
0-380-78234-0/$7.99 US/$10.99 Can

Dr. Jane Darlington's super-intelligence made her feel like a freak growing up and she's determined to spare her baby that kind of suffering. Which means she must find someone very special to father her child. Someone very . . . well . . . . *stupid.*

DREAM A LITTLE DREAM
0-380-79447-0/$7.99 US/$10.99 Can

Rachel Stone is a determined young widow with a scandalous past who has come to a town that hates her to raise her child.

THIS HEART OF MINE
0-380-80808-7/$7.99 US/$10.99 Can

A down-on-her-luck children's book illustrator is about to cross paths with the new quarterback of the Chicago Stars.